continued on next page . . .

Praise for Patricia Kay writing as *USA Today* bestselling author Trisha Alexander

For Margaret,

FAMILY ALBUM

PATRICIA KAY

Happy exercising!
Pat

BERKLEY BOOKS, NEW YORK

This is a work of fiction. Names, characters, places, and incidents either are the product of the author's imagination or are used fictitiously, and any resemblance to actual persons, living or dead, business establishments, events, or locales is entirely coincidental.

FAMILY ALBUM

A Berkley Book / published by arrangement with the author

PRINTING HISTORY
Berkley edition / September 2002

Visit our website at
www.penguinputnam.com

ISBN: 0-425-18632-6

BERKLEY®
Berkley Books are published by The Berkley Publishing Group, a division of Penguin Putnam Inc., 375 Hudson Street, New York, New York 10014. BERKLEY and the "B" design are trademarks belonging to Penguin Putnam Inc.

PRINTED IN THE UNITED STATES OF AMERICA

10 9 8 7 6 5 4 3 2 1

This book is dedicated, with much love, to my sisters: Gerri Paulicivic, Marge Ford, and Norma Johnson. Each year you mean more to me. I can't imagine life without you.

Acknowledgments

Special thanks to my writing buddies Alaina Richardson, Amanda Stevens, Heather MacAllister, and Kay David, who read this book as it progressed and gave invaluable feedback.

As always, I owe tremendous thanks to my editor, Cindy Hwang, who always makes my books better, and to my agent and friend, Helen Breitwieser, who has believed in me from the beginning. I would also like to thank another of my editors, Gail Chasan, for first giving me the idea that I had a mainstream voice. Thanks, Gail, for all your encouragement and support over the years.

Prologue

"Push, Hannah, push!"

Hannah groaned.

"You can do it."

Gripping the side rails, Hannah pushed as hard as she could.

"Al*most* . . . al*most* . . . keep pushing . . ."

Sweat rolled down Hannah's face. She clenched her teeth. "Unnngh," she grunted.

"Keep pushing, come on, come on . . ."

Oh, God. She couldn't push anymore.

"That's it. That's it. *Push*, Hannah!"

From somewhere came the strength to give another hard push. Suddenly Hannah felt something give way.

"Here he comes," one of the nurses said.

"Just one more push, honey," another nurse said. "Okay, okay. That's it."

"It's a boy," someone else said. The doctor?

Exhausted and depleted, Hannah collapsed back against the pillows. *A boy*. She'd had a boy.

The room had exploded into organized chaos as everyone did his or her job.

Then she heard the baby—a mewling that crescendoed into a squall. Her chest tightened at the sound. *My baby*. The words thundered in her heart.

"Nice set of lungs on him," Dr. Jennings said.

"Nice set of everything on him," someone else said with a chuckle.

"Good work, Hannah," the sweet-faced nurse they called Molly said.

A while later, after the doctor had tended to the afterbirth and they'd cleaned her up, Molly took her hand. "Do you want to hold him?" she asked gently, her eyes sympathetic.

Hannah had told the other nurse, the one who'd done her admission workup, that she didn't want to see the baby after it was born. That decision was made because the adoption agency's caseworker had told her it would be easier on her and better for everyone if she didn't see him at all. She had agreed. But she hadn't known how she would feel once the baby was actually here. Everything was different now. Now she couldn't bear the thought of giving him away without at least seeing him.

Today was her eighteenth birthday. Her baby, due over a week ago, had been born on her birthday. It was almost as if he'd waited so he could come today.

Surely that was a sign. Surely their sharing a birthday meant they had an even more special connection. *I have to see him.*

Hannah's eyes filled with tears. "Yes," she whispered. "Yes, I want to hold him."

A few seconds later a tiny bundle was placed in her waiting arms. Hannah gazed down into that perfect little face. Seeing those two dark eyes, that precious nose and mouth, feeling the warmth of his little body, caused such a welter of emotions that Hannah trembled with the force of them.

Nicholas.

The name came from some secret recess in her brain. She hadn't even known she'd chosen a name, yet there it was. Nicholas. It had been her mother's maiden name.

Cradling the baby closer, Hannah drank him in. And then, in a moment that would haunt her for years to come, he turned his head toward her breast, his little mouth searching. Hannah's breasts ached in response, and the tears that had been hovering unshed rolled down her cheeks. She bit her lip to keep from crying out.

"I'd better take him now," Molly said softly.

"Yes," Hannah managed. *Goodbye, my dearest boy. I love you.*

Yet even as she was handing him to Molly, she wanted to snatch him back. Hold him fiercely to her. Say, "No, no, I've changed my mind, I'm keeping him."

But how could she?

She was only eighteen. Unmarried. Uneducated except for a high school diploma. What kind of life could she give him? Especially since she had no support, not from his father, not from her family. Only Aunt Marcy. And it wouldn't be fair to expect Aunt Marcy to take on this kind of responsibility. She had her own family to think of, her own problems.

You made the right decision. He'll have a much better life without you. He'll have two parents who will be able to give him all kinds of opportunities you can't give him. He'll be happy. This is best for him. Don't compound your mistakes by making another one. Wanting to keep him is selfish, and you know it.

So Hannah handed her baby to the nurse.

She was mature enough to know that over time, the pain she felt today would lessen. But it would never completely go away. Because the image of her son was engraved on her heart, and there it would stay until the day she died.

One

Los Angeles, late May, 1999

The young man in the faded crewneck sweater and baggy jeans swiped a strand of long hair from his face as he stared at the imposing electric gate, the six-foot-high stone wall, and the winding driveway leading to the large Spanish-style home beyond.

Money. The place stank of it, he decided as his hungry brown eyes took it all in.

The house was partially obscured by a canopy of leafy trees and dense, flowering oleander bushes, but he could still tell it was built of a creamy stucco and had a gleaming red tile roof. From his vantage point across the street from the entrance, he saw several gardeners working—one was pruning a privet hedge, another was planting some kind of flowers, still another was using a leaf blower whose high-pitched whine grated on David's nerves. And just a few minutes ago he'd seen a pool-cleaning truck leaving the premises.

Yeah, they had the bucks all right, the kind most people only dreamed of having, although from what he'd seen of this section of Bel Air, there seemed to be a shitload of people here who did.

He knew the family living in that house would wear designer clothes, eat at the best restaurants, drive the latest-model cars, and could buy just about anything they wanted.

Thinking about the way they lived, a terrible ache compressed his chest.

He thought about all the years he'd been shunted from one foster home to another. He thought about the loneliness, the beatings, the worn-out castoff clothes, the taunting and bullying at all the schools.

He could still hear the voices: *Hey, snot nose, you gonna eat those boogers for lunch? Watsa matter, dorkface? Your mama put your grandpa's pants on you today?* And then the raucous laughter, the poking and pushing.

It was only because David was so stubborn and so determined not to let anyone, *anyone,* keep him from his objective that he'd survived. He learned to tune out the insults, to ignore the bullies, to withdraw into himself the way a turtle does. Mostly he'd been successful, but there were times when he couldn't keep the pain and anger from seeping in, and on those days he usually went home with a bloody nose or worse.

He hadn't fit in anywhere. Not with the preppies or jocks, not with the nerds or Goths, not even with the druggies and gangs.

He'd been a lonely, scared kid who nobody liked.

Standing there on that shaded, tranquil street, watching the sprinklers feed the thick, beautiful lawns, knowing that inside those cool, elegant homes were maids and cooks and housekeepers and pantries filled with expensive and exotic foods, he thought about all the days he'd gone to bed hungry and all the nights he'd lain sweating in bed in the suffocating heat of south Florida as he listened to yet another drunken fight between his latest set of foster parents.

There might be foster families somewhere who really loved the kids they took in, who worried about them and protected them, who made sure their bellies were full and their clothes were clean, who never abused them or made them feel worthless, but you couldn't prove it by him.

Why? David asked himself for at least the hundredth time since he'd known where she was. *Who* she was. Why had she given him away? Why hadn't she wanted him?

He'd been four when Claudia Conway, the woman he'd

believed to be his mother, had told him he was adopted. He'd been too young to understand exactly what that meant, even though she'd explained it to him gently and told him how much she and his adoptive father loved him. At the time, David had felt so special, especially when he thought about how his mom and dad had chosen him to be theirs. He'd been happy—*really* happy—a normal little kid in an ordinary neighborhood in Homestead, Florida, with a dad who was an electrician and a mother who worked in a day-care center.

Just two years later everything changed. His adoptive father, Herman, was killed in a freak accident. Never very strong emotionally, Claudia fell apart afterward. Sinking into a deep depression, she gradually lost all touch with reality, and ended up in a mental hospital. With Claudia gone, there was no one to care for David.

Herman's only brother, who lived in Indiana and had never even seen David, was in his sixties and in poor health, so he couldn't take him. And Herman's parents were dead.

So at seven and a half David ended up a ward of the courts. Later he'd learned that a child that old is considered past the prime adoption age. Most Caucasian couples looking to adopt want an infant, but in a pinch they'll take a toddler. A boy David's age has already formed his personality, already has a value system in place, and is not going to unlearn his bad habits nor be able to banish his memories—good or bad. Added to those general negatives, David had spent eighteen months with a mother who could hardly lift her head in the morning, let alone pay any attention to him. Out of his fear and pain was born the habit of acting out so that she would notice him.

So though technically becoming eligible for adoption when he was placed under the guidance of the Florida courts, realistically there was very little chance anyone would want him. He wasn't even cute, as he'd overheard one of the caseworkers say carelessly when he was in earshot.

No, he thought bitterly, he hadn't been cute. He'd been neglected for too long. He was scrawny, had severe allergies, and his dark, lusterless eyes were used to hiding what he was really feeling.

Thus began the long succession of foster homes. He would stay in a place until his behavior, which became progressively worse, was deemed intolerable, or the family in question would, for one reason or another, stop keeping foster children.

Twice he ran away. Twice he was caught and returned to the system. No one noticed that the system had failed him utterly.

Yet despite all of the trauma, despite his rage and loneliness and fear, David had one thing no one could take away from him.

He was smart. And somewhere, buried deep in his unhappy psyche, was the knowledge that no matter how unbearable his life became, no matter how tempted he might be to quit, he must stay in school, at least long enough to get his high school diploma. For the one thing David knew without question was that he would never become what so many disadvantaged kids did become—a drug addict or a criminal.

At eighteen he finished high school with solid grades. If he'd wanted to, he could have graduated in the top percentile of his class, but he hadn't cared enough to work *that* hard.

The day after graduation, he'd packed his meager belongings, unearthed his hidden stash of money saved from his part-time jobs as a lifeguard and working at Burger King, and hit the road.

For the past two years he'd worked as a waiter in one of the best restaurants in St. Augustine, saving as much money as he could. During his time off, he'd haunted the Internet with one goal in mind: to find the woman who had given birth to him. He wasn't sure why, he just knew it was something he had to do.

Now here he was, mission accomplished. He knew who his mother was and where she lived. Her name was Hannah Turner Ferris, and she lived right there in that house—the one he'd been watching so carefully for hours. By now he knew a lot about her. He knew she had been married for fifteen years to Simon Ferris, the owner and CEO of the Ferris Sporting Goods chain of stores. He knew that after she'd given birth to him in a Tampa hospital, she'd attended the Ringling School of Art in Sarasota. He knew that shortly after her graduation from the school she'd moved to Los Angeles and gone to work for a big advertising agency. And he knew he had a sister, that his birth mother and her husband were the parents of a teenage daughter named Jenny.

A sister.

He stared at the house again. His sister lived there. Had lived there all of her life. Whereas he . . .

His jaw tightened.

Had his mother ever thought about him? Had she ever wondered where he was and how he was doing? Or didn't she care?

He was so lost in his painful thoughts, he didn't hear the vehicle approaching until it stopped a few feet away. He instantly stiffened. HAMILTON SECURITY SERVICES was lettered on the side of the SUV, and as David watched, a tall, brown-uniformed guard emerged. A gun was holstered at his waist.

David's heart was beating too fast, but he kept his face expressionless, saying nothing as he watched the guard walk toward him.

"You lost?" the guard said. He didn't smile.

"I don't think so."

"What are you doing here, then?"

"Just sightseeing."

"Sightseeing."

"Yeah, you know . . ." Smiling innocently, David pulled a map from the back pocket of his jeans. "Looking at the homes of the stars." He congratulated himself on his foresight. "Did you know Charlie Sheen lives there?" He pointed to a house two doors down.

"No, he doesn't."

"But . . ." David showed him the map. "Look. It says so right here."

"I don't care what that map says. It's wrong. And the

homeowners here don't take kindly to people who don't live here wandering around these streets. Especially young guys like you. They're inclined to think maybe you're casing their homes. Trying to find out who's there and who's not so you can rob them."

"I'd never do anything like that." David's indignation wasn't faked.

"Maybe not. However, I'd like to see some ID. You got a driver's license?"

David nodded and pulled out his wallet. "It's a Florida license. I haven't had a chance to get a California one yet."

The guard studied the license carefully, comparing the picture to David. Finally he handed it back. "Okay, maybe you're legit. Still, it's time for you to move along. You don't belong here."

No, David thought as he headed toward Sunset Boulevard and the bus stop. He didn't belong there. But that wasn't his fault. That wasn't his fault at all.

For two days David thought about what to do. Part of him wanted to take off. Just take off, put her and her family and everything about her out of his mind, just the way she'd put him out of her mind.

That was the part of him that hurt. The part that wanted someone to buy him birthday presents. The part that wanted someone to spend Christmas with. The part that wanted someone to love him.

The other part of him, the bitter, angry part, seriously considered just walking up to the front door and, when she answered, looking her straight in the eyes and saying, "Surprise. I'm the kid you dumped twenty years ago."

She'd probably shit a brick right there on the doorstep, be totally freaked out. For a while, he contemplated the pleasure of shocking her. But as appealing as that scenario was, there were problems with it.

For one thing, he had to get *to* the door. Which meant he had to get through the security gate, and that wouldn't be easy. From what he'd seen, visitors had to stop and buzz the house and identify themselves. Yeah, right.

Anyway, he didn't really want to do that. What would be the point? No, he needed to give this whole business some serious thought. Decide just what it was he ultimately wanted.

Short term, he *did* know. He wanted to meet his mother and her family. See what their lives were really like. Once he'd accomplished that, he would figure out what to do next.

So he spent a week scoping out everything he could concerning his mother's life. He soon realized he wasn't going to be able to survive in L.A. without a car or, at the very least, a motorcycle.

Although the motorcycle would have been his first choice, he knew he'd be less noticeable in a car. The question was, could he afford one? He had a little more than six thousand dollars saved, but unless he found a job right away, that money was going to go fast. It was already going.

He picked up a copy of the *Los Angeles Times* and studied the classifieds. It was obvious his best bet was to visit some used-car lots. Luckily, he knew a bit about cars, because one of the other guys at one of the foster homes he'd lived in was a car buff. Billy had shown David a few things, some legal, some not, including how to hot-wire a car. Remembering what he'd been taught, David began to make the rounds.

By the end of his first week in L.A., he was the owner of a six-year-old Ford pickup which he'd gotten for twenty-five hundred bucks. It needed some body work and a new paint job, but David didn't care about that. The mileage wasn't too bad, the truck ran well, and the tires wouldn't need replacing for at least a year.

Once he had wheels, it was easy to follow not only his mother, but her husband and their kid—he was having a hard time thinking of her as his sister. Soon he knew where the husband's office was located, where he parked his car, where he ate lunch, and where he worked out.

He knew where his mother shopped, where she ate lunch, and where she got her nails done and her hair cut.

He knew where the kid stabled her horse, where she had her music lessons—he wasn't sure what instrument she played yet, but he thought it might be violin because of the case she carried—and where she hung out.

One of the places the whole family frequented was their country club. It was so typical of the difference in their lives that the kid not only had a pool at her house, but she could swim at that fancy club, too, whereas the only place he could swim was in the ocean. David hated the ocean, which reminded him of Florida and the life he'd left behind.

But maybe them belonging to that club was a lucky break for him. Places like that always needed help, didn't they? And he had experience both waiting tables and as a lifeguard. If that club had any openings, it would probably be a piece of cake for him to get a job, because he had great references. Legitimate references.

So the following day—a Thursday—he drove to the club and asked the guard at the gate where the employment office was.

"You got an appointment?" the guard asked. He eyed David's truck suspiciously.

David gave the guy his most polite smile. "No, but I'm a certified lifeguard, and I've got experience as a waiter. I just thought I'd fill out an application in case any openings come up."

The guard picked up the phone. David couldn't hear what he was saying, but he figured he was calling the office.

After hanging up the phone, the man poked his head out and waved David on, saying, "Okay. You can go on up to the office. Just drive to the top of the hill. The main building is on the right. Drive around to the back. There'll be a sign on the office door."

Five minutes later David sat in a small reception area filling out an application. A half hour later he had a job. As he'd figured, there were several openings. He had his choice of lifeguarding or working in the dining room. Although he knew he'd make more money waiting tables, he figured he had a better chance of meeting and possibly getting chummy with the kid—which might mean he could meet the rest of the family—if he took the job at the pool. If he needed more money, he could always get a part-time job waiting tables at a restaurant at night.

The office manager, an older woman, seemed thrilled he'd come in. "Would you be willing to help out in the restaurant when we're shorthanded?" she asked after a few minutes of talking about his experience.

"Sure."

"The thing is, one of our waiters quit yesterday and another called in sick just a few minutes ago. He's got the flu and will be out all weekend." She pushed her hair back from her face in a harried gesture. "It's going to be impossible to find someone else so fast, but if you could see your way to helping us out . . ."

"You mean *tonight*?"

"No. Tomorrow night and Saturday. Those are our two busy nights."

Tomorrow was his birthday. Did he really want to spend it waiting on a bunch of rich people all night? But what the hell. He didn't have anything better to do. And it would mean extra money he could use. Plus he'd be making points with this woman. So he said, "Sure, no problem. I can help out."

"Oh, that's *wonderful*. I'll tell Julio—that's Julio Sanchez, our waitstaff manager—to get with you. He'll show you the ropes. Now, what about the lifeguarding? Can you start next week? The pool's closed on Monday for servicing, but reopens at eleven Tuesday morning."

"Tuesday's great.

"Wonderful. Your shift will be from eleven until seven." She told him how to find Julio and then the pro shop. "I'll call them both and tell them you're coming. The pro shop will get you outfitted with a couple of suits and robes."

"Okay. Thank you, Mrs. Shaver."

"My pleasure, David. We're looking forward to having you here as part of our little family." She stood, and they shook hands.

These rich people were really something, he thought as he walked to the main part of the club. *Our little family.* David almost laughed. Who the fuck did she think she was kidding? He was no more a part of their little family than he was part of the Ferris family.

That night he celebrated by buying himself a TV set and a six-pack of beer. Then he ordered his favorite pizza with mushrooms and extra cheese. He didn't even mind the noise outside. It was funny, he thought. When he'd first found out his mother lived in the L.A. area, he'd imagined Hollywood as being some big glitzy place with palm trees on every corner.

In reality it was the armpit of L.A., from what he could see. Unfortunately, it had turned out to be the only area he could afford.

His apartment was near Vine and Santa Monica Boulevard, and the most distinguishing thing about it was the constant noise—radios and TV sets blaring, people fighting, kids crying.

But David didn't care, because he knew living there was temporary. Besides, when you'd lived in some of the places he'd lived, you didn't expect satin sheets and maid service. It was enough to have a roof over your head.

He slept better that night than he'd slept for a long time.

Two

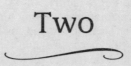

"You're so lucky, you know that?"

Hannah nodded. Jill Richman was her best friend and had expressed the same sentiment dozens of times. "Yes, I do know it," she answered softly. *A lot luckier than I deserve to be* . . . The melancholy that had descended from the moment she'd opened her eyes this morning weighed heavily, making it hard for her to return Jill's smile.

Jill sighed. "Long-stemmed roses and emerald earrings waiting for you when you wake up. What I wouldn't give for a husband like Simon."

"He *does* spoil me."

"Spoil you! That's an understatement. He treats you like a queen. I mean it, Hannah. If you ever get tired of him, just point him in my direction."

"You know you wouldn't trade Pete for ten Simons."

"Oh, yeah? Just try me."

Sometimes Hannah wasn't sure if Jill was kidding or not. She wondered if Jill and her husband were having problems. This wasn't the first time she had made a similar remark.

"Of course," Jill added, "you *do* bend over backward to please Simon. I'm not sure I could be that accommodating."

"I like pleasing him."

"But don't you, just sometimes, wish you could do what *you* wanted to do instead of what he wants to do?"

"But what Simon wants *is* what I want. Besides, he's

never told me I couldn't do something I wanted to do."

Jill made a face.

"You don't believe me, do you?"

"It's not that I don't believe you. It's just that I don't know another woman who doesn't occasionally wish she didn't have to consider anyone other than herself."

"Would you ladies like a refill on your iced tea?"

Hannah and Jill looked up at the same time. Neither had heard their waiter approach. Hannah was reminded of a line from a favorite Carl Sandburg poem. *The fog crept in on little cat feet*. Their waiter even looked catlike, she thought, with a lithe dancer's grace and sleek dark hair combed straight back. She supposed he, like every other good-looking waiter and waitress in L.A., was an aspiring actor. Poor guy. She wondered if he had any idea what the odds were of ever making it in the movie industry.

Once he'd refilled their iced-tea glasses, Jill said, "I thought you'd probably cancel out on today, since it's your birthday."

"I never miss First Friday, you know that." But Hannah had considered canceling. She hadn't been sure she could keep a smile on her face today. Yet the prospect of staying home, where there would be no buffer between her and her thoughts, was even worse.

She and Jill volunteered at their church's First Friday sale every month, then had lunch together afterward. It was a tradition, one Hannah normally looked forward to. In fact, working at First Friday was how Hannah had met Jill. So in the end, she'd decided keeping to her normal activities was preferable to the alternative.

"I just thought you'd probably be going out tonight."

Hannah sighed. "We are. I didn't want to, but Simon insisted."

"Where are you going?"

"To the club." Hannah hadn't wanted to do that, either, because she figured Simon would call ahead and make sure there was a birthday cake for her, plus there would be people there they knew, who would probably make a fuss, too.

But what could she say? Especially when Simon was so pleased by his idea.

"I love you, darling," he'd said. "I want us to celebrate." She hadn't been able to refuse him.

"What's the matter? Aren't you looking forward to going out?" Jill said.

"Not really . . . birthdays aren't my thing . . . but it's no big deal." She made her voice more upbeat. If Jill suspected the truth—that her birthday was always the worst day of the year for her—she would want to know why.

If only she could tell Jill. If only she could unburden herself and talk about that day twenty years ago.

But how could she? If Simon knew the truth, it would be different. But he didn't. When he'd asked her to marry him, she hadn't wanted him to know. She'd told herself the reason was that he would think so much less of her, and she couldn't bear that. Besides, she'd rationalized, the past wasn't important.

But the real reason was that she wasn't in love with him. She loved him, yes. She admired him and respected him. He made her feel safe. He gave her the security she had always wanted.

It was years later, after she'd fallen deeply in love with him as opposed to caring for him, that she realized what a disservice she'd done them both.

By then it was too late. The time for telling him was fifteen and a half years ago, *before* she'd married him. Since she hadn't then, she would now have to keep her secret forever. Every birthday she would have to smile and laugh and pretend to be happy, when all the time she was aching inside, thinking of that other person who was also celebrating a birthday today.

Nicholas.

Today he was twenty.

Twenty.

My baby. My beautiful, beautiful son.

Most of the time, Hannah managed to bury the memory of those two days in that Florida hospital, because to remember was too painful, but on their shared birthday, the memories tormented her.

"Are you taking Jenny with you tonight?" Jill asked.

At the mention of her daughter, Hannah managed a genuine smile. She and Simon were crazy about their only chick and rarely left her out of their plans. "No. This is the weekend her class is taking their end-of-the-year trip. They left this morning and won't be back until Sunday afternoon."

"That's good, then. You and Simon can have a romantic weekend on your own."

"Yes, but you know, we'd both rather have Jenny with us. I mean . . . she's fourteen. She's growing up. Soon she won't want to do things with us. So we're trying to make the most of this time we have left with her."

Jill made a face. "I wish I felt that way. I can't *wait* until Keith is out of my hair." Keith was Jill's husband's sixteen-year-old son from a previous marriage—a boy who had given Jill a hard time for years.

Hannah nodded sympathetically.

"You did it right, Hannah. Not only is Simon a terrific catch and a great guy, but he came unfettered."

Hannah thought about her mother-in-law. "Not completely."

"Yeah, I know, his mother can be a pain in the ass, but at least she doesn't *live* with you."

"True."

"You know," Jill said with a frown, "I've never understood why she doesn't like you."

Hannah shrugged. "She doesn't think I'm good enough for Simon." *And she's right*. Hannah knew she had to shake her dark thoughts. Brooding was pointless. *Focus on your blessings, not on the mistakes you've made or the things you can't change*.

She did have so much to be thankful for. A wonderful husband, an adored daughter, fulfilling work, a few good friends, a beautiful home . . . yes, she was extremely blessed. Much more so than she deserved.

By now Jill had finished her grilled sea bass, and Hannah had eaten all she wanted of her chicken piccata. Both women dabbed at their mouths with their napkins, then settled back to wait for the check.

It came a few minutes later, and Hannah reached for it.

"No, Hannah, let me," Jill said.

"You paid last time."

"But it's *your* birthday."

From the determined look on Jill's face, Hannah knew it would do no good to argue. "Oh, all right. But next time it's my treat."

After looking over the bill, Jill put it and her American Express card in the folder. Once Jill had taken care of the bill, the two women made their way to the exit. Jill's Lexus was parked right across from the door, and they stopped in front of it.

"Where are you off to now?" Hannah reached into her purse for her sunglasses.

"I have a dress to pick up at Saks."

"Have fun."

They hugged goodbye, Jill climbed into her car, and Hannah headed for her BMW convertible, which Simon had bought her the previous Christmas.

Hannah eased her way into traffic on Pacific Avenue and headed toward Wilshire Boulevard. Although it was only a little after two, traffic was heavy, but that was normal for a Friday. Everyone, it seemed, quit early on Fridays.

The June sun felt good on her shoulders. To her left, the ocean was dotted with pleasure craft, the beach crowded with sun worshipers.

Despite the traffic, she made good time and reached the house well before three. After parking her car in its slot in the four-car garage, she walked slowly toward the back door. The scent of jasmine and gardenias, the tinkle of wind chimes, the rich scarlet bougainvillea tumbling over the low wall that enclosed the back terrace, and the excited barking of Jenny's Labrador puppy—all the sights and sounds that usually brought her so much pleasure—failed to erase the melancholy that wouldn't begin to fade until this day was finally over.

"Hi, Martha," she said as she walked into the spacious

kitchen where the housekeeper was polishing silver. Hannah tossed her purse onto the kitchen table, then toed off her sling-backs.

Martha Kudeska, a sturdy woman with salt-and-pepper hair and a cheerful disposition, smiled a greeting. "Did you have a nice day?"

"Yes, very nice, thank you."

Martha studied her for a moment. "You look tired. Why don't you have a rest before you have to get ready for to-night?"

The housekeeper's motherly expression and kind eyes were nearly Hannah's undoing. Suddenly the suppressed sadness of the past twenty years nearly overwhelmed her. "I am tired," she said. "I think I will go and lie down for a while."

Hannah made it to the master bedroom before her control slipped. Stumbling into the bathroom, she locked the door behind her. Then she buried her face in a towel and let the tears come.

Three

~~~~~

Simon Ferris was two weeks shy of his thirty-sixth birthday the first time he set eyes on Hannah Turner. He was immediately captivated. She reminded him of the young Grace Kelly, with a clean, classical beauty and an innocent purity of expression and manner.

Even her coloring—blond hair, fair skin, and cool green eyes—fed into the fantasy. He could hardly take his eyes off her, even as he told himself she was too young for him.

Afterward, Simon wondered if he would still have switched advertising agencies if he hadn't met Hannah and known she would be part of the team servicing his account. At the time he told himself he'd made the decision to go with Chandler-Rossetti because they were better than his old agency, that the campaign they had designed was a winner. That the decision was strictly a business one and Hannah and her appeal had nothing at all to do with it.

Yet from day one he made certain he was present at every meeting concerning Ferris, Incorporated, rather than leaving subsequent decisions about their advertising campaign to John Jacobson, his V.P. of Marketing.

The more he saw of Hannah, the more interested he became. Gradually he realized she was much more mature than her chronological age. She was also smart and creative. She thought outside the box. Some of the best, most innovative ideas to come out of the meetings originated with her.

He also was intrigued by the fact she never came on to him. Ambitious, attractive women *always* came on to him. But Hannah didn't. She was friendly but businesslike, and there were no sexual undercurrents in the way she looked at him or spoke to him. She seemed either unaware of or unwilling to recognize his interest in her as a woman. Her attitude was so unusual, it only made Simon find her more desirable instead of less.

Two months after first meeting her, Simon asked Hannah to have dinner with him. Normally he would not have waited that long, but nothing about Hannah or his feelings for her was normal.

At first she hesitated. Simon figured her reluctance either had to do with him being a client or the difference in their ages, or maybe a combination of the two. Never one to avoid an unpleasant reality, he said, "If you're not interested, at least tell me why."

She'd met his gaze unflinchingly. "The truth is, I'm flattered, but you *are* a client. I'm not sure it's a good idea to mix business and pleasure."

"If I give you my word that nothing you ever do will change my opinion of the value of your work for my company, would that make a difference?"

"Well . . ."

"I do give you my word." He grinned. "Even if you decide you can't stand me and tell me so, you'll still be handling my account."

She'd laughed. "I don't think I'd ever say anything like that."

"Good. Then you'll have dinner with me?" When she didn't immediately agree, he pressed harder. "What if I told you you're one of the most extraordinary women I've ever met and I want to get to know you more than I've wanted anything in a long time?"

He could see she was flattered but not convinced.

"Just one dinner. That's all I'm asking for."

"You're a hard man to refuse."

"Does that mean yes?"

She'd laughed again. "I guess it does."

He was as excited as a teenager when he pulled into the parking lot of her Santa Monica apartment complex that long-ago Friday night.

Although they'd had many wonderful evenings since, he would never forget that particular evening. She literally took his breath away, even though she was dressed very simply, in a mossy green sleeveless linen dress and matching high-heeled sandals. She wore her hair longer then, and he remembered how she'd pulled the sides back and up, securing them with hair combs studded with tiny pearls. Her only jewelry had been small pearl earrings and a dainty gold watch.

Her hands had fascinated him. Small and graceful, with slender fingers, her nails were filed short and unpainted, and she wore no rings. The women in his circle of acquaintances sported expensive manicures and wore multiple rings on both hands, the bigger and more expensive, the better.

He took her to Bernard's, long known as the place to go if you wanted pampering, elegant surroundings, and a romantic ambience. And even though she was young and unsophisticated compared to most of the women he'd dated over the years, she seemed to fit not only Bernard's, but Simon, too.

Simon had never considered himself the romantic sort. Certainly he wasn't flowery or poetic. His style was straightforward and practical. But sitting across the table from Hannah that night, watching the candlelight play across her face, seeing her enchanting smile and the way she absorbed everything, listening to her delightful laugh, he knew he had been destined to meet this woman. That she was the missing piece of the puzzle that was his life. That she matched him in a way no other woman had ever matched him, and that she was the person he wanted to spend the rest of that life with.

He didn't care that she was only twenty-three. Age was relative, anyway, he thought. He certainly didn't feel as if he were nearly thirty-seven, and he didn't look it, either.

People always thought he was younger until they got to know him or had been on the opposite end of a business deal where they'd made the mistake of underestimating him. It was only when his dark hair began to sprout gray wings in his early forties that people believed him when he told them his age.

After that first date, as he and Hannah spent more and more time together and he got to know her on the inside— her thoughts and feelings, her beliefs and morals—his sense that she was his destiny only became stronger.

He loved everything about her—the way she looked, the way she sounded, the way she laughed, her attitude about her job, her enthusiasm for life.

But most of all he loved her honesty and her high standards. She was the most moral person he'd ever known— someone who believed in and lived the Golden Rule. She drank very little, she didn't smoke, she didn't use vulgar language, and she believed in God.

In short, she was perfect. A lady. A well-brought-up lady. Someone he could be proud of—as wife, and later, as mother. Just the thought of having a baby with Hannah filled him with a burst of happiness.

She would be a wonderful mother. She would love and nurture her child, instilling him or her with all of her own values and beliefs. Her child would be cherished and considered a precious gift. She would never treat her child as a commodity, a throwaway, as his own mother had.

Even after all these years, the reminder that his mother hadn't wanted him because he was an inconvenience, because he interfered with her lifestyle, disgusted him. From the day he was born, she had shown no interest in him, had passed him off on anyone she could find. When he was thirteen months old, she had decided he was just too much trouble to keep at all, and she'd quickly found a way to relieve herself of the burden.

Luckily—and he *was* lucky as well as grateful—he had been taken into the home and hearts of two of the greatest people who ever walked the face of the earth. Granted, his adoptive mother could be overbearing at times, but she was still a wonderful woman, and she loved him unconditionally. In fact, Simon knew it was no exaggeration to say Madeleine Chappell Ferris would lay down her life for her son.

And his dad . . . Simon smiled thinking about his adoptive father. His dad had thought the sun rose and set on Simon's head. The only other person who had ever inspired that kind of unquestioning devotion in his father was Jenny. Until Hugh Ferris's death three years ago, he had doted on his granddaughter, and she on him.

Simon missed his father. He guessed he always would. Hugh had taught Simon what it meant to be a man, and by his example, how to be a good husband and a firm, yet kind and loving father.

He was still thinking about his parents when he reached the house. After opening the security gate with his remote, he drove into the garage and cut the ignition. A few seconds later the excited yapping of Jenny's Lab greeted him.

"Missing your mistress, are you, Vixen?" Simon said as he rubbed the puppy's head. "She'll be home in a couple of days." The puppy followed him into the kitchen.

As he entered, Martha looked up. Spread on the kitchen table in front of her were what looked like lists. Simon smiled. Martha had a list for everything. Once he'd teased her that she'd probably still be making lists in heaven. Her laughing answer had been, "If Gabriel needs help organizing things, I'm his woman."

"Is Mrs. Ferris in her studio?" Simon asked after they'd exchanged greetings.

"No, she's been taking a nap, but I believe she's awake now. I heard the shower a little while ago."

When Simon walked into the master suite, he could hear the water running in the bathroom. He tapped on the door, then nudged it open. Hannah, clad only in a lacy beige bra and matching panties, was just turning off the tap. "Hi." She smiled at him as she returned her toothbrush to its holder.

"Hi." Leaning over, he gave her a lingering kiss. She tasted like peppermint toothpaste and smelled like Joy, her favorite perfume. "How's my birthday girl?" he said softly.

"Fine."

"Martha said you took a nap."

She nodded. "I was tired. I'm always tired on First Friday."

"Feel better now?"

"Yes. What about your day?"

"Typical Friday. Meetings all morning. Boring lunch." He grinned. "I'm glad to be home." Unbuttoning his knit shirt, he added, "Looking forward to tonight."

She nodded. "Speaking of, I'd better start getting ready."

"How about a glass of wine?"

"Are you having one?"

"I thought I would."

"All right. I'll keep you company."

Later, shoes kicked off, glass in hand, he relaxed on the bed and watched her dress. He could watch her for hours. Sometimes he wondered if she had any idea how much he loved her. He knew she hadn't loved him in the same way he'd loved her when they were married, but it hadn't mattered to him. He'd wanted her any way he could get her.

She loved him now, though. He was as sure of that as he was of anything in this world.

"What do you think?" She held up two dresses, one a shimmery gold lace studded with sparkly stuff, the other a dark blue satin column.

"The gold."

She nodded and replaced the blue dress in her closet. When she stepped into the gold dress, he put his glass of wine on the nightstand, got off the bed, and walked over to her. "I'll zip you up."

She turned around, lifting her hair so it wouldn't catch in the zipper. When he got the dress zipped, his hands lingered at her neck, and his eyes met hers in the mirror. For just a moment a shadow darkened their depths.

It was funny how she acted on her birthday. She probably thought he didn't realize her birthdays bothered her, but he knew her so well. Birthdays definitely disturbed her. He couldn't imagine why. If wasn't as if she was obsessed with aging. She wasn't one of those women who were constantly looking in the mirror and examining their faces for wrinkles or anything, so why did she always get what he'd come to think of as the birthday blues?

Early on in their marriage, he'd asked her about it. All she'd said was that birthdays had never been much fun in her house. At the time Simon had accepted that answer. God knows nothing could have been much fun in that house where she'd grown up, not with a father like hers. Now, though, he wondered if there was some other factor involved, maybe even one she wasn't conscious of herself.

"You'd better get ready, too," she said, moving away from him. "It's almost seven."

As Simon changed from his casual Friday clothes into a dark pin-striped suit and crisp white shirt, he decided he would make tonight so wonderful, Hannah would forget whatever it was that troubled her about the day.

And he would love her so thoroughly tonight, she would be back to her normal, contented self in the morning.

Smiling, he began to hum.

Four

⁓

As a birthday treat, David had breakfast at IHOP—sausage and a stack of pancakes—then bought himself two CDs and a boom box. What the hell. If he had to work tonight, he might as well spend the money on himself.

After all, it *was* his birthday.

If wasn't like anyone else was going to acknowledge it. David was used to never getting birthday cards or presents, but that didn't mean he had to ignore the day, too.

He spent the rest of the morning and the early part of the afternoon hanging out at Venice Beach.

At four o'clock he headed to his apartment. As he got ready to go to the club, he admitted to himself that he was kind of nervous about what kind of reception he'd get from the waitstaff when he reported in.

But he needn't have worried. He quickly realized there wouldn't be any trouble. The manager of the club restaurant, Julio Sanchez, was a decent guy, and the other three waiters working that night turned out to be longtime employees who didn't feel threatened by David's presence. Actually, he thought with relief, they seemed glad to have him there.

The oblong room held thirty tables around its perimeter, with a dance floor in the middle and a slightly raised plat-form at one end. Two walls contained floor to ceiling windows that overlooked a flower garden on one side and the golf course on the other. As the sun lowered in the west, the scene was bathed in red-gold light. It looked like a pic-ture postcard, David thought, too perfect to be real.

At six-thirty the five-piece band began to set up. David knew just by looking at the musicians the kind of stuff they'd be playing tonight, which wasn't exactly cutting edge.

"Those four tables are gonna be yours tonight and to-morrow night," Julio said. "That one . . ." He gestured to-ward what was probably the choicest table in the room since it occupied the one corner where the two windowed walls met. ". . . is reserved for a VIP. Member of the board of directors and his wife. It's her birthday, so give them extra-special treatment."

David almost said, *It's her birthday, huh? It's my birth-day, too*, but then he thought better of it. Sanchez might think he was angling for some kind of special treatment himself. Besides, hadn't he learned a long time ago it was always better to keep your own counsel?

David eyed the table. A crystal vase filled with pale pink roses sat in the middle, surrounded by small crystal candle-holders alight with votive candles. These VIPs were already getting special treatment, because the other tables only had one candle and a single rose decorating them. "Wouldn't you rather have one of the regulars waiting on them?" he asked.

Julio shook his head. "No. They all have their own tables and regulars who sit there. They wouldn't like being switched."

David wondered in amusement what the VIP wife would think if she knew it was his birthday. Not much, he'd bet. The women who belonged to this club wouldn't enjoy having anything in common with the hired help.

"Their reservation is for seven-thirty," Julio added. "Mr. and Mrs. Simon Ferris. Just so you'll know."

David hoped his face didn't show the shock he felt. His heart knocked against his chest with several painful thuds before it settled down to something approaching his normal heartbeat. *My mother's going to be here tonight. I'm to wait on her.*

"Okay," Julio said. "Looks like Lauren is seating your first table. Questions?"

"I don't think so." *We have the same birthday.*

"Good." Julio patted his back. "These people, they're mostly pretty nice, but some of them are demanding and won't tolerate mistakes. So be on your toes and ask for help if you need it."

As David waited on his first table—a party of four consisting of a middle-aged couple and their two teenage children—he told himself to settle down and pay attention to what he was doing. But his mind was whirling with the knowledge that in less than forty minutes he would see his birth mother up close. He would actually *talk* to her and get to observe her in a way no amount of watching from a distance could provide.

I was born on her birthday.

He hadn't known that. The information he'd dug up about her hadn't contained the date of her birth, and he'd never thought to try to find it. It was enough for him that he knew who she was and where she lived.

For the next half hour he worked hard to keep his cool and not think too much about what was ahead. He was listing the specials to his third set of customers when, out of the corner of his eye, he saw the hostess leading a couple toward the reserved table.

Once again his heart betrayed him. Yet despite the way it pounded, he managed to keep his voice sounding normal while he finished taking the order.

He wanted to carry the order to the kitchen before approaching his mother and her husband. That way he'd have enough time to get himself under control. But he knew he shouldn't, that they would expect him to come over immediately. All he had time to do was take a couple of deep breaths, then he walked over to their table.

They looked up as he approached.

Until that moment he hadn't known how he would feel,

so he wasn't prepared for the intensity of the pain that knifed through him.

Green. Her eyes were green.

And she was beautiful.

He swallowed.

My mother . . . He stared at her. Did he look like her at all?

Wrenching his gaze away from *her* was one of the hardest things he'd ever had to do. Somehow he managed it. Turning to her husband, he pasted on his best professional smile and said, "Good evening. I'm David. I'll be your waiter tonight."

"Hello, David," Simon Ferris said. His blue eyes were friendly.

"What happened to Blake?"

The question came from *her.* David slowly met her gaze again. "He's out sick with the flu."

"Oh, that's too bad."

Was it David's imagination, or was she giving him a funny look? Once more addressing himself to her husband, he said, "What would you like to drink tonight?"

"Since tonight's a celebration," Simon Ferris said, smiling across at his wife, "we'll have a bottle of the Cristal ninety-five."

David had enough experience with upscale restaurants to know that Ferris had just ordered one of the most expensive champagnes on the menu. More in control now, he turned back to his mother yet again. "Yes, happy birthday, Mrs. Ferris."

"Thank you."

Her smile seemed strained. Was there something wrong? She sure didn't act like she was happy. Then a chilling thought hit him. Was it him? Did she recognize him or something? No. That was stupid. How could she? She'd never seen him before.

Just then, the busboy came to fill their water glasses and bring them their complimentary hors d'oeuvre of pâté and toast rounds, so David made his escape.

As he brought their wine order and table three's food order into the kitchen, the orchestra began to play.

The irony of the situation didn't escape him. His mother was out there, all dolled up, not a care in the world, celebrating her birthday by having a great dinner and drinking three-hundred-dollar champagne.

And he was in here, celebrating *his* birthday by waiting on her.

Five

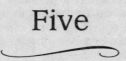

Hannah stared after their waiter. She knew it was her guilty conscience and the fact that all day she'd been thinking about the son she'd given up so long ago that made her think the waiter looked like Mark, but nevertheless, she felt shaken.

You're imagining things.

"Hannah?"

She blinked.

"You looked as if you were a million miles away."

"Sorry." She picked up her menu, even though they'd eaten at the club so many times over the years, she could have recited it from memory. But holding the menu gave her something to do until she could gain control of her thoughts once more. "What are you going to have tonight?"

Simon grinned. "Probably the lamb chops."

"You're such a creature of habit," she teased. Simon adored lamb chops and ordered them almost every time they ate here.

"What about you?"

"I believe I'll have the crab cakes."

"And you're *not* a creature of habit?"

This time Hannah didn't have to force a smile. Dear Simon, she thought, looking at his kind face with its loving expression. He was such a good man. If only he didn't think she was so perfect. That was his only flaw—putting her on a pedestal. So many times she'd wanted to tell him it wasn't fair, that she couldn't possibly live up to his expectations, but she knew it was best for both of them if she didn't go there.

"Since we've decided on our dinner, would you like to dance?"

Hannah realized the band was playing "Unforgettable," which happened to be one of Simon's favorites. "All right."

At least when they were dancing, she didn't have to talk or look into Simon's eyes. She could just let herself be held and lose herself in the music.

As they slowly circled the floor, she thought about how much she'd always loved dancing with Simon. Not only had he taken lessons when he was younger—something he'd admitted half sheepishly—but he had a natural rhythmic feel for the music. She closed her eyes and nestled closer, savoring the safe harbor his arms provided.

But all too soon the song ended. Simon glanced toward their table. "Our champagne is here."

Hannah realized their waiter was standing by the table waiting for them. As they walked toward him, she saw that her first impression of him hadn't been her imagination. The boy did resemble Mark. He had the same slight build and dark hair, but it was his eyes that really arrested her. They were the same shape and color of Mark's—that mix of brown and gold that had so captivated her as a girl.

She bit her lip. She knew there were thousands, perhaps hundreds of thousands of people with eyes of this color. Still . . . seeing this boy *today* was upsetting.

This kind of thing had happened to her before—several times, in fact. Once when she'd accompanied Simon on a business trip to Chicago, she'd spent an afternoon at Bloomingdale's, and the young man who had waited on her in the shoe department had borne an uncanny resemblance to Mark. She had been so shaken by the encounter, she'd left without buying anything. For days afterward she'd kept thinking about the boy, until even Simon had noticed her distraction.

And another time, when they'd been on vacation in New

York, she'd stood next to a man at the ticket office at Lincoln Center who could have been Mark's brother. That time she'd forced herself to put the man out of her mind.

And she couldn't count the number of times she'd seen a boy that would have been the age of Nicholas and wondered if, just possibly . . .

And now, on this day of all days, here was another one. God was punishing her. He didn't want her to forget.

Stop it. You're going to make yourself crazy.

All the while the boy was uncorking the champagne and pouring some for Simon to taste, she studied him. She couldn't help herself. He was nice looking. Not quite handsome—his face was a bit too narrow for that—but attractive. Girls probably liked him.

"Would you like to order now?" he asked.

He had a nice voice, too. She wondered if he was also an aspiring actor, the way the waiter at lunch had been.

"Darling?" Simon said.

Hannah cleared her throat. "I'll have the crab cakes."

The boy nodded and smiled, then turned to Simon.

Hannah took a deep breath. She was totally unnerved by this boy. It didn't matter that she knew she was overreacting, that his similarity to Mark was only a coincidence and didn't have some deeper, darker meaning. She couldn't help the way she felt.

It seemed to take the boy forever to finish with their order. But finally he was done and left them. Hannah sighed in relief, but she knew this was only a short reprieve. The waiter would be back and, with him, more unwanted reminders of the past.

Simon raised his champagne flute. "Happy birthday, sweetheart."

Hannah picked up her glass. "Thank you."

After drinking the toast, Hannah tried hard to smile and keep up her end of the conversation, but she was afraid she wasn't doing a very good job of it. Again, she was grateful when Simon wanted to dance. By now there were other couples there that they knew, and when the dance was over, they stood and talked to several of them.

When the waiter brought their salads, Simon led her back to the table. She tried not to look at the boy, but her eyes seemed to have a mind of their own. Thankfully, it took him only a few minutes to serve them. Still, she was constantly aware of him as he worked and served the other tables, and she couldn't relax.

By the time dinner was over, she knew she wasn't going to be able to keep up the pretense that she was enjoying herself much longer. She already knew she was going to plead a headache so they could leave early. But that would have to wait awhile, because she was certain Simon had arranged for a birthday cake to be served.

Sure enough, as soon as the busboy had cleared the table, their waiter—followed by two of the other waiters—returned carrying the restaurant's specialty and Hannah's favorite, German chocolate cake, topped with lighted candles.

"Happy birthday to you," they sang as they walked. "Happy birthday to you . . ."

Hannah glanced over at Simon, who was beaming.

"Happy birthday, Mrs. Ferris . . . happy birthday to youuuuuuu."

Their waiter set the cake on the table, then stood back as the other waiters, joined by the rest of the diners, all clapped.

"Make a wish, darling," Simon said.

For just a moment Hannah raised her eyes to find the waiter's gaze pinned to hers. Quickly she looked away. She only had one wish. *Please, God, help me get through this night.* She took a deep breath and blew out all the candles.

The waiters cheered, then all but the Mark-look-alike went back to their own work. While he cut the cake and served a piece to each of them, then brought them coffee, she kept her gaze resolutely trained on Simon and Simon alone.

It was another hour before she and Simon finished their cake and coffee because well-wishers kept stopping by their table. Then it took another fifteen minutes to get the bill and for Simon to approve it and sign it.

"It's still early," he said. "We don't have to leave yet."

Hannah knew he would have liked to stay on and dance,

but no matter how much she wished she could please him, she simply couldn't endure another minute of this evening. "I'm sorry, darling, but I'm afraid I've got the beginnings of a terrible headache. Do you mind if we leave?" This wasn't a lie. Her head had begun to throb a good half hour ago.

"Of course not."

Hannah felt terrible when she saw the immediate concern in his eyes.

On the way home Simon turned on KCSN, their favorite classical station. Tonight they were featuring works by Puccini. Hannah leaned her head back against the headrest and closed her eyes.

It didn't take long to reach the house. Simon stopped to allow her to get out before pulling the car into the garage. By the time he'd parked and closed the garage door, she'd already unlocked the back door and walked into the kitchen, where Martha had left a night-light burning.

The house was very quiet. Hannah was sure Martha was probably already asleep in her quarters. Hannah removed her strappy sandals and headed for the master bedroom suite. Halfway down the hall she heard Simon locking the back door and knew he would soon follow.

He'll want to make love tonight.

She couldn't. Not tonight. Not when she was in this state of mind. Not when all she wanted was to close her eyes and blot out the day and everything in it.

But she didn't want to hurt him, either.

As was her custom, Martha had turned down the bed and switched on the bedside lamps. She'd also laid out Simon's black silk pajama bottoms and Hannah's pale blue satin nightgown.

By now Simon had walked into the bedroom. "Headache any better?" he asked.

Hannah shook her head. "Not really."

"Why don't you take a couple of Advil and go right to bed?"

Hannah could have cried. He was telling her that he knew she wasn't in the mood for anything but sleep tonight and that it was okay with him. As she had thousands of times before in their married life, she wondered what she had ever done to deserve him.

She gave him a grateful smile. Ten minutes later she slipped into bed. Simon, who had changed into his pajamas, put on his robe and came and sat on the edge of the bed beside her. "I'm going to read awhile, but I'll go into my study so the light doesn't disturb you." He leaned over and kissed her gently. "You have a good night's rest."

Whether it was the work of the wine or the pain medication or a combination of the two, Hannah had no trouble falling asleep. It was almost as if her mind had been on overload all day and couldn't wait to shut down.

She didn't even hear Simon come to bed, and slept soundly until about three o'clock in the morning, when she abruptly awoke, trembling and heart pounding, from a horrible nightmare in which she was standing outside a huge stone fortress. Inside the fortress were all the people she loved, but she couldn't reach them. The walls seemed to have no opening at all, and no matter how she screamed and beat her fists against the stones, they couldn't hear her. She couldn't get to them. She was shut out, completely alone and so afraid.

Simon reached for her. "Hannah, sweetheart, what is it? A bad dream?"

Hannah burrowed into Simon's arms. She couldn't stop shaking. The dream had been so real.

He rubbed her arms and kissed her forehead. "It's okay," he soothed, "it's okay. I'm here."

"Oh, Simon, I was so afraid."

"I know." He tipped her face up and kissed her lips.

She clung to him, returning his kiss with something like desperation. Suddenly all she wanted was to be close to him. To have him hold her and love her. To chase the demons away.

He responded immediately to the need she couldn't articulate, and his arms tightened as the kiss deepened.

"Hannah . . ." His voice was ragged.

They kissed again and again. His hands became more

insistent as they cupped and stroked and kneaded in all the ways he knew would please her.

She strained against him. She couldn't wait. "Simon," she moaned, digging her nails into his back.

With a cry, he plunged into her. Almost weeping, she wrapped her legs around him and moved urgently against him, even though he tried to hold back. "Now!" she cried. "I want you now!"

He shuddered, and then she felt the hot rush of his release deep inside her. Moments later her own release came in shimmering waves that left her completely spent.

Afterward, he held her close. "Are you all right now?" he murmured.

She wove her fingers through his chest hair. "Yes."

Just before she drifted back into sleep, Hannah thought that if she could only stay wrapped in the safety of Simon's arms, nothing bad would ever happen to her again.

Six

When they'd bought the house shortly after their marriage fifteen years ago, Simon had insisted Hannah needed a place of her own—somewhere she could paint or draw without being disturbed, so he'd had a spacious studio wing added. At the time Hannah had thought the studio an extravagance. Now she couldn't imagine being without it.

When Jenny was younger, Hannah's studio had been a place of refuge—a quiet haven amidst the constant chatter and tumult of life with a preschool-age child. But gradually, over the years, Hannah had begun to take on freelance assignments.

Now the studio was her workplace, the place where she was Hannah Turner Ferris, artist and illustrator, instead of plain Hannah Ferris, wife and mother.

Not that she didn't love being a wife and mother. Those were the two most important roles in her life. But she wasn't a whole person unless her life included the work she loved, as well.

What had she ever done to deserve Simon? she wondered as she changed into her favorite outfit of faded jeans and an old T-shirt. He had always known what it was she needed. Hannah had never been in therapy or had counseling, but she was smart enough and educated enough to know that she'd unconsciously been looking for a father figure—someone who would take care of her and give her the happy home she'd never had.

As always, any reminder of her harsh, unbending, unforgiving father filled her with sadness. Now sixty-nine, Joshua Samuel Turner had spent all his adult years as the minister of a small church in the Nebraska town where Hannah had grown up. He was eligible to retire, but Hannah knew he never would. The only way he would ever leave the pulpit was if he were forced out or he died.

She sometimes wondered how the members of the church felt about him, whether they sometimes wished for a minister who was a bit more liberal and understanding of human failings. Her father took the church's fundamentalist teachings literally and demanded absolute obedience and piety from his flock, but no more so than he demanded from his wife and three daughters. In fact, if anything, he was harder on his family than his congregation.

It seemed to Hannah that the entire first seventeen years of her life had been spent trying to win her father's approval and love—an impossible goal, she now knew. Only Leah, the youngest of Joshua Turner's three daughters, had been able to manage that, and Hannah knew the slightest infraction on Leah's part would change her father's attitude in an instant.

Poor Leah. I wouldn't be in her shoes for anything in the world.

Thinking about Leah—actually, thinking about any of the members of her family—depressed Hannah, so she pushed her unwelcome thoughts from her mind. She'd finally gotten past her birthday melancholy, and she did not want to invite further despondency by thinking about her bleak girlhood.

Scraping back her heavy, wheat-colored hair, she secured it with a band, then shoved her feet into her favorite clogs and walked down the hall to her studio. The enormous room faced north, giving her the best possible light. One wall, the one overlooking the side yard, was made up entirely of floor-to-ceiling windows. The wall that faced the front of the house also had windows, but these were set higher, and below them sat a seven-foot-long black leather couch.

The rest of the room was filled with cupboards that held her supplies, her huge drawing table and stool, an adjoining desk, a built-in sink and attached counter, and several filing cabinets.

Hannah's work-in-progress was taped to the drawing table. She walked over to look at it. Hannah was known for her bold, innovative watercolors, and this painting of a homeless woman sitting on a bench in Griffith Park was striking in its stark intensity.

Rarely without her camera, Hannah sometimes spent days on end walking the city streets or park trails. She took hundreds of photos of people and places that interested her, many of which ended up as subjects for a body of work a critic had recently dubbed brilliant.

Although she occasionally painted what she termed "pretty" pictures, Hannah preferred darker, more realistic subjects. Homeless people, in particular, fascinated her. When she'd first started photographing them, she'd been afraid they would object. Hannah being Hannah, if they had, she would have had to stop. But rather than object, most of her subjects seemed to love the attention. This old woman had especially enjoyed being the focus of Hannah's camera and had preened and posed willingly.

When the session was over and Hannah felt she had enough photos, the woman grinned, exposing a smile missing a couple of front teeth.

"I still have it, don't I?" she'd said.

Her question pierced Hannah's heart, and she knew she'd never forget the look on the woman's face when she asked it.

The photo Hannah had chosen to paint of the several dozen she'd taken that day was one where the woman had given her a coy smile—almost a flirtatious smile—and looked up at Hannah through her eyelashes. The end result was a poignant reminder that once this woman had been young, and probably pretty. That once someone might have loved her. That once she'd belonged somewhere.

That was the look Hannah wanted to capture, and she felt she was almost there. Excited now, ready to get to work, she filled two containers with fresh water, then settled onto her stool and chose a #2 sable brush. She worked steadily all afternoon, completely lost in her work. So lost she jumped when, just past three-thirty, the phone on her desk buzzed.

Eyeing the blinking line on the multibutton phone, she punched the intercom button and said, "Yes, Martha?"

"Sorry to disturb you, Mrs. Ferris. But it's your sister."

"Which one?"

"Sarah."

Hannah laid down her brush and pressed the blinking button. "Hello, Sarah."

"Happy belated birthday!" her sister sang out.

"Thank you."

"I'm sorry I didn't call you Friday."

"That's okay." She hadn't been disappointed because she hadn't expected a call. She loved Sarah, who was two years younger, but Hannah had no illusions about her sister. Sarah only contacted Hannah when it benefited her to do so, and usually that meant she wanted something. Which meant she wanted something today. "How have you been?"

"Fine, but let's not talk about me," Sarah said archly. "First tell me what you did to celebrate Friday."

"Nothing much. We went out to dinner and made it an early night."

"And that's it? Christ, if I had your money, I'd be jetting off to London or Paris or the French Riviera."

Hannah winced. She might have rebelled against her father's tyranny, but her religious training was too deeply imbedded, especially when it came to the sanctity of the Lord's name. Simon felt the same way. Neither of them swore or used vulgarities of any kind.

"So what did he buy you?" Sarah continued.

For a few seconds Hannah considered waffling, then was immediately irritated with herself. She was not going to lie to Sarah.

"Emerald earrings, huh? Wish I had that kind of sugar daddy," was Sarah's rejoinder.

Hannah gritted her teeth. She hated when Sarah intimated

that she had married Simon because of his money. Simon's money had been irrelevant to her decision, but she knew Sarah would never believe that.

"Well, hey," Sarah went on, obviously unfazed by Hannah's lack of response, "what the hell. Got it, spend it. Which reminds me . . . I'm a little behind on my rent, and I was wondering if you could help me out."

"How much do you need this time?" Although it wasn't intentional, Hannah couldn't help the tinge of exasperation that had crept into her voice.

"Six hundred should do it. Wait. Better make it seven-fifty." Sarah's own voice was breezy.

And why not? Hannah thought wearily. Wasn't it perfectly acceptable to ask your sister with the rich husband to bail you out when things were tight?

The trouble was, things were always tight for Sarah, because Sarah hadn't just rebelled against their father's harsh disciplinary and moral code, she'd also cast off his work ethic and the firm belief that God helps those who help themselves.

Since she'd graduated from high school and bid goodbye to their hometown and their grim father, she had managed to exist by a combination of her wits, the least amount of work she could get away with, and a long line of men who were willing to pay to have a beauty like Sarah on their arm.

Unfortunately, after eighteen years of hard living, Sarah's looks were beginning to fade, and it was no longer as easy to find well-heeled boyfriends to support her in the style she favored. More and more, she was calling on Hannah to help her out of jams.

Hannah sighed. "All right. I'll write you a check for seven-fifty and get it in tomorrow's mail."

"I really need the money tomorrow. Couldn't you wire it to me this afternoon?"

"Sarah," Hannah said as patiently as she could manage, "it's almost four o'clock, way too late to get to the bank. The lobby closes for business at three."

"You could call them. They'd arrange a wire transfer for

you, you know they would. Hell, they'd jump through hoops for the wife of one of their most important customers. C'mon, Hannah. It's no big deal. I really have to have the money tomorrow." The breezy tone had disappeared, and now a note of desperation colored Sarah's voice.

Hannah wanted to say no. But she knew what would happen if she did. Sarah would start to cry, and pretty soon she'd make Hannah feel guilty, even though Hannah knew she had nothing to feel guilty about. At least not on *this* score, she thought wryly. "Okay, Sarah, okay. I'll call the bank when we hang up. Where do you want them to send the money?"

Happy now that she'd gotten what she wanted, Sarah rattled off the information, then said a nonchalant goodbye.

Hannah sighed again as she replaced the phone. Why did she always cave in to Sarah? Hannah knew she wasn't doing her sister any favors by continuing to enable her to lead a life of irresponsibility.

Yet it was so difficult to refuse, because Jill had been right the other day. Hannah *was* lucky. And Sarah wasn't. Hannah supposed the argument could be made that a person made her own luck, but Hannah knew that wasn't entirely true. Certainly one didn't choose one's parents.

Anyway, the bottom line was, Sarah was her sister, faults and all, and Hannah loved her.

Hannah flipped through her Rolodex until she found the number for her bank. She had just finished arranging for the transfer of money when there was a soft tapping at the door.

"Come in," she called out, the frown brought about by Sarah's call fading, replaced by a smile of anticipation.

A second later Jenny walked in. Vixen was right on her heels.

Every time Hannah saw her daughter after not having seen her for a few hours, she marveled anew at her good fortune, for Jenny was any mother's dream child. Pretty, smart, sweet, a gifted horsewoman and violinist, Jenny was as perfect as a girl could get.

But she was growing up so fast. Already her coltish figure was changing from that of a girl to that of the woman she would soon become. Even her school uniform of dark blue pleated skirt and white blouse couldn't hide the promise of the future.

Jenny had inherited her father's thick, dark hair and Hannah's green eyes—a winning combination, especially combined with her gorgeous skin, which glowed with good health and tanned effortlessly. Already three inches taller than Hannah's five-feet-four—another trait handed down from her father—she showed no signs of stopping the growth spurt that had accelerated a couple of years earlier.

Yet despite her beauty, Jenny was so unspoiled and unaware of her allure. Thank God, Hannah thought as she smiled at her lovely daughter, who had plopped onto the black leather sofa. Vixen jumped up beside her. Although the puppy wasn't allowed on the furniture, Hannah hadn't the heart to chase her off. Jenny absentmindedly scratched behind the puppy's ears, but she seemed distracted.

"Tired, sweetie?"

"Uh-huh."

Hannah sat on the other side of Jenny and took her free hand in her own. "Glad school's out?" Today was the last day of school at the private academy Jenny attended in nearby Brentwood.

"I guess."

Hannah frowned. Jenny was a naturally cheerful child. Something must be wrong. "What's the matter? Did something happen today?"

Jenny shrugged.

"What?" Hannah pressed.

"Nothing." But Jenny didn't meet Hannah's eyes.

"Sweetie . . ." She rubbed her thumb over Jenny's knuckles. "You know you can tell me anything."

Still not meeting her mother's eyes, Jenny nodded.

"Jenny, you're scaring me. What *is* it?"

"Do you think I'm fat?" Jenny blurted. She finally looked at Hannah.

Hannah was astounded by the question. Jenny wore a size seven. By no stretch of the imagination could her daughter be considered fat. If anything, Hannah felt Jenny could use a few more pounds. "Fat? Good heavens, no! What ever put that idea into your head?"

Another shrug.

More gently Hannah said, "Come on, Jenny. Did someone call you fat?"

Jenny swallowed. "Yes," she whispered.

"Who?"

"Melanie Birch."

"Melanie *Birch*?"

Jenny nodded.

Hannah wanted to laugh, but she could see from the expression on Jenny's face that her daughter actually thought Melanie Birch might be right. *Tread carefully. Remember how sensitive a fourteen-year-old can be, especially about her body.*

"Sweetheart, let's just think about this for a minute. Isn't Melanie Birch the girl who ran against you for student council? And lost?"

"Yes, but—"

"And isn't Melanie Birch the one who came in second in the Medal class at Old Oaks in April? The girl you beat for the second time?"

"Y-yes."

"Now, isn't it possible, just possible, that this same Melanie Birch might be a teensy bit jealous of you?"

"I don't know."

"Jenny . . ."

"Well . . ." Another shrug. "I guess so."

"You *know* so." Hannah painted a mental picture of the girl in question. If memory served, Melanie Birch was shorter than Jenny and stick thin. No curves whatsoever. Hannah eyed Jenny's sweetly rounded breasts, her flat abdomen, her long, slender legs, and high-arched feet. "You are so far from being fat, it's almost laughable. Trust me, sweetie, Melanie is jealous of you, and because she couldn't think of anything else to say, and because she knows all girls your age—shoot, all girls, period—are terrified of being thought fat, she latched on to the one area where she thought she might shake your confidence."

"You think?"

"I *know*."

After a moment a small smile played at the corners of Jenny's mouth.

Hannah squeezed her hand, then leaned over and kissed Jenny's smooth cheek. "Jenny, you're beautiful. You're beautiful and you have a gorgeous body and you are not the least bit fat."

Jenny pulled her hand from Hannah's and threw both arms around Hannah's neck. "I love you, Mom."

Hannah breathed in the wonderful essence of her daughter. There was a lump in her throat. "I love you, too, pumpkin."

When they drew apart, Hannah knew her eyes were glistening with tears. Jenny's, though, were shining happily.

"Martha said Aunt Sarah called you," Jenny said. "Is she coming out to visit?" Her voice was eager.

One of the things Hannah was most proud of was the fact her daughter really loved her sisters and was completely unaware of any tension between them. "No, she just wanted to wish me a belated happy birthday."

Just then Hannah saw—out of the corner of her eye— Simon's Infiniti pull into the driveway. She rose. "Dad's home early today. Why don't you go out and say hi while I clean my brushes?"

As Jenny, followed by Vixen, went off to greet her father, Hannah said a silent prayer of thanks. She might have made a lot of mistakes in her life, but marrying Simon and having Jenny were not among them.

And yet, even as she sent up her acknowledgment of God's beneficence, she felt a trickle of uneasiness. Because Hannah knew, more so than most, that what has been given can, in the blink of an eye, also be taken away.

Seven

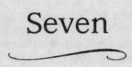

The excited yapping of Vixen, followed by a happy, "Hi, Daddy!" from his daughter, brought a smile to Simon's face. Coming home to his wife and daughter was the best part of his day.

"Hey, Princess," Simon said, throwing his arm around Jenny's shoulder and giving her an affectionate hug. At six-three Simon was a head taller than Jenny, but she was still growing. "How was the last day of school?"

"Great."

"Glad it's over?"

"Yeah, I guess. I'll miss Courtney, though."

Simon gave Jenny a commiserating smile. Courtney Jamison was Jenny's best friend but would be spending the summer with her dad, who lived on the East Coast.

Sometimes Simon wondered about these parents who seemed to think bouncing their kids around like rubber balls was no big deal. Did they ever even *consider* the kids when they got their quick and easy divorces? From everything he'd read and heard recently, divorce affected kids a lot more than the experts had first thought. Even adult children were affected, sometimes so strongly it negatively influenced their own relationships, even years later.

"Well," he said, "at least you can e-mail each other all you want."

Jenny seemed to brighten.

"And I'll tell you what," he added impulsively, "if your mother agrees, maybe you can go and visit Courtney for a week later in the summer."

"Dad! Do you really mean it?" she squealed.

"I wouldn't have said it if I didn't mean it."

"Will you ask Mom tonight?"

He squeezed her shoulder again. "Yes. But don't you say anything about this until I have a chance to talk to her, okay?"

"I know, I know." Jenny grinned. "You have to butter her up."

Simon laughed. "I wouldn't put it that way. It's just that your mother and I have an agreement about not making decisions where you're concerned unless we've talked about them first."

"You know, Dad, I really like that you and Mom never argue. Some of my friends, well, their parents never do anything else. I don't know how they stand it."

"I know, honey." Simon had heard enough talk in the locker room at the club and on the golf course to know he and Hannah were the exception. Who was it that had said most men led lives of quiet desperation? That certainly seemed to be true of a lot of today's marriages.

By now they'd walked into the kitchen, and Simon was immediately assaulted with the tantalizing aroma of freshly baked rhubarb pie, his favorite. "What's the occasion?" he asked Martha, who was slicing mushrooms. To Jenny, he said, "Maybe your mother is trying to butter *me* up."

Martha chuckled.

"What else is on the menu?"

"All your favorites," Jenny chimed in. "Steak, mushrooms, French fries, and salad."

"Now I *know* something's going on."

Anyone listening to the conversation and hearing the menu might have thought the Ferris family needed to make a change in their eating habits, Simon thought in amusement. But long ago he and Hannah had decided that once in a while, they could indulge themselves, especially when the majority of the time they ate a healthy, low-fat diet.

"Where *is* your mother?" he asked Jenny.

"Cleaning up in the studio." She reached into an open container of grape tomatoes and popped one into her mouth. "Ummm, Martha, these are soooo good."

"They should be," Martha said dryly. "They cost enough."

"I'm going to go check my e-mail and write to Courtney so when she gets to her dad's, there'll be a note waiting for her," Jenny said. She grabbed a couple more of the tomatoes.

"Jenny, remember, don't say anything to Courtney about what we discussed."

"I *know*, Dad. I won't."

Simon headed for Hannah's studio. The door was open and she was leaning over the sink washing out her brushes. She didn't turn around, so Simon knew she hadn't heard him enter. Walking softly, he came up behind her and dropped a kiss on her ear.

She jumped. "Simon! You scared me!" But she was laughing.

He was so glad to see she was back to her normal, cheerful self. The melancholy that had started with her birthday and lingered through the weekend seemed to finally be gone. "Sorry. I couldn't resist. You looked so cute standing there."

She shut off the water and dried her hands on a towel, then looped her arms around his neck and lifted her face for a kiss. As their lips met, she pressed closer, and Simon felt the familiar stirring of desire that his wife so easily brought about. "You vixen," he said huskily as they finally broke apart.

"I think you might have me mixed up with the dog." Her eyes sparkled.

"She does share some of your traits."

"Excuse me?"

Pulling her close again, he nuzzled her ear. "You're both soft. You both have cute rumps. And you both like to be petted." To demonstrate, he stroked her behind. "I rest my case."

"Unhand me, you sex maniac." Laughing, she pushed his hands away and twisted out of his arms. "I've got to finish cleaning up."

"Sex maniac, huh?" He eyed her suggestively, doing his best imitation of a lecherous old man. "Jenny's busy with e-mail, Martha's busy in the kitchen, and it's two whole hours before dinner . . . plenty of time for a quickie."

Grinning, she shook her head. "Later."

"Promise?"

"Cross my heart."

For the rest of the evening, even as he enjoyed the one predinner cocktail he allowed himself, the easy conversation and laughter between the three of them, and the delicious dinner, a part of him was impatient for the evening to be over.

And yet he knew the waiting and the anticipation would only enhance his pleasure when it was finally time to say good night to Jenny and he and Hannah could retire to their bedroom and the promised delights to be found in its king-size bed. Tonight, he knew, there would be no desperation to her lovemaking, no underlying sadness, no tears. Tonight she would be all his—body, heart, and mind.

Later, lying in bed spoon fashion, their naked bodies sated and cooling after making love, Simon thought again how fortunate he was. If he'd been given the choice of selecting the perfect family, he wouldn't have asked for anything different from what he had.

His one disappointment in that regard was his and Hannah's inability to have another child. Since Jenny's birth, Hannah had had two miscarriages, and her OB/GYN had finally told her it would be dangerous for her to keep trying.

So Simon had buried his desire for a son to carry on the family business—a business that his grandfather Ferris had begun and that he, Simon, had built from a regional chain of sporting goods stores to a national chain that had done more than a billion dollars' worth of business last year. Now he rarely thought about the *what-if*s. He had more than most—*far* more than most—and he knew it.

Moving his hand from where it rested lightly against Hannah's waist, he cupped a small, perfect breast. Absently, he stroked her, and her nipple hardened. He smiled and buried his face in her neck.

God, he loved her. She was one in a million. How had he gotten so lucky? From the very beginning they'd had a good sex life. In fact, he thought their sex life was even better now than it had been in the early years. As a result he found himself wanting her more as each year went by.

As he had earlier, he thought about some of his acquaintances—especially the men he played golf or squash with. How they often grumbled about their wives and their lack of interest in sex.

Simon never said a word. First of all, he didn't believe in talking about his private life. And second, he would never make Hannah the subject of locker-room talk.

Simon had always believed women belonged on a pedestal. If you couldn't feel that way about the woman you were married to, you had no business marrying her.

"Sweetheart?" he said.

Hannah sighed deeply. "Hmmm?"

"Jenny and I were talking earlier." He went on to tell her about the conversation they'd had concerning her friend Courtney and the possibility of her going to Connecticut to visit this summer. "What do you think?"

"I don't know, Simon. Summer seems to go by so fast, and what with all her shows and going to France, she's going to be awfully busy."

"I was thinking in terms of three of four days."

She didn't answer for a moment. Then, "I suppose she really wants to go."

"Yes."

She sighed. "Oh, all right, but first I'd want to talk to Courtney's mother."

"Her mother?"

"Yes. Just to see what she has to say about Courtney's dad, since we've never met him."

"I didn't think of that."

"I mean, I'm sure he's fine. I've only heard good things about him from Courtney. Still, I think it's best to be safe."

"You're right. But if he gets a clean bill, would you be agreeable to Jenny going?"

"I guess so." Then she chuckled. "You know I'd much rather she stayed close to home, but I guess I can't keep her tied to my apron strings forever."

Simon smiled. "Our chick is growing up."

"Yes."

Turning a bit so she could look into his eyes, she said, "Oh, Simon, I wish we could always protect her. Make sure no one ever hurts her."

"I know."

"We can't, though, can we?"

"No. All we can do is hope that the way we've brought her up and the things we've taught her will let her make wise choices."

"But if she doesn't—"

"If she doesn't, she'll always know we're here, that she can come to us no matter what."

They fell silent after that, each lost in his own thoughts. Gradually Hannah's breathing changed, and Simon knew she'd fallen asleep. He lay quietly thinking for a long time.

Finally, as the numerals on the bedside clock changed to show it was almost midnight, he pressed a soft kiss against her hair, whispering, "Sleep well, my love."

Then he gently eased his arm out from under her and closed his eyes.

Eight

⁓

"Did you check out the new lifeguard?"

Jenny grinned. "Oh, yeah."

"He's, like, totally hot."

Angie DeCarlo, who didn't go to Jenny's school but was the daughter of one of Jenny's dad's friends, leaned back on her elbows. In so doing, Jenny noticed, she had made her chest stick out a little more, which Jenny was sure had been her intention. Jenny couldn't help being a little jealous of Angie, for she was small and blond and sexy, and the boys all liked her, whereas she, Jenny, was too tall and had straight dark hair and wasn't sexy at all. She sighed. "He's really cute."

"Wonder how old he is?" Angie reached for the bottle of sunscreen they'd been sharing.

Jenny shrugged. "Eighteen?"

"At *least*." Now it was Angie's turn to sigh. "Too old for us."

Angie, like Jenny, was only fourteen, although her fifteenth birthday would be in the fall, whereas Jenny wouldn't turn fifteen until next March. Practically another whole year. God, how was she going to stand waiting? More than anything, Jenny wanted to get her learner's permit so she could drive. In her mind, driving and dating went hand in hand.

"You know who he looks like?" Angie said, shading her

eyes and staring at him unabashedly. Without waiting for Jenny to answer, she said, "Brad Pitt."

"Brad Pitt's blond." The subject of their intense interest had brown hair, but it was thick and wavy and worn kind of longish like Brad Pitt had worn his in a couple of movies. "And taller."

"I know, but I still think he looks like him."

"I think he looks more like Johnny Depp." Jenny was totally in love with Johnny Depp.

"Oh, you and Johnny Depp," Angie said disparagingly. "I don't know what you see in him."

Jenny rolled her eyes. They'd had this discussion before. The thing was, if a person didn't get what it was about Johnny Depp that was so cool, there was no way you could explain it to them.

Just then the new lifeguard, who had been standing at the other side of the pool watching some of the younger kids play a game of water tag, began to walk back to his station on the side of the pool where Jenny and Angie were sunning themselves. He smiled as he approached.

Jenny's heart beat faster. Oh, wow, she thought. He was even better looking up close than he had been from a distance. He had gorgeous brown eyes and a really great smile, which, to her complete astonishment, he seemed to be directing toward her instead of toward Angie. Jenny's mouth went dry.

"Hi." He stopped in front of them. "I'm David Conway, the new lifeguard."

"Hi," Angie drawled, dragging out the word like it was two syllables instead of one. She gave him her flirtiest smile.

Jenny was tongue-tied. Somehow she managed to croak out a hi, but she couldn't think of another thing to say. Oh, what was *wrong* with her? Here was the best-looking boy she'd seen in a long time, and he was being friendly and she was acting like a stupid kid! She completely forgot he was far too old for her, and that he was probably just being friendly because he wanted the people who belonged to the club to like him.

Angie got gracefully to her feet. Her small, curvy body

was shown to advantage in her hot-pink bikini. At that moment Jenny hated her. "I'm Angie DeCarlo. And this is my friend . . ." She gestured to Jenny.

Before she could finish, Jenny jumped up. "Jenny Ferris." She wished she wasn't wearing her boring old green tank suit from last year. Why hadn't she bought that cute striped two-piece with the little-boy bottoms that she'd seen at Stussy when she'd been there with Courtney and her mom last week?

"Hi, Angie. Hi, Jenny. You guys come here often?" A breeze lifted his hair, and he unconsciously smoothed it back.

"All the time," said Angie.

Jenny gave her a sidelong look. They didn't come here all the time. They came maybe twice a week. But she'd bet Angie would now want to come every day if David Conway was going to be there. Honestly. Angie could be such a slut sometimes. *Slut* was Jenny's new favorite word, although she didn't use it in front of her parents.

"Great. Guess I'll be seein' you around, then."

Jenny felt weak in the stomach when he smiled again. Especially since he once more seemed to mean the smile for her. She wondered how old he really was. Maybe he was only seventeen. Seventeen wasn't too old for her, was it?

"Do you go to school around here, David?" Angie said before he could walk away.

Suddenly Jenny was glad Angie was with her, because if anyone could get the information Jenny craved, it would be Angie.

"No, I just moved here from Florida. Anyway, I graduated from high school a couple of years ago, and I'm not sure if I'm going to go to college." As he said this, something changed in his eyes, but whatever it was, it disappeared so fast Jenny thought maybe she'd imagined it. She did a quick mental calculation. Her heart sank. He was probably nineteen or twenty. And no amount of rationalizing would make nineteen or twenty a suitable age for someone who was only fourteen. That was one of her dad's favorite words: *suitable*. She could just hear him.

"Now, Jenny," he'd say kindly—he *always* spoke kindly to her—"a twenty-year-old man is completely unsuitable company for a fourteen-year-old girl."

If she was older, it would be different. Nobody thought it was unsuitable for a twenty-year-old girl to date a twenty-five-year-old guy. Shoot, her own father was fourteen years older than her mother. But she knew there was no hope as far as David Conway was concerned. Even if he was interested in her, her parents would never let her go out with him.

"Well, I'd better get back to my station," David said. "Nice to meet you girls."

As he walked away from them, Angie muttered under her breath, "I'm in love, Jenny. Really, truly, deeply in love." Angie's voice rose dramatically.

"Oh, you're pathetic."

But Jenny's heart wasn't in it, because she knew she was just as pathetic, maybe even *more* pathetic, because at least Angie was honest.

For the rest of the afternoon, Jenny watched him from behind her sunglasses. The way he walked, the way he talked to the little kids—he was so *nice* to them—the way he paid attention and did his job instead of acting bored or spending his time flirting like so many of the lifeguards did.

Even after she went home, she kept thinking about him. And that night, at dinner, even though she knew it was probably not a good idea, she couldn't seem to stop herself from bringing his name into the conversation.

"Oh?" her mother said when she told them there was a new lifeguard. "Who is it? Anyone we know?"

"Nuh-uh. He just moved here from Florida. His name's David Conway." The name was like See's Chocolate on her tongue. She wanted to add, *He's really cute, and he smiled at me*, but she knew that would be, like, crazy.

First of all, there was the age thing. Second of all, she *never* talked about boys she liked in front of her parents. Once, she'd told her mom about a crush she had on a boy, and she could see the alarm in her mother's eyes, and the next thing Jenny knew, she was getting a lecture about sex and hormones and birth control and all kinds of embarrassing stuff.

Anyway, Jenny knew all about sex and hormones and birth control. At her school they'd been taught much of that stuff in their health class when they were eleven. Besides, she read *Seventeen* and other magazines, and she'd listened to the older girls talk.

She'd decided then that she wasn't going to tell her mom about boys until there was really something to tell, like being asked out on a date or something. Her mom just got too weirded out.

After that her parents seemed to forget about David, and Jenny had to content herself with daydreaming about him. And that night, in her sleep, she had a real dream about him. In the dream he called her, and her parents miraculously said it was okay to go out with him because he was so nice and so polite and they knew he'd take good care of her.

So he came to the house and picked her up and they went to the movies, and afterward they went to Benny's, the local hamburger place where the coolest kids hung out, and everyone stared at her. The boys were curious, and the girls, well, Jenny could see they were so jealous they could hardly stand it. They were all wondering who he was and how Jenny knew him, but Jenny just ignored them and let them wonder, the same way they normally ignored her.

Then when he brought her home, he told her what a good time he'd had and how he'd like to see her again and how much more mature she was than most of the girls he'd dated. And then he'd kissed her, and it was one of those dreamy kisses, all sweet and romantic, not one of the yucky kind that you saw in so many movies that were all open mouths and tongues and stuff.

Jenny hated that. She knew those kinds of kisses were supposed to be totally awesome, but Jenny thought she'd like the other kind much better.

She woke up the next morning still thinking about the

dream. She knew this crush on David was hopeless, but she couldn't seem to stop thinking about him.

She couldn't wait to see him again. Trouble was, today it would be almost impossible to get to the pool. This morning she was going to be out at the stables, and when she was through there, she'd have to hurry home and get cleaned up for her violin lesson at two.

Normally, she loved Wednesdays and couldn't wait for them to come. Spending the morning with Beauty, her nine-year-old Dutch Warmblood mare, was her favorite thing in all the world. It wasn't the only time she went to the stables, but it was the only time she and Beauty jumped. That was so they'd both remain fresh for the tough weekend competitions.

And she loved her violin lessons, too. Her teacher, Mr. Derrick, thought she had a lot of promise and had been encouraging her to consider making music her major in college. So she rarely missed a lesson, at least not voluntarily.

But maybe today, just this one time, she could pretend not to feel good enough to have her lesson, and she could go to the pool instead.

But as soon as she had the thought, she knew it wouldn't fly. Like her mom would let her go to the club if she was too sick to have her lesson. Not.

She sighed. The soonest she could see David again would be tomorrow, and she guessed she'd have to be satisfied with that. But wait a minute! Maybe that was best, anyway. Maybe after her lesson this afternoon she could persuade her mom to take her to Stussy, and she could get that cute bathing suit after all.

Smiling now, she bounded out of bed and began to get ready for her day.

Nine

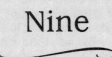

Hannah had just come back from dropping Jenny at the stables and was in her studio hoping to get a good three hours' work in before she had to pick Jenny up again when the phone rang. She glanced over and realized it was her business line. Sighing, she picked up the receiver.

"Hannah Ferris."

"Hannah, hello. It's Morgan McFarland."

"Hi, Morgan." The slight frown over the disturbance to her morning disappeared. Morgan McFarland owned one of the most prestigious galleries in the greater Los Angeles area and had shown and sold several of her paintings over the past two years.

Never one to beat around the bush, Morgan said without preamble, "I've got a proposition for you."

"Oh?"

"In September I want to feature you and your work to launch the opening of our new location in Beverly Hills."

For a moment Hannah was struck speechless.

"Well?" he said impatiently, his British accent more pronounced than usual. "Are you interested?"

"Morgan, of course I'm interested. I just—"

"You just what?"

Hannah took a deep breath. "I-I'm not sure I'm ready for something like this."

"If I think you're ready, you're ready."

Hannah almost laughed at Morgan's imperious tone. "How many paintings would you want?"

"At least forty, perhaps fifty."

Hannah bit her lip. At the most she had twenty-five paintings ready to display. Even supplying him with forty would mean she'd have to work nonstop all summer to be ready for a September show. And Simon wanted to take her and Jenny to France this summer. *Jenny.* Who would chauffeur her back and forth from the stables, the club, her violin lessons? And what about the horse shows? Hannah hadn't missed a single show since Jenny began to take part in competitions. The summer show season was the biggest, and Jenny was one of the most promising of the younger competitors with quite a few wins under her belt already. "I just don't know, Morgan. I'm not sure I can have that many paintings ready for you," she finally said.

"It's your choice, Hannah. If you can't do it, I'll have to find another artist to feature."

And he could do that easily, Hannah knew. "Can you give me just a couple of days to see what I can work out?"

"I'll give you until Friday."

"Morgan, I don't want you to think I'm not grateful. I am. I want, more than anything, to do this. It's just that we had some things planned for the summer, and I'm not sure I can cancel them."

"Yes, well. It's up to you. Call me on Friday."

After they'd hung up, Hannah sat thinking. She knew Morgan's offer was a fantastic opportunity. She also knew such opportunities didn't come along very often. Many people felt those who became successful at their chosen professions owed a lot of their success to luck. Hannah knew that wasn't true. When it came to careers, people made their own luck, which she believed meant taking advantage of every opportunity presented.

If you don't do this, you'll always regret it.

Five minutes later she picked up the phone.

"Sure," Simon said, "I'll meet you for lunch. What's up?"

"I'll tell you when I see you."

Later, settled at their table at the Yorkshire Grill, which

was only a few blocks from Simon's office on Figueroa, Hannah told him about the call from Morgan McFarland. She didn't elaborate, just unemotionally recounted the offer.

Simon listened quietly. When she was finished, he said, "This is a great opportunity, isn't it?"

Hannah nodded.

"How long would it take you to get ready?"

"I'd have to work nonstop through the summer."

Their eyes met. She'd always loved Simon's eyes. They were a dark, compelling blue, and in them she'd never seen anything but a deep and abiding love.

"We wouldn't be able to go to France," he said.

"No."

"And you'd have no time to spend with Jenny or accompany her to shows."

Hannah sighed. "No." Just then their waiter approached to take their orders. Once he was gone, she said, "That's the worst part, I think, missing the shows. It's not that I worry about her going on her own. I mean, you know how protective Grace is." Grace O'Malley owned the stables where they boarded Beauty. She was also Jenny's coach and trainer. A more trustworthy woman couldn't be found. She was like a mother hen with the girls, guarding and watching over them just as their own mothers would. "And it's not just the shows," Hannah continued. "She's got so many things going on this summer. Just getting her to and from places takes a lot of my time. And I had wanted to spend time at the club with her, plus take in some movies and do some shopping. You know, girl things."

"Getting her to and from places is easily solved," Simon said. "I'll have Ricardo do it." Ricardo Perez was Simon's assistant—a young man who did anything and everything to help make Simon's day run smoother.

"But, Simon, *you* need Ricardo."

"It's not a big deal to have him ferry Jenny around this summer. He's out several times a day running errands for me, anyway. He can just organize his trips to include her needs." Simon smiled. "He'll probably enjoy it. He thinks Jenny's pretty special."

"What about the shows?"

"Why don't I talk to Grace about the schedule? Maybe I can go to some of them."

"And the trip to France?"

"We can do that later in the year."

"But Jenny will be in school later in the year."

"She'll learn more going to France and meeting her cousins than she will in school. Besides, she can get her assignments in advance. If necessary, we can take a tutor along." He reached across the table and took her hand. "You can't pass up this opportunity, Hannah. You know that."

"But—"

"No *but*s. I want you to do this. If you don't, you'll always wonder what might have happened if you had. We can work everything out."

Hannah smiled crookedly. "Your mother's going to have a fit." She was referring to the fact that Madeleine Ferris had been looking forward to showing off her successful son and beautiful granddaughter to her relatives, none of whom had approved when she'd married Hugh Ferris and stayed in the U.S., a country they considered filled with unsophisticated and vulgar people.

"I'll take care of my mother."

"Simon, are you sure? I really am going to have to give my total concentration to work. I may be working a lot of evenings, too."

He squeezed her hand. "I'm sure."

She sighed deeply. "Jill's right."

"Jill? What does she have to do with this?"

"She told me last week that you were one in a million, and you are."

"Darling, I love you. It's that simple."

But Hannah knew it wasn't that simple. Simon was an extraordinary man. There wasn't a selfish bone in his body, and he truly cared about her career.

When she thought about how close she'd come to not marrying him, it was frightening. To think she'd believed she wasn't in love with him. She hadn't known the meaning of love. Thank God, now she did.

"All right," he said, releasing her hand. "It's settled. And just in time. Here comes our lunch."

They finished eating in plenty of time for Hannah to drive out to the stables to get Jenny. She had decided she would tell her daughter about the change of plans on the ride home.

"Gee, Mom, that sounds great," Jenny said.

"I won't be able to come to many of the shows."

"I know. It's okay. It'll be really cool to have Dad come. The other girls'll be jealous. Their dads hardly *ever* come."

"What about Ricardo? Will you mind him chauffeuring you around this summer?"

"Nuh-uh. That'll be cool, too. My own driver." She grinned to show she was teasing.

"I just feel bad because we'd planned so many things to do together."

"Mom, really, I'm fine with this. Since you'll be busy, I, um, can go to the club more often. Angie was saying just yesterday how she'd like to go every afternoon, but she didn't want to go by herself. Now I can go with her."

Hannah smothered a smile. She knew Jenny didn't realize it, but it hadn't taken Hannah more than a glance at her daughter's face the night before when she'd mentioned the new lifeguard at the pool to see that Jenny probably had more than a passing interest in him. Hannah decided that, busy or not, she'd have to carve out at least one afternoon to check this boy out.

"Gran will probably be upset, though," Jenny said.

As always, the mention of her mother-in-law brought an involuntary sigh to Hannah's lips. Now Madeleine would have one more reason to disapprove of her. "Yes, I'm sure she will."

"She really wanted us to meet all our French relatives."

"Dad said we could go over in the fall."

"Without *me*?"

Hannah grinned. "No. You'd go, too."

"But I'll be in school."

"Your father feels you'll learn more from a trip to France than you can learn in school. He said if necessary we'll hire a tutor and take her along."

"Mom, *really*?"

"Yes, really." Hannah flipped her right turn signal on. "So you think I should do this, even if it means I won't be available at all this summer."

"Yes, I do."

Hannah wasn't sure if she was happy or disturbed by the fact that Jenny didn't seem the least bit disappointed by the change in their plans. She really was growing up. For a moment Hannah wondered if she was doing the right thing. Wasn't Jenny more of a priority right now than her career?

"But you know, Mom, if I'm going to be spending a lot of time at the pool, I'm going to need another bathing suit. So I was thinking . . . could you maybe take me to Stussy before we go home? Beause there's this really cool bathing suit that I saw there. I really love it, and if I wait, it might be gone."

With effort Hannah set aside her doubts. She was being silly. Just because Jenny wasn't upset by the change in their summer plans didn't mean she was losing her daughter. Jenny was simply growing up and becoming more independent. And after all, wasn't that what Hannah *wanted*? "How can I say no when you're being so reasonable?" she said lightly.

But as she turned the car around, and they headed for the popular shop, one last worry niggled at her, and she thought it would be prudent not to wait too long to check out this boy that she knew perfectly well was the real reason behind Jenny's easy acceptance of Hannah's summer commitments. Because if he turned out to be someone Hannah didn't want around Jenny, she needed to know.

What she would do in that case, she hadn't a clue. She hoped she was worrying for nothing. She hoped he turned out to be a nice boy and no threat to her daughter's well-being.

Because Hannah knew how powerful adolescent hormones were, and how quickly a life could change when you thought you were in love. How you could lose all sense of proportion and propriety. How you could forget everything you'd been taught.

Keeping that in mind, she would check out this boy carefully, because the last thing she wanted was some hunky hormonal opportunist taking advantage of her fourteen-year-old daughter.

Please God, don't let her be hurt. Above all, don't punish her for my mistakes.

For ever since the day Jenny had been born, that had been Hannah's greatest fear. That someday her sins would catch up with her, and her punishment would be having to watch her daughter pay the price.

Ten

"I'm very upset by this, Simon." Madeleine Chappell Ferris's aristocratic face had settled into a disapproving frown that accentuated the deep grooves on either side of her mouth. "You know how much I was counting on this trip. I cannot believe you're canceling it."

Simon wondered if his mother had any idea how unattractive she looked when she was unhappy, a state of mind she seemed to choose over optimism and cheerfulness more and more often as she aged. But he kept any hint of censure out of his voice, because after all, she was nearing her eightieth birthday, and maybe she'd earned the right to be cranky. Besides, despite her faults, he loved her, and he knew she loved him. "I thought we could go in September instead. For your birthday."

"For my *birth*day! But I had supposed we would have a big party *here* for my birthday."

Simon suppressed a sigh. "Of course we'll have a party here. I just meant as this is a special birthday, it warrants more than a party. The weather in Burgundy will be nicer in September, too. And the continent won't be overrun with children. You know how you hate traveling when all the kids are out of school."

She sniffed, not placated. Her dark eyes were hard when they met his. "I still think Hannah is being extremely selfish."

"Yes, I know. But I don't agree." This last was said firmly. Simon always took Hannah's side in any discussion where his mother had a criticism of her, which happened almost every time they were alone. It frustrated him that his mother had this attitude toward his wife. He couldn't understand it.

Yes, Hannah hadn't been to the manor born, but neither had he. His mother conveniently forgot that he was adopted, that his background was far inferior to Hannah's. After all, she'd been born to respectable parents and was intelligent and well-educated. The same couldn't be said of his parents. Simon's father had run out on his mother before he was born, and his mother had discarded him as if he had no more value than a pair of old tennis shoes.

There was certainly nothing to be ashamed of in his wife. In fact, he felt she was a tremendous asset to him. Over the years they'd been married, both business associates and friends alike had said time and again what a lucky man he was and what a charming woman Hannah was.

As far as he knew, Hannah had never been rude or discourteous to his mother, either. In fact, she was unfailingly thoughtful and attentive, always deferring to Madeleine and always remembering her station in the family. Yet his mother persisted in this unfathomable disapproval and dislike of his wife.

Smothering another sigh, he continued quietly, "I *want* Hannah to do this show, Mother. It's a wonderful opportunity, and I'm proud of her for being chosen. Jenny is, too."

His mother's lips tightened, and she looked out the window, but he knew she wasn't seeing the sightseers, the traffic, or the coast beyond. The two of them were having lunch at a little French restaurant near his mother's high-rise condominium apartment in Malibu.

Simon had grown up in the family home in Brentwood, but shortly after his father died, his mother had decided she didn't want the responsibility for the upkeep of the large home. Even though Simon had advised against it, she'd sold the home and bought the condominium. He'd tried to tell her it wasn't a wise idea to uproot herself from all her friends, that she wouldn't like being isolated from everything familiar, but his advice had fallen on deaf ears. Now she was paying the price, because ever since she'd moved to Malibu, she'd been unhappy, a situation that worsened weekly.

He studied her as she continued to ignore him. Today she was impeccably dressed, as always, in a pale peach linen suit, white silk blouse, and her favorite pearls. Her hair, which she still insisted on dying the black of her youth, was brushed back into a severe chignon. She wore too much makeup, but Simon had noticed that many elderly, wealthy women who were trying to hold on to their youth were guilty of the same thing.

Still, she was a lovely woman and could be even lovelier if she smiled more often. It saddened him that she'd become so discontented in the past few years. It wasn't all because of the move. He guessed his father had kept her on a more even keel than any of them had realized, for Hugh Ferris had been a naturally upbeat person.

"You'd defend Hannah no matter what she did," his mother said tightly as she finally turned away from the window.

"If that's true, it's because she never does anything to upset me."

"You know, Simon, just once I wish you could be honest with me."

"And by that you mean . . . ?"

"I mean no one is perfect, and why you persist in pretending Hannah has no faults is ludicrous."

Simon told himself to count to ten. "I didn't say she didn't have any faults. I'm sure she does. But whatever they are, they don't affect me. She's been a wonderful wife. I couldn't ask for better."

And if you keep this up, I might just decide your age or our relationship doesn't give you the right to constantly harp about my wife.

"Now, come on, Mother," he added, forcing himself to respond more kindly than he actually felt, "let's stop arguing, okay? I'm sorry you're disappointed, but Hannah and

Jenny and I can't go to France until after Hannah's show, and that's that. But if you still want to go, that's fine. I'll ask Eileen to make the arrangements." Eileen was his secretary.

"You know I don't want to go without you and Jenny."

This time Simon didn't even try to hide his growing loss of patience. "Then stop being difficult. We'll all go in September." So saying, he turned his attention to his roast chicken.

After a few minutes of silence that simmered with her anger and righteous indignation, his mother finally seemed to accept the inevitable and began to tell him about the baby slam she'd made the day before at her duplicate bridge group.

"You should have seen Charlotte's face when I trumped her ace of spades," she crowed. "She thought with her three aces she couldn't help but set us. But I was void in spades and Nancy was void in diamonds, and we got our tricks before Charlotte ever had a chance."

His mother was an avid bridge player. When Simon's father had been alive, they played duplicate at the tournament level and had been quite good. The game was the one thing that still interested her, although many other pastimes had succumbed to age and ennui.

"Good for you," he said when she'd finished giving him a rundown of yesterday's game. He smiled at her, forgetting his earlier irritation. "I almost feel sorry for Charlotte, having to play someone as sharp as you."

She smiled back, pleased at the compliment.

After that, the remainder of their lunch together was pleasant, and by the time Simon kissed her goodbye and installed her in the backseat of her Lincoln Town Car—driven by her longtime chauffeur, Anton—he could almost forget that they'd nearly quarreled earlier.

Yet as he drove back to the office, he couldn't help remembering her intractable attitude toward Hannah. He would never forget the first time he'd taken his wife home to meet his parents.

He'd been so excited, so proud, so sure his parents would

adore Hannah the way he did. So he was entirely unprepared
for his mother's reaction. Unprepared and bewildered. At
first he'd thought maybe he was imagining that she didn't
like Hannah, but as the evening progressed and that cool,
assessing expression in her eyes remained, he knew he
hadn't imagined anything.

Hannah had felt it, too, and when the evening was finally
over and they were on their way to her apartment, she'd
brought it out in the open. "Your mother doesn't like me,"
she said quietly.

"I don't know what got into her tonight." He wouldn't
lie to Hannah. She was too important to him, and he felt
honesty was essential if their relationship was going to go
where he wanted it to go. "I'm sorry. Whatever it was, she'll
get over it."

"Maybe she won't."

Something in her tone scared him. "Hannah, whatever my
mother thinks, it doesn't matter." When she didn't answer,
he said with more urgency, "She's just possessive."

"It's more than that."

"Hannah, I love you, you know that."

She sighed deeply. "Yes, I do, but—"

"Let's not talk about this now. Let's wait until we get to
your apartment, okay?" He wanted to be able to take her
into his arms. He wanted to kiss away any doubts she had
that what his mother thought would make any difference to
him or to their plans. Damn his mother! He was going to
have to get a few things straight with her. He would talk to
her tomorrow, because he had no intention of letting her
ruin this for him.

He did his best to reassure Hannah that night, but he knew
he'd only been partially successful. As she'd sadly said, she
didn't want to be the cause of any kind of estrangement
from his family. "You're their only child, Simon. They want
the best for you."

"*You're* the best for me."

Hannah's eyes filled with tears. "Maybe I'm not."

"Why would you *say* anything like that?" he'd cried. "If
I looked the entire world over, I'd never find anyone better

for me than you." With that, he'd gotten down on his knees in front of her. "Hannah, I love you. I love you more than I ever thought I could love anyone. And I want you to marry me."

"I don't know if I can. I just . . . it's bad enough that I'm not on great terms with my parents. It would be intolerable if I drove you away from yours." A tear ran down her face, and she brushed it away. "Think about if we have children." At the word *children*, her voice broke. "I want our children to know their grandparents. I can't bear the thought that . . ." Too upset to continue, she groped in her pocket and pulled out a tissue.

"Sweetheart," he said, getting up and sitting beside her. He cradled her in his arms. "You're making too much of this. I told you, my mother is possessive. She'll get over this. She'll realize that she's not losing me, and she'll come around. I promise you."

But he knew Hannah wasn't convinced. And the next morning, instead of going to the office, he headed straight for his parents' home. When he arrived, they were sitting in the enclosed sunroom at the back of the house over their usual morning coffee and croissants. His mother was reading the *Times*, his father *The Wall Street Journal*.

Both gave him welcoming smiles.

"Good morning," he said, kissing his mother's cheek and giving his father a warm smile.

Lucy, their housekeeper, walked into the room. "Hello, Mr. Simon. Would you like some coffee?"

"Please." He sat down. Outside, the December sun shone brightly. He said nothing until Lucy came back with a table setting for him and had poured his coffee. It was only when she'd left them that he plunged in. "I wanted you two to be the first to know. I've asked Hannah to marry me."

His mother, who had been in the process of putting jelly on a croissant, dropped the knife. Jelly spattered onto her powder-blue robe, but she seemed not to notice. "You haven't!"

Her exclamation overlapped his father's equally surprised, "I had no idea things were that serious, son."

"Yes, Mother, I have. And yes, Dad, things are very serious between us. I love Hannah very much and I hope she'll have me."

"Hope she'll *have* you!" his mother said. "And just why wouldn't she have you, I'd like to know?"

"Maybe because last night you made it so obvious you didn't like her."

"Just who *is* this girl, anyway, Simon?" his mother retaliated. "From what I could see, she's a nobody. Not only that, there's something about her that bothers me. I can't quite put my finger on what it is. Not yet, anyway. The thing is, you know nothing about her or her people. Whereas it's easy for her to see that you are a catch. One of the most eligible bachelors in Los Angeles. Not to mention one of the richest."

"Hannah doesn't care a thing about our money. She—"

"They *all* pretend they don't care about money, Simon," she interrupted scornfully. "Hugh." She gave Simon's father an exasperated look. "Will you please say something? You can't think this is a good idea."

"On the contrary," Simon's father said, "I think Simon has made an excellent choice. I liked Hannah very much. She's a lovely young woman."

"I simply do not believe this! Why, you know *nothing* about the girl. How can you say he's made an excellent choice?"

"I trust his judgment."

"Thank you, Dad."

"Men *have* no judgment when it comes to their libido," his mother said furiously. "You *all* think with your penises. *What?*" she added, glaring at Simon. "Won't she put out for you until she has you hooked?"

"Madeleine!" Simon's father said, aghast.

Simon stared at his mother. He had never heard her talk that way before. Suddenly furious himself, he jumped up, nearly spilling his coffee in the process. "I don't have to sit here and listen to this. I'm just going to say one more thing, and then I'm going before we all say things we'll regret later." His gaze didn't waver. "I love Hannah. And I'm going to marry her. You, Mother, can either accept that and welcome her into our family, or not. It's your choice. Dad . . ." He gave his father an apologetic look. "I'm sorry about this. See if you can talk some sense into her, okay?"

He drove home in a rage. Afterward, he realized it was a miracle he hadn't had an accident on the way.

The next day his mother called and asked him to meet her for lunch. She apologized and said if he was determined to marry Hannah, she wouldn't stand in his way. It wasn't the kind of unconditional apology he had hoped for, but he knew his mother's pride wouldn't allow her to grovel, so he didn't push it. It was enough that she was going to try to meet him halfway.

After that she had been very polite to Hannah. She'd even managed a smile when they'd announced their engagement and had gone along with his father's wish to host an engagement party for them. The party was lavish and elegant. He could find no fault with it or with his mother's behavior, although she hadn't gone so far as to give him the ancestral ring that had belonged to her grandmother—the one she had always led him to believe would be his to present to his future wife, and Simon hadn't pressed the point. A ring was just a ring. He would buy Hannah her own ring.

Despite her outer compromise, his mother's inner feelings about Hannah had never changed, and Simon knew it. So did Hannah. Yet they both accepted what couldn't be changed. Still, there were times, like today, when Simon wanted to throttle his mother.

When he arrived back at his office, the first thing he did was to call Hannah.

"How'd it go?" she said.

"She wasn't happy with the change in plans, but she'll get over it."

"You know, I was thinking, maybe you shouldn't postpone the trip. You and Jenny could go with her. She never really cared about me coming along, anyway."

"There is no way I'm going without you."

"Simon . . ."

"No."

"But—"

"No."

She sighed, the sound carrying clearly over the wire. "She's getting older," she said softly. "It's not a good idea to put things off."

"Hannah. It's only three months. And my mother is as healthy as a horse. She's not going to die anytime soon. In fact," he added dryly, "she'll probably outlive me." Silently he added, *She's just nasty enough.*

He was immediately sorry for the thought. His mother wasn't really nasty. She was just stubborn and set in her ways. Sometimes he thought that even if she *did* finally see that Hannah was a great person, she could never back down and admit it.

"Okay, you've convinced me," Hannah said. "I didn't really want you to go without me."

He heard the smile in her voice, and he smiled in return. "Good. That's settled, then. Listen, Hannah, I'd better go. But I'll be home by five, since we'll have to leave no later than six-thirty tonight."

"Oh, that's right. With everything else, I almost forgot about tonight's dinner."

Simon sat on the board of a prominent Los Angeles children's shelter, and tonight was their annual fund-raising dinner followed by a silent auction. It was being held at the Century Plaza Hotel.

After they'd hung up, he swiveled his chair around and gazed out at the hazy L.A. skyline. Angelenos never referred to the polluted air as smog. It was always much more generously called "haze." He smiled. He loved his city and its positive take on things. Sure, it had its problems, but what great city didn't?

And just like that the irritation of the past couple of hours faded away. So what if his mother persisted in her unwarranted dislike of his wife? Her attitude made no difference to him. All marriages had their problems, and in the scheme of things, his mother's attitude was minor.

Because the bottom line was, he had everything he had ever wanted in Hannah and Jenny.

And nothing else mattered.

Eleven

Things couldn't have worked out better if she'd planned them, Jenny thought happily. It was Tuesday, five days since her mom had told her about the change in their summer plans, and this was the third time Jenny and Angie had come to the club pool since then.

Today when they'd arrived, she'd been afraid maybe David wasn't working, because she didn't see him. But shortly before eleven he walked out of the locker room. The sight of him in his red bathing trunks with the club logo on the side caused her to feel slightly breathless. He looked great.

Jenny had never realized how much she liked a boy to have a good body. David's body looked strong, even though he wasn't big. But you could tell he worked out or something, because he had nice muscles and awesome legs and arms. Of course, he was from Florida, so he'd probably done lots of swimming.

He had a great tan, too, much darker than it had been when he'd first started working there.

He was so cute. Every time she looked at him, she felt weak, the same way she felt when she looked down from someplace high up. That sort of half sick, half excited feeling in the pit of her stomach.

She wondered if this was what it felt like to be in love, as if you were sort of perched up on top of a mountain and might topple over at any minute.

"Here he comes," Angie said under her breath.

"Who?" Jenny said innocently.

"Oh, don't act like you don't see him. I know you like him just as much as I do."

"You're crazy. He's too old for us. You said it yourself."

"So? Doesn't mean I can't *think* about him, does it?" Angie's voice fell suggestively. "Wonder what it would be like to have sex with him?"

"Angie."

"What?" said Angie innocently. She grinned. "Would you rather I said fuck?"

"Angie!" Jenny said through gritted teeth. She looked around nervously. She saw that Mrs. Taggard, whose daughter Jessica was in Jenny's Sunday School class, was looking at them. Oh, God. Had she *heard* Angie? If she told Jenny's mom, Jenny would die.

And her dad! He would ground her for weeks if he thought she talked like that. Worse, he might say she couldn't hang out with Angie anymore, and *then* who would she come to the club with?

"You're such a baby," Angie said.

"I told you. My parents would kill me if they heard me say that word." Or any of the other words Angie used so freely.

"They're not *my* parents."

"They wouldn't let me do stuff with you anymore, either. They'd say you're a bad influence."

Angie giggled. "Well, I am."

Jenny couldn't help it, she laughed, too. "Anyway, you've never done it, so I don't know why you act like you're so experienced."

"Jeez, Jenny. Saying the word *fuck* isn't that big a deal. *Everybody* says it."

But Jenny noticed Angie had lowered her voice this time. "That doesn't mean it's okay."

"Y'know, if you're gonna keep being such a baby, maybe I'd *better* find someone else to hang out with."

Out of the corner of her eye, Jenny saw David approaching them. "Shut up," she whispered urgently. "He's coming."

Both girls automatically sat up straighter, and it was all Jenny could do to keep from smoothing her hair back. Her heart picked up speed as he came closer.

"Hey," he said, smiling down at them.

"Hi," Angie said brightly.

"Hi," Jenny echoed weakly.

For a minute nobody said anything else, and Jenny frantically tried to think of something really clever, something that would impress David, but for the life of her she couldn't think of anything.

"So do you girls ever go in the water?" David said. He grinned.

"Not if I can help it," Angie said. She tossed her head. "Ruins my hair."

"What about you, Jenny?" he said.

When he smiled at her like that, Jenny felt like she was going to melt. "I like the water," she managed to say without sounding too stupid.

"Well, come on in, then." He blew his whistle. "Adult swim. Everyone under twelve out of the pool for ten minutes," he called. Once the pool was cleared of the younger children, he motioned for her to follow, walked to the edge, and dived in.

Jenny didn't wait for a second invitation. Without looking at Angie, she leaped to her feet, walked to the spot where David had gone in, and executed a perfect swan dive herself.

When she surfaced, David's face was only inches from hers.

"Hey, nice dive," he said.

"Thanks." She was mesmerized. Up this close she could see the tiny golden glints in his otherwise dark eyes and the fuzz above his upper lip. She had the almost irresistible desire to touch him.

"You take lessons?"

"Uh-huh." She could hardly breathe. Things were going on in her body that felt completely foreign to her.

"Thought so. You're pretty good."

Jenny felt warm all over. She knew Angie was probably croaking and wishing she hadn't said she didn't go in the water unless she had to, because she would probably kill to be here with David right now.

"So do your parents come to the pool, too?"

"Not much."

"Why not?"

"Well, my dad works and so does my mom."

"Yeah, I heard your mom was an artist."

Jenny frowned. "You *did*?"

He shrugged. "Yeah, someone mentioned it. She must be famous, huh?"

"No, not really." Jenny didn't want to talk about her parents, but she wasn't sure how to change the direction of the conversation.

"She paints, right?"

"Uh-huh."

"In oils?"

"No, mostly in watercolor." She couldn't understand this. Why did he care?

"So if I wanted to see something she'd painted, where would I go? Are her paintings for sale anywhere?"

Maybe he was just being polite. "Not right now, but in September they will be. Are you an artist yourself?"

"Me?" he said. "I can't draw a straight line."

"Then why—"

"Hey, are you gonna stay out there forever?"

David and Jenny both turned. Angie stood at the side of the pool. Jenny could tell from the way she had her hands on her hips that she was mad. Jenny smothered a smile. It was rare for her to make Angie jealous, but it felt good.

David looked at the clock mounted on the outer wall of the locker room. "Ten minutes is almost up. Guess I'd better get back to work. Nice talkin' to you, Jenny."

"You, too."

"What were you talking about out there?" Angie demanded when Jenny climbed out.

Jenny shrugged and reached for her towel. "Nothing important." But she smiled as she remembered how he'd complimented her dive. Impulsively she threw down the towel. "I think I'll go back in the water for a while. Practice my diving."

"Hey," Angie called as Jenny walked away, but Jenny ignored her.

Glancing over to see what David was doing now, Jenny saw that he'd climbed up into his chair and was watching her. Instead of diving from the side as she'd done before, she walked self-consciously around the pool to the diving board. She knew David was still watching her as she climbed up and walked out to the end of the board.

Which dive should she do? she wondered. She really only knew how to do two or three well. Of those, the back flip was the showiest dive she'd learned. Disregarding the fact that she hadn't executed the dive since last summer and was probably really rusty, she turned around and bounced the board experimentally. She felt almost giddy as she sucked in her breath and positioned her feet at the edge of the board.

She bounced once, twice, then propelled herself up and out, bringing her knees up close the way she'd been taught. She never realized she wasn't far enough out. She never saw the board. The first awareness she had that she'd made a mistake was when pain shot through her head.

A second later the entire world went black.

Twelve

The instant David realized the kid was in trouble, he leaped from the chair and raced around to the spot where he'd last seen her. Taking a deep breath, he dived in. He saw her immediately. She was lying motionless at the bottom of the pool. Blood stained the water around her head, and he realized she'd probably hit it on the board.

It had been a long time since David had rescued anyone, but he knew what to do. Within seconds he had the kid in a secure hold and was kicking his way to the surface of the water. As soon as he broke free, he yelled, "Somebody call 911. She's hurt."

A woman whipped out her cell phone, and several others ran to the edge to help him. He handed Jenny up as gently as he could, then heaved himself up and out. Breathing hard, he knelt beside her and pressed his fingers to the side of her neck. Relief coursed through him as he felt her pulse beating.

But she wasn't breathing. Pinching her nose shut, he began rescue breathing. After five breaths she suddenly began to cough. He quickly turned her head to the side, and a second later water erupted from her mouth and nose.

After that everything was a blur. People were everywhere, shouting to one another, and then, overriding everything else, the sound of a siren.

Once the EMTs were on the scene, David stood back and

managed to keep everyone else out of the way, too. Jenny's eyelids fluttered, and she moaned as they lifted her onto a stretcher.

"Are her parents here?" asked a female EMT.

"No, but I know the family," one of the women said.

"She's with me," Angie said. "Her name's Jenny Ferris."

"Has anyone called the family?" the female EMT asked.

"I'll call right now," the woman said. "Do you know the number?" Angie nodded yes.

"Good," the technician said, "because we can't take her anywhere without permission. And she really should be checked out by a doctor."

Five minutes later, after reaching Simon Ferris and getting his permission to transfer her to the UCLA Medical Center, the technicians loaded her into the ambulance.

After they had gone, several of the bystanders patted David on the back. One man who looked as if he'd just come off the golf course said, "Good work, son."

By now Tony, David's boss, had joined the group. "Tell me exactly what happened," he said to David,

"Is she gonna be okay, do you think?" Angie said. She looked scared to death.

"She'll be fine," the woman said. "She's in good hands."

"Yes," Tony said, "she'll be fine."

David wondered if they really believed what they were saying or if they were just trying to make Angie feel good. He hoped they were right, because even though she didn't know it, Jenny was his *sister*. But even if she hadn't been, she was a nice kid, and he wouldn't have wanted anything to happen to her. Besides, he couldn't help but realize what had happened today was going to give him a perfect way to meet the family.

People continued to talk about what had happened for a while, but before long they lost interest and things settled back to normal. All afternoon, as David worked, he wondered how Jenny was doing. He told himself he wasn't worried, not really, just concerned the way anyone would be concerned. Jeez, he wouldn't want *any* kid to get hurt. He decided that when his shift was over, he would ask Tony if there had been any news.

But shortly before five, Tony, accompanied by a tall, good-looking man that David immediately recognized as Simon Ferris, walked out into the pool area and headed in his direction. David took a deep breath and told himself not to be nervous.

"David," Tony said, "this is Mr. Ferris, Jenny's father. He wanted to talk to you."

"Hello, Mr. Ferris. It's nice to see you again."

"Again?" He frowned.

"Yes. I'm sure you don't remember me, but I waited on you and your wife the night of her birthday."

"Of course. I thought you looked familiar, and now I know why." Simon Ferris smiled and shook David's hand with a firm grip. "I can't tell you how grateful I am for what you did earlier today."

"I just did my job, sir."

"You saved my daughter's life. I owe you more than I can ever repay."

David was embarrassed by the praise. He hadn't done anything so special. Any good lifeguard would have done the same. "I'm just glad I could help. How *is* Jenny? She okay?"

"She's got a concussion, and she had to have quite a few stitches, but she's going to be fine."

"I'm glad."

"My daughter has told us a little about you. She said you just moved here from Florida?"

"Yes, sir."

"She mentioned something about college. Are you planning to go to school in the fall?"

"I don't know. I'd like to, but . . ."

"But what?"

David shrugged. "The truth is, I'm not sure I can afford it."

Ferris nodded and studied him for a few seconds. "Maybe I can do something about that."

"I couldn't take your money, sir."

"How about a job instead? My company offers a tuition-reimbursement program to employees. So you could go to school, if you wanted, and we'd pay for it."

David stared at him. He could hardly believe what Ferris was saying.

"I could use a quick-thinking young man like you in my organization."

"I . . ." David cleared his throat. "I don't know what to say."

Ferris smiled. "Then say yes."

David's mind was racing. In all the scenarios he'd dreamed up about getting to know the Ferris family, he'd never imagined he could get himself hired by Simon Ferris.

"If you're worried about your job here, I'll square it with the club," Ferris pressed.

"I . . . it's just . . . well, you don't have to do this, Mr. Ferris."

"I know I don't. I want to."

David finally allowed himself to smile. "What kind of business do you have?" He figured it was a logical question, one Ferris would expect him to ask.

"Have you ever heard of Ferris Sporting Goods?"

"Who hasn't?"

"I'm that Ferris."

David grinned. "You're kidding."

Ferris just smiled.

"You're not kidding."

"No."

"What kind of job are we talking about?"

"You'd start out in the shipping department so you could learn the product line. Where you'd go from there is entirely up to you." When David didn't immediately answer, he added, "It's a good job. I think you'd like it." He smiled. "It was *my* first job."

"Really?"

"Yes. My father believed in learning the business from the ground up. He always said you couldn't understand the problems unless you'd experienced them. So what do you say?"

David nodded. "It sounds good. Really good. I know I'd like it. The only thing is, this is a nice place. I don't want to leave them shorthanded."

"Don't worry about that. I told you. I'll make sure it's okay with them. Now, do we have a deal?"

"Yes." David grinned. "We have a deal."

After giving David instructions on where to report, he gave him a business card. "I wrote my cell phone number on the card in case you need me and can't get me at the office. Now I'll go talk to Tony and see if next week is notice enough for you to give here. If not, we'll work around it, okay?"

"Okay."

They shook hands again, then Ferris left. David stood watching him go. Euphoria gripped him. The whole incident with Jenny today . . . it was almost as if fate had taken a hand in his life. He was sorry she'd hurt herself, but because she had, things had worked out perfectly for him.

He had no doubt Simon Ferris would square things away here at the club. Someone of Ferris's importance was always catered to. Why, they were probably falling all over themselves right now, saying, "Yes, sir, Mr. Ferris," "Whatever you want, Mr. Ferris."

In fact, David imagined that his boss and his boss's boss would be relieved that there weren't going to be any accusations of negligence. What was one little lifeguard as opposed to a lawsuit?

Not that David or the club was at fault in what had happened with Jenny. She was the one who had attempted a dive she obviously wasn't equipped to do.

Still . . . people like the Ferrises didn't get blamed when things went wrong. Someone else usually took the fall. It scared the hell out of him to think about how different today could have turned out—if Jenny had been more seriously hurt or if he hadn't known what to do and done it so quickly.

"My ass would have been grass," he muttered.

But neither of those things had happened. And now he was going to go to work for Simon Ferris.

Thirteen

Hannah spent the day at Venice Beach. She shot half a dozen rolls of slides, and now she was pleasantly tired, but happy. She was getting more and more excited about her show, which she'd decided she would call "Street Life." In addition to her paintings of homeless people, she planned to include paintings of ordinary and not-so-ordinary Angelenos at play. And what better place to find the entire spectrum of the populace than Venice Beach?

Today she'd seen everything: beachcombers, souvenir hawkers, gay couples strolling, winos lying on the beach, mothers pushing babies in strollers, hard bodies Rollerblading, kids bopping to rap music, a couple of street musicians, some old men playing bocci, and the ever-present tourists in their Bermuda shorts, white athletic shoes, and Sure-Shot cameras.

Yes, a very good day, she thought. She had some great material to work with. She still had plans to shoot in a couple of other areas of L.A.—Rodeo Drive, the nightlife around Sunset, and Watts—but for now she had enough to keep her busy for at least a month or more.

It was late when she arrived at the house, nearly six. Simon's car was already in its slot in the garage. She smiled. She was looking forward to the evening—a cool shower, a change of clothes, some wine, a good dinner . . . The smile was still on her face when she entered the kitchen.

It didn't stay there long. She took one look at Martha's expression and knew something had happened.

"I tried to call you," Martha said. "But your cell phone wasn't working."

Oh, God. "The battery's low, and I forgot to charge it last night. What happened? Is it Jenny? Is she okay?"

Heart in her throat, Hannah rushed back to Jenny's room, where Martha said she would find Simon, who would explain everything.

Ten minutes later Hannah was sitting at Jenny's bedside, holding her groggy daughter's hand. Love and guilt were mixed together in that universal emotion parents feel when they haven't been there to protect their child from harm.

"Oh, sweetie, I'm so sorry," Hannah said. She still felt shaky at the thought of what could have happened. How the outcome of today's accident could have been so much worse than a concussion, a small shaved place on the head, and a half dozen stitches.

"It's okay, Mom." Jenny's voice was barely audible as she drifted back into sleep.

"She'll probably sleep for hours," Simon murmured. "That painkiller they prescribed for her is pretty strong." He inclined his head toward the door. "Let's go talk where we won't disturb her."

Hannah reluctantly let go of Jenny's hand. Bending over, she kissed Jenny's smooth cheek. Love nearly overwhelmed her, and she had to blink back tears. Fighting for control, she followed her husband to the room they called the library, but was really Simon's study. Hannah sank into the soft leather sofa.

Simon poured her a glass of wine, then came and sat next to her. He told her what the doctor at the medical center had said. How Jenny should be kept quiet. How there could be no riding and particularly no jumping for at least a month and possibly longer. "After that she should be fine. They'll want to check her, of course, but they anticipate no problems."

"Thank God. Was she very disappointed about the jumping? She'll miss most of the shows this summer."

Simon nodded. "Yes, she cried when she realized the season was probably over for her, but you know, although I certainly wish this had never happened, it's probably a good lesson for her." He smiled ruefully. "Some people never learn that actions carry consequences, but now Jenny has, and she'll be a better and wiser person because of it."

"I hope you didn't say that to her." The words were out of her mouth before she could stop them.

"Hannah . . ." He looked pained. "Don't you know me better than that?"

"I'm sorry. Of course I do. I'm just so upset, and I know Jenny's crushed about the shows."

He sighed. "I know, but it could have been a lot worse. We owe that lifeguard a huge debt of gratitude. It was his quick action that saved her. The paramedic I talked with told me seconds can make a difference when it comes to drowning deaths."

She shuddered. Dear God. She couldn't have borne losing Jenny. Even the thought made Hannah feel sick.

Simon put his arm around her. "Come on, now, sweetheart." He kissed her temple. "There's no sense in dwelling on *what-if*s. Jenny is fine. By the end of the summer she'll be as good as new."

Hannah nodded, but she couldn't shake off the conviction that if she'd only been there today, none of this would have happened.

"I can see by the look on your face that you're starting to feel guilty. Don't do that to yourself. What happened today was an accident. Not your fault. Not anyone's fault."

How did Simon always know what was in her heart? "You're a good man," she whispered.

He kissed her gently. Then he told her about the offer he'd made to the lifeguard.

"A job? You don't think he would have rather had a reward?"

"He said he didn't want money. And I have to tell you, Hannah. That really impressed me."

Hannah understood. Most people, knowing who Simon was, would have leaped at the chance to cash in with a fat reward. "He sounds like an extraordinary young man."

"I think he is."

"Simon, is this the same lifeguard Jenny's been talking about so much?" She didn't add *the one she has a crush on*, but it's what she was thinking.

"I think he might be."

She bit her lip, remembering how she'd been so quick to be suspicious of the boy. "I want to meet him and thank him, too."

Simon smiled at her. "That would be nice. I think he'd really appreciate it. But you know, you have met him."

"I have?"

"Yes. He was the boy who waited on us the night of your birthday."

Hannah froze. Vividly she recalled the boy in question. He was the one who had reminded her so strongly of Mark.

"It seems he was pressed to do double duty in the restaurant because he's had experience as a waiter."

Simon took her free hand, rubbing his finger over her knuckles. The diamonds in her wedding band and engagement ring sparkled in the ray of sunlight that slanted through the window. "We're so lucky Jenny's okay."

"Yes."

For a long moment they were silent. Hannah sipped at her wine and told herself it was silly to place any significance in the fact that the boy who had so disturbed her on her birthday should be Jenny's rescuer. "Do you have a phone number for the boy?"

"No, but he'll be at the pool for the rest of this week and all of next. He doesn't start working for me until a week Monday."

"I'll go see him tomorrow, then."

"Good."

They sat quietly awhile longer. Hannah finished her wine and declined more. "I'm going to go shower and change for dinner, okay?"

"Okay."

As Hannah headed back toward the master bedroom, she couldn't resist peeking in on Jenny one more time. Jenny was sound asleep, her chest rising and falling evenly and slowly. Lying there with that ugly bandage on her head, she looked so young and fragile. So terribly vulnerable to life and all its dangers.

If only I could always protect her.

But Hannah knew that was a futile wish. Short of locking Jenny up for the rest of her life, there was little Hannah or anyone else could do to ensure her safety and happiness. As Simon had pointed out many times, all any parent could do was give a child a solid foundation and then pray that what they'd been taught would stick.

The next morning, after assuring herself that Jenny would be fine in Martha's care, Hannah headed for the club. It was ten-thirty, and the pool opened at eleven.

Told David Conway had just come on duty, she walked out through the bathhouse to the pool area where she found him opening umbrellas and otherwise setting up for the day. He hadn't yet seen her, so she took advantage of the moment to watch him unobserved.

Seeing him in a bathing suit was very different from seeing him in a waiter's uniform. That night at the club he'd worn his thick, dark hair tied back in a tiny ponytail. Today it was cut shorter, but still too long for her taste.

Why had she thought he looked like Mark that first day? Nothing about him seemed familiar today. Probably the only reason she'd imagined he resembled Mark had been her state of mind that night. *He's just an attractive young man*, she thought in relief.

Just then he turned and spotted her. For an instant he seemed to stiffen, but Hannah decided that must have been her imagination, because by the time she reached him, he gave her a friendly smile, which she returned easily now that her misgivings were gone.

"Hello, David. Do you remember me?"

"Yes." He removed his sunglasses, and his eyes met hers squarely. "How are you, Mrs. Ferris?"

"I'm fine, thank you. My husband told me what you did

yesterday, and I just wanted you to know how grateful I am."

"I'm glad I could help."

"You did a lot more than help. You literally saved Jenny's life."

He shrugged.

"She thinks a lot of you."

Another shrug. "She's a nice kid."

Just the way he said *kid* told Hannah she had nothing to worry about as far as Jenny's interest in him was concerned. He was obviously too old for Jenny. More important, he knew it. Unfortunately, now that he was facing her and she could see his eyes, her uneasiness returned with a vengeance, because no matter what she'd told herself only moments earlier, those eyes were eerily like Mark's, as was the shape of his face.

"Well . . ." She couldn't think of anything else to say. "I guess I should let you get back to work."

As Hannah walked away, she had an almost irresistible urge to turn around, because she knew he was watching her. She could feel his eyes boring into her back. She wondered if he had sensed her discomfort.

I'll never be free of this. Never.

Remembering what she'd given up was her penance, the ongoing price for her sins.

Fourteen

Everything was ruined. Ruined! Tears ran down Jenny's face. And it was all her fault. If she hadn't been showing off, trying to impress David by doing a fancy dive, none of this would have happened.

Now he was going to go to work for her father, and she would never see him again. How could she have been so stupid? Even the fact that David had saved her life, and now her parents thought he was wonderful, didn't help. If she couldn't see him, what good did it do her to have her parents like him?

And almost as bad, Jenny wasn't going to be able to compete in the Santa Barbara show this weekend or any of the other summer shows, including the ones in Calistoga and San Jose.

She felt so stupid! She could just imagine what Angie was going to tell everyone. They'd probably all laugh at her. And the worst thing of all was having to have her head shaved. She was going to look so *awful* when they took the bandage off. Oh, God. Jenny wished she could die. She was so humiliated.

Her tears fell harder, and even though she'd been trying to cry silently—if Martha, who was cleaning the bathroom across the hall heard her, she would call her mother—an involuntary sob escaped her. Sure enough, less than five minutes later her mother—who Jenny knew felt guilty because she hadn't been there when Jenny got hurt—knocked at her door. Hurriedly Jenny dried her eyes on the corner of the sheet and wiped her nose against the sleeve of her pajamas.

The door opened a crack. "Sweetie? You okay?"

"I'm fine, Mom." Jenny loved her mother, but right now she wished she'd quit obsessing and just go back to her studio and leave her alone to be miserable in peace.

No such luck. Her mom came in and sat on the edge of Jenny's bed. She had one of those worried looks on her face, the kind that meant she wasn't going to go back to work any time soon.

"Honey, I know you're disappointed about the shows you're going to miss."

Jenny swallowed and avoided her mother's eyes. "Yeah."

"It's not the end of the world, honey. It's just one season. It's not as if you're never going to compete again."

"Mom! Will you *stop* it? I know how much I'm going to miss. I'm not stupid." Jenny knew she had probably hurt her mom's feelings, but right now she didn't care.

"Honey, listen, maybe I can rearrange some things so I'll have more time to spend with you."

Before her mother could say anything else, Jenny said, "I don't want to talk anymore."

"Jenny . . ."

Jenny knew she was going to start crying again. "Please, Mom, I'm tired. I want to go back to sleep."

Her mother sighed, and for a minute Jenny was afraid she wasn't going to listen, but she finally got up. "I'll leave you, then. But if you decide you want to talk, just call me, okay?"

"Okay."

But when her mom had gone, Jenny knew she wasn't going to fall asleep again. She didn't even want to. She'd only said that to get rid of her mother. Climbing out of bed, Jenny dispiritedly turned on her computer. Maybe there would be e-mail from Courtney. Momentarily, that thought cheered her up. But no. There wasn't. *Shit!* She didn't even feel guilty over thinking the word *shit*, even though her mom and dad hated foul language. That's what they called it. Foul language.

Lots of the girls at school said stuff a lot worse. Her parents thought her school was so great because it was private and there were only girls there and it cost a lot of money, but those girls weren't any better than the girls she knew who didn't go to exclusive schools. They just pretended to be in front of the teachers and their parents. Some of them even went to raves, and a lot of them used drugs. Jenny heard them talking about Ecstasy and other stuff like that. Scary stuff.

Courtney, who was Jenny's best friend, didn't do any of that crazy stuff, but she sometimes used words that would make Jenny's parents cringe if they knew.

Thinking about Courtney made Jenny frown. Where was she? Jenny had written to her several times a day for the past three days, and there hadn't been any answer. Tears pricked Jenny's eyes again. Everyone had abandoned her. Everyone. The only ones who wanted to talk to her were her parents. And they were the last people she wanted to talk to. If only she hadn't attempted that stupid dive!

She reached for the box of tissues, and just as she pulled one out of the box, her bedside phone rang. She snatched it up.

"Hello?"

"Hello, Jenny?"

Ohmigod! Her heart leaped. It was David.

"It's David. David Conway."

Jenny finally found her voice. "I-I know. Hi, David."

"I was wondering how you're doing."

Her heart pumped madly. "I-I'm doing fine."

"I hear you've got a concussion."

"Yes, that's what they said." Oh, why couldn't she think of something clever? She sounded like a total dork!

"That's too bad. Does it hurt?"

"No, not really." It *had* hurt the first couple of days, but she was feeling pretty good now. "I'm glad you called. I-I wanted to thank you. You saved my life, my dad said."

"I'm glad I was there."

Suddenly Jenny felt better than she'd felt in days. "I'm glad you were there, too," she said softly.

For a few moments neither of them spoke. Then David said, "Your dad offered me a job, did you know that?"

"Uh-huh. He said you're starting to work for him in a week."

"Yeah."

Because she had to say something, she said, "I-I'm glad." She knew that working for her dad would be a good opportunity for David, much better than being a lifeguard at the club. Suddenly she realized how selfish she had been to think only of herself. If she *really* cared about David—and she *did*—she would *really* be happy for him, not just say she was happy for him.

"Thanks. I'm kind of glad myself."

Jenny smiled. "What're you going to do there? Do you know?"

"Your father said I'd start out in the shipping department."

"Oh, that's cool. Hector, the manager there, he's a real nice guy. You'll like working for him."

Silence fell between them again, and Jenny searched frantically for something else to say. But she couldn't think of a thing.

"Well, guess I'd better let you go," he finally said. "I just wanted to say hi."

"Okay, well, um . . . thanks for calling." She held her breath, willing him to say something about calling her again before he hung up, but he didn't.

Still, she thought as she replaced the phone and tried to stifle her disappointment, he must care something about her. After all, he'd called her, hadn't he?

That thought made her feel better. He didn't *have* to call her, after all. Suddenly she couldn't wait to tell Courtney about the phone call. Opening her e-mail program, she started a new message.

Courtney!
David just called me! It was, like, so totally awe-

some. He wanted to know how I was doing and he
told me about the job and everything. I don't think he
would have called me if he didn't like me, do you?

Oh, I wish you were here. I wish you'd gotten a
chance to meet him. I know he's too old for me, but
who knows, maybe he'll wait for me to get older.

He's soooooo cute. I told you he looks kind of like
Johnny Depp, didn't I? And he's so nice, not like the
younger boys at all. He never says stupid things, and
he doesn't stare at my boobs like some of them do.
God, they're so immature! He doesn't use four-letter
words, either, which I totally appreciate. As my dad
would probably say, he's a gentleman.

Jenny giggled as she typed the word *gentleman*. Yet was
it so off the mark? David *was* a man. She sighed and returned to her e-mail message.

Answer me as soon as you get back from wherever
you are, okay? I'm, like, *so bored.*

Jenny sighed again as she signed the e-mail, then pressed
Send. Until just lately, she had never been in a hurry to
grow up. But now she wasn't sure she could wait to be
nineteen or twenty and old enough for David. 'Cause he
was cute, way too cute to still be available. Anyway, how
did she know he didn't have a girlfriend already? It wasn't
like she ran around in the same crowd with him or anything.
For all she knew, he could be going steady.

The thought made her feel sick. She could just imagine
the kind of girl he would pick—someone small and sexy
and blond. Someone like Angie, only older. Someone who
knew what to say and do.

She swallowed against the lump in her throat, and once
more—as they had so often in the past few days—her eyes
filled with sorry-for-myself tears.

I'll never be small and sexy. I'll never even be tall *and
sexy!*

In that moment Jenny hated everything about herself. She

was such a loser. Boys didn't care a thing about girls who rode horses and played the violin. Just the opposite. Boys probably thought she was a total dweeb.

Maybe she should forget about boys and devote herself to horses. Horses didn't care if you were sexy or popular. If you loved them, they loved you back.

She imagined herself competing at Spruce Meadows, which was the most awesome of the horse shows and the one everyone wanted to take part in. She'd learn to do some of the fanciest jumps, and she'd be so good, she'd have no trouble qualifying for the U.S. Equestrian team.

She'd compete in the World Cup, then the Olympics. She could just see herself marching into the Olympic stadium with the rest of the U.S. squad. And in the competition she'd be flawless. She'd win the gold—an *individual* gold, not just the team gold.

Her parents would be in the stands cheering for her, and after the games were over, she'd come back home to a parade and she'd appear on all the talk shows and she'd be offered all kinds of endorsements and she'd even be asked to do the commentary for all the horse events on ESPN.

Lost in her daydream, she jumped when Vixen, who had been sleeping at the foot of her bed, suddenly licked her hand.

"Oh, Vixen, you love me, don't you?" She leaned over, put her face next to the puppy's, and let Vixen lick her face. "I love you, too," she whispered. "With you and Beauty, who needs boys, anyway?"

Fifteen

It surprised David how much he enjoyed working in the shipping department at Ferris's company. He hadn't expected to, but he found the work interesting. The department itself was housed in a huge warehouse in La Puente, one of the dozens of small towns that made up the greater Los Angeles area. La Puente was east of the city and it took him anywhere from thirty to forty minutes to get there, first on the Hollywood Freeway, then on the San Bernardino Freeway.

At first, when David was told he'd be starting work at seven in the morning, he thought he'd hate it. But he quickly realized he was better off coming in early and leaving early because he missed the worst of the rush-hour traffic, although in L.A. there was never a time when traffic was light.

Hector Garcia, his boss, explained that since their East Coast stores opened at nine-thirty, which was six-thirty in L.A., it was best for them to be available at least by seven.

"Or else," he said, "we'd be missing out on the best time to talk to the people in our stores about problems or whatever."

"But don't you handle most of the problems over the Internet or with e-mail?"

"We do a lot on the computer, yes, but sometimes you just need to talk to people in person. You'll see."

David did see. He hadn't been there two days when he

realized Hector was right. Some things couldn't be handled with e-mail. Soothing someone's frustration, for instance. Or asking someone for a favor. David had even handled one of the sticky situations himself when their East Coast distributor balked at requiring all new hires to be tested for drugs, a requirement which had gone into effect for all Ferris contractors on the first of that month. He'd insisted that other employers in his area didn't require drug tests, and if he had to, he would have a tough time recruiting people.

David did some quick research on the Internet and was able to give the manager a list of more than two dozen companies that did require drug tests. "It's getting more and more common," David assured him.

"Did you have to be tested?" the manager asked.

"Sure did."

"And you didn't mind?"

"Nope. Why should I? If I was the one doing the hiring, I'd want to be sure the person was clean."

Hector had complimented David on the way he'd handled the problem. "If you'd argued with Charlie, he would have just gotten madder. Instead, you did the exact right thing. You gave him facts. He couldn't argue with facts."

David quickly caught on to the rhythm of the work and began to learn about the merchandise. Hector started him out filling orders and talking to the buyers when they had problems with a particular order. When, after a couple of days, David felt comfortable with that phase of the business and could locate soccer balls as opposed to basketballs or tennis rackets as opposed to badminton rackets, Hector started teaching him about their suppliers.

"We sell millions of kids' uniforms," Hector said. "In fact, uniforms for soccer and Little League make up more than twenty percent of our business. And our biggest supplier is Berryman, whose manufacturing plant is in Taiwan. You'll be dealing with James Cho, who's the general sales manager."

"Papa, you'd better warn him about James." This came from Maria, Hector's daughter. She looked at David. "James can be a real pill."

"Yes," Hector said, "Maria's right. James can be hard to deal with sometimes, but in the end we usually get our way, because he depends on our business just as much as we depend on his. One hand washes the other, so to speak."

"Don't take any crap off James," Maria said later, when her father had gone off to the loading dock to supervise the unloading of a new shipment of athletic shoes.

"Thanks, I'll remember that."

Maria got up from her desk and walked to the refrigerator that stood in the corner of the office. David couldn't help but admire the way she looked from behind. She probably had the finest ass he'd seen in a long time. It was high and round, just like Jennifer Lopez's. In fact, Maria kind of looked like the sexy actress.

Ever since the first day David had worked there, she had been sending out vibes that told him she was interested and available. But David knew it would be a major mistake to get involved with his boss's daughter. So he'd ignored the looks and little smiles and would continue to ignore them. Still, no reason he couldn't appreciate her finer qualities or look at that gorgeous ass when he had the opportunity.

She opened the refrigerator and bent over. Her short skirt rode up. David smiled. She knew she was giving him a good view, and she knew he was looking. Oh, yeah. She was definitely one sexy babe. And it was too bad he couldn't take her up on what was being offered.

She finally straightened and turned around. Their eyes met. "Want some?" she said with a slow smile.

David could feel his body react to the loaded question. He was glad he had some files in his hand, for he was able to hide that reaction by holding the folders in front of him.

Her eyes were knowing. "Coke, that is."

He shook his head. "No, I'm not thirsty. I think I'd better get back to work."

"Another time, maybe," she drawled.

David let out his breath as he escaped into the warehouse. He could feel Maria's dark eyes on him. He wondered if her father knew what a hot little number his daughter was. If David had wanted to, he knew he could have had Maria in his bed tonight. No, Hector probably didn't know. If he did, he wouldn't let her out of the house alone.

David hadn't had a girlfriend in nearly a year. Not since Beth. He frowned thinking of Beth. He'd met her when they'd been in the same training group of new hires at Rafael's, the upscale restaurant in St. Augustine where they'd both worked. He'd been immediately attracted to her. She was just the type of girl he'd always liked, tall and blond and outdoorsy. She was also quiet and really nice, other qualities he liked almost as much as the way she looked. She'd liked him from the beginning, too.

Within a week they went out on their first date—just a walk on the beach after they'd finished work for the night, but soon they were spending every night and every free day together. It wasn't long before they were sharing each other's bed, too.

Remembering how good they'd been together, David felt that empty ache again, the one that he'd never been completely successful at banishing, even though he'd been the one to break off the relationship.

Trouble was, Beth started talking about getting married. That had alarmed him because he had no desire to get married. He was only nineteen years old, way too young to be thinking about marriage. He was hoping to go to college eventually. He didn't want to be a waiter all his life; he wanted to make something of himself. Sure, he really liked Beth, they were great together, and the sex—geez, it was fantastic—but marriage? The whole idea scared the pee out of David.

So even though he didn't want to, he told her he thought things were getting too heavy and it was best if they cooled it for a while.

She'd been hurt. And it had made David feel bad to see the pain in her eyes. Hell, she'd looked as if he'd punched her or something. Her blue eyes had filled with tears, and her bottom lip trembled.

"But I thought . . ." She'd swallowed. "I thought . . . I thought we loved each other."

"Beth . . ." He'd felt like such a jerk.

The tears overflowed, and she'd angrily wiped them away. She'd given him one last wounded look before gathering up her things and leaving his apartment.

The next day she gave her notice. The following week she was gone. He'd only seen her a few more times. He'd heard from one of the other girls who worked there that she'd moved to Pensacola, where her older brother, who was in the Navy, was stationed.

Four months later that same girl told him Beth had married a sailor.

"She said to tell you hi," the girl added.

David didn't sleep well that night. He kept wondering if he'd been wrong to let Beth go like that. He also wondered if she really loved the sailor, or if she'd married him on the rebound.

But the next day he told himself to forget about her. Beth and her marriage weren't his problem. As nice as she was and as much as he'd cared for her, he was too young to get serious about anyone.

But the thing about sex was, once you were having good sex regularly, you really missed it when you no longer had it. David knew he could have found any number of willing partners, but he was kind of old-fashioned. He liked sex, sure, but he didn't like having it with just anybody. He knew guys weren't supposed to feel that way. They were supposed to always be horny and ready to jump in the sack. In fact, he couldn't think of any of the friends he'd had in the past couple of years who would've walked away from Maria the way he had just now. They'd all think he was crazy for not taking what she was offering.

He grinned, remembering how Maria had looked bending over the refrigerator. Hell, maybe he *was* crazy.

Shaking his head, he walked over to a beat-up filing cabinet that held the shipping department forms. He quickly found what he was looking for: an inventory checklist for athletic shoes. Then he headed toward the section where he'd find their current stock. But before he had taken more than half a dozen steps in that direction, someone called his name. Turning, he saw Simon Ferris approaching.

David hid his surprise and smiled. "Hello, Mr. Ferris."

"Hello, David."

As he had each time David had seen him, Ferris wore an expensive-looking suit. Today's was gray pin-striped, paired with a light gray shirt and burgundy tie. He walked and talked with that confident air all wealthy, powerful men possessed.

"How's the job going?"

"It's going great, Mr. Ferris. I really like the work."

"Hector tells me you're doing a terrific job."

David grinned. He'd have to remember to thank Hector.

"I was wondering if you'd like to have lunch with me."

The invitation took David by surprise. "Uh, sure. That'd be great."

Ferris smiled. "Good. Do you like Mexican food?"

"Sure. Who doesn't?"

"There's a little Mexican place not far from here. We'll go there. First, though, I have to talk to Hector. Let's say fifteen minutes?"

"Okay." David stared after him. Why had Ferris invited him to lunch? Was it just because of what had happened with Jenny at the club? Did Ferris still think he owed David? Or was there another reason? What it could be, David had no idea. It wasn't like Ferris knew who he really *was* or anything.

A half hour later, settled in a booth across from Ferris, David decided the older man's invitation had been prompted by nothing more than a desire to know him better. And that suited David just fine, because there was nothing he wanted more than to learn everything he could about his mother's family.

"Tell me about yourself, David." Ferris squeezed lemon into his iced tea and stirred.

"What would you like to know?" David dipped a chip in the salsa.

"Did your parents move to California, too? Or did you come on your own?"

"My parents are dead, sir."

"Oh. I'm sorry."

"Thanks."

"They must have been young."

David nodded. "My mother was only fifty-three. My dad died at fifty-one."

Ferris frowned. "*I'm* fifty-three."

David had figured Ferris was older than his mother, but he didn't look fifty-three. He looked more like he was in his forties.

"So how old were you when this happened?" Ferris continued. He reached for a chip.

"I was six when my dad died, twelve when my mom died."

Just then, their waiter appeared with their food. He set the platters of steaming enchiladas down. "The plates are hot," he warned.

For a few minutes the two of them busied themselves with their food. Then Ferris said, "What happened to you after your mother died?"

"Same thing that had been happening. When my dad died, my mom had a kind of breakdown, so from the time I was seven and a half, I lived in foster homes."

Something in Ferris's eyes changed, and David knew the older man felt sorry for him. And for some reason, that made David angry. For one crazy moment he wanted to shout at his benefactor, just blurt out everything, but he managed to control himself. That really *would* be crazy. David's shitty childhood had nothing to do with Simon Ferris, not unless he was David's birth father, and David didn't think so. From what he'd been able to find out about his mother and her background, Simon Ferris hadn't entered her life until well after David was born.

Just be cool, he told himself. Get to know him better. Then figure out when and how you want to reveal the truth.

"That must have been tough," Ferris finally said.

"Yeah." David shrugged. "But I survived."

Ferris looked as if he wanted to ask another question, but he didn't, and David was glad.

After that they turned their attention to their food and didn't talk much. When they did, it was about the company.

After they'd finished their lunch and were waiting for the check, David said, "How's Jenny doing?"

"Much better."

"That's good. Tell her I said hi."

"Why don't you give her a call and tell her yourself? I'm sure she'd love to hear from you."

"Okay, thanks. I'll do that."

A few minutes later, bill paid, they headed out to Ferris's car. When they reached the warehouse, Ferris pulled up to the door and said, "I'm not coming back in, so I'll drop you here."

"Okay. Thanks for lunch."

"My pleasure, David."

David waved goodbye and walked inside. To reach his desk, he had to pass by the office. Maria was working at her desk. A wall separated them, but she was visible through the big window that allowed Hector to keep an eye on what was happening outside the office. When she saw him, she waved and beckoned him in.

"So how was your lunch?" she said when he walked into the office. Her dark eyes were avidly curious.

"It was good."

"No, I meant, how'd you like having lunch with the boss? And why'd he ask you to lunch, anyway? Did he want something?"

David almost said it was none of her business what Ferris had wanted or not wanted, but quickly thought better of the urge. He shrugged. "Just wondered how I was doing. You know, whether I liked the job or not."

She frowned. "He could have asked you that right here. He didn't have to take you to lunch."

"So? What's your point?"

"I just wondered why he's so interested in you. Is there something you're not telling me?"

David chose his words carefully. He might not think it smart to get involved with Maria on a personal level, but he didn't want to make an enemy of her, either. Even if she hadn't been his boss's daughter, he wouldn't have wanted to piss her off.

"Look, it's kind of embarrassing, but the truth is, I was a lifeguard at the country club the Ferrises belong to, and Jenny had a diving accident during my shift. I pulled her out of the water and did rescue breathing." He shrugged again. "They think I saved her life."

"Well, well, well," Maria said. "And to think I just thought you were a pretty face."

David laughed in spite of himself. It was really too bad about Maria. He had a feeling they could have some good times together. She laughed, too.

"You like to dance?" she asked when their laughter subsided.

"Not really."

"It's a lot of fun." To illustrate her point, she got up and swiveled her hips while humming Latin music. "I could teach you," she added softly. In her eyes was a blatant invitation.

"Not me. I'm hopeless."

For a moment he thought he'd blown it and made her angry.

But after a moment she just shrugged. "Okay, fine, but you don't know what you're missing."

David went back to his desk feeling pleased with himself. He also felt more hopeful about the future than he'd felt in a long time.

Sixteen

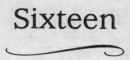

That could so easily have been him.

Simon drove back to his office on autopilot, his mind occupied with David's disclosure at lunch.

Foster homes.

What must David's life have been like? Simon had wanted to learn more, but something had held him back. Was it guilt because he himself had been adopted by wealthy parents who adored him and gave him everything any boy could want? And David hadn't been?

If not for Madeleine and Hugh, Simon could have grown up exactly the way David had, with no real home and no one to care about him or provide for his future.

But David did have one thing Simon didn't. Good memories of his birth parents. At least he knew that while they were alive, they loved him and wanted him.

Simon, on the other hand, had been a disposable commodity. He wondered if a person ever got over the knowledge that his mother hadn't wanted him. That she'd tossed him away with no more thought than you might give to an unwanted piece of furniture.

Sheryl Reis had been the sister of a man who worked for Hugh Ferris. She had gotten pregnant by her boyfriend, a sailor stationed in San Diego. He'd had no interest in marriage or fatherhood, and when he'd been shipped out right before Simon's first birthday, that had been the end of his involvement in her life.

It was quickly apparent to her brother that Sheryl had no interest in being a parent, either. She neglected her baby son and kept talking about how he "cramped her style" and was a big "noose around her neck."

Because Sonny Reis knew how much Hugh and Madeleine Ferris wanted a child and that they were in the process of starting the adoption process, he approached his boss and told him about his sister and her little boy.

The adoption was handled privately. Money changed hands. And Simon, who had been neglected and unwanted for so long, now had two parents who were so thrilled to have him they could hardly bear to leave him alone for a minute.

But David hadn't been so lucky. And yet, despite his background, he'd turned out to be a fine young man. One his parents would be proud of if they were alive to see him today.

Simon decided then and there that he wanted to do more for David than just give him a job and assist him with college tuition. What that might be, Simon wasn't sure. Right now he'd just make sure he kept an eye on the boy, and when the right opportunity to help him presented itself, he would be there.

Seventeen

Hannah had been working steadily since very early that morning and by nine o'clock was engrossed in a painting of a toddler holding a cone of cotton candy. The photograph she was working from had been taken the day she went to Venice Beach, and she hoped the finished product would be as enchanting as she remembered its subject being that day.

Normally Hannah didn't paint many children—they triggered too many unwanted and painful feelings—but in this show she knew she needed balance, and a few paintings of younger subjects would provide that element better than anything else could.

Concentrating heavily, she jumped when the phone rang.

"It's your sister Leah," Martha said when Hannah picked up.

Hannah frowned. Leah only called on special occasions, and today wasn't one of them. She punched the blinking button. "Leah? Hi. What's up?"

Her sister's voice was thick with tears. "Oh, Hannah, it's Father. He's had a heart attack."

Hannah's own heart skidded. "Is . . . is he . . . ?" She couldn't finish.

"He's alive, but—" Leah's voice broke. "They're not sure if he'll make it." Hannah could hear her blowing her nose.

Hannah wet her lips. "Wh-when did it happen?"

It took Leah a moment before she could answer. "This

morning, about eight. The alarm had just gone off and Mother had gotten up to put on the coffee . . . you know how she does . . . and . . . and Father was still in bed. Usually he's downstairs by eight-thirty, but this morning he didn't come down and Mother got worried, so she went up to check on him. She found him on the floor. Apparently he'd fallen when he got out of bed. He . . . he was barely breathing. Sh-she called 911 and, thank the Lord, they came within ten minutes and the paramedics were able to get him stabilized. They took him in to the county hospital in Beatrice, and they've got him in Coronary Care."

Hannah's mind had been racing as Leah gave her the details. She knew she would have to go to Nebraska, because if her father died, and she didn't go, she would be sorry the rest of her life. Maybe she didn't have the best relationship in the world with her father, but she did love him. She wouldn't allow herself to think about the show and all the work she still had to do and how she was already stretched to the limit time-wise. Some things in life were more important than work obligations, and this was one of them. If she had fewer paintings ready than she'd hoped, so be it.

"Mother didn't call me until after ten, and I didn't know the seriousness of his condition until I got to the hospital myself, or I would have called you sooner," Leah said. "I'm scared, Hannah. The doctors tell us these first twenty-four hours are the most crucial. If . . . if he survives them, then they'll know better what his prognosis is, but I have to tell you, they didn't sound hopeful to me. Y-you'll come, won't you?"

"Yes, of course I'll come. As soon as we get off the phone, I'll call Simon and see about getting a flight out this afternoon."

"I'm so glad."

Hannah could hear the relief in Leah's voice. Her youngest sister, although a rock in many ways, didn't cope well with being in charge. Every important decision in her life had been made for her; consequently she had no confidence in her own ability or judgment.

Hannah felt numb after they'd hung up. Navigating through life was like walking through a minefield. You never knew what was in store for you. You could go along for weeks, months, years even, with no problems, and then, bam, something exploded in your face and turned you and your life upside down.

As she pressed in the familiar numbers to Simon's office, she worried about Jenny. How was she going to go off for an indeterminate time and leave Jenny? Especially now, when she was depressed and miserable and hurting?

Hannah forced herself not to think about the McFarland show. Somehow she would get the work done, even if, after she returned from Nebraska, she had to work twenty hours a day to do it.

"Don't worry about Jenny," Simon said when she'd explained what had happened. "My mother will be happy to come and stay. You know she dotes on her granddaughter. It'll be nice for the two of them to have some private time together."

Hannah knew Madeleine would love it; she wasn't so sure about Jenny.

"How soon do you want to go?" His tone said everything was settled.

"As soon as possible."

"All right. Let me connect you with Rose. She can make the arrangements for you." Rose was the company's travel coordinator. "While you're doing that, I'll call my mother."

A half hour later Hannah had reservations on a United flight from LAX to Lincoln. Rose had also rented Hannah a car to be picked up at the Lincoln airport. The flight didn't get in until nine-thirty, so it would be eleven or eleven-thirty when she finally arrived in Jordan, the town where Hannah had grown up, but it couldn't be helped. It was already almost ten. There was no way Hannah could have gotten out sooner. She hadn't even told Jenny she was going yet, then she had to pack and make a list for Martha and call Morgan McFarland and probably half a dozen other things. It was giving her a headache just to think of everything that needed doing in the next few hours before she left for the airport.

Simon was so sweet. When he'd called her back to say his mother was delighted to be able to help out, he'd offered to go to Nebraska with her, but Hannah didn't want him to. She knew her parents made him uncomfortable in the best of times, and this was far from the best of times. Plus, with Simon there, Hannah's loyalties would be divided. She would want to be at the hospital with her mother and sister. . . .

Hannah clapped her hand over her mouth. Sarah! She hadn't even thought to ask Leah if she'd called Sarah, but she was sure Leah hadn't. Sarah was a pariah in Leah's world. Hannah didn't think her sisters had spoken in years.

But no matter what had happened between them in the past, Sarah had a right to know about their father. Hannah tapped her fingernail against the phone. Should she call her? Would Sarah care?

Hannah thought about how Sarah had left Jordan. The day after she'd graduated from high school, she'd cleaned out her bank account, bought a bus ticket for Chicago, and never looked back. She'd once told Hannah that she didn't care if she ever saw their parents again.

"I especially hate him," she said. "He's the cruelest man I've ever known. And our long-suffering mother . . ." Sarah's mouth had twisted. "She's almost as bad."

"How can you say that?" Hannah had cried, appalled.

"I say it because it's true," Sarah said bitterly. "She knew how miserable our lives were, because hers was just as bad—maybe even worse—but would she lift a finger to help us? Oh, no, not her. She's too mealy-mouthed and too afraid of rocking the boat to speak up to defend her daughters or try to make our lives a little better. Well, fine. If that's the life she wants, she's welcome to it. But I want no part of it, Hannah, and that includes her."

Over the years Hannah had tried talking to Sarah, to no avail. Sarah had washed her hands of Jordan and everyone in it.

Still . . . this was their father. Making her decision, Hannah flipped through her Rolodex, then pressed in the numbers for Sarah's apartment. The phone rang four times, then Sarah's voice mail kicked in.

"Sarah," Hannah said, "it's ten o'clock Thursday morning. Leah just called to tell me Father has had a heart attack. It's pretty serious. I'm flying home later today. I thought you might want to know. I . . . if you want to go home, too, call Simon's office. He'll make the arrangements for you." She hesitated for a moment. "Sarah, I hope you'll come." She swallowed. "No matter what, he's our father."

She sighed deeply as she slowly replaced the phone. She had done everything she could. The rest was up to others.

Eighteen

As the plane banked steeply left to angle into the proper position for its approach to the Lincoln airport, Hannah tightened her seat belt. She had always been a nervous flyer, and never more so than upon landing. Most people she knew were frightened of takeoff, but she knew landings were considered the most dangerous part of any flight, and she couldn't banish the butterflies until the plane had safely touched down.

Although today she wasn't quite as nervous. Somehow she didn't think God would let anything bad happen to her when she was on her way to see her father.

She looked down. She could see the airport lights, winking white and red and blue. They would be on the ground soon.

She concentrated on breathing deeply and let her thoughts drift back to Jenny, where they'd been most of the flight. Hannah still felt bad about leaving her. Jenny had been good about it, she hadn't whined or complained, but Hannah could see the disappointment in her eyes when she'd told her she was leaving for an indeterminate time.

"I wish I could go with you," she'd said.

"I do, too, honey, but it's still too soon after your accident. Besides, it won't be much fun there. I'll probably be spending most of my time at the hospital."

"I know, but what if Grandpa dies? I should be there."

"He's not going to die." She made her voice sound convincing, even though she was anything but.

Later, as she packed, Hannah thought about how Jenny could sometimes surprise her. Hannah wouldn't have guessed that it would be that important to Jenny to see her grandfather, but it was evident from the way she'd reacted to Hannah's news that despite their lack of closeness, she cared.

Hannah had done her best to remedy that lack of closeness. Ever since Jenny's birth, she'd made a strong effort to take her daughter to visit her grandparents for a week each summer.

On most of those visits Jenny had seemed to enjoy herself. Hannah's mother, Rachel, always did everything she could to make the visits special for Jenny. She'd let her help make cookies and bake bread, and she'd sewn sweet little pinafores for Jenny to wear. She'd taken her out to the meadow behind their home to pick clover and Queen Anne's lace that they'd weave into necklaces, which had delighted Jenny. Once she'd even managed to overcome Hannah's father's disapproval and had accompanied Hannah and Jenny and Leah to the county fair. And in later years, after Leah's children were born, Jenny had her younger cousins to play with and love.

But when Jenny was in the presence of her grandfather, it had been a different story. It was obvious from the very beginning that Jenny was afraid of him. *And why not?* Hannah thought sadly. *I was afraid of him, too. We all were.* Joshua Samuel Turner was not an easy man to love. He was taciturn and humorless. He struck fear into the hearts of most children and not a few of their parents, Hannah suspected. It was so ironic that a man who believed so strongly in the word of God could be so completely devoid of compassion and understanding. So completely unable to show affection or love.

Hannah sighed. She felt sorry for her father. He had missed out on so much. Yet beneath the sorrow, there was also anger, for his inability to bend had caused everyone else in the family to miss out, too.

Why does love have to be so hard? It was a question she had asked herself many times.

"Flight attendants, be seated for landing," the pilot said in the scratchy voice that came through the speaker.

In spite of Hannah's unspoken fears, the landing was smooth and trouble-free, with only a couple of bumps as the 737's wheels hit the runway.

Within minutes Hannah had retrieved her hand luggage from the first-class overhead bin and was exiting the jetway. A half hour later she'd collected her large suitcase and was headed toward U.S. 77 in the rented Buick Riviera Simon's travel coordinator had arranged for her.

During the forty-plus-mile drive, Hannah thought about what she would find when she reached her parents' home. She prayed her father was still alive. It would be horrible to arrive and find that he hadn't made it.

I have to get there in time to say goodbye to him. Until the phone call from Leah, Hannah hadn't realized how much she needed some kind of closure with her father. Yes, she'd visited over the years, maintaining at least a surface harmony with her parents, but there hadn't been any real communion, at least not with her father.

Not with Mom, either.

Because how could there be true intimacy when there were so many things that remained unsaid between them? Hannah knew that unresolved conflicts and buried resentment and hurt festered until they either exploded or poisoned the relationship.

This visit home was going to be so different from all the others. Not only because of the reason for it, but because Aunt Marcy—her father's older sister—would be there, too. Hannah smiled thinking of her aunt. She hadn't seen her since the previous Thanksgiving, when she and Simon and Jenny had made the trip to Tampa to spend the holiday with her aunt who, at seventy-two, was slowing down.

She hadn't slowed down sufficiently not to cook enough food to feed ten families, though, Hannah remembered with amusement. Although there had only been eight of them at the table, it had been loaded with enormous quantities of all

the traditional foods Hannah remembered from her childhood: a twenty-two-pound turkey stuffed with old-fashioned
bread dressing, cranberry-orange relish, caramel sweet
potatoes, creamy mashed potatoes, brussels sprouts liberally
doused with butter, creamed peas and onions, homemade
biscuits, and Aunt Marcy's wonderful gravy. And, of course,
homemade pumpkin and apple pies and real whipped cream.

"None of that fake stuff for me," Aunt Marcy had declared,
her green eyes—the one physical trait she'd shared with Hannah—alive with pretended repugnance.

"I see you're not worried about cholesterol," Simon had
said.

"Oh, phooey!" *Phooey* was Aunt Marcy's favorite word.
"All that garbage about cholesterol and triglycerides and
counting this and counting that is just silly. Why, if a person
just eats in moderation and gets off his backside and uses
his legs to get from one place to another, he'll never have
to worry."

Hannah and Simon had exchanged a smile.

Remembering, Hannah smiled again. Dear Aunt Marcy.
Sometimes it was almost impossible to believe that she and
Hannah's father had been born to the same two parents, but
they had. There was a physical resemblance between them,
but there the similarities ended. Perhaps they were so different because they had been treated differently as children.

At any rate, Aunt Marcy was wonderful. And she never
changed. You could always depend on her for sensible advice, support, understanding, and unconditional love. All the
things Hannah had not gotten from her parents. All the
things Hannah had striven so hard to give her own child.

Child.

Hannah swallowed. Tears pricked her eyes as she pictured
her daughter and the way she'd looked propped against the
pillows this morning. So innocent. So beautiful.

I wonder . . .

As she always did when her thoughts veered in this for-
bidden direction, she tried to cut off the thought. But tonight, driving down this southern Nebraska highway—a
highway she'd traveled so many times in her youth, heading

toward what might be the end of her father's life—her mind refused to cooperate.

Nicholas . . .

A tear trickled down her cheek, and she knuckled it away. He was such a beautiful baby. It had nearly killed her to give him away.

For years afterward, her arms had ached every time she saw a baby. They'd only stopped aching when Jenny had been placed in them. That physical ache might be gone now, but it had never been completely forgotten.

Where was her beautiful boy now? Was he happy? Did he ever think about her? Did he ever wonder where or who she was?

Hannah had wanted so badly to keep him, but she had known it wasn't possible. If her parents had been the kind of people who would have been supportive, she might have, but they weren't. Her father would have expunged her from his life. He had no tolerance for sinners, unless those sinners publicly repented. Hannah shuddered as she remembered some of those public purges.

In particular, she remembered Katrina Hale. Katrina had been two grades ahead of Hannah, a pretty redhead with bright brown eyes and an infectious laugh. The daughter of a farmer, she'd been one of the most popular girls at their consolidated high school.

Like Hannah's, her family was very religious. Her parents were longtime members of Hannah's father's church. Her father was an elder, her mother the president of the women's club. Hannah knew her father didn't approve of the way they'd raised Katrina.

"Too permissive," he'd said more than once, giving his wife and daughters an ominous look. "No good will come of it. Just asking for trouble letting that girl run wild the way they do."

Hannah had wanted to say Katrina Hale wasn't wild. She was just high-spirited. She liked to have fun. But she knew what would happen if she tried to defend Katrina. Her father would coldly quote scripture to prove his point.

Just as Joshua Turner had predicted, Katrina got pregnant

in her senior year. No one tried to hide it. Katrina's father told Joshua that his daughter and her boyfriend—a farmer's son Katrina had met in FFA—were going to get married and he asked Joshua to marry them. Joshua said he would perform the marriage only if Katrina would get up in front of the congregation and admit her sin and ask God for forgiveness and promise to lead a good life from now on. Hannah still remembered how she felt as she watched Katrina Hale's public humiliation. How her father had made the girl grovel, how he'd given her a tongue-lashing that had caused her face to turn red and tears to run down her face. When Katrina cried, Hannah had felt sick. It was all she could do to keep from bolting from the church. All that kept her in her seat was the certain knowledge that if she ran, she would pay for it later.

In that terrible moment she had known she could never, ever endure that kind of disapproval and public indictment from her father. So when the same thing happened to her less than two years later, there was never any question about whether she would let her parents know. She couldn't. Not ever.

Just then, she reached the turnoff for Jordan, which was five miles east of the highway. She shook off her gloomy thoughts and concentrated on navigating the narrow road, which was not well lighted. The last thing she wanted was to end up in a ditch because she wasn't paying attention.

Soon the lights of the little town she had called home for the first seventeen years of her life became visible. Jordan was small by anyone's standards—only a bit more than two thousand inhabitants, not even enough for their own high school. Most of the people who lived there worked in Beatrice or on the surrounding farms. A few made the forty-mile trip into Lincoln every day, and a few others, like her father, made their living caring for the needs of the populace.

Hannah slowed to twenty-five miles per hour as she entered the town proper. It never changed, just looked older and more weathered. Other than that, the same houses, the same businesses, and the same churches graced Main Street.

She drove past Webb's Drug Emporium (bought out by Henry Dixon ten years ago, who didn't change the name), Miller's Grain and Feed Store (this was the third generation of Millers to make a living with the store), Susie's Snip & Style (now run by the original Susie's daughter), the Jordan Elementary School, the white clapboard First United Methodist Church (in Jordan, you either belonged to the Methodist Church or Hannah's father's church), Calico Corner (where her mother had purchased all the fabric used in all the dresses she'd sewn for her daughters), and finally, on the left, surrounded by hundred-year-old maple, white poplar, and cottonwood trees, the Church of the Disciples and the parsonage that sat behind and slightly to its right.

She saw that the downstairs lights were on. Someone must be home. That was a good sign, Hannah thought. If her father's condition had worsened, they would all be at the hospital. Pulling into the driveway, she parked at the back of the church. By the time she had turned off the ignition, gathered up her purse, and climbed out, Leah was coming out the front door and down the steps.

"Hannah! Oh, it's so good to see you!" She threw her arms around Hannah and hugged tight.

"It's good to see you, too."

Leah released her.

"How is Father?" Hannah walked around to the trunk and unlocked it.

"He's improved somewhat. The doctors are feeling more hopeful."

Relief flooded Hannah. "What about Mother? Is she asleep?"

"No, she refused to leave the hospital."

Hannah wasn't surprised. She wouldn't have expected anything else from her mother. "Have you heard from Sarah?"

"No." The answer was clipped. "Why? Did you call her?"

"Yes. She wasn't there, though, but I left her a message."

"She won't call, Hannah. And frankly, I think it's best if she doesn't."

"Oh, Leah, how can you say that?"

"Because it's true. She's nothing but a troublemaker and you know it."

Although Hannah would have liked to deny Leah's claim, she knew it was probably futile. It saddened her, though, that Leah couldn't be more understanding. Still, she couldn't resist one last attempt at healing. "Isn't forgiveness one of the main tenets of Jesus' teachings?" she said softly.

But Leah had turned away and was bending down for Hannah's carryon. Hannah sighed. It was no use. She was wasting her breath.

A few minutes later they entered the old-fashioned kitchen, which, except for new tile flooring that had been installed a few years back, looked exactly the same as it had when Hannah lived there. She and Simon had tried to give her parents new appliances a couple of Christmases ago, but they wouldn't accept them.

"Why do we need a dishwasher or a new stove?" her mother said. "There's only the two of us. I can wash the dishes. And our stove is just fine."

"Give the money you would have spent to further God's work," Hannah's father added.

Hannah remembered how she'd clenched her jaw at her father's pious remark and how Simon had simply shrugged. *Can't say I didn't try*, his silent expression said as his eyes met Hannah's.

"Nothing ever changes," Hannah remarked now.

"No." Leah smiled.

Hannah studied her sister. Leah and Sarah looked a lot alike, although Leah had done her best to disguise her good looks. Her blond hair was cut short, in a plain, no-nonsense style, and she wore no makeup. Her blue eyes, very like their father's, were hidden behind glasses. She wore a light blue cotton dress. It was sleeveless, loose-fitting, and covered her knees. Her sandals were more functional than feminine. No jewelry adorned her ears or hands.

She dresses like an old lady, and she's only thirty-two.
"Are you still homeschooling?"

"Yes. Thomas and I feel very strongly about my continuing to teach the children at home."

Hannah smiled. "I can't wait to see them." Leah had three, a boy and two girls. Samuel was ten, Elizabeth eight, and Mary four. They were very nice children, too. That was one area where Leah had done a magnificent job.

"Samuel wanted to stay up and wait for you to come in, but Thomas and I felt that wasn't a good idea, because I figured you'd want to go to the hospital as soon as possible."

"I do."

"Well, let's get your things upstairs, and then we can go."

They continued to catch up on family news as they carried Hannah's luggage up and deposited it in the room Sarah and Leah had once shared. Hannah's old room, the smallest of the three bedrooms, had long ago been turned into a sewing room for her mother.

After Hannah had taken a few minutes to freshen up, the sisters were on their way to Beatrice and the hospital.

They didn't talk much on the drive; each was lost in her own thoughts. But as the lights of the hospital came into view, Leah said, "You'll be shocked when you see him, Hannah. He looks so much older."

Hannah nodded. She remembered how much Simon's father aged during the course of his illness and how hard it was on Simon to watch his father's health deteriorate.

"I'm worried about what Mother will do if Father dies," Leah continued.

Hannah had wondered about the same thing.

"They don't own the parsonage, you know."

"Yes, I know."

Leah sighed. "Thomas said she can come and live with us, but—"

"But that would be tough on all of you."

"Yes, but I don't think she can afford to live on her own. I don't think they have any savings."

By now Leah had parked in the front lot, but neither sister made a move to get out of the car.

"Leah." Hannah knew she would have to proceed carefully, for Leah, unlike Sarah, was proud and had never seemed to care about Hannah's financial status. "I don't want you to worry about Mother or about money. If Father dies, we'll work it all out as a family. Besides, she certainly won't be destitute. She'll get Social Security, and I'm sure the synod must have some kind of retirement benefits for widows of their ministers."

"I honestly don't know if they do. We've never talked about anything like this. I think we all thought Father would live forever."

"Let's not worry about that now, okay? If the worst happens, we'll figure out what we're going to do. But for now, let's just go into the hospital and see Father."

After a moment Leah nodded. Then, arm in arm, the sisters headed inside.

Nineteen

Rachel Turner sat in the waiting area outside Coronary Care and prayed silently. As she prayed, she knitted on a dark blue sweater. The work didn't require much of her attention. She had made dozens of these sweaters over the years—sweaters earmarked for the clothing donation box that the church sent monthly to their missionaries in various needy countries around the world. Sometimes she made mittens or scarves or baby blankets, but mostly she made sweaters. She had this particular pattern down to a science, barely even had to think as her hands expertly handled the needles.

She was alone in the waiting area. Earlier there'd been several other families sitting there, too, all with the pale, strained faces that were so common to the loved ones of coronary patients. But everyone else had left by midnight, and the hospital had settled into its quiet, nighttime routine. Now the only sounds in the waiting area were the *click, click* of her knitting needles and the occasional wail of a siren outdoors.

Rachel was tired, but she forced herself to keep working. She had had a strict upbringing. Her parents had stressed that idle hands were an affront to God, and she'd faithfully tried to instill that and other of her parents' and husband's strongly held views into the minds and hearts of her daughters. She knew she'd been successful with one and moderately successful with another but a total failure with the third.

At the reminder of the wayward Sarah, the pain and loss brought on by the family's estrangement weighed heavily on her mind. She wondered if she'd been wrong not to call Sarah. She had known Leah wouldn't; she had no use for her sister. Hadn't for a long time.

Rachel sighed heavily, both the sweater and her prayers temporarily forgotten. Of all her children, Leah was the most like Joshua. It saddened Rachel to realize how uncharitable and even self-righteous Leah could be, yet she knew she was as much to blame for Leah's shortcomings as Joshua was.

Rachel was spineless. Long ago she'd faced that undeniable truth about herself. She had no excuse for her failure to stand up for herself or her daughters. She had taken the easy way in her marriage, because she had learned early on that to challenge Joshua or to undermine his teachings in any way would invite his wrath and subsequent punishment, thereby plunging them all into an atmosphere of such fear and misery as to be almost intolerable.

Once, after Joshua had given her a tongue lashing in front of one of the neighbors—a woman named Peggy that he didn't approve of because he said she wasn't a fit companion for Rachel—the woman had asked Rachel why she put up with being treated like that. "I'd be out of here so fast, it would make his head spin," she'd declared.

"Where would I go?" Rachel said.

Peggy had given her a look filled with pity. "Anywhere would be better than this, Rachel. Here you have no dignity."

Rachel cried that night. She'd locked herself in the bathroom and let the tears pour down her face until there were no tears left. Peggy didn't understand. How could she leave? Divorce simply wasn't an option. Not only did Rachel not believe in divorce, but what would she do on her own? She had no skills, no money. She'd never even held a job. There was no way she could support herself, let alone her children.

Maybe if she'd somehow managed to get up the courage

to make a break right after her parents died, when she'd had a small inheritance . . . but she hadn't. She'd always been too frightened to seriously consider striking out on her own.

And before she knew it, that money was gone—used for the church and its charities—something Joshua deemed much more important than his family or anything they might need or want.

"We have a roof over our heads, food on our table, and God to look after our souls. Why do we need money?" he'd asked coldly when Rachel had the temerity to question what had happened to the money. She knew better than to call it *her* money.

The most she'd dared say in response was a timid, "I-I thought maybe if the girls wanted to go to college, we might help—"

"College!" he'd exploded. "And of what use is college to a woman? A woman is meant to marry and have children. Colleges teach women to defy their parents and follow the devil."

Colleges prepare women to support themselves so that they can live the way they want to. Rachel actually trembled in reaction to the rebellious thought.

That night, almost as if he'd known what she'd been secretly thinking, he'd pulled her to him roughly. And as she had from the first day of their marriage, this, too, Rachel endured. She'd learned never to cry out, never to act as if he were hurting her or she didn't want him to touch her, because that would only incite him to more punishing behavior. So without so much as a whimper, she tolerated the sharp bites on her nipples, the way he forced his engorged penis into her even though she was dry and it hurt so terribly, the way he gripped her shoulders so hard she knew there would be black and blue marks all over them in the morning, the way he kept pumping and pumping until he finally collapsed and rolled off her, spent.

He was her husband, she told herself as she waited to hear the snores that would let her know it was safe to get out of bed and clean herself up. She had to submit to him; that was God's law. She'd been wrong to question him and have those wicked thoughts. Tonight, Joshua wasn't punishing her, he was only doing what all men did. Just because it hurt didn't mean he was cruel. Sex was never meant to be enjoyable for a woman.

Over the years she kept telling herself that obeying her husband and keeping the peace was important for the children's sake as well as for her own. But down deep, she knew she was lying to herself. If she'd been braver, stood up to Joshua once in a while, maybe they would all have been better off.

Maybe I would have loved him.

Maybe we wouldn't have lost Sarah.

"Mother?"

Rachel jumped. She'd been so lost in her thoughts she hadn't heard the approach of Leah and Hannah. Putting down her knitting, she stood as quickly as her arthritic knees would allow her and opened her arms to Hannah.

Her eyes misted over as she held her eldest daughter close and breathed in the faint fragrance of roses that clung to Hannah's clothing. "It's so good to see you," she whispered.

"I'm glad to be here."

As they drew apart, Rachel saw that Hannah, too, was teary-eyed. She was such a lovely woman, with shiny, thick hair and the prettiest eyes. Rachel was so proud of her. As always, Hannah wore beautiful clothes. Tonight, even though they were rumpled from her hours of traveling, anyone could see that the black linen pants, black and white silk sleeveless sweater, and matching black jacket had probably cost a small fortune. Rachel self-consciously smoothed down her own cheap rayon dress, ashamed because she looked so dowdy.

Just once, she thought over the giant ache in her heart, *I'd like to look like Hannah does. I'd like to wear a beautiful outfit and have someone who knows what they're doing style my hair and show me how to use makeup to make me look better.*

"How's Father doing tonight?"

Rachel forced a smile. "A little better."

"When's the next visiting time?" This came from Leah.

Rachel blinked. She'd almost forgotten Leah was there. *What's wrong with me tonight?* She looked at the clock mounted on the opposite wall. It was just a little past twelve-thirty. "They'll let us go in at one. He'll be sleeping, though."

"That's all right," Hannah said. "I just want to see him." Her eyes—Marcy's eyes—were gentle. "You look tired, Mother. You're not planning to stay here all night, are you?"

"I won't leave until he's out of danger. I'd never forgive myself if something happened and I wasn't here."

"You won't be any good to Father if you're exhausted."

"It's no use, Hannah," Leah said with a tinge of impatience. "She's stubborn."

"My place is here," Rachel insisted. She could never say it aloud. Sometimes she couldn't even admit it to herself, but somehow she felt that by staying close she could make up for another thought—a horrible, wicked, guilty thought that lay like a venomous snake hidden behind all the prayers for Joshua's recovery: the one that whispered so softly and seductively that if Joshua died she would finally be free.

Just then the charge nurse came through the double doors of the Coronary Care unit. She stopped when she saw Rachel and the girls.

"Oh, Mrs. Turner, I didn't realize you were still here."

Grateful for the distraction from her terrifying feelings, Rachel smiled at the nurse. She liked the woman, who was kind and helpful. "Miss Lang, you've met Leah. This is my oldest daughter, Hannah. Hannah Ferris. She's just come in from Los Angeles."

Hannah and the nurse shook hands. "Your father is doing much better, Mrs. Ferris," the nurse said. She glanced up at the clock. "In about five minutes you can go in and see him, if you like."

"Yes, that's what my mother said."

"The cardiologist was here earlier, and he said your father's prognosis is much improved since this morning. If he doesn't worsen through the night, by morning he should be out of the woods."

At her words Leah took Rachel's hand and squeezed it.

Rachel wondered if Leah would still want to touch her if she had known how weak and sinful her mother really was.

The nurse continued to talk to Hannah and bring her up to date on everything that had been done for Joshua, then she said she'd be back in a few minutes and hurried off toward the elevators.

Five minutes later she returned with a can of Coke and a bag of potato chips. She gave them a sheepish look. "I'm a junk-food addict."

"There are worse things," Hannah said.

"Can we go in now?" Leah asked.

Nurse Lang nodded. "Follow me."

Rachel let the girls go first. She was suddenly reluctant to look at Joshua, as if her earlier, evil thoughts might somehow show on her face . . . or worse, cause her husband to become weaker.

Oh, please, God, she prayed, *don't punish Joshua on my account. He's a good man, and he's been your loyal servant for a long time. Just because I don't always see the wisdom behind his actions doesn't mean he's done anything wrong. I'm the one who's weak. I'm the sinner who is always questioning your laws. If you have to punish anyone, punish me.*

She took a deep breath. She felt stronger now. Silently she followed her daughters to her husband's bedside.

Twenty

Hannah thought she was prepared for what she would find when they entered the Coronary Care unit, but it was still a shock when she caught her first glimpse of her father. Joshua Turner was a tall man with a commanding presence. The man lying in the hospital bed bore little resemblance to the father she knew. Gone were the forbidding expression, the sternly set mouth, the strength and countenance that were the very essence of the man. In their place lay a man who looked shriveled and frail, a man whose face seemed blurred and indistinct, a man who was all too human.

He's old, Hannah thought. Old and sick. Somehow, even though her head had known he'd had a heart attack and that the attack was serious, she hadn't expected him to look so weak. He was hooked up to all kinds of tubes and monitors, which beeped softly in the eerie half light.

Walking over to the bed, she had to fight back tears. Almost as if he felt her presence, his eyelids fluttered slightly, then went still. Leah had walked around to the other side of the bed, and her gaze met Hannah's.

Hannah took a deep breath. Within her, all kinds of emotions competed for dominance. Sadness. Concern. Love. Anger. But mostly she felt regret. Regret for all the things she had missed, all the things he had missed. Regret for not being the kind of daughter he'd wanted and for him not being the kind of father she'd needed. And overriding everything else, regret for not ever being able to be honest with him, for having to hide most of what made her the woman she had become.

We've never really known each other, she thought sadly. *Will we ever? Or is it too late?*

"Father?" she murmured. She touched his arm. "Father, it's Hannah."

He didn't stir.

"He's not going to wake up," her mother said softly after a moment.

"No." Hannah took one last look at her father. Then she gave her mother a sad smile and said, "We should go. Leave him to sleep in peace."

Back outside in the waiting area, Hannah made another stab at trying to persuade her mother to come home with them, but she was adamant.

"I can't leave him," she said. "If they say he's out of danger in the morning, then I'll come home."

Hannah finally gave up, and she and Leah, after making their mother promise to call them should there be any change at all, left.

Once they were on their way back to Jordan, Leah said, "If Father recovers, I wonder if they will make him retire."

"They?"

"The church elders. They could, you know. They have the power."

"But isn't Thomas a church elder?"

"Yes, he was elected when his father died and left a spot open."

"Well, wouldn't he have some influence then?" Hannah couldn't imagine what her father would do if he was made to retire. The church was all he cared about. She knew that in his mind he might as well be dead if he could no longer minister to his flock.

Leah hesitated before answering. "I wouldn't say this to anyone else, but Thomas thinks Father should have retired a few years back."

"Oh?" Hannah was surprised. She knew Leah was very much under their father's influence and had assumed her husband—as the son of one of her father's staunchest supporters when he was alive—probably felt the same way.

"Thomas is more modern in his thinking than his father was. He believes Father is behind the times."

"Well," Hannah couldn't help saying, "we've all known that forever."

"There's nothing wrong with old-fashioned morality," Leah said stiffly. "If more people followed God's rules, we would have a much better world to live in."

Hannah stifled a sigh. "I'm sorry, Leah. I didn't mean to offend you. I just meant that—"

"Oh, I know what you meant. Thomas feels the same way. He's alarmed by the fact that none of the young people like coming to our church. He says one of these days we won't have enough members to keep the church functioning if we keep losing so many to the Methodists or to no church at all."

"That's a good point."

"It's just that I can't imagine our church without Father. It will break his heart if he's forced out, Hannah. He's given the church so much. It's his life." Her voice wobbled. "Maybe it would be better if he *did* die. At least that way he'd never know that his beloved church no longer wanted him."

Hannah used to hate when her father quoted scripture to her whenever he wanted to ram home a point, but just then, a familiar line of Scripture ran through her mind: *As ye sow, so shall ye reap*. Yet she knew if she were to say what she was thinking aloud, she would hurt her sister needlessly. Why destroy Leah's illusions? Especially when to do so would change nothing.

"I'm so ashamed," Leah said. Her voice was thick with unshed tears.

"You? What have you got to be ashamed of?"

"To think that my husband is the ringleader, that he might be the one responsible for Father losing his church. It's horrible."

"Leah, if Father does have to retire, it won't be your fault or Thomas's fault. After all, everyone has to move aside and let someone younger take over at some point in their lives. And Father *is* sixty-nine. In fact, he's closer to seventy."

Yet despite her assurances to her sister, Hannah couldn't imagine how her father would survive without his church to tend to.

"Remember what I said before? How we shouldn't worry about what might happen? I think that's still good advice. I think we should just concentrate our efforts and energy on helping Mother cope and leave everything else in God's hands. Isn't that what Father believes in? That God knows best and will show us the way?"

Leah didn't answer for a moment, then she sighed deeply. "You're right. I must have faith. Things will all work out."

After that, they didn't talk, and soon Leah was pulling into the parking lot at the church. "I'm not going to get out," she said. "Try to get a good night's sleep, and I'll see you in the morning."

"Okay. What time does Aunt Marcy get in?"

"Her flight arrives at eleven. Thomas is going to go to the airport and pick her up, then bring her straight to the hospital."

"What about us?"

"I've made arrangements for Mrs. Burton to watch the children for me, so I'll come by for you about nine."

They said good night, and Leah left. Hannah walked into the unlocked house—her parents never locked their doors—and turned on the light. The empty kitchen with its dark cabinets and stained countertops depressed her. How had her mother stood this ugly old house for so long? Even the yellow gingham curtains that Hannah knew her mother had made didn't do much to brighten the place.

Hannah looked at the teakettle sitting on the stove. Maybe she would make herself a cup of tea. She knew she should have been tired; it had been a long and stressful day and was already past one-thirty in the morning, but she was too on edge to be sleepy. Besides, she had promised Simon she'd call him after seeing her father. And she wanted to call Sarah again, too. But first Simon.

Forgetting about the cup of tea, she slipped off her shoes and poured herself a glass of water, then she walked into the living room and sank into the comfortable old chair her mother usually occupied. This room was a bit more cheerful than the kitchen, but not by much. Sighing, she reached into her purse for her cell phone.

Simon answered on the first ring, and she knew he'd been sitting with the phone at his side, waiting for her to call. "Hi," he said.

"Hi."

"How was your trip?"

"Okay. No problems."

"Good. Have you seen your father yet?"

"Yes." Hannah went on to describe how he'd looked and a little of what she'd felt when she'd seen him. She then told Simon about the conversation she'd had with Leah, both before going inside the hospital and on the way home.

"Poor Leah," he said when she'd finished.

"Yes, I don't envy her having to cope with whatever happens next."

"Well, I don't want you worrying, too, darling. We'll do whatever it takes to make sure your parents are comfortable. You know that, don't you?"

Hannah smiled. Oh, she loved him. He was the most generous man she'd ever known. "Yes, I know."

"So what do the doctors think about your father? Will he make a full recovery?"

"They hope he will. I should know more about his prognosis tomorrow."

"How's your mother bearing up?"

"She's doing okay. She refused to come home, though. She's spending the night at the hospital."

"Does she have a bed there?"

"No. When Leah and I left her, she was sitting in the waiting area. Knitting." Although Hannah couldn't see him, she knew Simon was shaking his head.

"I miss you," he said after a moment.

Hannah snuggled deeper into the chair. "I've only been gone a few hours."

"I miss you when you're gone five minutes," he said softly.

She closed her eyes. "I miss you, too. And Jenny. Tell her I sent my love."

"I will."

"When is your mother coming?"

"She's already here. She arrived about three o'clock, Martha tells me."

Hannah heard the amusement in his voice. "Does Jenny seem any happier now?"

"She brightened up when she saw the gift boxes in my mother's arms."

Hannah couldn't help laughing.

"You never told me what Morgan had to say when you called him," Simon said.

Hannah sighed. "He wasn't happy. But he could hardly order me to stay home. He calmed down, though, when I told him I had twenty-eight paintings ready and promised I'd have at least twelve more done before the show."

"What if you have to stay in Nebraska for a couple of weeks?"

"Oh, God, please don't even *think* that." Hannah was sure she'd go crazy if that were the case.

"All right. I'll think only positive thoughts."

"Good. So what was your day like?"

"Busy. Meetings. A problem with one of our biggest suppliers. The usual."

They talked a few minutes more, then he said, "It's getting awfully late. We'd better say good night so you can get some sleep."

"I guess you're right."

But instead of going to bed, Hannah sat there for a long time after they'd hung up. She thought about her marriage and how lucky she was to have Simon. She thought about Nicholas and how much she wished she had told Simon about him when he asked her to marry him. Then she thought about her parents' marriage and how different it was from her own. She tried to remember if she'd ever heard her parents say they loved each other, the way she and

Simon did all the time. She couldn't think of a single in-stance.

Finally, beginning to feel punchy with exhaustion, she knew she'd better heed Simon's advice and try to get some sleep. Putting her cell phone back in her purse, she got up. Then she remembered that she'd planned to try to reach Sarah again, and she took the phone back out. Although it was already one in the morning in Las Vegas, Sarah was a night owl. Most nights she didn't even get home until one or two.

Once again, she got her sister's voice mail. "Darn you, Sarah," she muttered after leaving another message. "Why haven't you *called* me?"

She was halfway up the stairs on her way to bed when her cell phone rang. Her Caller ID showed it was Sarah returning her call.

"Sarah! Finally."

"Hello, Hannah."

"I'm so glad you called. You got my message about Fa-ther?"

"Yeah, I got it."

"Are you coming home, then?"

"No."

"Oh, Sarah, why not? Can't you let bygones be bygones? He may not make it, you know."

"Guess what? I don't give a damn. In fact, I hope the bastard dies."

Shocked, Hannah gasped.

"I mean it."

"How can you say something like that, Sarah? He's your *father*."

"And a piss-poor one at that."

"You know, you're not perfect, either. You've made mis-takes. We all have. Can't you find it in your heart to forgive him?"

"You just don't get it, do you? I expect as much from the sanctimonious Leah, but I thought you were smarter."

"What do you mean?"

"I mean our father is a horrible, vicious, violent man.

Made worse by the fact that he pretends to be so pious and holy. He spouts that religious mumbo jumbo until you want to throw up, yet underneath he's a pig."

Hannah's hand shook. The venom coming out of her sister's mouth made her feel sick.

"Let's cut through the crap, okay?" Sarah's voice had gotten louder. "I'm not telling you anything you don't know, so you can stop pretending."

"I don't know what you're talking about. Yes, he was stern and a tough disciplinarian and he has narrow-minded views, but calling him a pig and violent! Why are you saying such terrible things about him?"

"Jesus H. Christ, are you telling me you really *don't* know?"

"Don't know *what?*"

"Listen, you were in that bedroom down at the end of the hall, but Leah and I slept right next door to our sainted mother and father. And the walls between our rooms were thin. Maybe Leah has blotted everything we heard out of *her* mind, but I never will. I know how he hurt our mother. I heard what went on. And I saw the marks on her body, too. More than once."

Hannah shook her head. "You're lying. He never hurt her. Not like that. Not physically."

"Oh, yeah? Believe me, my sheltered sister, I'm telling you like it is. What I said before stands. I hope he dies. And I hope, if there really is a God, He sends that father of ours straight down to hell where he belongs."

Hannah couldn't stand listening to Sarah anymore. "I'm hanging up," she said stiffly. "You've always blamed Father for everything bad in your life, but he didn't force you to do the things you've done. He didn't force you to choose lousy men or live the kind of life you've lived. *You* made those choices. I know he wasn't an ideal father, but I think he loved us in his way. And I think he loves Mother, too."

"Fine," Sarah said. "You live in your little dreamworld. You keep pretending we had a normal childhood and normal parents. I hope you can keep on pretending your entire life. But I can't. You say I made my own choices. Did you ever stop to think that I would have made entirely different choices if I'd been given a chance? No one offered to send *me* to college. No one offered to let me live with them so I could get out of that godforsaken town and make something out of my life. Hell, no. *You* were the favored one, Hannah, so you don't have any right to look down your nose at me and my choices. Even Leah fared better than I did. At least somebody *loved* her. Nobody loved me, and nobody wanted me. So don't you *dare* sit in judgment of me. Don't you *dare*!"

Then she hung up on Hannah.

Twenty-one

"Good morning!" Madeleine opened the slats of the blinds in Jenny's room. The morning sun poured in, spilling liquid gold across the carpet.

Jenny rubbed her eyes. " 'Morning, Grandma."

Madeleine smiled at her granddaughter. "Did you sleep well?"

"I guess so."

Madeleine sat on a corner of the bed. "You don't sound sure."

Jenny sighed dispiritedly. "I was dreaming about Beauty."

"I see."

"I know she misses me. I wish—"

"Sweetheart, listen to me. If you do exactly as the doctor says, you can probably go out to the stables to see Beauty next week."

"Really? Did Dad say so?"

"Yes, as a matter of fact, he did. We talked about it just last night."

Jenny smiled for the first time that morning.

"Now . . . Martha's making French toast for breakfast, and I even talked her into frying some bacon for us, so why don't you get up and get dressed?"

"Bacon, yum. Mom doesn't let us have bacon very often."

"Yes, well, I consider this a special occasion." She eyed the bandage that still patched Jenny's head. Every time she thought about what might have happened to her grand-daughter, she shuddered. It simply didn't bear thinking about. Madeleine loved Jenny with a fierceness she had never imagined possible. She supposed part of the reason was never giving birth herself and adopting Simon when he was nearly past the baby stage.

But Jenny . . . Madeleine had seen her just minutes after her birth. Looking at her granddaughter that first time . . . she would never forget it. Something stirred inside her that was the most powerful emotion she'd ever experienced.

She would always remember how Jenny's beautiful eyes, even that soon after her arrival into the world, had looked so alert and aware and had stared at her grandmother with such intensity. Madeleine had felt an onslaught of love so powerful it had stunned her, and that love had grown over the years. Sometimes she thought she loved Jenny even more than she loved Simon, if such a thing were possible.

After Jenny, followed closely by Vixen, who was her de-voted shadow, slowly shuffled into the bathroom, Madeleine walked around the room. She looked at the gaily patterned daisy wallpaper that Jenny had chosen, the ruffled curtains with matching bedspread and dust ruffle, the collection of carved wooden horses on top of her dresser, the ribbons and medals displayed so proudly, the Madame Alexander dolls that sat in prim rows on the top shelf of her bookcase and along the back of her window seat, the copy of *Misty's Twilight* on her nightstand, the scuffed sandals standing side by side in the corner.

The neatness of the room attested to the fact that Jenny was far superior to most girls her age, Madeleine noted with satisfaction. She'd always known her granddaughter was more intelligent and special than other girls, and this beau-tiful room and the way she kept it only reinforced her opin-ion.

Just then Jenny—again closely followed by the dog—walked out of the bathroom. She'd taken off her pajamas and brushed her hair and was now dressed in khaki shorts, the ever-present ball cap she'd taken to wearing to hide the shaved place on her head, and a Roxy T-shirt. She sat down on the bed and reached for her sandals.

A few minutes later the two of them walked out of the bedroom and headed toward the back of the house. The closer they came to the kitchen, the more tantalizing the smells. Mingling with the aroma of freshly brewed coffee was the mouthwatering scent of frying bacon.

Even Madeleine, who wasn't obsessed with food the way some of her friends were, felt her mouth water.

As they entered the kitchen, Martha, who was taking slices of bacon from the frying plan and transferring them to a paper-towel-covered plate, looked up. "Perfect timing. Breakfast is ready."

"Oh, good," Jenny said. "I'm starved."

They sat at the table—which was already beautifully set, Madeleine was pleased to see—and Martha began to serve them. Madeleine poured a bit of cream into her coffee and took a sip. Delicious. She hoped Simon and Hannah realized how lucky they were to have such a good cook in Martha, which you certainly were never guaranteed when you hired a housekeeper. Madeleine had always been fortunate in her help, but she knew she was in the minority, at least to hear her friends tell it.

For the next few minutes she and Jenny ate silently. When Madeleine finished, she dabbed her mouth with her napkin and looked up at Martha. "The French toast was wonderful. Just the way I like it, thick and creamy."

"Thank you, Mrs. Ferris. Would you like another piece?"

"Me? Oh, no. One is my limit." Madeleine patted her flat stomach, of which she was inordinately proud. "I *will* have some more juice, though."

Martha poured fresh orange juice into Madeleine's glass. "How about you, Jenny? More French toast?"

"I've already had three pieces, Martha." Jenny grinned.

"You're young and growing."

"Well . . ."

Martha had just walked over to the stove when the phone rang, causing all three to look at the portable unit that sat on the counter by the door.

"I'll get it." Martha walked over and picked up the receiver. "Ferris residence." As she listened, her gaze moved to Jenny. "Yes, David, she is. Just a moment, please."

David? Who was David? Madeleine wondered. She looked at Jenny, whose face had flushed a bright pink.

Martha handed Jenny the phone. "It's David Conway."

Jenny's voice sounded breathless as she answered. "David? Hi."

Conway. That name was familiar. *Who is he?* Madeleine mouthed to Martha.

Martha leaned over and whispered, "The boy that rescued Jenny at the pool."

Ah. Madeleine turned back to Jenny. The child was definitely flustered. Clearly this wasn't just any boy. This was a boy Jenny was interested in, if her reaction to the phone call was any indication. Madeleine picked up the lifestyle section of the morning *Times* and pretended to be reading it while she surreptitiously gave her full attention to the one-sided conversation.

"Yes," Jenny was saying, "I do feel better. Uh-huh. No, I can't do the stuff I normally do, not for a week or two. Uh-huh. Now? Oh, I was just having breakfast with my grandmother. She's here 'cause my mom had to fly to Nebraska on Wednesday. Why? Because my grandfather had a heart attack. Uh-huh. Yeah, her father. Yeah, they're both still alive. Well, my dad said she called last night, and it looks like my grandfather will be going home tomorrow." She listened for a bit. Then her expression changed and her eyes, already shining from the phone call, widened. "Today? You want to come and see me today? I . . . oh, no, that's fine. That's great. I'd *love* to have you come, I just was surprised you wanted to, that's all. Sure. Um, what time? Okay, yeah, that'd be fine. Do you need directions? No? Okay. Great. Okay. I'll see you about eleven, then."

"Tell him he's invited for lunch," Madeleine interjected before Jenny could hang up.

Jenny grinned. "My grandmother said to tell you you're invited for lunch." She laughed. "You will? Great. That's great. Okay. Bye."

After hanging up and handing the phone back to Martha, Jenny, trying to sound offhand but sounding anything but, said, "That was David Conway, the boy who pulled me out of the pool and saved my life. He has today off 'cause he had to work Saturday. He's working for Dad now."

"Yes, your father told me," Madeleine said. "I'm looking forward to meeting him."

Jenny shoved her chair back. "I've gotta go take a shower. I have to figure out what to wear and all."

"Be sure to wear that shower cap."

"I know, Gram. I can't get this bandage wet." Jenny's eyes were still shining.

After she'd left the kitchen, Madeleine looked at Martha. "Well. I'm really looking forward to meeting this boy."

Martha nodded. "Yes."

Madeleine put the paper down. "What can you tell me about him?" She tried to think back about what Simon might have said, but all she could remember was that the boy was a lifeguard at the club pool and that Simon had offered him a job in the shipping department of their company as a thank-you for what he had done for Jenny.

"Well, I did hear Mr. and Mrs. Ferris talking about him."

"And?" Madeleine prompted. "What did they say?"

"Nothing much, really. Mr. Ferris just said David was a nice kid, and Mrs. Ferris said she agreed, but she was a bit worried because she thought Jenny was too interested in him, and he was too old for her."

Madeleine mulled over this bit of information as she drank a second cup of coffee, then she thanked Martha again for the lovely breakfast and headed for the guest room. She didn't take showers and had had her bath last night before retiring, but she did want to redo her hair and check her makeup before the boy arrived. First impressions were very important.

Madeleine finished her preparations for the day by ten o'clock and was relaxing in the sunroom, which overlooked the pool and backyard, when Jenny—looking adorable in red cropped pants and matching top, walked in. This time she wore a silver ball cap.

"I wondered where you were, Gram."

Madeleine noticed that Jenny had somehow managed to wash her hair, because it looked shiny and clean. And she'd put on lip gloss and eye shadow. "I see you washed your hair. You didn't get that bandage wet, did you?"

"No, I was really careful. I didn't put my head under the water at all."

"Well . . ." Madeleine smiled at her. "You look lovely, dear."

Jenny blushed. "Thanks."

Madeleine waited a few seconds. "Something tells me you like this boy a lot."

The blush deepened, and Jenny toed the carpet. "I do."

"Tell me about him."

After a moment's hesitation Jenny sat down in one of the cushioned wicker chairs. "What do you want to know?" she asked shyly.

Madeleine smiled. "Anything. Everything."

"Well, he's really cute. He has dark hair and brown eyes and . . . I think he kind of looks like Johnny Depp except his nose is bigger. Do you know who Johnny Depp is?"

"An actor?"

Jenny grinned. "Yeah. Anyway, David hasn't lived around here for very long. He moved here from Florida."

"Oh? How old is he?"

"Um, I'm not sure. Nineteen or twenty maybe."

As much as Madeleine hated to admit it, Hannah was probably right. He probably *was* too old for Jenny. But Madeleine would reserve her final opinion on his rightness or wrongness until she'd met him. She was certainly not going to take anything Hannah said as gospel. The reminder of her daughter-in-law caused her to frown. She knew Simon couldn't understand why she still had reservations about Hannah, but she couldn't understand why *he* didn't.

Even after all these years, Madeleine had never met Hannah's parents. Every time she asked about them and why they never visited, Simon said they were set in their ways and didn't like to travel.

"Her father doesn't like to leave his church," he always said.

Fiddle, Madeleine thought. She'd bet anything that family of Hannah's wasn't the upstanding, perfect family Simon would like her to think they were. In fact, she had the distinct feeling there was something strange about them. She *had* met the one sister, Sarah, and she certainly hadn't left a good impression, which only reinforced Madeleine's suspicions about the other Turners and what it was about them that Hannah preferred no one to know.

"I hope we've got some Coke. I'd better go check," Jenny said, getting up.

"Martha's made iced tea. That goes better with chicken enchiladas, anyway."

"Is that what we're having for lunch?"

"Yes. That and some rice and a salad."

"Plain rice?"

"No, Mexican rice."

"Oh, good. David'll like that, I think."

Madeleine smiled. "Yes, I'm sure he will."

"I still think I'll see if there's any Coke."

"You go on, dear. Let me know when he arrives."

After Jenny left, Madeleine went back to thinking about Hannah's family. Last night, after Hannah had called Simon, Simon had relayed some of the conversation, and Madeleine again had the distinct impression there were things he wasn't telling her. She'd subtly tried to pry them out of him, but he was guarded when he talked to her about anything to do with Hannah, and she supposed she didn't blame him.

Once, when Hugh was alive, he'd asked her why she couldn't be more charitable toward Hannah.

"After all," he'd pointed out in his mild way, "you remember how angry and hurt you were by your family's attitude toward me."

"That was different." And it *was* different. Her family had been ignorant of America and Americans. They'd formed their opinions from the movies they saw and the books they read, and because some of the American tourists they'd come in contact with were obnoxious. But they hadn't ac-

tually known anything about the United States or Americans
of refinement. Certainly, Hugh was as refined and intelligent
a man as anyone could ever ask for, and he came from an
impeccable background and family. Probably more impeccable than hers, if the truth be known.

Dear Hugh. Madeleine missed him so much. They'd had
a very good marriage, one of the best. In the three years
since he'd died, she'd had a tough time adjusting to life
without him.

Hannah wasn't Hugh, though. Yes, she was lovely looking. Madeleine would give her that. And she knew how to
dress and conduct herself. But she was very reticent when
it came to talking about her family. She'd offered the information that her father was a minister and that her mother
had always been a homemaker, but she never volunteered
anecdotes about her childhood or elaborated about her life
in Nebraska in any way. When Madeleine had asked about
her sisters, she'd said her youngest sister—Leah, if Madeleine remembered correctly—was married to a local man
and had three children. Then she'd changed the subject.

Madeleine had learned more from Jenny than she ever
had from her mother. It was Jenny who had told Madeleine
about her cousins, Jenny who had mentioned that her grandparents didn't own a television set because her grandfather
didn't approve of that kind of entertainment. It was Jenny
who let slip that her mother and her grandfather didn't get
along well, too.

"She doesn't know I realize that, Gram," Jenny had said,
"so please don't say anything to her. I think she feels bad
about it."

Madeleine would never have said anything to Hannah,
anyway, but because the information came from Jenny, she
would be doubly careful. She thought too much of her
granddaughter to ever compromise her. Besides, if she did,
how would she ever find out anything useful again?

Jenny had also told Madeleine that her aunt Leah home-
schooled her children. Madeleine found that piece of information interesting, too. She supposed the homeschooling
came about because of the family's strong religious beliefs.

However, Madeleine actually approved of homeschooling, especially if you couldn't afford a really good private school, because God knows, most public schools had little to recommend them. And it was obvious from Jenny's description of their house and the fact—also innocently passed on—that Leah's husband worked on a production line for some kind of manufacturing company, that the family didn't have much money. Still, at least the younger sister sounded respectable and sensible. A point in her favor was that Jenny thought so highly of her.

The other sister was different. She was a wild one. No other word for it. She'd wanted Madeleine to believe she was a dancer in a big Las Vegas show. Ha! Madeleine suspected Sarah was a stripper, or worse. And even if she wasn't, did she actually think dancing in a Las Vegas show would *impress* Madeleine? If the girl hadn't been related to Simon by marriage, Madeleine might have been amused by her foolishness, but since her poor judgment was a direct reflection upon Hannah and, by implication, upon Simon, Madeleine was simply disgusted.

Shaking her head, she reached for her glass of water. On her doctor's orders, Madeleine was trying to train herself to drink at least a couple of glasses of water a day, but it wasn't easy. A true Frenchwoman, she preferred coffee or wine. Just as she put her glass back down, she heard the distant chime of the doorbell. A glance at her watch showed it was a few minutes before eleven, so that probably meant the boy had arrived.

A few minutes later Jenny, followed by a handsome boy who was, Madeleine was pleased to see, dressed quite nicely in clean khaki pants and a new-looking pale blue knit shirt, entered the sunroom.

Jenny, eyes glowing, said, "Gram, this is David Conway." She smiled shyly at David. "David, this is my grandmother, Mrs. Ferris."

"It's nice to meet you, Mrs. Ferris." He walked over to her and extended his hand.

Madeleine studied him carefully as they shook hands. Yes, quite a good-looking boy. She could see why Jenny was smitten, for smitten she was. Unfortunately, Madeleine was afraid her daughter-in-law was correct in her assessment of the situation, though. It was obvious just looking at the boy that he was too old for Jenny. But there was no harm in Jenny's having a crush on him. After all, she wasn't allowed to date yet, anyway, so the only way she would see him was if he came to the house, especially now that he was working at their company and was no longer at the club pool. So really, there was no reason to worry. Why, Madeleine herself remembered how, at fifteen, she'd had a crush on her piano teacher. All girls had crushes on older men at one time or another. It was a natural part of growing up and becoming aware of your femininity.

"Look what David brought me, Gram," Jenny said. She held out a fluffy white stuffed bear. Her eyes glowed.

"That was nice of you, David." He seemed embarrassed, so Madeleine added, "Please sit down." She looked at Jenny. "Perhaps my granddaughter will bring you something to drink."

"Oh. Yes. Would you like a Coke, David? Or something else? We've got Sprite and Coke and root beer. And Martha made iced tea, too."

He smiled. "A Coke sounds great."

"What about you, Gram? Do you want anything?"

"Thank you, dear, I'm fine." Madeleine gestured to her glass of water.

After Jenny left to get David his drink, Madeleine said, "We all owe you a debt of gratitude, David."

"No, you don't, Mrs. Ferris."

"Oh, but we do. You saved my granddaughter's life."

"I just did my job. What anybody would have done."

Madeleine liked that the boy was modest. "Well, perhaps, but Jenny is very special to us, and we are extremely fortunate that you were so quick-thinking and knowledgeable." Seeing that she was embarrassing him, she decided to change the subject. "Jenny tells us that you've recently moved here from Florida."

"Yes, ma'am."

"Whereabouts in Florida?"

"St. Augustine."

"Is that where you grew up?"

"No, ma'am. I grew up in the Miami area. I only moved to St. Augustine after I graduated from high school."

"I see. What about your parents? Do they live in Miami, or did they move, too?"

"My parents are both dead. Actually, I grew up in foster homes."

The information was offered so dispassionately, it took Madeleine a moment to realize what he'd said. "Oh. I'm sorry."

He grimaced. "Yeah, me, too."

Something about the expression in his eyes caused Madeleine to feel a twinge of uneasiness. Under that polite facade of his, the boy was a scrapper and much more sophisticated and world-wise than Jenny.

Just as she was about to ask him another question, Jenny came back into the sunroom carrying a tray that contained two glasses filled with ice, two cans of Coke, and a small glass dish containing cashew nuts.

By the time Jenny had unloaded the tray and put the dish of nuts on a wicker end table close to David, the moment was lost. Or perhaps not . . .

"I'm sorry about your parents, David," Madeleine said. "Were you very young when you lost them?"

"I was six when my dad died, twelve when my mother died."

Again the facts were given flatly, but Madeleine was sure the boy wasn't as nonchalant as he'd have them believe. How could he be? She couldn't help feeling a stirring of sympathy. After all, he couldn't help what had happened to him. Actually, considering the way he'd grown up, she admired him for turning as out as well as he had. Even so, she wanted much more for her granddaughter than the David Conways of the world could ever provide. "That must have been rough."

He shrugged.

"There were no relatives you could have lived with?"

"No, ma'am. There weren't." His tone didn't invite further questioning.

"I'm sorry. I didn't mean to pry."

"That's okay."

"Well, I'm sure you young people want to go and talk privately, so please don't think you have to stay here and entertain me. Jenny, perhaps you'd like to take David to the game room."

Jenny gave Madeleine a grateful smile. Then she turned to David. "Do you like to play pool, David? My dad has a pool table. There's also a dartboard, and we've got PlayStation."

He grinned. "Pool? Do you play pool?"

"Uh-huh. My dad taught me."

"Cool."

After they'd gone, Madeleine continued to sit and think about the boy. He'd had a hard life, she suspected, even though a person wouldn't guess it from looking at him. It was only when he'd talked about his past that a hint of those darker days had been in the depths of his eyes and in the subtle shift in his tone of voice. It was also clear to her that there was much he hadn't said.

Well, it was a pity. Because as loath as she was to side with Hannah on anything, in this instance, she had to agree with her. Even if David Conway had been younger, he wasn't suitable for her granddaughter. Jenny deserved only the best, and a boy raised in foster homes with a questionable history and future was not a candidate.

Madeleine sighed. She would have to be careful, though. It wouldn't do to let Simon know why she felt this way. He was sensitive about his own heritage, and she didn't want him to ever think it entered into her feelings about him, because it didn't. He, however, had been raised in a completely different environment. She and Hugh had given him all the advantages, not the least of which was an atmosphere of love and nurturing.

So she would be careful what she said about David. But

she would work behind the scenes and discourage Jenny's interest in him anytime she got the chance.

Satisfied with her plan of action, she put her feet up and closed her eyes.

Twenty-two

*"**I do wish you'd been** able to bring Jenny along with you."*

Hannah smiled at her aunt, who sat across the table from her. Marcy Harris was seventy-two, but she didn't look it. Tall, but not as tall as her brother, Joshua, she was naturally slender, and her soft, creamy skin belied all the years she'd lived in Florida. She was religious about wearing sunscreen, and before sunscreen became widely used, she wore a big floppy hat to protect her. Her light brown hair had long ago turned gray, and she kept it cut short and simply styled. And her green eyes were still as beautiful as they'd ever been. The fact that Hannah also had those eyes had always been a source of great pride to her, because next to Simon, she admired her aunt more than anyone else in the world.

A widow now, her aunt had married at eighteen. She'd always said Russell Harris had been her salvation, because he hadn't been able to find a decent job in the Jordan area, so had struck out for Florida where he had a cousin who had promised to get him work. They'd settled in the Tampa area, and she'd been there ever since.

"I wish I could have brought her, too," Hannah said. "But neither Simon nor I thought it would be wise, considering Jenny's still recuperating from her accident."

"Thank goodness she suffered nothing worse than a concussion."

"Believe me, Simon and I have said many prayers of thanks since the accident happened."

Her aunt nodded and took another swallow of her tea. It was morning, the fifth morning Hannah had spent in Jordan, and the fourth since her aunt had arrived. Soon the two of them would accompany Hannah's mother to the hospital, where they would collect Hannah's father, who was being released today, and bring him home.

Hannah herself was returning to California tomorrow. Part of her felt guilty and felt she should stay to help her mother. She knew her father would not be an easy patient while he recuperated from his near-fatal heart attack. But her mother had urged her to go.

"Jenny needs you," she'd said.

Hannah had nodded, relieved, but she knew Jenny was perfectly fine without her. She'd talked to her daughter every day since she'd left, and Jenny seemed to be having a fine time with her grandmother.

No, the reason Hannah felt guilty was because her desire to get back to California—which she obviously had not been able to hide from her mother—had to do with her conflicted feelings about her father. The trouble was, he made it so difficult to be around him.

If her father had still been in danger, she would have stayed. But he was on the mend; both his cardiologist and the resident cardiologist agreed.

And it wasn't as if Hannah couldn't come back if they really needed her. Still, she continued to fight the feeling that she wasn't the good daughter she was expected to be. *Like Leah is.* Because no matter what Sarah had said, Leah *was* a good daughter. She always had been. That's why Sarah thought their parents loved her and not Sarah. Hannah didn't think Sarah's perception of the situation was accurate at all, but she understood how Sarah might believe it was.

Hannah sighed.

"What's wrong, Hannah? That's the second time you've sighed in the past five minutes."

"Oh, I don't know. I guess I'm feeling guilty about leaving."

Marcy was leaving tomorrow, too. No one had urged her to stay, which secretly amused Hannah. Although her aunt loved her brother, they had never seen eye to eye on anything. Marcy had told her once that he was so much like their father, it was scary.

"I would have thought your father'd suffered enough under Dad that he would have bent over backward to be different. Instead, he's worse." Her aunt had shaken her head sadly. "I couldn't wait to get away from Dad. But Joshua, he turned into a clone."

As a result of the siblings' differences in philosophy and life choices, Hannah knew it only made life more difficult for her mother when Aunt Marcy was there, for Hannah's father was constantly criticizing everything she said and did, and eventually she would get tired of listening and the fireworks would begin.

"Now, don't you feel guilty," her aunt said now. "Your mother's used to being a martyr. She likes it." Marcy grimaced. "I'm sorry. I shouldn't have said that. It was unfair."

Hannah shrugged. "I've had the same thought many times."

"I've never understood why any woman would put up with the stuff my brother dishes out." This last was said in a much lower tone of voice, as if Hannah's aunt had just realized that Hannah's mother was upstairs and might be able to hear them.

Hannah, too, lowered her voice after glancing toward the hall to make sure her mother wasn't, even now, on her way down to the kitchen. "She's frightened, Aunt Marcy. She's never been on her own; I don't think she'd have any idea how to manage."

"Maybe so. But she has you. I'm sure she knows you and Simon would be glad to help her."

Hannah frowned. "I don't know. She's never even hinted that she's unhappy, so I've been reluctant to bring up the subject."

It was a good thing they *had* lowered their voices, for just as her aunt started to answer, they both heard the sound of footsteps on the stairs.

"So," her aunt said brightly, "what time does your flight leave tomorrow?"

"Simon's supposed to call and let me know. He said he'd ask Rose—she's the travel coordinator for the company— to try to get me on a flight that leaves about the same time yours does. That way we can go to the airport together."

Her aunt smiled. "That would be nice."

"I'm ready," said Hannah's mother, walking into the kitchen.

Hannah turned. "You look nice, Mother." Rachel wore a lilac print dress made out of polished cotton. "Is that new?"

Her mother smoothed down the skirt self-consciously. "Yes. I made it a couple of weeks ago."

"Pretty color, Rachel," Hannah's aunt said. She got up and carried her cup to the sink. After rinsing it out and placing it in the dish drainer, she said, "Shall we go?"

Hannah gathered her things, and the three headed outside to Hannah's rental car.

They didn't talk much on the way to the hospital, and Hannah was glad. Most subjects had been exhausted over the past few days. Moreover, Hannah was accustomed to having big chunks of quiet time during the day, something that was in short supply this week.

Was there something wrong with her, she wondered, that she didn't enjoy being with her family much? She loved them all, but she wasn't sure she liked any of them. With the exception of Aunt Marcy, of course.

Aunt Marcy was such a sweetheart. What would she have done without her? If not for her, Hannah wasn't sure what might have happened to her. Remembering how her aunt had helped her all those years ago when she'd felt so desperate, she was flooded with thankfulness. She would never be able to adequately repay her.

It was about ten o'clock when Hannah, her mother, and her aunt finally reached the hospital. Hannah's father sat waiting for them as they walked into his room. He looked so much better than he'd looked when Hannah had first seen him that night in Coronary Care. He had color in his face now, and he looked a lot stronger. His thick gray hair was freshly washed and neatly combed, and he was dressed in the dark trousers and white shirt her mother had brought for him yesterday. His blue eyes, still piercing, reflected impatience.

"It's about time," he said curtly.

Hannah smothered a sigh. Her mother was really going to be in for a bad time until her father was fully recovered and could once again take over the full complement of duties at the church. She pushed the worry about what Leah had told her—that the elders might force her father to retire—to the back of her mind. No sense borrowing trouble. When and if that happened, they would figure out a way to deal with it. But what that way would be, Hannah had no idea. Her poor mother. Hannah wouldn't be in her shoes for anything.

"Rachel," he snapped. "Don't just stand there. Help me up."

"Oh, Father," Hannah said. "I'll do it." She walked over and held out her hand. For a moment she thought he was going to refuse her help, but after a moment he took her hand and allowed her to give him the support he needed to stand. Once he was on his feet, he seemed steady enough, although Hannah knew it had taken a lot of effort just to do this one small thing they all took for granted.

Hannah's mother picked up his small suitcase, and her aunt reached for the two flowering plants he had received.

"Is there anything we have to do before we go?" Hannah asked.

"Yes," answered a female voice.

They all looked around. A dark-haired nurse Hannah hadn't seen before stood in the doorway. "Reverend Turner isn't allowed to leave unless he's in a wheelchair. I've called for one and it'll be here in a few minutes. Also, Mrs. Turner . . ." She looked at Hannah's mother with a question in her eyes. When Rachel nodded, she said, "You'll need to sign a couple of forms."

"I can sign my own forms," Hannah's father said. He glared at the nurse.

The nurse started to say something, then must have

thought better of it, because she brought the forms over to him. He pulled the rolling tray table over and shakily signed the forms. During the thirty seconds or so it took him to accomplish this, Hannah's eyes met her aunt's. Marcy's expression seemed to say *stubborn ass*, a term she'd used more than a few times in connection with her brother.

Hannah's gaze moved to her mother, who was worrying her lower lip. *Thank God I don't have to take care of him, because if he kept up this kind of behavior, I would probably strangle him in a matter of days.*

"We might as well all sit down," her aunt said after the nurse left with the signed forms. "I know these hospitals. They say a few minutes, but sometimes that means a half hour or more."

"I don't want to sit down. I just got up."

"Well, Joshua," she answered softly, unruffled by her brother's dark look, "suit yourself, but you're going to be awfully tired of standing if it takes as long for that wheelchair to come as I'm afraid it might." So saying, she parked her trim frame on the end of the bed.

Hannah looked at her mother and willed her to say something. But her mother, too conditioned to keep her mouth shut no matter what, didn't utter a word.

"Father," Hannah said, exasperated with them both, "please sit. You don't want to jeopardize your health, do you? Then it'll be that much longer before you can go back to work."

He looked as if he were going to argue, but then he abruptly sat back in his chair. Hannah's mother edged over to the bed and perched on the other end from her sister-in-law. Hannah, with a mental eye roll, leaned against the wall. It was going to be a long twenty-four hours before she could escape to the airport.

While they waited for the wheelchair to arrive, Hannah attempted to make light conversation, but her father was having none of it. To everything she said, he replied with a scowl. Finally she quit trying, and the four of them waited in silence. Although it didn't take the half hour her aunt had been afraid it might, it did take nearly twenty minutes—a twenty minutes that seemed endless.

Finally, though, the wheelchair arrived, pushed into the room by a tall black male nurse who had the dark blue uniform that Hannah knew belonged to the Physical Therapy unit. "Okeydokey," he said cheerfully. "It's time to go." He wheeled the chair over to Hannah's father, then leaned down to lift him up.

Hannah noticed that her father didn't protest the nurse's assistance at all. No, she thought sadly, he only bullied people who were least likely to fight back.

Once her father was settled in the chair, the nurse wheeled him out the door. The three women followed. When they reached the main entrance, Hannah said, "I'll get the car," and left the others waiting.

Five minutes later she pulled up under the covered entranceway, and the nurse pushed her father outside. Once her father was safely deposited into the front passenger seat, Hannah put his suitcase and the plants in the trunk, made sure her mother and aunt were belted in, then climbed into the driver's seat and began the trip home to Jordan.

They didn't even attempt to talk on the way. Her father stared out the window, and the two older women were quiet, as well. Hannah wished she could put the radio on, but she knew it would irritate her father if she did; he didn't approve of modern music.

When they were halfway home, the sky darkened, and within minutes rain pelted the car. Hannah had forgotten how fast a summer storm could arise in this part of the midwest. When she was a kid, she'd loved the summer rainstorms. She and her sisters would sit on the glider on the front porch and enjoy the respite from the heat. She didn't even mind the thunder or lightning, although she remembered that Leah had always been frightened of it. But Hannah and Sarah loved the noise and the wind.

Hannah had especially loved when it would rain at night. She'd lay there in her bed and listen to it hit the roof and pretend she was high up in the tower of a castle on the Cornish coast. Reminded of those days, she smiled. She

guessed her fantasy about Cornwall came from reading the
dogeared copies of the Daphne du Maurier novels she'd
found in the attic. She had always meant to ask her aunt if
the books had belonged to her, because she couldn't imagine
they had been her mother's.

*Funny how I knew, even then, it was best not to bring
them to my parents' attention.*

Hannah remembered now how she'd sneak and read the
books under the covers at night, then hide them deep in her
closet during the day.

"You're driving too fast, Hannah."

Hannah jumped, startled by her father's voice when she'd
been so deep into her own thoughts. "I'm only going thirty-
five, Father." The speed limit on this stretch of road was
fifty.

"It's raining. You don't live around here, so you don't
know how slick these roads get when it rains."

Hannah sighed and slowed down to thirty. It was useless
to argue with him. He never gave up until he got his way,
and the longer you resisted, the more disapproving he became. Sometimes that disapproval could last for hours, even
over something as minor as this.

The last half of the drive home seemed to take forever,
but finally she pulled into the driveway. The rain had
slowed, but it was still coming down steadily.

"I'll park as close to the front steps as I can get," Hannah
said, "then I'll run in and get some umbrellas."

They managed to get her father inside without too much
difficulty, but even with the shelter of the umbrellas, Hannah
and her mother got fairly wet from the effort and Hannah
shivered once they were indoors.

Earlier, they'd set up a rented hospital bed in the dining
room, which was where Hannah's father would be until he
was capable of climbing stairs again. Thank God the church
had spent some money a few years back and added a small
bathroom downstairs, or it would have been impossible for
him to recuperate at home, which, for years, had only had
the one bathroom upstairs.

He grumbled the whole time she and her mother spent

getting him settled in the bed—for the trip home had exhausted him, even if he wouldn't admit it—but finally he was in. They had taken the leaf out of the dining room table and pushed it into the corner. They'd also pushed the antique tea cart up next to the bed. After covering it with a piece of oilcloth Hannah's mother had unearthed, it would serve as a place for her father to put his glass of water, his reading glasses, a box of tissues, his Bible, and a bell.

"What's *that* for?" He frowned, pointing to the bell.

"In case you need me, Joshua," Hannah's mother said. "You can ring."

The frown remained, but he didn't tell her to take it away.

Only after making sure he wanted nothing more did Hannah go upstairs to change into something dry. Once she had, she headed for the kitchen to join her aunt, who was busily mixing up tuna salad for their lunch. When Hannah asked about her mother, her aunt said she'd gone down to the basement, saying she had to put in a load of laundry.

It couldn't have been five minutes later that the bell they'd given Hannah's father rang furiously.

"Where's your mother?" her father demanded when she entered the dining room.

"She's downstairs putting in some laundry. What do you need, Father?"

"I need a lamp. I can't see to read."

"Oh, okay. I guess we didn't think of that."

"Your mother doesn't think of anything."

"Now, Father, that's a bit unfair, don't you think?"

He looked at her as if she'd suddenly grown two heads, and Hannah realized how unused to being contradicted he was. Actually, it surprised her that she *had* contradicted him. "I'll get a lamp from the living room." She felt proud of herself as she unplugged the floor lamp that sat behind her father's favorite chair in the living room and brought it into the dining room, where she set it up within his easy reach near the head of the bed. "If you want to sit in the living room and read, we'll have to get you another, but for right now, this should be okay."

"There's no need to spend money on another lamp that we won't need when I'm completely well."

"You can always use it. I'll buy it for you. It'll be my get-well present."

"That money would be put to much better use in the church donation basket."

Hannah started to say, *Oh, all right, have it your way,* then stopped. "Father," she said patiently, "I am buying you a lamp. It would be nice if you would just say thank you and quit arguing with me." Ignoring the astonished look on his face, she walked out of the room.

Back in the kitchen her aunt had finished making the tuna salad and was slicing a loaf of wheat bread.

She looked up. "How about slicing that tomato for me?"

"All right." Hannah opened a drawer and found the paring knife.

Once lunch was ready, Hannah called to her mother, then walked back to the dining room to see if her father felt like eating.

He didn't look up. "I'm not hungry." He continued reading the Bible.

"All right. Call or ring your bell if you change your mind, and I'll fix you a sandwich."

"Your mother can do it."

"Father, why is it so hard for you to accept help from me? I'm just trying to give Mother a hand while I'm here." When he didn't answer, just kept on reading, she shook her head and went to join the women.

"I'd better fix your father a sandwich before I sit down," Hannah's mother said.

"I asked him if he wanted anything, and he said he wasn't hungry."

"Are you sure?"

Marcy smacked the table. "For heaven's sake, Rachel, stop dithering and sit down. Don't you think Hannah knows what Joshua said?" It was clear she was quickly losing patience with Hannah's mother.

Although she slid another fearful glance in the direction of the dining room, Hannah's mother did finally sit. But she had no sooner taken her bread and started to put some of the tuna salad on a slice when the bell jangled again. She jumped up, nearly overturning the glass of iced tea Marcy had poured for her.

"What is *wrong* with that man?" Hannah's aunt muttered. She looked at Hannah. "I'm not sure I'll last until tomorrow. Think we could get out of here tonight?"

Hannah couldn't help it. She laughed. And a moment later her aunt laughed, too.

They were still laughing when her mother came back, and although she didn't comment or ask what they were laughing about, Hannah had the sudden, sad feeling she knew.

Twenty-three

Jenny was so glad her mother was home again. It wasn't that she didn't like having her grandmother there. It was just that things felt different when her mother was home. They felt *right*.

She could tell her mom was glad to be back, too. Yesterday, after she'd unpacked and all, she kept smiling and saying stuff like "I missed you so much." She must have given Jenny twenty hugs. She even hugged Vixen, who kept licking her face and making her laugh.

And last night she and Jenny's dad kept looking at each other during dinner, and Jenny knew they were thinking about later, when they'd be alone. Jenny knew they still made love, unlike some of her friends' parents, who didn't. She thought about Baylee Grunwald, who sat next to her in the violin section of orchestra. Baylee said once that her mom and dad didn't even sleep in the same room anymore.

And Charlotte Hathaway, who played the cello and heard Baylee talking, said her parents were both having affairs with somebody else. "And it isn't the first time, either."

At first Jenny thought Charlotte was exaggerating, saying what she had just to try to shock Jenny and Baylee, but Charlotte insisted it was the truth. She'd said she knew about her dad because only a week earlier she'd heard him talking on the phone. He hadn't even lowered his voice, because he didn't know anyone else was there. He'd been talking to some woman, and Charlotte heard him say he couldn't wait to see her and she should be sure to wear that sexy lace teddy she'd worn the last time they were together. Then Charlotte went on to say she'd seen her mother with her tennis coach.

"They didn't know I could see them, because they were behind some bushes. But I did, and they were kissing, and he shoved his hand down her shorts. It was gross!"

Jenny *was* shocked. And she could tell Baylee was, too. Charlotte hadn't acted like what she'd said was any big deal, and Jenny couldn't understand that. If her parents were doing stuff like that, she'd be totally freaked out. Plus she'd be disgusted, and she'd never feel the same way about them. People who were married shouldn't act like that. They should be honest with each other and respect their marriage vows. Didn't they care that they had promised to love each other and be true to each other until the day they died? Didn't their vows mean *anything* to them?

Jenny could kind of understand why actors and actresses couldn't seem to stay married. Like, if you were always having to kiss other people and stick your tongue in their mouths—not to mention all those scenes where they were naked together—it would probably be hard to remember you were married. But *normal* people shouldn't act that way. Normal people should remember they were supposed to be setting examples for their children.

Jenny was so grateful she didn't have to worry about that kind of thing. Her parents loved each other, plus they were really good people. They always told the truth, and they never kept secrets from each other.

She liked when they got mushy and romantic around each other, too. It made her feel good to see them kiss or hug. It made her feel safe.

When I get married, that's the way I want it to be with me and my husband.

Thinking about getting married caused her thoughts to drift in the direction of her favorite person. She hadn't been able to stop thinking about David since he'd visited her on Monday. That night, when her dad came home from work, she'd wondered if she should tell him about David's visit, but her grandmother had solved the problem for her and told him herself.

"That was nice of him," her dad had said.

Jenny had hoped they'd talk about him some more, but the subject changed, and she couldn't figure out a way to bring David's name back into the conversation.

She hugged herself as she thought about how nice Monday had been and how much fun the two of them had had together.

After they'd talked to her grandmother, they'd gone into the game room and played pool for a while. David had won the first and second games, but Jenny had played really well in the third game and she'd beaten him. She could tell he was surprised, but he didn't act all weird like some of the boys she knew who couldn't stand for any girl to get the best of them, no matter what they were doing. David had just grinned and raised his hand for a high five.

And then, after the pool games, she'd shown him around the house. He'd seemed really interested and had looked at everything and asked questions. When they'd gone into her mom's studio, he'd seemed totally impressed and had spent a long time looking at the paintings that were stacked around the walls.

"She's really good, isn't she?" he'd said after looking at a painting of one of the homeless people she liked to paint so much.

"Yes," Jenny said proudly. Then she'd told him about the show her mom was getting ready for.

"When's the show going to be?"

"In September."

"She paints a lot of homeless people, doesn't she?"

"Uh-huh."

"Why?"

"Because she said they have character in their faces."

He hadn't said anything to that, but after a few minutes, he asked another question. "Did your mom always like to paint?"

"Well, she always liked her art classes in high school, and

then she went to this really neat art school in Florida instead of going to college."

"Your mom went to school in Florida, huh? Whereabouts?"

"Sarasota."

"The Ringling School, you mean?"

"Do you know it?"

"You forget. I grew up in Florida."

Jenny smiled. "I know, but Florida's a big place. I guess the reason she went to school there is because she was staying with her aunt at the time. Aunt Marcy lives in Tampa."

"Why was she staying with her aunt?"

"I don't really know. I just remember her saying something about no jobs in Nebraska where she grew up, so after she graduated she went to live with Aunt Marcy."

Once she'd finished showing him around inside, they took a walk outside. He said he really liked their pool, and Jenny got brave and told him if he'd like to come and swim, just to call her.

"I might do that," he'd said.

Jenny had been so happy, she'd almost burst.

Soon after, it had been time for lunch. Jenny'd hoped he didn't mind having lunch with her grandmother, but he didn't seem to. And she was thrilled that her grandmother seemed to like him so much. Her grandmother was pretty particular. She didn't like just anybody. She was especially picky when it came to manners, but David easily passed in that area. It made Jenny feel good to see how polite and well-mannered he was and to know that he'd made a good impression—not just on her parents when they'd met him—but on her exacting grandmother.

Having David there almost made up for not being able to ride Beauty or participate in any of the horse shows this summer. If she thought she would see him again, regularly, she would think her accident was completely worth what it had cost her. Trouble was, she just didn't know how he felt about her. He seemed really friendly when he called and really glad to be there when he came on Monday, but when he left he hadn't said anything about coming back, and

Jenny wondered if he'd completely forgotten about swimming in their pool.

She desperately needed to talk to someone about the situation, but who? Not her mom. And not her dad or her grandmother. And she didn't want to talk to Angie, because she didn't trust Angie to keep her mouth shut.

Why did Courtney have to go away this summer? she wondered. E-mail just wasn't as good as talking on the phone or in person.

Jenny listlessly turned on her computer and watched as it booted. Courtney hadn't even answered her last e-mail, and Jenny had sent that one yesterday morning. The trouble was, Courtney had made a friend in Connecticut, a girl who lived next door in the same apartment complex as Courtney's dad and his girlfriend, and now Courtney had all kinds of things to do and places to go. Whereas, she, Jenny, had nothing to do but read and hang around the house.

It was just so unfair, Jenny thought, completely forgetting that only moments ago she'd been thinking that it wasn't so bad to have had the accident, since it had caused David to call and come over.

If only she could figure out a way to see him again. Too bad her birthday wasn't coming up. She could have a party and invite him.

For the rest of the day she thought about ways she could engineer another meeting. And then, almost as if God had heard her, her father solved her problem.

It happened at dinner. One minute Jenny was eating her salmon and feeling sorry for herself, and the next, she was hearing David's name. She blinked and looked up.

"That boy is definitely promotion material," her father was saying to her mother.

"Simon, he's only been working at the warehouse a couple of weeks," her mom said. "How can you possibly know that so soon?"

"Trust me, Hannah. I know people. That boy is smart, and he's a hard worker. Hector told me Friday that David is the best employee he's ever had. That you only have to show him something or explain something once and he's got it."

Jenny beamed. "Did you go out to the warehouse Friday, Dad?"

"Yes."

"Gee, I wish I could've gone with you. I'm so tired of being stuck here in the house, and I haven't seen Hector or Maria for so long."

"Jenny . . ." Her mom looked hurt. "You know I told you if you get really tired or bored that I'll stop work early, and we can go see a movie or something."

Jenny was immediately sorry she'd said what she did. She certainly hadn't wanted to make her mom feel guilty, and that's exactly what she'd done. "I didn't mean it that way, Mom. I just meant—"

"We know what you meant, Pumpkin," her dad interrupted. "And I promise, the next time I go to the warehouse, I'll come and get you."

Her mom frowned. What was wrong now?

"At any rate, Hannah," her dad continued, "I'd like to invite David to dinner some night. I'll probably go out to the warehouse again this Friday. . . ." He smiled at Jenny. "Yes, you can go then, too." He turned back to Jenny's mom. "I thought I'd ask him to come some time next week, maybe Wednesday night if that's convenient for you."

Jenny's heart was pounding so hard she was sure her parents could hear it. She was going to see David on Friday. And her dad wanted to have him come for dinner next week! *Please say yes, Mom. Please say yes.*

"Why do you want to invite him to dinner, anyway?" her mom asked.

Now her dad frowned. "Because I like him, and I'd like to get to know him better. Besides, we still owe him, Hannah."

"You've given him a good job. Surely that's payment enough."

Jenny couldn't understand why her mom, who was normally so nice and so generous, was acting like this. Why, she almost acted as if she didn't *like* David. Jenny couldn't understand it. How could *anyone* not like David?

"Come on, Hannah, where's the harm?" her dad said. "He's a nice kid, and he's all alone here. I think he'd really appreciate our asking him to dinner."

Her mother sighed. "Oh, all right, Simon, if you want to, go ahead."

"If he can't come Wednesday, I'll ask him for another night."

"Fine."

Jenny was thrilled. If she'd been alone, she would have jumped up and started dancing around the room. As it was, she could hardly contain herself, and for the rest of the meal, all she wanted to do was get finished and go to her room and e-mail Courtney, because telling Courtney—even if she didn't write back right away—was better than telling no-body.

The best part of all this—almost better than the fact David would be coming over soon—was the fact that her dad liked David so much. So if a miracle happened and David *did* ask her out on a date, maybe her father *wouldn't* say no. Maybe he'd think it was fine for her to go out with him. And even though her mom was acting kind of weird about David, she'd eventually come around, too, because she never disagreed with Jenny's dad for long.

Oh, Jenny was so happy.

The only question was, how was she going to wait until Friday?

Twenty-four

———

"Darling, what's the matter?" **Hannah,** who was brushing her hair in preparation for the evening, looked up. Her eyes met Simon's in the mirror. "Nothing's the matter."

"Hannah . . ." Simon's eyes, so deep and blue and clear, so steady, held no reproach, but his tone said he didn't believe her.

Hannah held his gaze for a moment, then sighed and put down her silver-backed hairbrush, part of a monogrammed set that had been a gift from Madeleine a couple of birthdays ago. "I'm sorry, it's just that I can't get rid of the feeling that it's a mistake to encourage this boy to think he's going to be part of our circle of friends."

She could see Simon was taken aback by her statement. He was probably even disappointed in her. But she couldn't help it; this was how she felt.

"It's not like you to be a snob, Hannah."

"I'm not a snob. My not wanting this Conway boy to become a part of our lives has nothing to do with him personally." She ignored the little voice that said she wasn't being entirely truthful. "It has to do with the fact that Jenny has an enormous crush on him, and he is entirely too old for her."

Simon smiled. "Is that all?"

"Isn't that enough?"

"Oh, come on, surely you're not really worried about

Jenny. First of all, having a crush on someone older is normal at her age. I don't think there's anything to worry about. David is not interested in our daughter in that way. He thinks of her as a kid."

"I wish I could be as sure as you are."

"Hannah, you worry too much. Trust me on this one, darling."

"You know, other than what he told you about his parents being dead and being raised in foster homes, we really don't know a *thing* about his background. I mean, why did he move here? It's not like he had a job or anything. He just came."

"You left Nebraska and moved to Florida," Simon pointed out in that quiet, reasonable way of his.

"That was different. I went to live with my aunt. To go to school there. This boy is on his own." She bit her lip. "Maybe he's running away from something."

"Hannah, listen to yourself. You're being paranoid. David probably just wanted some adventure. L.A. seems romantic to kids. Thousands of them move here every year. You know that."

"That's because most of them want to be actors."

"I still think you're manufacturing problems where none exists. Give the boy the benefit of the doubt, okay? And if it'll make you feel better, I'll ask him why he decided to come to L.A."

Hannah knew he was becoming impatient with her. In his shoes, she would probably feel the same way. She wished she could explain her disquiet, but she couldn't, because it wasn't based on reason, it was based on feeling and intuition, two things that were anathema to most men. Even Simon, as understanding and fair as he was, operated on logic, not emotion. And feeling and intuition had no place in a logical argument.

"Now, come on," he said. "Finish getting ready and let's have a glass of wine before he gets here." He leaned over and kissed her lightly on the mouth. "Okay?"

"Okay." She made herself smile. "I'm not quite ready, though, but you go on. I'll be there in a few minutes."

Her smile faded the moment he was out the door. If only it was as easy to banish her misgivings as Simon made it seem. She stared at her reflection in the mirror. She hoped Simon was right. She hoped this evening would prove her completely wrong. She hoped her negative feelings about David Conway had a simple explanation. That they were rooted in his resemblance to Mark and had no basis in reality.

Sighing, knowing she was getting nowhere, she finished fixing her hair and reached for her emerald earrings. After putting them on, she inspected her makeup one last time, then went to join Simon.

Both he and Jenny were sitting in the living room. Simon held a glass of red wine, and Jenny was drinking her usual evening treat of a mixture of ginger ale and cranberry juice. Hannah smiled at her. She looked adorable in a short black skirt and silvery knit top that hugged her body and showed far more of her budding curves than Hannah would have liked. Instead of the ball cap she'd been wearing ever since the accident, she'd pulled her hair back and put on a wide black headband, which covered the shaved place on her head. All of the excitement and anticipation she was feeling shone in her face.

Hannah's heart swelled with love. *Darling Jenny, you've got to learn to mask your feelings. When you put them out there like that, you're just asking to get hurt.*

"Shall I pour you some wine?" Simon asked.

"I'd love some. What are you having?"

"This is that Australian shiraz I bought last week."

"That sounds good." Hannah walked over and joined Jenny on one of the two pale gray suede sofas that flanked the fireplace.

Simon poured her wine and brought it over to her, then returned to his seat across from them. For a long moment no one spoke. On the mantel the clock ticked, from outside came the distant hum of traffic and the bark of a neighbor's dog, out in the kitchen were the sounds of Martha bustling about, at Jenny's feet Vixen twitched and whimpered in her sleep. The afternoon sun slanted across the Aubusson carpet, intensifying its rich ruby and sapphire tones.

Hannah took a deep breath and sipped at her wine. She crossed her legs, then uncrossed them.

A moment later Martha entered carrying a tray. She set it on the coffee table in front of them. It contained a plate of stuffed mushrooms, a bowl of artichoke dip, and a container of water wafers as well as four small plates and napkins. She had no sooner put the food down on the coffee table than the buzzer signifying someone at the front gate sounded.

Simon stood. "I'll get it." He left the room, and Hannah heard him talking through the intercom system by the front door. A few moments later she saw a black truck drive up the driveway and park in front of the house.

"David's here," Jenny said breathlessly.

As if to echo her announcement, the clock on the mantel began to chime the hour.

"Right on time," Hannah murmured.

Jenny jumped up. Her cheeks were flushed. Hannah so wanted to tell her daughter what she'd been thinking earlier about not wearing her emotions out there for everyone to see, but she knew now was not the time, so instead Hannah sent up a silent prayer. *Please watch over her. She's so vulnerable to being hurt.*

Hannah also rose to her feet as Simon ushered the boy in. She noted that David had taken care with his appearance. His khaki pants and black shirt looked new. He'd gotten a haircut, too, and although it wasn't preppy-short, it wasn't as long as it had been before.

"Hi," Jenny said, beaming.

"Hi, Jenny. Hello, Mrs. Ferris."

"Hello, David. Glad you could come."

"Thank you."

After asking him what he'd like to drink, Simon walked to the bar and poured David a Coke. Then they all sat, Hannah next to Jenny, David on the same sofa with Simon. Hannah gestured to the laden tray.

"David, please help yourself."

"Thanks."

For the next few minutes they made small talk. Once the plates were filled and everyone had had a chance to sample the appetizers, Hannah said, "Simon tells me you're really enjoying working at the warehouse."

"Yes. The work is interesting, and Hector's a great guy to work for." David turned to Simon. "How long has he been your supervisor?"

"Eight years. But he's been an employee of the company for twenty-one years."

"Wow. I can't imagine working anywhere that long."

"We have a lot of longtime employees."

"That's because they're treated so well," Hannah said.

"I'll bet they miss you at the club," Jenny said. "You were the best lifeguard they've ever had there."

David looked uncomfortable.

"Well, you *were*." Jenny grinned. "Hey, you saved my life."

"Let's change the subject," David said.

"You're embarrassing him, Jenny," Simon said.

"Sorry." But she didn't look sorry. She looked adoring.

"Mrs. Ferris," David said, "I was sorry to hear about your father. Is he okay?"

"Thank you. He's doing fine."

"Jenny told me he's a minister."

"Yes."

"What church?"

"It's a small denomination. I'm sure you've never heard of it."

"It must have been tough being a minister's kid."

"Yes, my father was pretty strict. Much stricter than the parents of my friends."

"You grew up in Nebraska, right?"

"Yes."

"And went to school in Florida?"

Now Hannah was uncomfortable. She was also even more disturbed than she'd been earlier. When had all this conversation about her taken place? She knew David had visited Jenny while she was in Nebraska; both Simon and Jenny told her about the visit. And Jenny had mentioned he'd called her once, too. Still, the visit and the call must have been of much longer duration and been a whole lot more intimate than Jenny had let on. Now all of Hannah's misgivings came rushing back full force. Realizing she hadn't answered his question and that he was looking at her expectantly, she said, "Yes, in Sarasota."

"What about you, Mr. Ferris? Where did you go to school?"

"I got my degree at Stanford," Simon said.

"How about you, Jenny? Are you planning to go to Stanford, too?"

Jenny shrugged. "I don't know." She looked at Hannah. "Grandma would like me to go to the Sorbonne." Turning back to David, she said, "My grandmother Ferris is French, so she thinks French schools are best. Especially for girls. But Mom doesn't want me to go that far away."

"No," Hannah said, "I certainly don't."

Simon chuckled. "When you only have one child, David, you get pretty protective."

David's gaze moved to Hannah, and something in his eyes gave her the oddest feeling. She was relieved that before he had a chance to say anything else, Martha walked in and quietly announced that dinner was ready.

But questions swirled in her mind. Why was David so curious about their family? And why was she so suspicious of his motives?

She hated that she felt this way. He was obviously a nice boy. He was well spoken, he was intelligent, he was polite, and certainly no one could find fault with his appearance tonight. Added to that, he behaved exactly the right way with Jenny—friendly but not overly friendly, and with absolutely no indication that he was interested in her in a romantic way.

So what was Hannah's problem?

She didn't know.

She only knew she would be glad when the evening was over, and no matter what Simon said in the future, she did not want him to invite David Conway to their home again.

Entering the dining room, Hannah was glad she'd told Martha to remove the leaf from the table which, when it was in, seated twelve easily. Even now, with the leaf removed, the table was still too big for four, especially when Simon sat at the head and she sat at the foot, but tonight, instead of that arrangement, Hannah had instructed Martha to set the table with two plates on either side. Now the meal would be more intimate and conversation could flow more easily. But even more important, Hannah would be able to study David's expression as they talked, because she had placed him and Jenny side by side, and she and Simon sat across from them.

Jenny, of course, was thrilled to be next to David. Her eyes sparkled, and she couldn't keep her eyes off him. And even though he *was* too old for Jenny, Hannah couldn't help noticing how attractive they looked together.

As promised, Simon brought up David's move from Florida as soon as Martha had served the vegetable consommé.

"Are you finding California very different from Florida, David?" he said.

"There's a lot more traffic, that's for sure."

Simon smiled. "Certainly that's true of L.A." He let a few seconds go by, then added casually, "What made you decide to come to California?"

"It seemed to me there were more opportunities here," David said easily.

"Whereabouts in Florida did you grow up?" Hannah asked.

"The Miami area." He waited a heartbeat. Then, looking directly at Hannah, he said, "It wasn't just better job opportunities that brought me to California. I had another reason."

Later, Hannah would look back on this night and know that in that instant, she had a premonition of what was to come. Everything inside her went still, and the world around her seemed to hang suspended in time.

"See," he continued slowly, still holding Hannah's gaze, "a few months ago I discovered that my birth mother lives in L.A. So part of the reason I came was to look her up."

Hannah felt like someone was sitting on her chest and she couldn't breathe. No. No. It couldn't be. It simply wasn't possible. It wasn't. Simon was right. She was paranoid. This was just a cruel coincidence. It bore no relation to her or her life. The adoption had been closed. There was no way David could be the child she'd given up all those years ago. But the look in his eyes told her something different. Her heart told her something different.

She swallowed. Dear God.

"Your birth mother? You mean, you were adopted?" Simon asked.

David's gaze slowly left hers, and he gave his attention to Simon. "Yes. When I told you my parents were dead, I was talking about my adoptive parents."

"We have something in common, then, because I was adopted, too."

"Really?" David said.

Simon smiled. "Yes."

Hannah's head was spinning. She felt as if she were going to pass out. Her hands were trembling so badly, she had to put then in her lap to hide them. Yet no one else at the table seemed to think anything was out of the ordinary. How could they not? How could Simon sit there so calmly and talk to David as if this were a completely normal evening? *Oh, God, oh, God, what am I going to do?*

"Have you seen your birth mother?" Jenny was asking eagerly.

"I've seen her, but I haven't let her know who I am yet." He smiled crookedly. "Or that I know who she is."

Jenny's eyes got big. "Why not?"

David shrugged. "I don't know. Waiting for the right time, I guess." He looked across at Hannah. "I mean, she gave me away, didn't she? She might not be exactly thrilled to see me again."

Hannah's heart pounded like a crazy thing. She felt hot one minute, cold the next.

"It's always frightening confronting the unknown," Simon said softly.

Although Hannah would have liked to pretend she was

wrong in what she now guessed to be true, she couldn't
ignore all the similarities between her situation and his. David had been raised in Florida. Florida was where she'd had
her son, where he'd been placed for adoption. David was
the right age. And most damning of all, from the first day
she'd seen him, he'd reminded her of Mark.

And now that she was looking, *really* looking, she saw
other similarities. His hands. His hands were shaped exactly
like hers. And his mouth. She'd seen that mouth before on
Leah and on Leah's son, Samuel.

Dear heaven. So many emotions flooded her. Shock.
Fear. Guilt. Sorrow. Regret. But overriding them all was
love. An almost overwhelming love. It took all the strength
and willpower she possessed not to jump up and grab him
and crush him in her arms.

Nicholas. My baby.

Tears burned at the back of her eyes as Hannah tried to
calm herself. She had to. If she didn't, if she kept on this
way, she was going to fall apart right there.

"Gee," Jenny said, "it's kind of exciting, too, isn't it?"
She gave David another adoring look. "What's she like,
your birth mother?"

Again David's gaze flicked to Hannah. "She's beautiful.
Rich. Married. And she has a kid."

Any lingering doubt Hannah might have still harbored
evaporated at his words. She wanted to look away, but she
couldn't. It was as if his eyes had frozen her in place. But
inside she wasn't frozen. Inside she was a raging, churning,
chaotic inferno of emotion.

"Wow," Jenny said.

"Yeah," said David dryly, "wow."

Beside Hannah, Simon said nothing. She wondered what
he was thinking. Because of his situation, he had very little
sympathy for women who gave away their children. Hannah
was afraid to look at him. Afraid the feelings inside of her
would show in her eyes and on her face, and then he would
feel the same disdain and disgust for her that he felt for his
birth mother. Suddenly she was terrified. What would happen to them when Simon found out what she'd done? And

not only what she'd done twenty years ago, but how she'd lied to him by not telling him when he asked her to marry him? How she'd continued to lie to him all these years . . .

She remembered her first visit to a doctor when she'd suspected she was pregnant with Jenny. How, beforehand, she hadn't thought about having to give a medical history. And how, with Simon sitting there watching her, she'd been forced to lie as she filled out the form, saying "no" to the question "Have you ever been pregnant before?"

Her OB/GYN had known she'd lied as soon as he'd examined her.

"My husband doesn't know," she'd said. She'd been so ashamed. "Please don't tell him."

"It's not my place to tell him," Dr. Michaels said.

So many lies. Too many lies.

Somehow Hannah got through the rest of the meal. Somehow she managed to talk and laugh and eat as if she hadn't just gotten the shock of her life. As if her world hadn't just been turned upside down.

Throughout the remainder of the evening, every time David looked at her, she knew he knew that she had gotten his message. She also knew he wasn't going to expose her in front of Simon and Jenny, because he'd also figured out they had no idea that he existed.

Finally the meal was over, and Jenny asked if it was okay for her and David to play a couple of games of pool. When Simon said that was fine, Hannah grabbed at the opportunity to escape, saying, "You won't mind then if I excuse myself, will you? I'm not feeling well, and I think I'll go and lie down."

She walked over to David and extended her hand. When he took it, his touch was nearly her undoing, but she managed to unearth one last reserve of strength to give him a smile and say warmly, "Good night, David. It was very nice to have you with us tonight. I hope we'll see you again soon."

"Good night, Mrs. Ferris. Thank you."

Hannah knew Simon was puzzled, because all through the years they'd been together, Hannah had never shirked her duties as a hostess. Certainly she'd never let a small thing like a headache keep her from her guests. But all he said was, "I'm sorry, darling," and then he kissed her good night.

Hannah left wondering what David was thinking. Whether he knew that she was running away.

Gaining the privacy and safety of her bedroom, her shoulders sagged with relief, even as she knew this was just a short respite.

She kicked off her shoes and lay down on the bed. What she had feared for so long had finally happened. Her past had caught up with her. Very soon her secret would be exposed. What would happen next was out of her control. All she could do was pray that somehow she would be able to make things right. For David. And for all of them.

Twenty-five

David couldn't sleep. He kept remembering the look in his mother's eyes when he'd said the other reason he'd come to California was to find his birth mother. He knew the exact moment she'd realized who he was.

She'd been shocked. He could see it in the way her eyes widened, the way the green became darker.

What was she going to do?

Would she call him?

Or would she pretend nothing was different, maybe talk herself out of what she thought she knew?

Was she scared?

David thought she was. He was pretty sure neither Simon nor Jenny knew about him. So his mother was probably worried about what would happen to her perfect little world when they found out.

Part of him wanted to smash that world. Make her suffer the way he'd suffered. But another part, the part he'd been pretending didn't exist, just wanted to belong to that world. Just wanted her to love him the way she loved Jenny. Just wanted her to say she'd never wanted to give him away.

Yet how could that be?

She *had* given him away.

She doesn't want me. I shouldn't have come here.

Hot tears clogged his throat. He fought them, because he was tough, and tough guys never cried. But it was no use.

He'd been strong for too long. Finally he could fight the pain no longer, and for the first time since he was a scared little kid in a strange house with strange people, David cried himself to sleep.

Hannah slept fitfully. Finally she gave up, and at a little after three in the morning, she crept out of bed. As quietly as she could manage in the dark, she found her robe and slippers, then tiptoed out of the bedroom. She closed the door behind her, taking care not to make noise.

Simon didn't stir. For this she was grateful, because if he had awakened, he would have been certain to want to know what was wrong and why she couldn't sleep.

Hannah was not a good liar, despite the fact she'd been living a lie for a long time. But not telling Simon about her teenage pregnancy and putting her child up for adoption was a lie of omission. It wasn't as if she'd had to look Simon in the eye and tell him something that wasn't true. She knew that if he'd ever suspected the truth and questioned her, she would have caved in immediately and the whole story would have spilled out.

Moving silently, she made her way to the living room. She didn't turn on any lights. She didn't need them. Moonlight flooded her way.

Settling into a large armchair by the front window, she curled her legs up under her and stared out. It was a clear night with a full moon in an indigo sky. She couldn't see them, but she knew the stars were out tonight. She smiled sadly, remembering how, as a child, she always wished upon the first star she saw at night with such hope and trust. Those days of innocence were gone forever. Now she knew it took more than wishes to make dreams come true. Now she knew how hard life could be. How we make choices, and sometimes those choices hurt people.

She kept seeing David's face. She thought about how his adoptive parents had died. How he'd ended up in state care. What had those years been like for him? Years when she had been going to school, years when she'd had her first job, met Simon, married him. Years where she had always had a good place to live and people who cared about her.

But David.

Nicholas.

Her lower lip trembled, and despite what might happen, she knew what she had to do next. Tomorrow, as soon as Simon left for the office, she would call David at work and see if they could meet either for lunch or when he was through for the day.

The thought of actually talking to David, of acknowledging him as her son, of finding out about his life, both terrified and thrilled her. How did he feel about her? His behavior the night before had sent mixed signals. At times he'd seemed threatening, as if he was daring her, saying, *Here I am, I'm going to turn your life upside down, and there's nothing you can do about it*. At other times he'd seemed only young and sweet, the kind of young man anyone would be proud to claim as her own.

Tears hovered as she wondered about him. Had he been happy before his adoptive parents died? Had they loved him and cared for him the way she and Simon loved and cared for Jenny?

Jenny.

Dear God. Jenny.

In all of this, she hadn't once thought about Jenny until now. What was this revelation going to do to her?

Would she be upset? Even as she asked herself the question, Hannah knew the answer. Of course Jenny would be upset. All these years she had felt special. Hannah couldn't count the number of times she and Simon had emphasized just how special Jenny was and how much they loved her. Would she feel betrayed and angry?

Would these feelings be compounded by humiliation that the boy she had such a crush on was actually her half brother? How would she handle *that*? Would she hate Hannah? Would this disclosure ruin their relationship forever?

Please, God, let her be glad. Help me make her understand that David's existence is not a threat to her, that I love her and I will always love her, that what happened when I was seventeen doesn't change that.

But what if she didn't understand? Jenny was so young. Maybe too young. The young were so self-absorbed. They felt the entire world revolved around them, that when something traumatic happened that affected them, they were the only ones suffering.

Somehow, some way, Hannah had to make her daughter understand. Because the alternative didn't bear thinking about.

Even as Hannah agonized over Jenny, she purposely kept her mind from dwelling on Simon. She was afraid she knew exactly how *he* would feel when he knew the truth. He would feel completely betrayed. He would question everything about their lives together. In fact, she wasn't certain he would ever be able to forgive her for keeping David's existence a secret from him. She refused to think about what that might mean in terms of their future.

I had no choice. Maybe he'll be able to see that.

If only . . .

She didn't finish the thought. All the *if only*s in the world wouldn't help her now. The time for regrets and *if only*s was long past. Now it was time to move forward. To be honest with the people she loved and to pray that somehow they would find it in their hearts to understand and accept. And that maybe someday they would also forgive.

The next morning Hannah called her mother-in-law before attempting to reach David. She hated asking Madeleine for favors. Whenever she did, no matter how reasonable the request, Madeleine always managed to make Hannah feel as if she were fulfilling her mother-in-law's worst expectations. But today that reluctance was overridden by a higher priority.

When Madeleine answered, Hannah said, "I have to be gone for a while today, and Jenny's awfully bored. I was wondering if you were free. I thought maybe you might take her shopping and out to lunch."

"As it happens," Madeleine said in her familiar imperious tone, "my bridge game was canceled, so I'm at loose ends myself. I'll be happy to entertain Jenny since you're so busy." There was a slight emphasis on the word *you're*.

"Thank you," Hannah said. "Shall I tell her? Or do you want to call her?"

"I'll call her."

When they hung up, Hannah took a deep breath, said a quick prayer, and dialed the warehouse.

"Maria," she said when Hector's daughter answered. "It's Mrs. Ferris. How are you?"

"Just fine, Mrs. Ferris. How are you?"

"Good, thank you. And your mother? How's she doing? I haven't seen her in a long time."

"Oh, you know Mama. Still the same. Always on my case." Maria laughed.

Hannah made herself laugh, even though the last thing she felt like doing was making small talk or jokes. But she also didn't want to raise any questions in Maria's mind or cause her to think there was anything unusual in this call. "She's a mother," she answered lightly. "It's our duty to guide our children in the right direction." The irony of her statement wasn't lost on her.

"Yeah, I know," Maria said. "Well, what can I do for you, Mrs. Ferris? Did you want to speak to my father?"

Hannah took a breath. "Actually, I wanted to speak to David. Would you mind connecting me with him, please?"

"Oh, sure, okay."

Hannah knew Maria's curiosity was aroused, but it couldn't be helped. Unfortunately, all calls to the warehouse went through her.

A few seconds passed. Then David's voice said, "Service Department. David Conway."

Suddenly, Hannah couldn't speak. Her heart pounded.

"Hel*lo*?"

She cleared her throat. "David. This is . . ." She stopped. *This is your mother.* She closed her eyes. *Courage.* "This is Hannah Ferris."

Silence.

"David?" Hannah's eyes filled with tears. "David," she whispered. "Please say something."

A long moment passed. A moment in which Hannah saw clearly all the things she'd ever done wrong.

Finally he said coldly, "What would you like me to say?"

"I-I was hoping we could talk today."

"So talk."

She could almost hear his shrug. Almost see the dislike in his eyes and the bitter twist to his mouth.

Please don't hate me. "Not on the phone. Could . . . could you meet me for lunch?"

"I don't go out at lunchtime."

She wanted to say, *You went out to lunch with Simon.* "After work, then?"

"Fine."

"Where . . ." Hannah swallowed. "Where would be a convenient place for you?"

"I could come to your house."

"David . . ." Hannah stopped, at a loss.

"You don't want me at the house," he said after a long awkward moment of silence.

"It's just that—"

"There's a diner not far from here. We could meet there."

She knew he was hurt, but she didn't know what to say to remedy that.

After giving her the name of the diner and its location, David said they would meet at three-thirty.

Hannah was shaking when they hung up. The tears that had threatened during their conversation spilled over, and it was only by the sheerest force of willpower that she managed not to collapse entirely. She had to stay strong. She had to. If she fell apart, it would help no one.

She managed to get through the morning and early afternoon by throwing herself into her painting. It only partially worked, although the painting she was working on—a study of a lesbian couple walking along the beach arm in arm—was turning out to be one of her best paintings so far. Ordinarily she would be thrilled with it. But this was no ordinary day.

In the back of her mind was the constant awareness that

in only five hours, four hours, two hours, she would be face-to-face with her son.

Son.

The word caused shivers up and down her spine. It was a word she had so rarely allowed herself to think. Even with Aunt Marcy, the only person in the world to know the whole truth about her, the word had been spoken only a couple of times, and that was in the days following his birth. Since then, with unspoken agreement, they had pretended David didn't exist.

Oh, God, please forgive me. . . .

Finally it was time to leave. Hannah gave herself plenty of time to get to the appointed meeting place and pulled into the parking lot of the diner fifteen minutes early. For a while she sat in the car. When her watch showed it was three twenty-five, she walked inside and tried to ignore the butterflies in her stomach.

When David arrived, she was seated in one of the back booths. She'd ordered a glass of iced tea and had already fixed it to her liking, but she hadn't drunk any. She was too nervous to drink.

Her heart swelled with pride as he walked toward her. Now she saw only his good qualities. He was such a fine-looking boy. Today he wore the standard uniform of the young—baggy jeans and a dark T-shirt. He didn't smile as he slid into the seat opposite her.

She tried, but her own smile fell short. *Please . . .* Her mute plea didn't seem to reach him, for his eyes remained cold.

"Thank you for coming," she said.

He shrugged and slouched back in the seat. His entire body language was defiant.

She prayed that she would find the right words. "The other night," she began, "you said you'd found your birth mother."

He stared at her.

"You meant me."

His smile was bitter. And yet . . . behind the bitterness, she saw the pain. It wasn't there long, but it was there long enough for her to identify the emotion. She wanted so much to reach over and take his hand. To tell him how sorry she was if she'd hurt him. But he was so on guard and defensive, she was afraid he'd slap her hand away. She knew she had to proceed cautiously. Her entire future, his entire future, her whole family's future, depended on what happened today.

"I'm glad you found me, David," she continued softly.

"You didn't look glad last night."

"I was shocked last night, that's all. Since then I've had time to think."

He sat up so abruptly he made her jump. "Tell me something," he demanded furiously, "why'd you keep Jenny but not me?"

"Oh, David . . ." Tears welled up again.

"Why?" he said through gritted teeth. "What was wrong with me that you didn't want me?"

"Oh, God . . ." She fought the tears. "I—"

"What can I get you?"

They were both startled by the waitress's nasal voice.

"Nothing," David said.

The waitress just looked at him. "Nothing?"

"That's what I said." He glared at her, daring her to voice an objection.

"There will be a big tip for you," Hannah said hurriedly, "if you'll just let us talk, okay?"

The waitress shrugged and cracked her gum. "Hey, no skin off my nose."

When she was gone, Hannah leaned forward. The urge to cry had passed. "I didn't want to give you away. In fact, I would have given anything to keep you."

"Yeah, uh-huh, *sure*."

"I *would have*. But I couldn't."

"Couldn't? Or wouldn't even try?"

"I was barely eighteen. Unmarried. And I knew I couldn't count on any help from my parents. I had no job and no money. No way to support myself, let alone a baby. I was thinking of you when I put you up for adoption. What was best for you."

"No, you weren't. You were thinking about yourself."

His words cut deeply. They weren't true. The truth lay somewhere between what she'd said and what he believed. "You know, David, most things are not so black or white. When you're older, you'll understand that."

"I understand a lot more than you think."

Hannah so wanted to touch him. To reach out her hand and stroke his cheek. To tell him she'd never forgotten him, that he'd always been in her heart, that every time she'd seen a boy his age, she'd felt as if a part of her were missing.

I always loved you.

But his face was so closed. His eyes were so hard, so angry. He held himself so stiffly.

She had no rights where he was concerned. And he was letting her know that.

"Your husband and Jenny, they don't know about me, do they?"

"No."

"That's the reason you're here today, isn't it? You're scared I'm going to tell them. Rock your little rich boat."

"No, that's not true. I'm here today because I wanted to see you."

"Yeah, sure."

"It's true. I-I know I have to tell Simon and Jenny everything. But I wanted to talk to you first."

"Yeah, that's easy to say now. Why didn't you tell them about me a long time ago?"

Hannah swallowed. "I was ashamed."

"Yeah. That's what I thought."

"No, you don't understand. I was never ashamed of having *you*. I was only ashamed of the circumstances." At this her eyes filled with tears again. And no matter how she tried, she couldn't contain them.

He looked at her for a long moment. Then he expelled a breath, saying, "Oh, shit."

Hannah fished in her purse until she found a tissue. She wiped her eyes and blew her nose. "I'm sorry," she said when she was calmer.

"I didn't think Simon was my father."

She shook her head. "No. He's not."

"Who *is* my father? Does *he* know about me?"

"No, he doesn't know about you."

"Why the hell not?"

She didn't blame him for his anger.

"It . . . it's a long story."

"I'm not going anywhere."

"Look . . ." Now she did reach across the table, and surprising her, he allowed her to take his hand. She squeezed it, then released it, not wanting to push her luck. "I'll tell you all about him, but first, tell me about your life, okay? I-I need to know. Simon told me you were raised in foster homes. H-how did your adoptive parents die?"

"My dad died of an accident, my mom died of diabetes. I went into foster care when I was seven and a half because my mom fell apart after my dad died. She couldn't take care of me and ended up in a mental hospital."

"Were there no relatives?" Hannah's heart ached for him.

"No."

"W-was it so bad . . . living in foster homes?"

His lip curled. "It was shitty. A really shitty life. And to think, all that time you were living like a queen and my sister was living like a princess."

What could she say? What could anyone say?

"Now it's your turn," he said. "I want to know about my birth father."

She nodded and tried to think how to start. To buy time, she took a swallow of her tea. Finally she began.

"I led a very sheltered life, a very *strict* life . . . but you knew that. I told you as much on Friday night. My father . . . your *grandfather* . . . didn't believe in giving young girls much freedom. He felt we needed to be protected from the temptations of modern life. I wasn't allowed to date or go to parties. I'd never even been kissed . . . oh, once, behind the bleachers at a football game, but it was such a hurried, furtive thing, it hardly counted. Basically, I was naive, and I was romantic. Most of what I knew about love and sex came from books . . . and from listening to the other girls at school."

She paused, studying David to see if he was bored or impatient, but he'd settled back into his seat and was listening intently.

"Anyway," she continued, "because I'd skipped second grade, I was a month shy of my seventeenth birthday when I graduated from high school. Being so young presented problems. My father didn't believe in college for girls. He'd said over and over again that girls were meant to get married and have babies. Trouble was, even he realized that I was a bit *too* young to get married, and there were no jobs in or near Jordan—that's where I grew up, in Jordan, Nebraska—that my father would have considered appropriate for one of his daughters."

She grimaced. "I had wanted to go to work as a checker at the supermarket, but my father considered that kind of job beneath a daughter of Reverend Turner. Too much riffraff working there, he said. Not a God-fearing environment."

She took another swallow of her tea. "I wasn't thrilled about staying at home, but I didn't know how to change that. I thought about appealing to my aunt Marcy—my father's sister, who lived in Florida—but right then she was dealing with the news that her husband had lung cancer, and I hated to add to her problems. And then, about a month after graduation, one of the older women in my father's church—a widow who was highly respected—heard my mother mention how much I wanted to earn some money, and she told my mother about her son, who had a huge problem.

"This son, who was in his late twenties, was a lawyer with two small boys. His wife had walked out on him and the boys. She, the mother, said her son was desperate to find someone to watch them while he was at work. She wondered if I would be interested.

"By then I would have done anything to get out of the house. When my mother told my father about the job, at first he said no because the son lived in Beatrice—a town about twenty miles from my hometown. 'How will she get there and back?' he said. 'We'll be too far away to help if she needs help.'

"My mother pointed out that I had always been responsible and had experience baby-sitting in the church nursery. Mrs. Perry said I could ride the bus back and forth and her son would bring me home on any evening he had to work late. My father didn't have another legitimate objection. He still didn't want me to take the job—he didn't like the idea of not having me where he could keep an eye on me—but Mrs. Perry was one of his staunchest supporters—not to mention one of his most generous contributors—and he didn't want to alienate her, either."

Hannah remembered how thrilled she had been to have something else to look forward to other than just doing housework and helping out at the church. She still secretly harbored the hope that she would eventually be able to go to college, but she needed money to do so, and here was her opportunity to earn some.

"Mrs. Perry said she'd take me to meet her son and the boys the next day, and if I had any qualms about the job or felt I might not be able to do it for any reason, I would be free to say so."

Hannah smiled. "I wouldn't have refused to work for her son under any circumstances. This might be the only chance at a job I'd have.

"The next morning, she called for me at seven o'clock." She sighed deeply. "We got to Beatrice about thirty minutes later. That was the first time I saw your father."

Twenty-six

Nebraska, June, 1978

Hannah immediately liked the look of the house. A red-brick two-story, it had white shutters and a shiny black door with a brass knocker in the middle. Hollyhocks grew in riotous profusion on either side of the front stoop. An over-turned tricycle sat in the middle of the driveway and the lawn needed cutting; otherwise the house looked neat and well cared for. The thing Hannah liked best about it was its brightness; her own home was so drab.

"Hannah, would you please get out and move that tricycle so I can pull into the driveway?" Mrs. Perry said.

"Of course, Mrs. Perry." Hannah scrambled out of the car and hurriedly picked up the tricycle and placed it upright against the house.

Mrs. Perry pulled her eight-year-old Ford in and turned off the ignition. A few moments later Hannah stood behind the older woman at the back door. She knocked, then tried the knob, but the door was locked. She pressed her lips together and knocked harder.

"They should be up by now," she muttered. "He knew I was coming."

A tense few seconds passed as she tapped her foot, and Hannah bit her bottom lip. Although she had done nothing wrong, she knew what it was like to be on the receiving end of her father's displeasure, and she couldn't help feeling a twinge of sympathy for Mrs. Perry's son.

When he finally came to the door, it was obvious he hadn't been ready for them. His blue button-down dress shirt wasn't tucked into his dark pants, his hair was still wet from the shower, his feet were bare, and he had an harassed expression on his face.

Hannah felt an immediate kinship with him.

"Well, Mark, you certainly took your time coming to the door," his mother snapped.

"I'm sorry," he said wearily. "I was in the bathroom with the boys, and I didn't hear you knock." His dark eyes met Hannah's, and he smiled. "Hello. You must be Hannah. I'm Mark. Mark Perry. Come on in."

The kitchen, all warm yellows and cool blues, would have been pretty if it wasn't so messy. Dirty plates with a residue of what looked like spaghetti sauce were piled in the sink, crumbs littered the countertops and floor, a banana peel lay forlornly on the kitchen table. Mrs. Perry looked around and sniffed. "Honestly, Mark. I cleaned up this kitchen only yesterday. And now it looks like a freight train ran through it."

He ran his hands through his hair in a distracted gesture. "I know. It's just that I got home late, and the boys were tired. . . ."

His voice trailed off as a noisy pounding of feet announced the arrival of children coming down a stairway that was out of sight. A few moments later two little boys burst into the kitchen, yelling, "Grandma, Grandma!" One had the dark hair and eyes of his father. He looked to be about three. The other, who was probably a couple of years older, was fair, with light brown hair and blue eyes. Hannah guessed he took after his mother. Both boys were as cute as could be. The older one stopped short when he saw her, ducking his head shyly. The younger one, the one that looked so much like his father, gave her an impish grin. Her heart melted.

"These are my boys," Mark said with a proud light in his eyes. "This is Hank." He put his hand on the older boy's head. "Named after my dad, Henry."

"Hi, Hank," Hannah said. "How old are you?"

"Five," he mumbled, still not meeting her eyes.

He's shy, Mark mouthed silently.

Hannah nodded and smiled.

"And this little rascal is Robbie." Mark grinned at the younger boy.

Robbie frowned. "Me not a rascal."

"*I'm* not a rascal," Mark automatically corrected.

"I'm *not!*" Robbie shouted.

"Hush," Mrs. Perry said. "Your father is only teasing you. And you know better than to shout, don't you?"

"Dad's right," said Hank, frowning and finally finding his voice. "Robbie's bad."

In answer Robbie kicked his brother. Hank, after a second's hesitation, kicked him back.

"Boys!" Mark said. "Settle down. Stop that, Robbie. Next time you kick your brother, I'm going to put you in the corner."

"He kicked me!" Robbie said.

"Because you kicked me first!" Hank yelled.

Hannah smothered a smile.

"Quiet, both of you," their father said. "Sit down at the table, and I'll fix you some cereal."

"I hate to say it," Mrs. Perry muttered under her breath to Hannah, "but you're going to have your hands full with these two. They need a firm hand, something they never got from their mother." At the word *mother* her lips tightened.

Hannah knew the story. Her father had told it with great relish. Alexis Perry was an example of what happened when women were encouraged to behave like men instead of what God intended them to be: wives and mothers. Alexis Perry fancied herself a singer, he'd said with great contempt, and instead of being content to stay at home and take care of her husband and sons, she had gone off to follow the devil.

Joshua Samuel Turner had gone on at length about sin and sinners, about the temptations of the world and the temptations of the flesh, and of what happened to a person's immortal soul when he yielded to those temptations. All the while he had fixed his terrifying gaze upon each of his daughters in turn.

Acting as if he hadn't heard his mother, Mark took a box of Cocoa Puffs out of the cupboard and filled two bowls for the boys.

"That's not a very healthy breakfast, Mark," Mrs. Perry said. She looked around. "Don't you have any bananas left? What about orange juice?"

He grimaced. "I was going to stop at the store on my way home from the office, but it was so late. . . ."

Mrs. Perry shook her head. "Do I have to do everything? What do you need? I'll go get some groceries for you before I go home."

"We like Cocoa Puffs, Grandma," piped up Robbie.

"Oh, I'm sure you do. But I think you'd be better off with oatmeal. Or shredded wheat."

"Shredded wheat!" Hank said. He made a face. "Yuck."

"Do not say yuck to me, young man," Mrs. Perry said darkly.

Hank bowed his head. "Sorry," he mumbled.

"I'll go shopping for groceries tonight," Mark said hurriedly. "You don't need to bother." He looked at Hannah, who gave him a sympathetic smile.

She felt sorry for him. It must be terribly hard to be left alone with two small boys when you had a demanding job. Besides, what did men know about small children?

"And what is Hannah supposed to do in the meantime?" his mother demanded. "Is there anything here suitable for lunch?"

"We like SpaghettiOs," Robbie said.

"Or peanut butter and jelly," Hank piped in.

Before their grandmother could find more fault, Hannah said, "I'm sure I can find something to fix them, Mrs. Perry." She turned to their father. "I'm a good cook. I'll figure out something."

"Well . . ." Mrs. Perry said.

"Don't worry, Mom. I'm sure they'll be fine."

"Yes," Hannah echoed, "we'll be fine."

His mother didn't seem convinced, but she finally said,

"Well, if you're sure, I need to get going. This is the day the Ladies Guild visits the sick. And since I'm the president of the guild this year, I should be there."

"You go on, Mom," Mark said. "Thanks for bringing Hannah over."

"I've got to finish getting ready for work," he said after she'd gone. "Let me show you where everything is, then you're on your own. Okay?"

"Okay."

After he'd shown her where to find what she would need, he went upstairs, and Hannah sat at the table with the boys, who were messily eating their Cocoa Puffs.

"So, Hank," she said, "are you going to be in kindergarten this year?"

"Uh-huh."

"I'm glad I don't have to go to school," Robbie said.

"You'll like school," Hannah said. "It's fun."

"No, it's not!"

Hannah bit back a smile. Robbie seemed to be one of those children who would say black was white if you said it was black. His grandmother was right. He was going to be a handful. But he was so cute she didn't think she'd mind.

She looked at Hank. He was a sweet boy. She was going to love both of them.

When the boys finished their cereal, she rinsed out their bowls and put them in the dishwasher—what luxury to have a dishwasher!—then she scraped and rinsed the dishes that had been sitting in the sink and put them in too. After that she wiped off the table and counter tops and swept the floor. By the time she'd finished, their father was back downstairs.

Mark Perry no longer looked disheveled. His dark hair was neatly combed, his shirt was tucked in, he wore his suit jacket and a dark red tie and carried a briefcase. He was very handsome, Hannah thought. She wondered how old he was. He looked young, but his mother had said he was a lawyer. She knew he would have had to go to college and then to law school before he could practice law. That would have taken, what? Six or seven years at least. And Hank was five. Would Mark have gotten married before he graduated from law school? He must have. She was sure he wasn't thirty yet.

She watched him as he kissed the boys goodbye. He was good with them. It was obvious he loved them. How sad that their mother had left them. How could she? How could any woman leave her children and husband? Especially little boys that were so sweet and a husband that was so good-looking and seemed so nice. And a lawyer! Even though Hannah wanted to go to college and wasn't ready to get married, she did want to marry someday and have children of her own. If she was married to someone like Mark Perry, she'd never leave him.

That night, when she got home, and her parents asked her about the day, she told them it had gone very well. That Mr. Perry—she knew better than to call him Mark in front of her father—was a very nice man and seemed to be a good father. "And the little boys are really sweet. I'm going to enjoy taking care of them."

"It's such a shame about his wife," her mother said.

"Harlot," her father said. "The Lord will punish her for her wicked ways."

Hannah bit her lip. Was the Lord really so vindictive and vengeful? Her father seemed to think so, but Hannah hadn't felt that way when she'd read her Bible. It said the Lord was understanding of human frailties, that He would forgive you if you stumbled.

That night Sarah crept into Hannah's room. She sat on the end of Hannah's bed, feet curled up under her. "What's it like there? Do you think you're going to like it?"

Hannah grinned. "They've got a dishwasher and a color TV."

"I hate you," Sarah said. She had been begging their father to buy a television set for the past year, but he was adamant in his refusal. "A tool of the devil," he'd declared.

"Everything is a tool of the devil according to Father," Sarah had grumbled.

"Maybe I could come with you some of the time," she said now.

"Maybe." But Hannah didn't really want her sister to come to the Perrys' house with her, and if asked, she wouldn't have been able to say why. She only knew Mark Perry and his boys belonged to her, and she didn't want to share them.

The next day she rode the bus to Beatrice. She didn't mind, even though most of her classmates had cars and wouldn't be caught dead riding the bus. Hannah didn't drive. She would have taken driver's ed in school if she could have, but her father would have killed her if she'd tried to go behind his back. Driving was another of those things he didn't approve of for women. He was such a throwback to an earlier age, he didn't even believe women should be allowed to vote. In fact, Hannah couldn't remember the last time her mother had voted.

The bus let her out at the end of the Perrys' street. Mark's house was eight doors down on the left. Hannah hummed as she walked along. It was already warm; this was going to be another hot summer. Hannah wished she could have worn shorts, but she knew her father would never have let her. Shorts were not appropriate attire when you were working in someone else's home. She'd done the next best thing and had put on a cotton skirt—one of the dozens her mother had made for her and her sisters—and a cap-sleeved T-shirt.

"Good morning, Hannah." He smiled. "Don't you look nice today." Her heart gave a little leap, which flustered her. He looked nice, too, but she wouldn't have dared to say so. This morning he wore a gray pin-striped suit, white shirt, and black tie.

"Good morning, Mr. Perry."

"Please, call me Mark. Mr. Perry is my father." Turning around, he called up the stairs. "Hank, Robbie, Hannah's here." He gestured her in.

A minute later the boys raced down the stairs. Robbie's hair looked as if it hadn't been combed, and Hannah grinned as she realized he'd put his shorts on backward.

Noticing her expression, Mark said, "I just kind of let them go this morning. I have a meeting, so I've got to get out of here in about five seconds."

"I can take care of them. You go on."

"You don't mind feeding them breakfast?"

"Of course not."

"And you're sure you'll be okay?"

She nodded.

"I put my phone number on the refrigerator. If you need me, just call. Otherwise, I'll see you about six-thirty."

By now they'd walked back to the kitchen. He picked up his briefcase, which was lying on the kitchen table. "We went to the store last night, didn't we, guys?"

"Yep," Robbie said. "And we got Cocoa Puffs, yay!"

"Yay!" echoed Hank.

Hannah laughed.

"But we *do* have bananas and juice," Mark added.

Hannah was glad to see he seemed more relaxed today, probably because his mother wasn't there to give him disapproving looks. "Don't worry, I'll make sure they have a balanced breakfast."

Giving her another smile, he bent to hug and kiss the boys. Five minutes later he was gone.

Hannah fed the boys, cleaned up the kitchen, then shepherded them back upstairs to supervise teeth-brushing and hair-brushing. She also helped Robbie get his shorts on the right way. Before they went back down, she made the beds and straightened up their rooms. She was tempted to go into the master bedroom, but resisted the impulse. Mark had closed the door, and she had to respect his privacy. She was so curious, though, wondering if there would be a picture of his wife there. She'd looked in the other rooms, and she hadn't seen one. She hadn't even seen a photo album anywhere, which she thought was odd. Even her family had a family photo album.

Once the upstairs was neat, she suggested they walk down to the park, which she'd seen from the bus. It was only a block or so away. "Before it gets too hot," she said.

"Yay!" Robbie said. "I like the park."

"Mom didn't like to go there," Hank said.

"She didn't?"

"Nuh-uh." He frowned. "I don't think Mom is coming home."

"She is, too!" Robbie said.

Hank shook his head. "I don't think so." Sadness clouded his eyes.

"You're stupid!" Robbie shouted. He pulled his leg back to kick his brother.

Hannah grabbed him just in time. "Come on," she said, "let's go to the park." She wished she knew the right thing to say. "It'll be fun."

"Mom doesn't like bugs. That's why she didn't like the park," Hank said.

Hannah's heart sank. Hank wasn't going to be easily distracted from the subject of his mother. Obviously it was something that weighed heavily on his mind.

"Do *you* like bugs?" asked Robbie.

She could have kissed him. "Some of them. Ladybugs, for instance. Bees. Bees are the reason we have such beautiful flowers in the summertime."

"They *are*?" This was from Hank.

Hannah was grateful to see the sadness in his eyes had disappeared. But she knew this was only a temporary reprieve. The subject would come up again. How could it not? Poor little kids. They must be so confused. Well, she thought fiercely, she was going to do everything in her power to make sure they had a good summer. She knew she was a poor substitute for their mother, but she would do her best.

After an active hour and a half at the park, the boys were sweaty, dirty, and tired, so the three of them trooped home and, after cleaning their hands and faces, she got them settled on the living room floor with their LEGO set. While they played, she did what she could to straighten up the house.

Before she knew it, it was time for lunch. She found a box of Kraft Macaroni and Cheese in the pantry, as well as applesauce. That would do fine, she thought. After lunch was over, she suggested a nap.

"I too big for a nap!" Robbie said.

"We don't take naps anymore," Hank said.

"Oh. I didn't know that. Well, how about some quiet time? It's too hot to play outside right now, anyway."

For the next couple of hours they played more or less contentedly with Tinkertoys and Hank's collection of Matchbox cars, with only an occasional eruption of arguing or fighting.

While they played in their room, Hannah mixed a pitcher of lemonade, fixed herself a bowl of the macaroni, and with only a tiny twinge of guilt, watched TV. She decided she could easily get hooked on *One Life to Live*. Did people really *live* like that? she wondered. She could just imagine what her father would say if he could see some of the women on the show—the clothes they wore and the way they acted.

At three o'clock she gave the boys a snack of a cut-up apple and Ritz crackers, then let them put on their bathing trunks and go out into the backyard, where she turned on the sprinkler and let them play in the water.

The next day, she decided, she would bring her bathing suit with her. That way she could run around in the water with them.

By five o'clock they were ready to come into the cool house again. She poured them each a glass of lemonade and let them watch cartoons on TV while she made preparations for the family's evening meal. Cooking their dinner wasn't part of her duties; at least no one had said she should do so, but Hannah knew their father would be tired when he got home. Besides, she liked to cook, and, like caring for small children, cooking didn't normally fall under a man's expertise. But even if she didn't like to cook, she wanted to do whatever she could to make life easier for Mark.

Earlier she'd found some pork chops in the freezer, and she'd taken them out to thaw. Looking in the refrigerator she found lettuce, carrots, and tomatoes, so she could make a salad to go with them. Soon she had the pork chops ready to go into the frying pan, the salad made and staying cool and crisp in the refrigerator, and rice cooking on the stove. If she'd thought of it earlier, she would have made some brownies, too. Tomorrow, she promised herself. She'd seen a Betty Crocker brownie mix in the pantry, so she wouldn't have to worry about whether Mark had the ingredients for brownies from scratch.

At six-thirty, when Mark walked in the back door, he looked at the table already set for his dinner—the chops brown and tender, the salad dressed, the rice buttered and hot—all of it ready and waiting to be eaten. "I fed the children already. I hope that's all right."

His surprised gaze met Hannah's. "I don't know what to say. Even Alexis didn't . . . this is wonderful. You're wonderful."

Hannah blushed with pleasure.

That day established her routine. She caught the bus at seven, arrived at the house by seven-forty. Mark left soon after. She fed the kids breakfast, got them ready for the day, and cleaned up the house. They spent mornings at the park, afternoons in the backyard. The only day their schedule varied was Wednesdays, when the Beatrice library had a story hour in the afternoon. The boys loved to go to story hour. Hannah liked it, too. She got a library card for herself, the first she'd ever had, and spent their naptime reading books she knew her father would never have let her bring into the house.

She read Danielle Steel and Catherine Cookson. She read Helen MacInnes and Evelyn Anthony. She read *Gone With the Wind*. And one day, she read *Shanna* by Kathleen Woodiwiss.

She devoured *Shanna*. She hated to leave it at Mark's house, but she knew if she tried to smuggle that book into her own home, she would be taking a foolish chance. If her father were ever to see a book like that in her possession, there was no telling what he might do. He might even forbid her to come back to Mark's, forbid her to keep watching his children. She couldn't take that chance.

But she also didn't want Mark to know she was reading the book. Her face flamed at even the thought of him discovering it and maybe looking through it. Just the idea he might read some of the sex scenes and know Hannah had read them . . . Oh, she would die!

So she hid the book at the back of the pantry, behind some old thermos bottles that she knew he wouldn't move anytime soon.

That night she couldn't think about anything else. She even dreamed about the story. Dreamed she was Shanna, and Ruark was taking her clothes off, touching her and making love to her, bringing her to the heights of passion just the way he'd brought Shanna. But in her dream somehow Ruark wasn't really Ruark, because he had Mark's face and Mark's body.

The next morning it was hard for Hannah to look Mark in the eye. She was afraid if she did he would know what she had been thinking about and dreaming about. She felt so guilty, but not guilty enough to take the book back to the library before she'd finished it.

That afternoon, while the boys were sleeping, she read as fast as she could. And when she read the next scene where Shanna and Ruark made love, she squirmed in her seat. She felt hot all over, and she felt things she'd never felt before. She knew what she was thinking and feeling was a sin, but it didn't matter. She couldn't stop reading.

When she was finished with the book, she held it against her heart, which was beating madly. To have someone love her like that! It would be the most wonderful thing in the world.

That night, when Mark walked in the back door, and his eyes met hers, something different, something she'd never felt before, pierced her heart.

In that second she knew nothing in her life would ever be the same again.

Twenty-seven

Two days later, when Hannah brought the mail in, there was a postcard with the Statue of Liberty on it. Curious, she turned it over and glanced at the signature.

Alexis.

Hannah's heart beat harder. Alexis! As far as she knew, this was the first time Mark's wife had written. Hannah didn't even think she'd called them, because surely, if she had, the boys would have mentioned it. Since that first time they'd brought up the subject of their mother, they'd talked about her a lot.

They'd say things like they missed her, and that their dad told them their mom would be back soon, and once Hank had said he was sure she'd be back by Christmas because he'd made a wish on his birthday candles, and those wishes always came true.

It had made Hannah's heart ache to hear him. But in all those conversations, he'd never said his mom had called.

Oh, it was so awful. Hannah felt so bad for the children . . . and for Mark. None of them deserved this. The boys were so sweet and basically such good kids. Sure, they were rambunctious, but what little boys weren't? They rarely gave her any trouble. And Mark . . .

She swallowed. Mark was so handsome and wonderful, such a fine, good man. How could any woman leave him?

She knew it was wrong, but she couldn't stop herself from reading the card.

Hi, Mark,

I've found a gig singing at the Blue Moon Club in Greenwich Village. Just thought you'd like to know. Give the boys a kiss for me. I know you think I'm awful, but I would have died if I had to stay there any longer. I was never cut out to be a hausfrau.

Love, Alexis

Hannah had never felt such rage as she did when she read that card. Until then, she'd been willing to give Alexis Perry the benefit of the doubt, but now! Why, the woman was a selfish, horrible person!

Kiss the boys for me.

She hadn't said she was sorry. She hadn't said she loved them. She hadn't said she missed them. *I was never cut out to be a hausfrau.* Hannah guessed not! She hadn't said anything about coming home or calling. She hadn't even given Mark a phone number! Hannah wondered if it was possible that he already had a phone number. But if he did, if he'd talked to her, why hadn't Hank or Robbie said something?

Placing the postcard in with the other mail, she put it all in the basket that sat on the small table in the foyer where she always left the day's mail.

Alexis Perry didn't deserve to have a husband like Mark or children like Robbie and Hank. They were better off without her. Hannah hoped when Mark saw that postcard he would just wash his hands of his wife. Hannah's father didn't believe in divorce, and Hannah thought she hadn't, either, but today she'd changed her mind. Some people deserved to be divorced, and Alexis Perry was one of them!

Still thinking about the card, she took the boys out to the kitchen, where she let them play with Play-Doh while she mixed up tuna salad for lunch.

They had just finished lunch when there was a knock at the back door. It was Karen Griffin, who lived across the street. Hannah smiled. She liked Karen, whose little boy,

Johnny, was four and often played with Robbie and Hank.

"Hi," Hannah said.

"Hi, Hannah. Luke and I are taking Johnny to see that new Disney movie this afternoon. We wondered if Robbie and Hank would like to go, too."

"Yeah! Yeah!" Robbie and Hank shouted.

"Uh, boys, I don't know if—"

"Please, Hannah, *puh-leeze*," Hank begged.

Hannah looked at Karen. "I'll have to call their dad and ask him if it's okay."

"Okay. Just let me know. We're not leaving until one-thirty."

Hannah had to quiet the boys down—they were so excited—while she called Mark's office. She hoped he wouldn't be in court or in a meeting or anything, because unless he said it was okay, she couldn't let the boys go.

But he was in his office, and he said it was fine if the boys went. "You can go, too, if you want," he said.

"That's okay," Hannah said. She didn't want to horn in on Karen and Luke's time together.

The boys could hardly contain themselves until it was time to go. Once they were gone, Hannah cleaned up the kitchen, then decided she would treat herself to the afternoon soaps while they were gone. A little after two o'clock she heard a car in the driveway. She looked out the window and was taken aback to see that it was Mark.

She turned off the TV and walked out to the kitchen just as he came in the back door.

He smiled. "Hi."

When he smiled at her like that, Hannah felt it all the way down to her toes. Love for him flooded her. "Hi. I didn't know you were coming home early."

"Right after I talked to you, I found out I have to fly to Tulsa tomorrow afternoon to take a deposition, so I figured I deserved the rest of the afternoon off."

"Oh. Who's going to watch the boys for you?"

"I wanted to talk to you about that. Do you think you could stay the weekend? I probably won't get back until late Sunday night."

"I-I don't know. I'd have to call and ask my father."

"I would have asked my mother, but that's impossible right now. You know she fell and broke her hip."

"Yes." Hannah's mother had told her about Mrs. Perry last week.

"And my sister can't come. Her oldest has chicken pox. I'm really in a bind."

"I'll call my father right now."

"Thanks. While you're doing that, I'm going to go change."

There was no answer at Hannah's house. Her mother was probably at the church. Today was the day some of the women cleaned the church and put out fresh flowers. Hannah sighed. Oh, well, she'd call again in a little while.

She started gathering up her things. Since Mark was home, there was no reason for her to stay, unless he needed her to do some laundry for him or make something for them to eat tonight.

It was a while before she heard him coming back downstairs. When five minutes passed and he didn't come out to the kitchen, she got up from the table and walked into the hall. He stood with his back to her, and she could see that he was reading his mail.

Her heart sank as she belatedly remembered the postcard. She bit her lip, not knowing whether she should go back to the kitchen or just stay there. Maybe she should go. He probably wouldn't want her to see him reading that card. But even as she told herself this, her feet simply wouldn't move. It was like they were glued to the floor.

For the longest time he was very still. Then, startling her, he muttered an oath and threw the card down. When he turned, their eyes met. In his she saw frustration and an impotent fury. She also saw an underlying hurt that he normally kept hidden. She tried to convey everything she felt in her eyes, tried to show him that there were people who cared about him and his boys, that not everyone would betray him.

Much later, when she thought about that long moment when their gazes locked, she couldn't remember who moved first. She only knew that seconds later, she was somehow in his arms, and he was kissing her furiously. Her head spun as she clung to him and returned his kisses with all the passion in her young body.

The entire world receded. There was only Mark. The taste of him, the feel of him. His mouth, his tongue, his teeth, the bit of stubble on his chin, the faint scent of his lemony aftershave and, as he pushed her up against the wall and ground his body against hers, the heat of his arousal.

His hands, which at first had cradled her face, moved up and down her body, awakening every part of her. Hannah had never been with a man, had barely even been kissed, but she instinctively seemed to know what to do. It was as if she'd been made for this man. Her body was his. She would have done anything he wanted, because she wanted it, too.

When he finally tore his mouth from hers and scooped her up into his arms and carried her upstairs to his bedroom, she wasn't afraid. She was ecstatic. Mark wanted her. Her!

"The bed's not made, I'm sorry," he said when he'd shut the door behind them. His voice sounded rough, not like his at all.

"I don't care."

"Hannah . . ." For the first time he seemed to realize what they were doing.

Suddenly afraid he would change his mind, Hannah put her arms around him and lifted her face. He only hesitated a moment, then he lowered his mouth to hers.

Hannah's heart beat like a wild thing as he pulled her T-shirt out of the waistband of her skirt, then moved to cup her breasts. When he unhooked her bra, and she first felt his hands against her flesh, she gasped. And when his thumbs rubbed against her nipples, she whimpered.

The sound seemed to galvanize him, and again he lifted her, but this time he placed her on the bed. Then, holding her gaze the entire time, he hurriedly stripped off his clothes.

Hannah's breath caught as she got her first look at him naked. She couldn't take her eyes off him. She stared at his penis. She'd never seen a man's penis before. She swallowed. It . . . it was so big. For the first time she felt a thrill of fear. Yet there was excitement, too.

"Let's get your clothes off," he whispered.

She helped him. Suddenly she was as eager as he was to rid herself of the last barriers between them.

The next hour was one she knew she would always remember. The urgency of Mark's kisses, the way his hands and fingers made her feel, the way he said her name over and over again, and then, the way he finally pushed into her. It hurt, but she didn't cry out, because it felt so right to have him inside her, to be part of him the way she knew she had always been meant to be. She didn't have an orgasm that first time, but she didn't care. She gloried in the way he shuddered and cried out hoarsely. She clutched him tightly, wanting to hold him inside her as long as she could.

When his breathing slowed, he gathered her close. Smoothing her hair back from her face, he murmured, "I'm sorry, Hannah. I know that wasn't great for you. It was your first time, wasn't it?"

"Yes." She wanted to say she was happier than she'd ever been in her life, but she was too shy to put her feelings into words.

He kissed her cheek, his hand caressing her breast. "You're so lovely. Your skin . . . it's so beautiful."

"Y-you're beautiful, too," she whispered. Feeling bolder, she stroked his chest, loving the feel of the springy hair that dipped down into a V. She wanted to touch him down there, but she didn't have the nerve.

They made love again that afternoon, and this time Hannah did have an orgasm. In fact, she had two. The first one came by his hand, and it stunned her. She'd never felt anything like it before. No wonder people liked sex. The second one came after he'd entered her. This one was even more powerful than the first.

Hannah felt drunk with pleasure. She wished she never had to leave Mark's bed, but the boys would be home by four-thirty, and she knew that even though they were young and wouldn't understand the significance of what happened that afternoon, it would be wrong to take a chance on them seeing them like this.

It was hard for her to leave Mark that day. The only reason it was bearable was because before she left she managed to get her father on the phone, and even though he was reluctant, he finally said she could watch the boys over the weekend.

"Come early tomorrow," Mark whispered as they snuck a goodbye kiss in the kitchen.

"Yes."

That night Hannah was sure her family would know everything that happened to her that day, but miraculously, no one seemed to see that inside she would never be the same person again. Even Sarah, who was so nosy and seemed to sense when Hannah had a secret, didn't notice the difference.

Hannah couldn't sleep that night. She relived every moment with Mark. She could hardly believe what had happened, but her body told her it was real, for it tingled with a knowledge it hadn't before possessed.

Mark hadn't said he loved her, but Hannah knew he did. Maybe he didn't know it yet, but that was okay. It was enough that he needed her, and today had shown he did. That she could give him something important, something that would make him feel better.

The next morning she could hardly wait to get to the house. She'd packed a small suitcase. She'd be sleeping in Mark's bed tonight! The same bed where they'd loved each other. The same bed where she'd become a woman.

They managed only a few minutes alone before he left, but it was long enough for him to give her a hard kiss and whisper that he couldn't wait until they could make love again.

"Me, either," she said, her heart in her eyes.

"I'll see you Sunday night. You told your parents you were sleeping over, didn't you?"

"Yes, I said it would be too late to bring me home, that you couldn't wake the boys up and take them out." Hannah still couldn't believe she'd lied to her parents. It frightened her, but not enough. She knew she would lie ten times, a hundred times, if it meant she could be with Mark.

They weren't able to manage being alone often, but three or four times over the next couple of weeks, Hannah told her parents Mark was going to work late that evening, that she wouldn't get home before ten or eleven. He *did* work late, that part wasn't a lie, but he was home by eight when the kids went to bed. Then they had at least an hour, sometimes two, together. They didn't take a chance on making love in the master bedroom where the boys might hear them. Instead, they made love on the floor of Mark's study, which was downstairs. Mark spread a quilt on the carpet and they closed the door and only kept one dim light on. It was their own private, wonderful world.

Sometimes Hannah thought about those wicked women her father loved to talk about, but she didn't care. Her father was wrong. Nothing this wonderful could be bad. Most days she was so happy, she had to pinch herself to make sure she wasn't dreaming.

She lived for those hours, those stolen kisses, his hands and mouth and the feel of him inside her, the way he looked at her and said her name, the way he kissed her everywhere, the way he said she was so beautiful.

She no longer dreamed about college. She dreamed about Mark getting a divorce, which he had begun to talk about doing. Then, no matter what her father said, she and Mark would marry. Robbie and Hank would be her boys, *their* boys, and they would live the rest of their lives together.

Mark still hadn't said he loved her, but Hannah knew how he felt. She didn't need the words. Mark was an honorable man who could never have sex with a woman if he didn't love her.

And then, one beautiful bright September day, when Hannah had been there for three months and she and Mark had been lovers for three weeks, while Hannah was slicing apples to bake an apple pie for dinner, a taxicab pulled into the driveway. Hannah frowned. Had the cabdriver made a mistake? What was a cab doing there? She stood on tiptoe and watched curiously from the kitchen window as a tall woman with curly light brown hair got out. The cabdriver got out, too. He opened the trunk and took out a black suitcase. The woman opened her purse to pay him.

In that moment Hannah's heart stopped. She knew. She didn't even have to see the woman's face. It was Alexis Perry.

Like a sleepwalker, she put down the knife and the apple. Hand clutching her throat, she stared at the back door. A few moments later Mark's wife unlocked the door and walked in. Up close, she was beautiful, with perfect skin and Robbie's blue eyes.

She looked at Hannah. "Who are you?"

Hannah swallowed. "Th-the baby-sitter."

Alexis Perry nodded. "I wondered how he was managing. I thought maybe his mother would be here." She smiled wryly. "I'm glad she's not."

While Hannah was trying to think how to answer or what to do, she heard someone else pull into the driveway. She didn't even have to look to know it was Mark. He had said this morning he might come home early.

Her heart pounded. *Oh, God.* What would he say? What would he do?

He was smiling as he opened the back door. The smile died. He stared at Alexis.

She grinned. "Hello, darling. Surprised?"

"Alexis." He seemed stunned.

Alexis Perry walked over to him, placed her hands on either side of his face, and drew his face down to hers.

Hannah stood frozen. Her hands clenched at her sides, she stared at them. The kiss seemed to last forever. Finally Alexis moved back. Hannah couldn't see her smile, but she could hear it in the satisfied purr of her voice.

"You *did* miss me," she murmured.

Slipping her arm around him, she leaned her head against his shoulder. "Pay the sitter, darling. We don't need her any longer. I'm home to stay."

His eyes begged Hannah to understand as he groped in his pocket for his wallet. Hannah knew he couldn't say anything then, that he had to talk to his wife first. So she didn't make a scene. She told herself he would call her tonight. He would send his wife packing, and tomorrow things would be the same as they'd been.

Still, she felt numbed by the day's events as she rode home on the bus. She thanked God that neither of her parents were home when she got there. It was Ladies Guild day, so her mother would be visiting the sick. And her father was in his office at the church. She couldn't have handled questions; her hold on her emotions was too fragile.

By the time her mother returned, Hannah was better able to tell her calmly what had happened.

"Oh, I'm so glad his wife has come back," her mother said. "I'm sorry you've lost your job, though."

"She may not be staying long," Hannah said.

"What do you mean?"

"I mean Mar . . . Mr. Perry might not *want* her back."

"But Hannah, marriage is *sacred*. It doesn't matter whether he's happy about what she did or not, he must forgive her. That's God's law."

Hannah didn't reply. Let her mother think what she wanted to think.

All night Hannah waited for the phone to ring. It did ring, twice, but neither time was it for her. Once it was one of the elders wanting to discuss a problem with her father, and once it was a neighbor asking her mother if she could help her out in the morning.

Hannah told herself it had probably taken Mark all night to work things out with his wife. After all, he couldn't just throw her out, even if she didn't deserve anything better.

But he didn't call the next day, either. Finally, at noon, she couldn't stand it any longer, and she called his house. Alexis answered the phone. Hannah hung up.

Then she called his office.

"I'm sorry, but Mr. Perry is in court this afternoon. If you'll leave your name and number, I'll ask him to call you."

It was nearly six o'clock before he called. It was the worst possible time, because Hannah's family always ate their evening meal at six, and they'd just sat down to dinner.

Thank God the phone was in the hallway. If Hannah had had to talk to Mark with her father watching her, she couldn't have done it. As it was, she knew he could probably hear her. Still, she was so desperate by then, she didn't care. She would be careful what she said, but she had to know what was happening with Mark.

"I'm sorry I haven't called you before this," he said when she came to the phone.

"I-I did wonder if . . . if you were going to need me anymore."

"Hannah." He had dropped his voice. "I'm really sorry about everything, but my wife . . . she's . . . she's home now."

Hannah knew it was over. She wanted to die. In that moment she faced the truth. Mark didn't love her. He had never loved her. He had simply wanted what she gave so freely.

Hannah's father had been right. All along he'd been right. Hannah had been a fool.

She didn't even cry. She was too devastated and too ashamed to cry.

One week after Alexis Perry smashed Hannah's naive and silly dreams, Hannah was offered a job as a clerk in the hardware store owned by a church elder—a widower in his late forties who she knew her father was thinking of as a possible future husband for her. Hannah didn't want to take the job, but at that point she didn't have many choices.

Two weeks after Alexis Perry came home, Hannah missed her period. And two weeks after that, she knew she was pregnant.

Terrified, she knew she couldn't tell her parents. Briefly her mind considered an abortion, but she quickly shoved that idea way. First of all, she had no money. Second, she could never go through with an abortion even if she *did* have the money.

Desperate, she called her aunt Marcy from a pay phone. Her aunt never hesitated. "Don't you worry, Hannah. I'll take care of this."

And she did. She called Hannah's father and told him she

couldn't manage on her own anymore. "Russell is really getting bad," she said. "I need help, and I don't want just anyone. I want family here. Please let Hannah come to Florida."

A week later Hannah left Nebraska for good.

Twenty-eight

Drained from reliving the past, Hannah sank back in her seat. David was silent, and she wondered what he was thinking. "That's why you were born in Tampa," she said. "Why you were adopted in Florida."

His eyes met hers. "You never told my father?"

"No. I never saw him or spoke to him again."

"Do you know where he is?"

Hannah shook her head.

David didn't say anything for a while. "So I not only have a half sister, I have two half brothers."

"Maybe more. Maybe your father and his wife had other children. I don't know." Hannah had never wanted to know. Once she'd accepted that she and Mark were not going to be together, that he didn't love her the way she loved him, she had tried to totally obliterate him from her mind. Hannah might have been young, but she was mature enough to realize that in order to survive, she had to put the past behind her and live only for the future.

David studied his hands. A minute went by. Two. Three. Finally he looked up again. "When are you going to tell Simon and Jenny about me?"

"I-I don't know. It . . . it's not going to be easy. I can't just blurt it out."

He stared at her. "How do you think they'll feel when they find out?"

Hannah shook her head. "I don't know." But she was terribly afraid she did know.

His mouth twisted in a way she was beginning to recognize as his defense against pain. "I'll bet you wish I'd never been born."

"No! No, David, please don't say that. I've *never* wished that. Not even once."

His expression said he didn't believe her. What could she say? She didn't deserve his trust. In his eyes she had abandoned him, just as surely as Simon's mother had abandoned him. Never mind that Hannah's motives had been mostly pure. Motives didn't matter to David. What mattered was that he had grown up in a way no child should have to grow up. That he'd felt unwanted and unloved. And that he was laying the blame for that life squarely at her door.

Where it belongs, she thought sadly.

"But you don't really want me in your life."

"David . . ."

"Tell me something. Did you ever even think about me? Did you ever once wonder how I was or what I was doing?"

Once more she fought tears. "David . . ."

"*Did* you?"

"Yes, of course, I did," she whispered. "I tried not to, because it hurt so much when I did. That day you were born, when I held you in my arms for the first time, I-I couldn't forget how that felt. I cried every time I allowed that memory to surface. Your face, your eyes . . . haunted me. For years my arms ached every time I remembered holding you. And every birthday, oh, God, it was so terrible. I could never be happy on my birthday, because all I could think about was you."

"Yeah," he said, "I couldn't believe we had the same birthday."

"But it wasn't just on birthdays. I thought about you on every holiday, too. I thought about you every time I saw a boy the age I knew you would be. And any time I heard the name Nicholas."

"Nicholas?"

She nodded slowly. "Yes. That's what I named you."

He swallowed. "Nicholas is my middle name."

The look in his eyes wrenched her heart. Nicholas. His adoptive parents had given him the name Nicholas. Knowing that they had honored the name she'd put on his birth certificate filled something deep inside her, something that had been empty for a long time. "Your adoptive parents must have been really nice people."

He bowed his head.

She wanted so much to touch him. To smooth that dark head, to tell him everything was going to be different now. She took a deep breath. "David, you said I didn't really want you in my life. That's not true. I do. But you have to give me some time. I have to talk to Simon and Jenny before I can . . ." She stopped. What could she say? *Before I can make you any promises? Before I can be a mother to you*?

He raised his head, but he didn't answer for a long moment. And when he did, that hard shell he effected to cover his feelings was back in place. He shrugged. "Fine. If you have anything else to say to me, you know where to find me." He slid out of the booth, gave her one last impassive glance, then walked away.

Hannah scrambled in her purse for a twenty-dollar bill, then threw it down on the table and hurried after him. By the time she reached the parking lot, he was already in his truck and backing out.

"David! Wait!"

But he didn't acknowledge her. Didn't even look back. Just peeled out of the lot in a shower of gravel and roared off down the street.

Tears ran down Hannah's face. She had made a mess of things today. David had deserved something more from her, yet what else could she have said? Until she knew how Simon and Jenny were going to react to her news, she'd had nothing more to offer.

David drove home too fast. So fast he nearly hit the car in front of him as he exited the freeway.

Goddamn her!

Goddamn her to hell!

Who needed her, anyway? He sure didn't. He'd gotten along for twenty years without her, and he could get along without her for the next twenty, too. For the rest of his life.

She didn't want him. She'd tried to pretend she did with those tears and that story of hers, but the truth was, she hadn't wanted him before, and she didn't want him now.

His mouth twisted.

Why should she? She had a perfect life. Why would she want him? He'd just screw things up for her.

The light ahead changed to red, and David slammed on the brakes. The truck screeched to a stop.

Well, that was fine with him. The hell with her. The hell with all of them.

Hannah drove home blindly.

All she could think of was the way David had looked when he'd left her.

Oh, David, I am so, so sorry.

All the way home she thought about what she might have said. How she might have said it. She didn't do a good job today, she knew that. She wished she could turn around and go back. Try again. Maybe this time she would do better. Maybe this time she could show him how much she wanted to make things up to him.

But how could she?

How could she promise him anything until she had talked to Simon and later, to Jenny?

Suddenly, now that she'd begun and no matter how terrifying, she just wanted to get the truth out in the open. By the time she turned onto her street, she had decided she wasn't going to wait. She would tell Simon tonight. She would only wait until after they'd had their dinner and Jenny had gone to her room for the night, but then they would talk.

It would be hard to wait even that long. Hard to greet Simon and Jenny as if this was just an ordinary day when it was one of the most traumatic days of Hannah's life. But somehow she would manage. Because when she did tell

Simon, she knew it would be an emotional scene, and for that they needed privacy.

As always, when Hannah walked in the back door, Martha was in the kitchen. Today she was tossing a salad. A cooling lemon-meringue pie sat on the counter. She looked up and smiled.

"Hi, Martha. Is Jenny home?"

"Yes, she got home about an hour ago."

A few minutes later Hannah knocked softly on the closed door to Jenny's bedroom.

"Mom?"

"Yes."

"C'mon in."

Hannah opened the door. Jenny was sitting at her computer. She turned.

"Just wanted to let you know I was back."

"Oh, okay. Where'd you go, anyway?"

"I had a meeting." Not a lie, Hannah told herself. It was a meeting. Just not the kind she had inferred. *Soon I won't have to stretch the truth about anything.* "How was your afternoon with your grandmother?"

"It was fun. She bought me some new sweaters."

"Good."

"Guess what, Mom?" Jenny made a face. "I got an e-mail from Courtney, and she said she's thinking about staying in Connecticut."

"She *is*? Why?"

"She *says* it's because the schools are better, but she's met some boy. And I think she just doesn't want to leave him."

"Oh, honey, I'm sorry."

Jenny nodded glumly. "I think she's crazy. But maybe her mom won't let her stay." Then she brightened. "Mom, Angie's mother wants to know if I can go to lunch and the movies with her and Angie tomorrow. It's that new Drew Barrymore movie. The one I've been dying to see. Can I go?"

"I don't see why not."

Her smile got bigger. "Oh, good. I'll call Angie right now

and tell her. Oh, and Gram invited me to spend the night Sunday. She said she'd take me shopping again on Monday. For school stuff."

"All right. But don't make any plans for Tuesday."

"I know, I have my checkup. I hope Dr. Weinberg says I can start riding soon."

"Honey . . ."

Jenny sighed. "I know. Don't count on it. That way I won't be disappointed if he says I have to wait."

As Hannah headed to her own bedroom to change, she thought about what a good kid Jenny was, and how, even when she had reason to be moody or cranky, she rarely was. *She doesn't deserve the shock she's going to get.* Simon didn't, either, but Simon wasn't a child. Jenny, though, Jenny was her child. Like David, she had a right to expect more from her mother. *Oh, Jenny, I'm so sorry. I hope you'll be able to forgive me someday. . . .*

Hannah stood in her walk-in closet and tried to decide what to wear for the evening. Everything she fingered seemed wrong. Then again, was there a *right* kind of outfit to wear when you were telling your husband you were a liar? That you'd deceived him for all the years of your marriage? That you were not the woman he thought you were?

Finally she yanked a plum silk pants outfit off its hanger. While she dressed and cleaned her face and put on fresh makeup, she went over what she would say to Simon and how she would say it. She wished she could just get it over with as soon as he arrived. But for Jenny's sake, she knew she couldn't.

She was so lost in her thoughts, she didn't hear the door to the bedroom open, and she jumped when Simon said, "Martha said you were in here."

Hannah put a hand to her heart. "You scared me."

He smiled. "Sorry."

She looked at the bedside clock. It was only a little after six. Simon didn't normally get home before six-thirty. "You're home early."

"Yes. We've got a crisis with Fender." Fender was a manufacturer from the Sacramento area; they made scooters, and

Simon had signed an exclusive contract with them six months earlier. "I'm afraid I have to fly up there. I probably won't be back before tomorrow afternoon."

"You mean you're going *now*?" she said, dismayed.

"Yes. I'm sorry, darling. I know it's short notice, but it can't be helped."

"But why do *you* have to go? Couldn't Don go?" Don Gentry was Simon's chief of operations.

"Bill Fender's insisting he will only deal with me."

"I told you when you said you were going to sign with him that he was a prima donna."

Simon grimaced. "That you did." He put his arms around her and kissed her softly. "I married an exceptionally smart and wonderful woman."

Hannah hadn't thought she could feel worse. "Can't you wait until morning to go?"

"No, darling. I'm meeting Bill for breakfast. I need to be there tonight."

"I . . . but there's something I wanted to talk to you about later."

"Sweetheart, I *am* sorry, but this can't be helped. Why don't we talk now? We can discuss whatever it is while I pack."

Hannah shook her head. "No, that won't work. This is going to take some time. Besides, I want your full attention."

He frowned, tipping her head up so he could look into her eyes. "What is it? Why so serious?"

Hannah was so tempted to just spill everything right then and there. But how could she? Blurting it out when there was no time to talk quietly and calmly wouldn't be fair to Simon, to Jenny, or to her, not to mention David. She sighed. "Never mind, Simon. You're right. It can wait." *It's waited twenty years.*

Smiling now, he kissed her again. "Well, stay and keep me company, anyway. Tell me about your day."

Simon made short work of packing. Hannah noticed he put several shirts in his bag. "Why so many shirts if you're going to be back tomorrow?"

"Better to be prepared."

She didn't like the sound of that. She could wait until tomorrow to tell him about David, but she wasn't sure she could stand a moment longer.

"Don't worry," he said upon seeing her expression. "I'll get this wrapped up tomorrow."

"I hope so."

Once he was ready, he headed for Jenny's room to say goodbye, and thirty minutes later he was gone.

Hannah and Jenny were both preoccupied during dinner. Normally, when Jenny was this quiet, Hannah would be concerned and try to draw her out. Tonight, however, she was too wrapped up in her own problems. Besides, Jenny was a teenager, she told herself when she began to feel guilty. Teenagers were allowed to be moody once in a while.

After dinner Jenny said she was going to watch TV in her room, and she disappeared. Hannah decided she would take a bubble bath. Maybe that would relax her. An hour later she was in bed herself.

It took her a long time to fall asleep. And when she did, her sleep was filled with dark, disturbing dreams. She awakened Friday morning with a feeling of dread in her stomach. She told herself not to be negative. She was just anxious because she had wanted to get everything out in the open yesterday. Having to wait had just made more of her doubts surface.

She managed to rid herself of the bulk of those doubts by mid-morning, and by eleven, when Jenny left to go to lunch and the movies with Angie and her mother, Hannah was deeply engrossed in her work. Tonight, she told herself when her thoughts *did* veer in the direction of David. Tonight Simon and I will talk, and by tomorrow the worst will be over.

But Simon didn't come home that afternoon. Instead, about five, he called and said he was really sorry, but it looked as if he'd have to stay another day.

"Oh, Simon."

"I know," he said. "I don't want to, but Bill has a really

serious problem here. In fact, I've sent for Don. He's on his way, too."

But he didn't come home Saturday, either. It was, in fact, late Sunday night before Simon returned to L.A. By then, Hannah was nearly a basket case.

When Simon finally arrived at the house it was nearly midnight, and he looked exhausted.

"I never want to go through another three days like the last," he said, rubbing his eyes. He gave Hannah a tired smile. "I'm going to have a shower, and then I intend to sleep for ten hours straight. You don't mind, do you?"

What could she say? This was no time to talk about something that was going to cause the biggest crisis their marriage had ever faced. The *only* crisis, in point of fact.

He gave her a quick kiss, said how glad he was to be home, then headed for the bedroom.

As Hannah lay in bed listening to the water running in the bathroom, she told herself it wasn't the end of the world. What was one more day? And tomorrow, no matter what else happened, she and Simon would talk.

All day Monday she was on pins and needles. She could hardly work, she was so nervous. In fact, she wasn't sure she could wait until after dinner to talk to Simon. Suddenly the burden of her lies was too heavy to carry a moment longer.

She was waiting in their bedroom when he arrived. He gave her a tired smile.

"Another bad day?" she said.

He shrugged. "Not really bad. I just had a disappointment, that's all."

"What happened?"

"David Conway quit."

The words hit her like a sucker punch. "Q-quit?"

He nodded dispiritedly. "Yes."

"B-but why?"

"I don't know. He told Hector there was nothing for him here."

"When . . ." She swallowed. "When did this happen?"

"Friday. Hector didn't tell me because he figured I had

enough to worry about, so he waited until I got into the office this morning. He said he tried to talk David out of it, told him he thought he had a real future with us, but David just said he didn't think so."

Hannah was numb. "Does Hector know where David was going?"

Simon shook his head. "It's a damn shame, Hannah. I know you had reservations about the boy, but I really liked him. In fact . . ." His expression clouded with regret. "You'll probably think this is crazy . . . and maybe it is . . . but there was something about that boy . . ." His smile was self-deprecating. "I almost thought of him as a surrogate son."

Twenty-nine

Now, even if Hannah had wanted to put off telling Simon about David, she couldn't have. Praying for strength, she said, "Simon, remember how before you left for Sacramento, I told you I had something important I wanted to talk to you about?"

He frowned, and she could see him mentally switching gears. "Yes."

"Could . . . do you think we could go to your study and talk? This is going to take a while and we might as well be comfortable."

He gave her a quizzical look. "It can't wait until after dinner?"

She shook her head. "No."

"All right. Why don't I change first and meet you there? Say in about fifteen minutes?"

"Okay."

Hannah walked out to the kitchen to tell Martha where they'd be, then headed straight for Simon's study. While she waited, she thought about David. She was afraid she knew exactly why he'd quit, and the knowledge was like a stone in her breast. It was her fault. Everything was her fault.

What was she going to do?

She had no answers, and was still agonizing over the

question when Simon joined her. He had a cold bottle of Beck's beer in his hand.

"Did you want one?" he said when he saw her looking at it.

"No, thanks. I'm fine." She gestured to her half full wineglass.

He sat down beside her on the leather sofa and gave her an encouraging smile. Hannah took a deep breath. *Please God, let him understand. At least let him understand, even if he can't forgive.*

"For a long time," she began, "I've wanted to tell you about this, but I was afraid."

"*Afraid*?" he said incredulously. "Of *me*?"

She raised a hand. "Please, Simon, this is going to be difficult enough. Just listen, okay?"

He seemed about to protest, then stopped. "Okay. I won't interrupt again."

"Thank you." She took another deep breath for courage. "To answer your question, yes, I was afraid of what you would say. What you would think." She closed her eyes briefly. When she opened them again, she looked into his, trying to convey, not only with what she was about to say, but with what he would see in her eyes, how deeply she meant this. "I love you very much, Simon. You know that, don't you?"

"Of course I know it."

"I know you've always thought I took a long time to make up my mind about marrying you because I wasn't in love with you the way you were in love with me. That's not true at all. It was because I was afraid to be in love, and when I explain, you'll understand why. But, please, Simon, believe me when I say you mean the world to me, and our marriage, our family, is the most important thing in my life. I-I didn't want to lose that, and I knew that what I'm about to tell you would shock you and . . ." She swallowed. "And that it would change your opinion of me."

"*Hannah* . . ."

Her bottom lip trembled. "See, the thing is, something happened to me when I was seventeen. Something I never told you. Something no one except Aunt Marcy ever knew."

She made herself keep looking him straight in the eyes, even though she now wanted to look anywhere but. "I-I got pregnant. And on my eighteenth birthday I gave birth to a beautiful baby boy."

She could see the shock in his eyes, the way he stiffened and pulled away from her. Her voice broke, even though she was trying so hard to remain calm and in control. "I was unmarried, terrified, and totally incapable of keeping him and giving him any kind of life. So I went to Florida on the pretext of helping Aunt Marcy with Uncle Russell, who was very sick. I had the baby there and gave him up for adoption."

Simon simply stared at her. His blue eyes, eyes that had never looked at her with anything but love, now looked at her as if she were a stranger.

"David is *my* son, Simon." At this she could no longer hold back her tears, and they spilled out of her eyes. "I'm the birth mother he came to California to find. I-I am so sorry I deceived you about this, but I-I tried to block it out of my mind, because to think about it or to talk about it was too hard. It hurt me to give him away, and it hurt me to think about him, so I tried very hard not to. I know now that I should have told you when you asked me to marry you, but at the time I couldn't. I literally couldn't. In fact, it never even entered my mind that I should. And by the time I realized how wrong it was to keep this from you, it was too late. We'd been married several years by then, and you . . . you had become so important to me. I couldn't bear the thought of losing you."

Still he said nothing.

"Simon, I . . ." She wiped her eyes with the wadded-up tissue she had in her hand. "I hope you can understand and . . . and forgive me for not being honest with you."

"David is your son," he repeated.

"Yes."

"How long have you known?"

"What do you mean?"

"Did you know before he moved to L.A.? When I offered

him a job? When I invited him to dinner? Is that why you didn't want him to come?"

"No, of course not. You heard what he said at dinner— about not having contacted his birth mother yet. That was when I knew, when he talked about it that night . . . because of what he said . . . I-I put it together then."

"And does he know you know?"

Hannah was shaken by Simon's dispassion, even as she understood where he was apparently coming from. She was sure he felt just as numb as she'd felt earlier when he told her David was gone. In a way, she was glad he was so matter-of-fact. His attitude made her feel calmer, whereas if he'd been more emotional, she would probably have fallen apart. "Yes," she answered quietly, "I met him after work Thursday and we talked. He's had a tough life, Simon. And he's bitter, but he's also a really fine boy. But you know that. You said yourself how much you liked him, how he seemed almost like a surrogate—"

"Don't start using my words against me, Hannah."

Simon's tone and the way he had interrupted her so curtly chilled Hannah. He had never before talked to her that way, never before looked at her that way. "I only meant—"

"I know what you meant." Before she could answer, he said, "Who's the father?"

As with David, this was the part Hannah had dreaded the most. But Simon had a right to know, so she said another quick prayer, then began. When she was finished with her story, she could hardly look at Simon, because she was sure she knew what he was thinking, and she was afraid to see the censure in his eyes. For the longest time he said nothing, and when he did speak, what he said was not what she'd expected.

"Do you know where Mark is now?"

"No."

"Does David want to find him?"

"I don't know. I-I don't even know if I'll see David again."

"So you had no idea he was going to quit?"

"None. When we parted Thursday afternoon, it was with

the understanding that I would tell you and Jenny about him, and, depending on how you two felt about it, he and I would talk about where we were going from here." Suddenly the anguish she felt, and the worry about David and his emotional state, overwhelmed her, and tears welled in her eyes again. "I think I know why he quit, though. When I left him Thursday, he was upset. He accused me of wishing he'd never shown up and said he knew I didn't want him in my life. He feels as if I abandoned him, that all these years I've led this wonderful life with you and Jenny, whereas he . . ." She couldn't finish. She kept seeing the pain in David's eyes. Dear God. She'd hurt so many people. And all because she'd been young and weak.

Simon abruptly stood and walked to the window. With his back to her he said, "This is why you always hated your birthdays so much."

"Yes."

He was silent for a long moment. "So you're planning to tell Jenny?"

"Don't you think I should?"

Startling her, he whirled around. "It's a bit late to be asking my opinion, isn't it?"

"Oh, Simon, I . . ." She stopped. What was there to say? She'd already said how sorry she was. "I never meant to hurt you," she whispered.

"I don't believe you thought of me at all."

There was no answer to that, either, because he was right.

"So when are you planning to tell Jenny?"

"I-I'd hoped we could tell her together, tonight." When he didn't immediately answer, she added in a rush, "I have to try to find David, Simon. I let him down once. I can't let him down again. And if I go away, Jenny will be bound to ask questions. How will we answer them except with the truth?"

Long seconds went by before he answered. Then, still in that flat, expressionless voice, he said, "I'd prefer to wait until tomorrow. I have to digest all of this first. I'm not ready to face Jenny yet."

Hannah swallowed. "I understand."

"Do you?" There was no compassion in his eyes, no gentleness in his voice. "Do you have any idea what a shock this has been? Not *what* happened, but . . . no, that's not right. All of it has been a shock. I have to be honest with you, Hannah. I feel as if I don't know you any longer. I'm not sure I've ever really known you."

Hannah trembled inside. If only there was a speck of warmth in his eyes. But search as she might, she couldn't find any.

"Now, if you don't mind, I'd like to be alone."

Hannah's heart was pounding. "Simon, I'm so sor—"

"Please. Don't say anything else. Just leave. Because if you don't, I'm afraid I'll say things that can never be unsaid."

More frightened than she'd ever been, more frightened even than when she'd found out she was pregnant with David, Hannah left the study. Blindly she headed for her sanctuary, the one place in the house that was hers exclusively, the only place where she knew no one would disturb her.

When she reached the safety and privacy of her studio, she locked the door. For a long time she simply stood there and stared into space. She could barely breath, barely think. Two questions pounded in her brain. What was to become of them all? And would anything ever be the same again?

Hannah wasn't sure how she could possibly get through dinner without Jenny suspecting something was terribly wrong. But when she emerged from her studio an hour later, Martha told her that Simon had been called back to the office on some kind of emergency and, since he knew she was working and hadn't wanted to disturb her, had told Martha to tell her not to wait up for him, that he would probably be home late.

Hannah knew there hadn't been any emergency. This was just Simon's way of making things easier for both of them, and she was grateful to him.

Dinner that evening would forever be a blur in her mind. She guessed she talked to Jenny, but if asked, she couldn't have said what about. When Jenny went to her room after dinner, Hannah pleaded an upset stomach and told Martha she was going to read in bed and make it an early night.

She didn't sleep, though. She was too keyed up and too worried to sleep. She kept thinking about David and wondering where he was. Would he stay in L.A.? Or had he gone back to Florida? Or somewhere else?

Where was Simon? Had he really gone back to the office? Or was he driving around somewhere, thinking and deciding their fate?

And Jenny. What would she say? How would she take this news? Would she be as upset as her father was? Or would she, by some miracle, be happy?

At ten o'clock, no closer to answers than she'd been when she started, Hannah turned off the light and lay in the dark and prayed. It was midnight before she heard Simon come home. She turned on her side and closed her eyes, pretending to be asleep. He was very quiet when he entered the bedroom, but she knew what he was doing. She heard him undressing. She heard him in the bathroom. And she heard him as he approached the bed.

A few seconds passed before he got in beside her. She wished she had the courage to turn and say his name. To touch him. But she was too afraid. She prayed he would make an overture to her. But he didn't. Instead, she felt him turn on his side and face away from her.

Only about two feet separated them, but it might as well have been a thousand. She wondered if he knew she was awake. *Oh, Simon, how did this happen to us? How did I let this happen?*

Her heart felt as if someone had taken it and squeezed as hard as they could. This was a milestone in their marriage. She couldn't ever remember another time when they hadn't kissed good night.

Eventually Hannah fell asleep. The next morning, when she awakened, it was after eight, and Simon was gone. Her heart sank. She had so hoped they could talk this morning, that maybe he had softened after having a chance to think about everything. She wondered if he'd gone to the office again.

But when she went out to the kitchen to get a cup of coffee to take back to the bedroom with her, he was sitting having his breakfast.

He looked up, and their eyes met. "I-I thought maybe you'd gone to the office early this morning."

His smile was for Martha's benefit, Hannah was sure. "No, I thought I'd take my time this morning."

I can't do this. I can't. Hannah headed for the coffeepot, using the time to pull herself together.

"Mrs. Ferris, you sit down. I'll get your coffee for you," Martha said.

"I'm not ready for breakfast, Martha." Hannah continued pouring her coffee. "I'm just going to take this back to the bedroom with me."

"When you're done showering and dressing," Simon said pleasantly—still for Martha's benefit, Hannah knew— "come to my study. I wanted to tell you about what I decided last night."

Hannah didn't trust herself to speak. She simply nodded, smiled at Martha, and escaped the kitchen as quickly as she could.

Forty-five minutes later, feeling marginally better after showering, dressing, and putting on some makeup to fortify herself, she knocked on Simon's study door, then entered. He was seated at his desk and didn't move. She walked to one of the side chairs and sat down. She felt calm now, almost fatalistic. Whatever happened, happened. Sometime over the past hours she'd finally realized that the future was no longer in her hands. Other people controlled it, and there wasn't anything she could do, so worrying was futile.

"I've done a lot of thinking," Simon said. "At first I was so angry, I wanted to lash out and hurt you the same way you'd hurt me. But that was a childish impulse, and I quickly realized that would be wrong."

Hannah couldn't help the spark of hope that ignited, even as she told herself not to count on too much. Simon's next words doused the spark.

"I think, no matter what we may be feeling personally, we need to present a united front with Jenny, so that she knows she can count on us the way she always has."

"I couldn't agree more."

"And I also think you were right, we should tell her as soon as possible."

Hannah gave him a tremulous smile. "Thank you," she said softly. She prayed he would get up and come over to her and take her in his arms. Tell her everything was going to be okay, that he loved her and understood and forgave. But she could tell just by looking at him that what she wanted wasn't going to happen. In fact, she was terribly afraid their relationship was never going to be the same.

"Is Jenny awake yet?" he asked.

"I don't think so."

"I'll be in here getting caught up on some paperwork. Why don't you bring her in after she's had her breakfast?"

"All right."

Later, as Hannah told Jenny she and her father wanted to talk to her, she wondered what Martha was thinking. She'd been with them so long and knew them so well, she was bound to know something unusual was going on. What would she think when she found out? Would she think less of Hannah? Or would she take the news in stride?

Hannah's heart ached for Jenny, whose face reflected her bewilderment as she led the way to Simon's study. Of course the child knew something was wrong. It wasn't every day her parents called a family powwow.

At least this time Simon didn't sit behind his desk. He pulled a chair over so he could face Hannah and Jenny, who sat on the sofa.

"What's going on?" Jenny said, looking from one to the other. "Am I in trouble or something?"

"No, of course not," Hannah said.

Simon cleared his throat. "Jenny, your mother and I have something to tell you." He looked at Hannah. "Hannah?"

So for the third time, Hannah began to tell her story. She edited out some parts but not many.

Jenny's mouth dropped open when Hannah got to the part about finding out she was pregnant.

"Mom! Wh-what happened?"

"I had the baby. That's the reason I lived with Aunt Marcy. So no one in Jordan would know."

"Ohmigosh," Jenny said. She seemed stunned, but not in a bad way. "So that means that somewhere I have a sister or a brother?"

"Yes. A brother," Hannah said.

"Wow. Do you know where he is?"

"Yes."

"*Really*?" She grinned. "Gee, it's kind of cool to have a brother. How old is he?"

"He's twenty."

"Where does he live?"

This was the bad part. "Jenny . . ." Hannah reached for her hand. "Jenny, sweetheart, he . . . he lives here in Los Angeles."

Her eyes widened. "He *does*?" She looked at Simon, then back to Hannah. "Have you met with him?"

Hannah nodded. "Yes, I have."

"Wow. When am I gonna get to meet him?"

"You . . ." Hannah swallowed. "You have met him, sweetheart. It's David."

Jenny blinked. "David?" It took her a few seconds, but finally Hannah's words registered, and Jenny shrank back. Her eyes widened in horror. "*David? David is my brother*?"

"Yes."

"Dad? Dad! Did you hear what she said?" Her voice had risen to a shriek.

"Jenny, sweetheart," he began.

"No!" She jumped up. "No! It's not true! David's *not* my brother. He's not! You're *lying*! Why are you *lying* to me? Why?" Her face had turned an ugly, mottled red.

Simon and Hannah rose at the same time. They both tried to put their arms around Jenny, but she flailed at them. She was hysterical, crying and saying "No, no, no," over and over again.

"Stop it, Jenny!" Simon said, grabbing her arms.

"Leave me alone!" she screamed. She glared at Hannah. "I hate you. I hate you!"

Then she tore herself from his grasp, ran to the door, and

yanked it open. Hannah flinched as, a few minutes later, she heard the door to Jenny's room slam shut.

"That went well," Simon said.

Hannah bit her bottom lip hard. If she hadn't, she would have started blubbering like a baby. When she had some semblance of control again, she said in a shaky voice, "She'll be okay. She'll settle down. I'll go talk to her."

"I think it's best if you stay away from her, Hannah. *I'll* go talk to her later."

After that there was nothing left to say.

Thirty

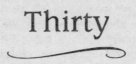

Jenny threw herself onto her bed and covered her head with a pillow to muffle her cries.

She couldn't believe it.

David. David was her brother.

Her mind kept screaming a denial. David *couldn't* be her brother. He just couldn't! She was horrified and humiliated as she remembered all the fantasies she'd had about him. All the romantic dreams. All the things she'd confided to Courtney.

Jenny moaned. Oh, shit! Courtney! What would Courtney say when she found out? What would she think? If she laughed at Jenny, if she made fun of her, Jenny would die. Then she had an even more horrifying thought. What if Courtney told someone? For the first time since Courtney had said she might stay in Connecticut, Jenny was glad and hoped she never came back to L.A.

Oh, God, *why* had this happened? Was her mom *trying* to ruin her life?

At first, when her mom had told her about the baby she'd had, Jenny had thought it was kind of romantic, but now! Now she was disgusted. She thought about how her mom had always told her she was special—"my only chick," she'd say—and how all the time she'd been lying, because Jenny hadn't been special at all! Her mother had had another child!

Jenny moaned again.

How could her mom have done this to her?

Just then there was a knock at her door, and she stopped crying. "Go away!" she yelled. "Leave me alone."

"Jenny, please let me in."

It was her father.

"Please, Jenny," he said. "I want to talk to you."

For a second Jenny thought about telling him to go fuck himself. She wanted to shock him the way he and her mom had shocked her. But she couldn't do it. Not to her dad.

"Jenny?"

She dried her eyes and got up. She walked over to the door and unlocked it. She took one look at her dad and started to cry again.

"Ah, Jenny," he said, so gently it made her cry harder. "Come here, Princess." He opened his arms, and she rushed into them.

"Did you kn-know?" she wailed.

"No, sweetheart, I didn't."

"How could she lie to us like that?"

Her dad sighed. "Jenny, I know this is hard for you to understand." He smoothed her head the way he had when she was a little girl. "It—it's hard for me to understand, too. But I know your mother had the best of intentions and thought she was doing the right thing when she kept this from us."

"What do you mean?" she cried. "Mom lied to us!" She blew her nose. "You've always told me the worst thing in the world is lying, that if you do something wrong, you should always admit it, that being honest is the best policy. And now you're saying it's okay she was dishonest?"

"That's not what I'm saying. I'm saying she thought she was doing the right thing."

"Well, she *wasn't*! And I'll *never* forgive her. Never."

"Jenny, honey, let's sit down and calm down and try to talk rationally, okay?"

Jenny did as her father asked, but she was perfectly rational right now. And no matter what her dad said to try to excuse her mom, she knew what the truth was. Her mom was a liar. Her mom had kept this huge secret, a secret that affected all of them, but most especially Jenny, and now Jenny's life was *ruined*!

Jenny picked at a loose thread on her quilt.

"Jenny . . ."

She looked up. Her dad was straddling her desk chair, and his eyes met hers. For the first time in all her fourteen years, she realized her dad was getting older, because she could clearly see the lines around his eyes. The realization frightened her. She couldn't imagine a world without her dad.

"I know you're hurting," he said gently. "But your mom is hurting, too. And she needs you right now. Don't shut her out."

It was so like her dad to make excuses for her mom. He was always protecting her and taking care of her. But Jenny knew better this time. She knew her dad was hurting just as much as she was. She could see it in his eyes, in the sad look around his mouth.

"You don't have to pretend with me," she said bitterly. "And if she's feeling bad, it's her own fault. She's the one who lied."

For a long time he didn't say anything. Then he sighed heavily. "All right, Jenny, I'm not going to push you on this. You obviously need some time to get used to everything. I'll explain to your mom and ask her to leave you alone for a while, okay?"

"Okay."

He got up and walked over to the bed. Reaching for her hand, he pulled her up. When his arms went around her, Jenny almost started crying again.

"We're going to get through this, Princess."

Jenny just cried harder.

"Just remember that we both love you."

"I love you, too, Daddy." The childish name just slipped out. She knew he wanted her to say she loved her mom, too, but the words just wouldn't come.

After her dad left her alone again, Jenny thought about the things he'd said. Why was he excusing what her mom had done? Why was he pretending it was okay when it clearly was not? He couldn't *really* think so. Maybe he just wanted to try to make Jenny feel better. That must be it.

Then she had a sickening thought. What if her dad really *did* forgive her mom and they decided they wanted David to come and live with them? Ohmigod! It made Jenny sick to even think of the possibility. How could she stand to live in the same house with David after the way she had acted around him? He probably thought she was the stupidest girl he'd ever met.

I can't. I won't live here if that happens.

The more she thought about it, the more she knew she couldn't stand being there at all anymore, no matter whether David came to live with them or not.

If only I was eighteen. If only I had my own money and could get an apartment of my own.

She thought and thought. And suddenly it came to her. She knew what she was going to do.

She picked up the phone and dialed her grandmother's number.

Thirty-one

Hannah put down her brush in frustration. Normally, no matter what else was happening in her life, she could still paint. In fact, painting had always been her refuge, a way to close out the rest of the world and anything that might be troubling her.

But not today. Today all she could think about, the only images she could see, were the faces of the people she loved the most. Every face held an accusation. Every face showed pain—a *pain* she had inflicted.

David. Simon. Jenny.

Of all of them, Jenny was the least equipped to handle what had happened. David was tough; he'd had to be. He was a survivor. And Simon was an adult. A rational, sensible, adult. But Jenny . . . Jenny was her precious sheltered daughter. She'd been raised to believe she was the center of their world. Finding out about David had to have completely rocked her universe. Especially considering her feelings for David. Right now she must be reeling from the morning's revelation.

What was going on between Simon and Jenny now? Hannah knew they were talking. She prayed Simon was getting through to Jenny, that somehow, some way, he could make her understand that what Hannah had revealed in no way affected the way either of them felt about her. That it changed nothing about her status in their family.

Simon had said he would let Hannah know how things went with Jenny before he left for the office. Hannah hoped she didn't have to wait much longer, because she was about ready to lose her mind with worry.

She spent another agonizing ten minutes before there was a knock on her door. "Simon?" she said eagerly.

The door opened, and Simon walked in.

"How . . . how did it go?"

He shrugged. "About the way I expected."

Hannah bit her lip.

"Look, you can't expect much from her right now. She's just a kid, and she's received a body blow. She's going to need time to come to terms with all of this. We're all going to need time."

"Will . . . she talk to me?"

"I'm sorry, Hannah, but she doesn't want to see you. I think the best thing for everyone is for you to give her some space."

Hannah nodded. She knew he was right, but still it hurt to know she had wounded her daughter so badly that Jenny didn't even want to talk to her. "I guess I just hoped that maybe . . ." She shook her head. "Oh, God. I don't know what to do now."

He frowned. "I just told you what to do."

"I don't mean about Jenny. I mean about David."

At the mention of David's name, a shadow crossed Simon's face. "What about him?"

"I just feel I can't wait too long. I need to find him. I *have* to find him." At the look on Simon's face, she said, "Not to make him any promises where you're concerned or where Jenny is concerned. I realize I have no right to do that. Just to let him know that I want him to be a part of *my* life."

Simon seemed to consider, then said, "Have you tried calling him?"

"Yes, but I don't have his number, and when I called Information earlier, there was none listed. I thought about calling Hector, but I didn't want him to start wondering why

I wanted to get in touch with David. I thought maybe you—"

"David has a cell phone," Simon said, interrupting her. He reached into his back pocket and pulled out his wallet, from which he withdrew a slip of paper. "Here. This is it. He gave it to me when I first offered him a job."

Hannah swallowed. "Thank you."

"Hannah . . ." Simon walked over to the sofa and sat on the arm. "I've been thinking. It might be best for everyone if Jenny and I take that trip to France after all."

Hannah knew she had no right to feel hurt. And yet she did.

"I haven't talked to her about it yet, because I wanted to tell you first," Simon continued.

Hannah sank back on her stool. Simon's gaze was unflinching, and there wasn't a shred of sympathy in it. She'd seen that look in the past, but it had never before been aimed at her. Until that moment, she hadn't realized just how deep a rift she had caused between them. Now she wondered if her marriage was going to survive. "You're not asking my permission."

His gaze never wavered. "No, I'm not."

"I guess there's really nothing more to say, then, is there?"

Simon decided he would call his mother before going to the office, so after leaving Hannah in her studio, he headed for his study.

"Simon! I was just about to call you," his mother said when he got her on the phone.

"Oh?"

"What in the *world* is going on there? Jenny called me a little while ago, and she was terribly upset, but she wouldn't tell me why. She just asked me to come and get her and said she wanted to stay with me for a while."

Simon really hadn't wanted to tell his mother the whole sorry story over the phone. But he couldn't see that he had a choice now.

She was silent at first, but when he got to the part that

David was actually Hannah's son, she exclaimed, "I knew there was something. I just knew it."

"You mean you suspected something about David?"

"No, of course not, I'm not clairvoyant. I mean I knew there was something Hannah was hiding."

"Oh, come on, Mother."

"I mean it, Simon. I always knew there was more to her than met the eye. At any rate, it's no surprise that Jenny's upset. What about you? How do you feel about all of this?"

"I don't know. I'm still in a state of shock."

"Yes, I can imagine."

"I suppose you feel vindicated now." He couldn't prevent the touch of bitterness in his voice.

"That's not fair, Simon. What I feel most of all is sorry for all of you. But right now the most important consideration is Jenny. Under the circumstances, I think it's probably a good idea to remove her from the turmoil and have her come and stay with me awhile."

"Yes, I agree. In fact, I was calling you to say that now might be the ideal time for you and I to take Jenny to France."

"Without Hannah, you mean?"

"Yes, without Hannah."

"Simon, is that wise?"

"I would have thought you'd be jumping for joy, since you've never liked Hannah, anyway."

"You thought wrong. Perhaps I have been hard on Hannah in the past, but that doesn't mean I want to see your family fall apart."

Simon shook his head. "Mother, you never cease to amaze me."

"I don't know if I should feel flattered or insulted by that remark, Simon."

"I just meant you are an amazing woman."

"Thank you. Now," she added briskly, "shall I come and pick Jenny up? Or will you bring her here?"

"I'll bring her."

"Fine. I'll be waiting."

• • •

Hannah had just worked up the courage to call David when Simon knocked at the door of her studio again.

She stared at him, heart pounding, as he explained about the call to his mother. "No! I don't want her going to your mother's. How will we ever repair the damage between us if she's not here? Simon, you know how your mother feels about me. There's no way she'll be impartial about any of this."

"I'm sorry, Hannah, but I don't really think we have a choice."

"Of course we have a choice. Jenny's just a child. If we say she can't go, she can't."

"Is that what you really want to do? Forbid her?"

Hannah knew she was being unreasonable, that if Jenny wanted to go to her grandmother's, nothing she or Simon could say would stop her. And did she really want to keep her at home against her will? Would that help anything? Oh, God. Why did this have to happen? "When are you going?"

"As soon as she gets packed."

"I want to talk to her before she goes."

"Hannah, I don't think—"

"You know what?" she cried. "I don't *care* what you think right now. I want to talk to my daughter."

He didn't try to stop her as she tore out of the room.

A minute later she stopped short in front of Jenny's closed bedroom door. She took several deep breaths to calm herself, then raised her hand to knock.

"Dad?" came Jenny's muffled voice.

Hannah turned the knob, half afraid the door would be locked. But it wasn't.

"It's me, Jenny," Hannah said.

Jenny didn't turn around. She was in the midst of packing her suitcase and she just kept folding clothes. "Go away," she said.

"Jenny . . ." Hannah walked toward her.

Jenny whirled around. "I *said* go away." Her eyes blazed with resentment and anger. And buried deep . . . raw pain.

"Sweetheart, all I'm asking is that you hear me out. Just a few minutes. That's all I want. And then I'll go."

Jenny gave her a hard stare, then deliberately turned around and resumed packing. Her movements were jerky.

Please, God, help me say the right thing. "Jenny, I know how angry you are and how hurt. I know you feel betrayed. I understand why you feel this way, and I don't blame you. In your shoes, I'd feel the same way, I'm sure. Maybe your dad's right, maybe we just need some time away from each other right now, so I'm not going to make a fuss about you going to your grandmother's or about you and your dad going to France without me, but before you go, I want you to know one thing."

Hannah's voice broke, but she pushed on. She had to say this. She had to try this one last time to get through to her daughter. "I love you, and I will always love you. Nothing that's happened can ever change that. I would rather have cut off my right arm than hurt you. I am sorrier than I can ever express, and I hope someday you'll be able to forgive me."

Hannah stared at her daughter's rigid back and willed her to say something. But Jenny remained silent. And finally Hannah had to concede defeat. Fighting tears, she whispered again, "I love you, Jenny."

And then she quietly left the room.

Thirty-two

❧

It took David three days to drive to St. Augustine. It was the first time he'd ever seen any of the country, and he was amazed by its vastness. Arizona, New Mexico, Texas. Driving across Texas, he couldn't get over how much open land still existed.

Briefly he toyed with the idea of not going back to Florida. Maybe he'd go to Dallas or Houston instead. Make a complete new start where no one knew him and he knew no one. But the idea didn't last long. Something in him, something he'd tried to deny for a long time, needed the security of something familiar, something that seemed like home, even if it wasn't.

As each mile sped by, as he put more and more distance between him and the woman he wished he'd never heard of, he told himself it didn't matter that she hadn't wanted him. It didn't matter that his fantasy of family was just that: a fantasy.

He reached St. Augustine late on the evening of the third day. He stopped at the first inexpensive motel he saw, paid for one night, then unloaded his few possessions from the bed of the truck. After that he was too tired to do much but fall into bed.

He slept until ten the next morning. After showering and shaving, he dressed and drove to the Denny's he'd seen a few blocks east of the motel, then proceeded to put away a Grand Slam breakfast.

It was nearly noon before he got back to the motel, and the first thing he did was call Rafael's, the restaurant where he'd worked before.

"Hey, Mike," he said when the manager came to the phone. "This is David Conway."

"Hey, David. You back from L.A.?"

"Yeah, and I need a job. I was wondering if you needed any waitstaff."

"Well, hell. I wish I'd known. I just hired a new waiter last week, and now I'm full up."

Damn. David had hoped he could just step back into a job at Rafael's, because he couldn't afford to be out of work for long, seeing as how his savings had suffered some serious hits recently.

"But hey, listen, I heard Blackie's is hiring."

"No kidding?" Blackie's was one of the most popular of the new restaurants, and according to the scuttlebutt, the waitstaff made great tips.

"If you want to try them, I'll give you a good reference."

"Hey, thanks, Mike. I think I will."

David didn't waste any time. By two o'clock he was filling out an application at Blackie's, and by three o'clock he had a job.

By six o'clock he also had an apartment in the same complex he'd lived in before. It wasn't much, just a sparsely furnished living room, bedroom, tiny kitchenette, and bath, but it was all he needed. He hung up his clothes, set up his TV, put away the few books and linens he owned, and he was pretty much set. Then he made a quick trip to the supermarket, bought a few essentials, and picked up some Hunan chicken and eggrolls at a Chinese restaurant he'd frequented when he'd lived there before.

It was nearly nine before he remembered to turn on his cell phone. He only turned it on to check the battery, not because he expected any messages. So he was surprised when he found he had one. He was shocked when he realized the message was from his mother.

"David," she said. "Simon told me you'd quit your job. I-I wanted you to know that I've told both him and Jenny about you, and also that I really want to see you again. You accused me of not wanting you in my life, David, but that's not true. I do want you in my life. I want that very much. Please call me. I'll be waiting to hear from you."

David sat staring into space for a long time after listening to the message. He wondered if she had any idea that he'd left L.A. Part of him just wanted to ignore her message. But the other part knew he wouldn't. If for no other reason than because he wanted to know what her reaction would be to the news that he was now thousands of miles away, he knew he would call her back.

He looked at his watch. It was about dinnertime in L.A. That was probably a good time to catch her at home.

He was taken aback when Hannah herself answered the phone. He was so surprised to get her instead of the house-keeper, for a moment he didn't say anything.

"David?" she said.

He realized she probably had Caller ID and recognized his number. "Yeah. It's me."

"Oh, I'm *so* glad you called. I've been waiting all day."

"I didn't check my messages until now."

"I was hoping that was the reason I hadn't heard from you and that it wasn't because you didn't want to talk to me."

He wanted to say he wasn't sure he *did* want to talk to her, but then he thought, the hell with it, she already had a pretty good idea of his opinion of her.

"Thing is," he said casually, "I was on the road, so I didn't have my phone turned on."

"On the road?"

"Yes." If she wanted to know where, let her ask.

"Are you back in L.A. now?"

"Nope. I'm in Florida."

"Okay. Then I guess if we're going to talk, I'll have to come there."

Whatever it was he'd expected her to say, it wasn't that, and it kind of took the wind out of his sails, making it hard for him to keep up his pretense of indifference.

"David? Would that be all right?"

He was tempted to say no, he didn't want to see her, but then he'd not only be lying to her, he'd be lying to himself. And all for the momentary satisfaction of thwarting her. Still, he didn't want her to think he was eager, because he was sick of people getting his hopes up, then smashing them back down again. "Hey, it's up to you. If you want to come here, come."

"Thank you, David. As soon as we get off the phone, I'll call and see what kind of flight arrangements I can make. Where, exactly, are you?"

"I'm back in St. Augustine."

After saying she would call him tomorrow morning and let him know when she'd arrive, they hung up.

David told himself not to count on anything from her. That way, when nothing significant happened, he wouldn't be disappointed.

He even told himself not to be surprised if she changed her mind. Hell, she might not even call him back. Nothing she did, nothing *anyone* did, would surprise him anymore. In the long run, most people didn't give a shit about anyone but themselves.

Despite these admonitions, he charged his phone all night and turned it on early the next morning. And when it rang shortly before ten and he saw the name Hannah Ferris on the display, he couldn't prevent the butterflies that suddenly erupted in his stomach, nor could he stop the spark of hope that flared.

"I'll be there this afternoon," she said. "My flight arrives at four-thirty. Can you give me directions to your apartment?"

"I could pick you up," he said, surprising himself.

"That's kind of you, David, but I've already rented a car. Just give me your address and tell me how to get there and I'll be fine."

All day he kept wondering what she would say when she got there. Once again, he told himself not to count on anything.

He figured the earliest she could possibly arrive was six, maybe even six-thirty, because he was a good hour from the airport, and by the time she got her baggage and picked up the car and did the paperwork and everything, she wouldn't get on the highway until at least five, five-fifteen. And even though it was a Saturday, who knew what traffic would be like.

Just as he'd figured, it was a few minutes past six-thirty when she arrived. He'd been standing at the window of his second-floor apartment watching for her. When he saw the dark blue Buick pull in and park, he knew it was her rental car. It gave him a strange sensation to watch her climb out, look around the parking lot, then locate his apartment. When she walked across the concrete to the steps closest to him, his chest tightened.

She was so pretty and she looked so young. Seeing her the way others would see her, he found it hard to believe she really was his mother. Today she wore dark tailored slacks and a red sleeveless top. The clothes looked expensive, but he was sure all her clothes looked expensive, because they were expensive.

He backed away from the window as she climbed the steps. He sure as hell didn't want her to think he was waiting for her.

When the doorbell rang, his heart started beating faster, which made him mad. *She* was the one that ought to be nervous, not him. He deliberately waited a few seconds before answering the door.

Her smile was tentative, as if she wasn't sure what her welcome would be. That made him feel better. Maybe she felt just as uneasy as he did. But that was crazy. Why should *she* be uneasy? She held all the cards.

He saw how she looked around when she walked inside. *Yeah*, he wanted to say, *it's not the Taj Mahal like you're used to, it's just a cheap furnished apartment.* Even *that* made him mad, because he had nothing to be ashamed of. He'd worked hard and earned the money to pay for this place; he had nothing to apologize for.

The couch sagged in the middle, so he offered her the

chair. Once she was seated, he asked her if she wanted something to drink. "I've got some Coke and some beer. Oh, and water."

Once again she gave him a hesitant smile. "Water sounds good."

He got her water and a beer for himself, then rejoined her. He sat on the couch, took a long swallow of his beer, and didn't say anything. This was her show.

She drank some of the water, then looked at him. "Why did you leave Los Angeles, David?"

The quiet question unnerved him. He shrugged. "Why not?"

"You told Hector there was nothing there for you."

"Seems to me that was true."

"Does that mean you're not interested in having any kind of relationship with me?"

"Hey, you're the one calling the shots."

"That's not true. You didn't give me a chance. Hector said you quit Friday, the day after we talked."

Give her a chance. Who the hell was she trying to kid? "I knew just from the way you acted you were hoping I'd disappear, so what's the big deal?"

"No." She leaned forward. "No. That's wrong, David. I was hoping nothing of the sort."

"Oh, yeah, sure, that's why you acted so happy you were practically dancing on the table."

"It wasn't that I wasn't happy. I was just concerned about Simon and Jenny and how they were going to react when they found out about you."

"And how *did* they react?"

Her expression told him everything he needed to know. "So why did you come here if that's the way they feel?" He drank more of his beer and gave her the coldest stare he could manage, the one that said *fuck you*.

"Look, David, their feelings have nothing to do with you personally. Their feelings have to do with me and the fact I kept such a big secret from them all these years. They're not angry with you. They're hurt and angry with me. I'm sorry about that, because I love them both. But that doesn't mean I don't want you in my life. It only means things may be difficult for a while."

He didn't want to like anything about her, but the dignified way she'd said what she'd did caused a stirring of admiration. It couldn't have been easy to admit she was the one in the wrong.

"Oh, David, I want so much for us to get to know each other. . . ." Here she faltered, and when her gaze met his again, there was a mute plea in the depths of her eyes. "I hope that's what you want, too."

Once more he shrugged. A long moment went by during which the sounds from outside seemed magnified by the silence that throbbed between them.

"If you want me to leave, I will. But that's not what I want. I want a chance to be your friend . . . and maybe, someday, your mother." Her voice dropped to nearly a whisper. "You may not believe me, David, but I love you."

David swallowed. He was terrified that he was going to humiliate himself by crying, but having her say she loved him had torn open something that had remained shut up tight for a long time.

Their eyes met, and suddenly they were both up, and they were hugging each other. The last thin veil of his self-control ripped away, David uttered a strangled cry and was powerless to stop the tears that erupted from his eyes.

How long they stood there holding each other and crying, he didn't know. All he did know was that he had finally come home.

"So where do we go from here?" Hannah asked. She and David now sat side by side on the couch. She kept wanting to touch him; she wasn't sure she'd ever get enough of touching him, this handsome boy that had so miraculously been returned to her.

He turned to look at her. "I'd like to find my father. And I'd like to meet my grandparents."

Hannah nodded. "I thought that's what you might say."

"Don't you want me to?"

"Now, don't start getting defensive again," she said gently, smiling to soften her words. He was so bristly, this man-child of hers, so quick to take offense where none was intended. She wondered if this was a learned technique to protect himself or if he'd been born that way. Certainly neither she nor Mark had had that particular character trait, but that didn't mean much.

"Sorry," he said.

"To answer your question," she said, "I think it's perfectly reasonable of you to want to meet your father. The problem is, he doesn't know about you, and I don't think it's fair for you to just spring yourself on him. That's providing we can even locate him."

"I can locate him," David said. "All I need is a computer."

"Is that how you found me?"

"Yeah."

"Whose computer did you use then?"

"I had an old laptop I bought secondhand, but it conked out on me right before I left St. Augustine, and I didn't want to spend the money to buy another."

"That's easily fixed. We can get one for you tomorrow. The stores here are open on Sundays, aren't they?"

"Yeah, in the afternoon. But I don't want you to spend money on me."

"Why not?"

"Because that's not why I tried to find you."

"David, I know that. But please don't deny me this small pleasure. It's such a little thing, buying you a computer, and it would make me so happy to do it."

For the first time since she'd arrived, he smiled, and the smile actually spread to his eyes. It made Hannah feel so good, she almost started to cry again. Love for him clogged her throat. "That's one problem solved, then," she said softly. "You have to promise me one thing, though, David. If we're able to locate your father, you have to let me contact him first. And if, after I tell him about you, he doesn't want to see you, you have to honor that."

She could see he wanted to refuse. But after a visible struggle he finally said, "All right."

After that they both agreed they were starving, and Hannah took him to dinner at the restaurant where he used to work, because he said they had the best seafood in town.

She couldn't get over how proud she felt to be seen with him. How proud *of* him she was, even more so as some of the waitstaff who knew him came by to talk to him, and especially so when the manager stopped by their table.

The man greeted David warmly, then gave her a frankly curious look.

"I'm David's mother," she said, holding out her hand.

"Mike Scofield," he said.

As they shook hands, Hannah caught a glimpse of David's face. He was trying hard to be cool, but the naked pleasure in his eyes was almost painful to see. *Oh, David, somehow I will make things up to you.*

"Pleased to meet you, Mrs. . . . is it Conway?"

"Ferris. Hannah Ferris." Hannah knew Mike Scofield was dying to know where she'd come from. She wondered what he knew of David's background.

"So, David," Scofield said, "did you call Blackie?"

"Yeah, thanks, Mike. I'm supposed to start Monday."

"Good, great. Well, nice meeting you Mrs. Ferris. You got a great kid here. He was one of my best employees."

"What was that all about?" Hannah asked when they were alone again.

"You mean about Blackie?"

"Yes. You didn't tell me you already had a job. I thought—" Abruptly she broke off.

"What?"

But just then their waiter approached with their food, so she waited to answer when they were once more alone. "You said you wanted to meet your grandparents. And if your father's agreeable, you'll be going to meet him, as well. And then . . . well, I'd hoped you would come back to Los Angeles with me."

"You mean to *live* with you?"

Hannah immediately realized her mistake. "I . . ." She swallowed. "I don't know about living with us, David. I'm not sure Simon . . ." She sighed. "I'm sorry. I just can't speak for him. To be perfectly honest with you, I'm not sure what's going to happen between us. He—he's very upset with me."

"Then what?" he asked.

"Well, I had hoped you'd come back and let me find you a nice place to live, somewhere close so we could spend time together. Once you were there and settled in, we could think about the future, whether you might want to go to school or get a job. There are some wonderful schools in and around L.A. You could go just about anywhere you wanted to. But nothing has to be decided this minute. First things first."

"Yeah, like eating our dinner."

His grin took her off guard, but it so delighted her, she grinned back.

By the time they'd finished the truly excellent seafood, it was almost ten o'clock, and Hannah was beginning to feel the effects of the past few traumatic days. When David commented that she looked tired, she admitted that she was. "If you don't mind," she said, "I'll drop you at home and then head on to my hotel. Maybe we can meet for breakfast in the morning."

"Okay. Where are you staying?"

"Um, the Radisson Resort."

He grinned again. "Figures. That's one of the nicest hotels in town."

That night Hannah slept better than she'd slept in days. She awoke refreshed and optimistic. Things were working out better than she'd dared hope with David, and maybe that was a harbinger for the future. Maybe Simon and Jenny would come around, too, and maybe the four of them could eventually forge a relationship that was healthy and happy and loving. She knew she shouldn't wish for something that might be impossible, but it was hard not to.

One thing Hannah knew for sure. No matter what happened with Simon and Jenny, she was not going to lose David again.

Thirty-three

Madeleine watched Jenny sort through a stack of pants, shorts, and tops as she decided what she wanted to take with her to France. "I like that blue outfit."

"You do?" Jenny looked at the blue cropped pants and sleeveless top doubtfully. "Do you think they wear cropped pants in France?"

Madeleine smiled. "Most popular fashions *begin* in France, my pet."

Jenny nodded and dispiritedly tossed the blue outfit on top of the pile she was taking. It hurt Madeleine to look at her, because it was so obvious Jenny wasn't happy. Even the long-anticipated trip to France hadn't lifted her spirits for very long. Madeleine wondered if now might be a good time to broach the subject of David and Hannah. She hadn't before now because she could see Jenny wasn't ready, that anything Madeleine tried to say would most likely fall on deaf ears. But she hated seeing her granddaughter so miserable, and if there was anything she could do to alleviate it, she would.

"Jenny . . . I was wondering . . . do you think you might be ready to talk about what's happened?"

Jenny stiffened.

"You're going to have to talk about it sometime, you know."

"Why?"

Speaking gently Madeleine said, "Because unpleasant and unhappy things don't go away just because we pretend they don't exist. It's important to talk about them, get our feelings out in the open so that we can begin to deal with them."

"Maybe I don't want to deal with them." Jenny's mouth was set in a stubborn line.

"My darling, I know you don't want to deal with them. But don't you see that you must? That you will just become more and more unhappy unless you face up to the problem?"

As suddenly as the stubborn look had appeared it disappeared, replaced by eyes filled with bewilderment and pain.

"But, Gram," Jenny cried, "talking won't make things *change*."

"Maybe it will. Maybe—"

"How? David will still be my brother. Nothing's going to change *that*."

"But if you talk about how you feel, perhaps your *feelings* will change."

"My feelings are *never* gonna change." Jenny angrily threw a white summer sweater onto her "take" pile.

"I thought you liked David."

Jenny didn't answer.

"I liked him a lot. It seems to me he'd be a really great kind of brother to have."

Still no answer. But Madeleine knew Jenny was listening, because she'd stopped sorting.

"I know he thinks a lot of you, Jenny. I could see that the day he came to lunch."

Suddenly Jenny's shoulders began to shake. Madeleine got up as fast as her arthritic knees would let her and walked over to Jenny, enfolding her in her arms.

"Oh, Gram," she sobbed. "He must think I'm so *stupid*."

"Why would he think that, sweetheart?"

"B-because . . . you *know* why. I-I *flirted* with him. I wanted him to be my *boyfriend*, not my *brother*. How can I ever face him again?"

Madeleine sighed. She smoothed Jenny's hair and let her cry it all out. The young were so intense. Madeleine had forgotten how serious everything was when you were young. When Jenny finally calmed down, Madeleine cleared a space on the bed so they could sit side by side. Holding Jenny's hand, Madeleine said, "All right, I understand you feel humiliated, but you never said anything to David about what you were thinking, did you?"

Jenny sniffed. "No."

"And quite honestly, Jenny, from what I saw of him that day he came to lunch, I don't believe he realized that you had a crush on him."

"But how could he *not*?" Jenny cried. "I mean, I was so *obvious*."

"No, you weren't. Yes, I knew you liked him, but that's because I know you so well. Remember, though, David already knew you were his half sister, so he was looking at you and thinking of you in an entirely different way, and it probably didn't occur to him that you would think of him in any context other than as a friend."

"You think?"

"I do."

"You're not just saying that?"

"No, I really believe it's true."

Jenny sighed.

"I know it might take some time, but don't you think you might, just possibly, once you get used to the idea, enjoy having David as a brother someday?"

The tiniest beginning of a smile played on Jenny's lips. When her eyes met Madeleine's, they were brighter. "Maybe."

Madeleine smiled. "Good. That's a good beginning. Now . . . do you think we could talk about your mother?"

The smile vanished. "She lied to me."

"Sweetheart, try to understand how your mother must have felt. She was barely older than you when she did something foolish that had serious consequences. Afterward, she did the best she could, and then she made a decision to keep that painful part of her past a secret. Perhaps she was wrong, but she did what she thought was best for everyone at the time."

"Well, it *wasn't* best! She should have told us. She should have told *me*. I'm sorry, Gram, I'll never forgive her for lying to me. Never."

For a long moment Madeleine said nothing. And then, still gently—for Jenny's pain was real and Madeleine shouldn't minimize its importance—she said, "There's just one thing I hope you'll consider. Someday you might make a mistake, too, and need the forgiveness of the people you love."

Then she squeezed Jenny's hand, got up, and walked out of the bedroom.

Thirty-four

Mark Perry stared out the window of his twelfth-floor corner office in the Woodman Tower. Downtown Omaha shimmered in the August heat. From his vantage point looking east, he could see the Central Park Mall at the edge of the Old Market, and beyond that the Heartland of America park—a scene that usually brought him pleasure since it wouldn't have been visible from his old office.

A year ago today Mark had been offered a full partnership at Lewis, McBain, and Fallberg, one of Omaha's most prestigious law firms, a position that had elevated him to one of the coveted corner offices.

Funny, he thought, how you could think you wanted something so much, then once you achieved it, it wasn't as great as you thought it would be.

He should be ecstatic. Partnerships at firms like Lewis, McBain didn't come easily, and he was only forty-nine years old—relatively young to be a full partner.

What was wrong with him? For weeks now, he'd been riddled by a vague discontent. It was nothing he could put his finger on, just a general malaise.

I'm bored, that's the crux of the problem. My life is boring. Nothing has turned out the way I imagined it would when I was young.

Still reflecting on his life, he was startled by the buzz of his intercom. He swiveled around and picked up his phone. "Yes, Cathy?"

"Mr. Perry, Mrs. Ferris is here to see you."

Mark looked down at the appointment sheet Cathy printed for him each morning. The Ferris woman was a new client. Supposedly she was a referral, although she'd been hesitant when Cathy had tried to find out just who had referred her. Mark wasn't even sure what she wanted from him. "Send her in," he said.

He straightened his tie and rose. A second later the door opened and a smiling Cathy stood back to allow an extremely attractive blonde who looked to be in her mid-to-late thirties to enter.

Cathy closed the door behind her, and Mark walked around the desk to shake hands. "Mrs. Ferris? I'm Mark Perry." It was only as their eyes met—hers a delicate shade of green that had always reminded him of new leaves in spring—that he suddenly suspected who she might be.

"Hello, Mark," she said.

"Hannah?" He couldn't believe it. He had never forgotten her. He had also never imagined he'd ever see her again. "Hannah? Is it really you?"

She smiled, and in that instant twenty years faded as if they'd never been. Like the color of her eyes, he had never forgotten her smile. He smiled, too. "I don't know what to say. You . . . you look wonderful."

"So do you."

All the promise she had shown as a young girl had been realized. She had grown into a beautiful, poised woman, and it was obvious she also had money, for the dress and jewelry she wore were expensive. Mark knew expensive. He'd had enough experience with Jodie, his second wife, to know when something cost a lot. That dress alone had probably set Hannah or her husband back close to half a grand.

Mark knew he was grinning like a fool, but he couldn't seem to help himself. Seeing her was such an unexpected and pleasant surprise. "It's great to see you, Hannah. Here, come sit down." He led her to the seating area in the corner, where four buttermilk leather chairs were grouped conversationally around a washed-pine coffee table. "Can I have my secretary bring you anything? Coffee? A soft drink? A glass of wine?"

She smiled again and crossed her legs. "A glass of ice water would be great."

"Coming right up."

Once Cathy had brought Hannah her water and the black coffee Mark was addicted to, he settled back in his chair and studied her more closely. Yes, the years had been very kind to her. "So what are you doing here, Hannah? Did you move back to the area?"

"No, I live in Los Angeles."

"Visiting, then?"

"Yes."

"I see you're married."

"Yes." But at the mention of her marriage, sadness clouded her eyes.

That was interesting. But not surprising, if Mark's experience with marriage was any indicator. "Children?"

Now she smiled. "Yes, um . . . two. And what about you? Are you and your wife still together?"

He grimaced. "No. I'm a two-time loser, as a matter of fact." At her blank look he added, "Twice divorced, in other words."

"Oh. I'm . . . I'm sorry."

He smiled wryly. "Don't be. I'm not." Not quite true. He was sorry about the exorbitant alimony he was still paying Jodie, but aside from that, he was well rid of both of his former wives.

"What about Robbie and Hank? How are they doing?"

As always, when someone mentioned Robbie's name, Mark was surprised anew by the intensity of the pain that stabbed him. "We . . . lost Robbie a few years ago."

"Oh, dear, I'm so sorry. What happened?"

"Drug overdose. Look, it's not a pleasant subject. Let me tell you about Hank instead. He's a history professor. Youngest one in his department. He's married and has a three-month-old baby." He smiled at the reminder of little Isabel.

He'd had no idea he would be one of those grandfathers who was totally bonkers over a grandchild.

"Serious little Hank." Her eyes met his. "I've never forgotten those boys, Mark. I really loved them."

And I really loved you, he thought. *I was just too stupid to know it then.*

For a long moment silence lay between them. Then she sighed. "Mark, the reason I'm here is because there's something I have to tell you. This is going to come as a shock, but it's something you have a right to know."

Suddenly he had a premonition of what she was going to say, and he went still.

"Twenty years ago I gave birth to a baby boy. That baby was yours."

Even though he'd been more or less prepared, Mark was still stunned.

"I gave him up for adoption and tried to wipe the whole thing out of my mind. But not long ago he managed to find me." Her smile was tremulous. "He's a wonderful boy, Mark. And he'd like to meet you."

Mark didn't know what to say. Another son. It was amazing. He had another chance. A grin split his face. "Where is he?" He jumped up. "Is he outside?"

She seemed taken aback by his reaction. "Um, no. He's not even here in Omaha. I-I wanted to see how you felt before I brought him here."

"Where is he, then?"

"He . . . he's in Florida, but he's waiting to hear from me. He knew we were meeting this afternoon."

A bit deflated, Mark sat down again. "Tell me about him. What's he like? What does he do?"

Her eyes softened. "He's had a tough life, but he's come through it, probably better than most could have. I'm proud of him, and I admire his strength and his courage." She went on, giving Mark details about the birth, his adoption, what happened after his adoptive parents died, and how he tracked her down. "As far as what he does, he's not working right now, but that's because I asked him to quit the job he'd just accepted—I'll explain that later—and go back to

L.A. with me. He's smart, and I'd like to see him go to college, and that's what he wants, too."

"When can I meet him? Can he come here? Or should I go to Florida?"

"He'll come here. He wants to come here. In fact, he wants to meet my family." At this she grimaced. "Whether that will happen is a debatable point, though."

Mark nodded. He remembered the things she'd told him about her family. He didn't imagine her father would be any too pleased to find out his oldest daughter had given birth outside of marriage.

"Anyway," she said, "how soon do you want him to come?"

"The sooner, the better."

"I'm so glad you feel that way. I was afraid you might not."

"Maybe if Alexis and I were still married, it would be different. But we're not, so there's no one to get upset."

"What about your mother?"

"She died two years ago."

"Your sister?"

"Marjorie's great. She'll be excited for me."

"What about Hank?"

"I can't say for sure, of course, but I think Hank will be thrilled to have a brother. He's really missed Robbie."

"I'll call David right now then." She opened her purse and took out a cell phone. A few minutes later she said, "David? Hi. Well, I'm here. In fact, I'm sitting in your father's office right now." After a few seconds she said, "Yes, he does. Do you want to call and see about a flight or do you want me to do it?" She smiled. "Okay. You've got my cell phone number. Call me back. I'll wait here until I hear from you."

After she'd disconnected the call, she said, "He'll call as soon as he's made his arrangements." She relaxed back in the chair and gave him a thoughtful look. "You can tell me this is none of my business, but I'm curious about what happened between you and Alexis."

He shrugged. "It was a combination of things, but at the

root of our problems was the fact the two of us wanted different things out of life. She was never really happy being married and a mother, and eventually, we just had to face that. We were divorced when Hank was ten and Robbie was eight."

"Five years after that summer," she said softly.

"Yes." He wondered what would happen if he said what he was thinking. She'd given him the idea that all was not rosy in her marriage. Maybe . . . But he pushed the thought away. He'd done enough rash things in his life. This time he'd be wise to think things through before acting upon an impulse.

"Did the boys stay with you?"

He nodded. "I had primary custody, but Alexis had generous visitation. Not that she exercised that right very often," he added with a trace of the bitterness he'd had a hard time banishing. He still blamed her for the bulk of Robbie's problems, because Robbie had been hurt the most by her neglect. Hank had been more resilient and mature for his age; he'd somehow understood that his mother's inability to be the kind of mother they wanted had nothing to do with him and his worthiness, but was instead a failure of hers. Robbie took her absence personally and couldn't handle the rejection.

"But you weren't soured on marriage if you married again," Hannah said.

He grimaced. "No, some people take a long time to learn a lesson."

"Oh, now, come on . . ."

"The truth is, I married on the rebound, and it was a disaster from the beginning. Jodie wasn't good with the kids, she spent money like it was water, and she was extremely possessive and demanding."

"How long did it last?"

"Eight years."

"So you never had any other children?"

"No. Jodie didn't want kids. She said my two were more than enough." He smiled. "We've talked about me long enough. Tell me about you. You said you had two children. Were you counting David?"

"Of course."

"So you've had just one child with your husband?"

"Yes, Jenny." At the mention of her daughter's name, her eyes sparkled the way they had when she talked about David. "She's fourteen."

"How does she feel about this brother you've sprung on her?"

The sparkle slowly faded, replaced by a worried frown. "She's upset. The problem is, she met David before Simon and I did—Simon's my husband—and she had a huge crush on him. So to find out he was actually her half brother was a shock. And of course she feels betrayed and hurt by the fact I kept him a secret all these years." She sighed. "She and Simon are in France right now, visiting his mother's relatives. I'm hoping that by the time they return, emotions will have settled down and we can all move forward."

"How about your husband? Is he okay with this?"

She shook her head sadly. "No, not really. But we'll work it out," she added with forced brightness. "It'll all work out."

He knew she was trying to convince herself more than she was trying to convince him. "What part upsets him?"

"It's complicated. And . . ." She took a deep breath. "I-I really don't want to talk about it."

"Well, I'm certainly not qualified to be giving anybody advice about marriage, but I do know one thing. If your husband really loves you, and if you have a good marriage otherwise, he'll get over this. And if he doesn't, then you'll have to make some tough decisions."

She nodded.

"Hannah . . ."

She raised her eyes.

Mark took a deep breath. "Hannah, I'm sorry about everything. So many times I wished I could make things up to you. What I did . . . it was inexcusable."

"No, Mark—"

"Wait," he interrupted. "It *was* inexcusable, and you know it. I was older. Married. Supposed to know better. You were just a kid, and I took advantage of you."

"It wasn't all your fault. I wanted what happened to happen," she said softly.

He shook his head. "It doesn't matter. I was the adult. Hell, I didn't even make sure you were protected!" He thought about how he hadn't used a condom that first time.

She sighed. "I'm not sorry I had David. I'm sorry about the pain it's caused others, but . . ." Her smile was tremulous. "I could never be sorry about his existence."

She started to say more when her cell phone rang. Mark handed her a notepad and pen. As he'd thought, it was David calling her back. When the call was over, she said, "He'll be here tomorrow morning at eleven. You heard me say I'd pick him up at the airport."

"*We'll* pick him up," he said. Then he reached for his phone and buzzed Cathy. "Cathy, cancel all my appointments for tomorrow and reschedule them for next week."

"What reason should I give?"

"Just say it's a personal emergency." He knew she was dying to know what was going on. He'd eventually tell her, but right now he didn't want to share this with anyone other than Hannah and Hank. Remembering Hank, he grinned. He couldn't wait to call him.

While he'd been talking to Cathy, Hannah had gotten up. "I'll let you get back to work now, Mark. I'm staying at the Westin Aquila. Do you want me to come here tomorrow, or do you want to pick me up?"

"I'll pick you up. In fact, why don't I come over about nine, and we'll have breakfast together, then go to the airport?"

"All right. That sounds good."

He walked her to the door. For a moment they stood there awkwardly, neither one knowing what to say. Then they both spoke at once.

"Mark, I'm glad—"

"I'm really looking forward—"

They stopped and smiled at each other. Then he said softly, "I made a bad mistake when I let you go, didn't I?"

"Oh, Mark, it wasn't—"

"It's okay, Hannah. You don't have to say anything. I

just . . . well, seeing you again, remembering what we had and what we could have had . . . it's just made me realize what I threw away." He put his hands on her shoulders, leaned over, and kissed her cheek. "Thanks for not holding any grudges."

"No thanks necessary." She smiled. "I'll see you tomorrow."

Thirty-five

~~~~~~~~~~

Hannah didn't know why she was nervous. After all, Mark wanted to be there, and he seemed genuinely thrilled about David, which still seemed to her a minor miracle. After Simon's and Jenny's reaction, and what she knew would be the reaction of her parents, she hadn't been counting on much from Mark.

Still, it wasn't every day a woman got to see the first meeting between her son and his father. How would David act? she wondered. She knew he was curious, but would he and Mark make the kind of emotional connection she and David had made?

She was so thankful for that. So grateful that, in spite of everything, David didn't seem to have any animosity toward her. Once he was convinced that she was sincere about wanting to be a part of his life, he had let go of his bitterness.

She glanced over at Mark, who was fidgeting in the seat next to hers. They had gotten to the airport early, only to find that David's flight would be twenty minutes late, so they'd had nearly an hour to kill. "Anxious?" she said.

Mark gave her a sheepish smile. "Yeah, I am. I was just thinking I wished I still smoked, because I could sure use a cigarette about now."

"You smoked?"

He nodded. "I started when I married Jodie, mainly because she smoked, but I got hooked and didn't quit until a few years ago. What about you? You pick up any vices in the last twenty years?"

Hannah chuckled. "Does a passion for popcorn count?"

"If that's the only vice you have, you're a much better person than I am."

They fell silent for a few minutes, then he said, "What does your husband do, Hannah?"

"He's the CEO of a family business."

"Oh? What kind of business?"

"You've heard of the Ferris Sporting Goods stores?"

"You mean he's *that* Ferris?"

"Yes."

He whistled.

After living in L.A. for so long, where everyone was so caught up in the entertainment business and millionaires were a dime a dozen, Hannah wasn't accustomed to anyone being impressed by Simon's position, but she could see that Mark clearly was.

"Your life now is a long way from Jordan, Nebraska," he said thoughtfully.

His comment about her roots was a sobering reminder of what was in store for her in the next few days. Telling her parents about David would be almost more difficult than telling Simon had been, Hannah was sure.

She was still thinking about the upcoming confrontation when the people around them began to stir. Mark stood and walked over to the window. "The plane's here," he said when he rejoined her.

The two of them joined the crowd that began to gather around the gate, and a few minutes later the door opened and the first of the passengers appeared. Hannah's stomach was full of butterflies. She couldn't help it. This was a momentous occasion in all three of their lives.

David was among the last group of passengers to emerge from the jetway. Hannah's heart swelled with love as she spied him. "David!" She waved. "Over here."

The next few minutes would always stand out in her mind. David seeing them. The expression on his face, a combination of excitement, wariness, and hope. And then the moment of meeting, the first time he and Mark came face to face.

Hannah's eyes were nearly blinded by tears as she watched them, father and son, greet each other for the first time. The similarities between them were even more pronounced today, and she marveled at the miracle of genetics.

"David," Mark said. He seemed shaken, too, by the enormity of the moment. He gripped David's hand with both of his and stared at his son's face.

"Hi," David said. His smile was uncertain. "I-I'm not sure what to call you."

"Why not call me Mark?"

The relief on David's face was palpable. "Okay. Great. Mark." He said the name as if he were trying it on. Then he grinned. "Mark."

Hannah knew she would never forget this moment. As she watched them, her hands itched for a paintbrush. She would have given anything to be able to paint them, right now, right here. To try to capture the way they were looking at each other this very second. She attempted to etch the scene in her mind so that sometime in the future she might be able to re-create it. The two dark heads—one tousled, one razor cut and threaded with gray. Their stance, their smiles, the all-male way they were checking each other out, sizing each other up. Her chest felt tight, as if her heart had expanded.

"Did you have a good flight?" Mark was saying.

"Yeah, it was cool."

"Hannah . . . your mother . . . booked you a room in the hotel where she's staying. We thought we'd go back there where we could talk, then maybe all go to lunch. If that's okay with you."

"Sure, that sounds great."

Mark eyed David's duffle bag. "Do you have any other luggage?"

"Nope." David grinned. "I travel light."

In that instant Hannah knew everything had been worth it. No matter what happened in the future, no matter what the cost to her personally, the only part of the past she would change would be her decision to give David up for adoption.

David didn't know what he felt. At first, when he'd met Mark, and then, during lunch, he'd been euphoric. But during the afternoon when he and Mark went for a drive by themselves and during dinner where he met his half brother Hank—who wasn't quite as ecstatic as Mark had led David to believe he would be—and later, throughout the evening when he and Mark talked for hours, he began to feel a kind of letdown, the way he'd felt as a swimmer when a big race was finally over.

He kept thinking, okay, so this has been nice, but what happens now? He couldn't really be a part of Mark's life, and it was obvious that Hank wasn't going to welcome him with open arms.

He thought about Simon and how good to him he'd been. He thought about Jenny, the way she'd looked at him so trustingly, how she'd cared about him. And he thought about his mother, how her life would probably never be the same because of him.

Suddenly he wondered if he'd done the right thing. Maybe the best thing for everyone would be for him to just pack it up, go back to Florida, and allow them all to get on with their lives.

Thirty-six

"But I don't understand," Hannah said. "I thought you were going to come with me. You said you wanted to meet your grandparents. You have an aunt and uncle and three cousins in Jordan, too."

"I changed my mind," David said.

Why wouldn't he look at her? What had happened with him and Mark yesterday to change his mind about Jordan? Had Mark *said* something?

"Look," David finally said, "I've caused enough trouble. You know your parents aren't going to be happy to find out about me. So why tell them?"

"David, I *have* to tell them."

"Why? I'm sure not gonna say anything. They're old, aren't they? And you told me how strict your father is. Why get him all upset? What's the point?"

"The point is that I've kept something important a secret from them. The point is that our relationship has never been open or honest. The point is that I *need* to do this, I *need* to tell them they have a grandson they never knew about. The point is, being honest with them is the right thing to do."

He shrugged. "Fine. But I still don't want to go."

She spent another hour trying to persuade him, but he wouldn't budge. In fact, he said he was going back to Florida the next morning, a day earlier than he'd planned.

"But *why*?" she cried. "Will you at least tell me why? Did Mark say something to upset you? Is that what this is all about?"

"This has nothing to do with Mark."

Hannah finally gave up. "All right, David, I'm not going to argue with you anymore. I'm going to drive to Jordan myself, and tomorrow or Friday I'll fly back to St. Augustine. Once I get there, we can decide how we'll get you back to L.A."

"I'm not sure I'm coming to L.A."

She stared at him. She couldn't believe how much things had changed in just twenty-four hours. Maybe he didn't think Mark had said anything, and maybe Mark hadn't, but *something* had happened. And Hannah had every intention of getting to the bottom of it, if not now, then as soon as she'd taken care of business in Jordan.

She had not risked her marriage and her relationship with her daughter—which were both still in jeopardy—to end up losing David. "It's clear to me that something is wrong, but now's not the time to talk about it. You go back to Florida, and when I get there, we'll talk."

For the second time in a month Hannah drove into Jordan. The town slumbered in the August heat. There'd been no rain in weeks, and the streets were dusty, the flowers wilted. Even the trees looked tired and ready for cool weather. It had always amazed Hannah that a state that could be so frozen and miserable in the winter could be so sweltering in the summer. At the very least there should be some kind of fair tradeoff for putting up with the snow and harsh winds of winter—mountains or the ocean or a gentle summer. Somehow she didn't think being considered part of the Great American Breadbasket was enough of a reward.

It had taken her a couple of hours to get there after leaving David this morning, so it was close to one o'clock when she pulled into the church parking lot. She had called ahead, so her parents knew she was coming. Her mother had been curious, Hannah knew, curious and surprised to find out Hannah was in Omaha, but she hadn't asked questions. She was too inured to being the unquestioning wife to feel entitled to ask anything.

Hannah had also asked her mother to tell Leah she was coming. She knew it might be difficult for Leah to get a baby-sitter on such short notice, but she hoped her sister had been able to manage it. Hannah didn't want to have to tell her story twice. Bad enough that she had to tell it once and that there would be others—like Sarah and Madeleine and Jill—all of whom would have questions, too.

Her mother had been watching for her and walked out onto the porch. They hugged. "How's Father doing?" Hannah said before they went inside.

"He's doing good. He's been wondering why you're here, though."

Hannah knew that was her mother's way of saying her father had been complaining and grumbling ever since she'd called. If the situation facing her hadn't been so serious, she might have laughed. At least her father was predictable.

Her mother led her back to the living room, where her father was sitting in his favorite chair, reading his Bible. He didn't look up immediately, but made a point of finishing the passage. He marked his place with a bookmark, put the Bible on the table beside him, then finally rose and came to meet her.

"Hello, Father," Hannah said as they embraced.

"Hello, daughter. It's good to see you."

"And you." Hannah stepped back. "You look very good. Very healthy."

"I feel as good as new." He looked at Hannah's mother. "Rachel, I'm sure our daughter is hungry and thirsty after her long drive."

Before her mother could scurry off to the kitchen, Hannah said, "No, Father, I had something to eat on the way." This wasn't true, but it was easier than saying she wasn't hungry and having to sit through a mini-sermon on the importance of fueling the body as well as the soul.

He frowned. "We waited lunch for you."

Smothering a sigh, Hannah said, "Then let's go out to the

kitchen. We can talk while you eat." She looked at her mother. "Is Leah coming?"

"No, she couldn't get a baby-sitter. She said to tell you to drop by and see her later."

Hannah didn't try to begin telling them about David until her father had his grilled cheese and fruit salad in front of him, and her mother had finally sat down to her own lunch. Even then Hannah stalled. Maybe they'd be more receptive to her news on a full stomach. She chatted about Jenny and Simon and the trip to France, instead.

Halfway through his lunch, her father put down his sandwich and gave her a hard look. "You didn't come all the way here to talk about your family's trip, daughter."

Hannah swallowed. "No, Father, I didn't." Her gaze swung to her mother, who had stopped eating mid-bite. "I came to tell you something that I've kept hidden for nearly twenty-one years."

Her father's gaze remained rooted on hers. Hannah forced herself to meet those intense blue eyes, even though she would rather have looked anywhere else.

"Do you remember the summer I worked for Mrs. Perry's son?" she asked quietly.

It only took her fifteen minutes to shatter an illusion and change their relationship forever.

When she finished, her father stared at her for a long moment during which there was barely a sound. Then he stood slowly. Without a word he left the room.

Hannah looked at her mother. Rachel's eyes were wide and scared. She didn't look at Hannah.

Hannah's heart sank. In that moment she knew she had been hoping that somehow, today, things would be different. But nothing had changed. There would be no support here.

Wearily she stood. She considered just leaving, was almost ready to say a quiet goodbye to her mother and walk out, when a long-buried anger suddenly pushed through the barriers she'd erected as a defense mechanism to enable her to survive her childhood.

No. She was not going to leave, skulk out like someone who had something to be ashamed of. If she did that, she was no better than the parents of that girl her father had humiliated all those years ago. For the first time in her life, she was going to face down her father.

Head high, she marched into the living room where he once again had his nose buried in his Bible.

"Father."

He didn't move, didn't even blink.

"Father," she said more loudly. "Look at me."

He calmly turned the page and continued to ignore her.

"Fine. Don't look at me. Keep pretending I don't exist. Keep pretending your grandson doesn't exist. Well, I'm here to tell you he does exist. And you know what? It's *your* loss if you don't want to meet him. Because he's a wonderful boy, someone we can all be proud of."

She shook her head. "I'm so disappointed in you, Father. You call yourself a minister, a man of God. Yet there is no compassion, no forgiveness in your heart. You know what else? I feel sorry for you. You must be a very unhappy man."

He finally raised his eyes. "I have nothing to be unhappy about. You, however, have much to answer for."

"Oh, for heaven's sake! It was just a youthful mistake. Can't you understand that? Everyone makes mistakes. Okay, fine, censure me if you want to. But not David. He doesn't deserve that." Although she felt more like screaming, she fought to soften her voice. "Father, please, just meet him. Can't you do that much?"

"I have no desire to meet the spawn of your adulterous relationship. He is not welcome here. You are no longer welcome here, either." So saying, he turned his attention back to his Bible.

Hannah stood there another minute. She had just turned to go when her mother entered the room.

"Joshua," her mother said.

"Do not disturb me when I am reading my Bible." He didn't look up.

"Joshua," her mother said more forcefully, "this is my home, too. And Hannah will always be welcome here, as will my grandson."

That got her father's attention. He slammed his Bible shut and, eyes blazing, got to his feet. He glared at Rachel. "How dare you speak to me like that!"

Hannah was frozen in place. She couldn't have moved or spoken if her life depended on it. She also couldn't take her eyes off her mother, who suddenly seemed to have grown taller and stronger.

"I have every right to speak to you any way I want to," her mother said. "I am your wife, not your child or your slave. You are a mean man, Joshua. Mean and cruel. I've followed you blindly for too many years, but that's over. No more. I love Hannah and I want to see my new grandson. And I'm going to. Hannah?" She turned to look at Hannah. "Wherever you're going now, I want to come with you. Is that all right?"

"Oh, Mom, it's more than all right. It's *wonderful*."

They left Hannah's father standing there. Neither of them looked back.

There was another scene with Leah, but this one didn't last as long and it wasn't as ugly. And by the time Hannah left her sister, Leah even bent enough to give her a hug and wish her luck. Still, Hannah knew Leah would never defy their father as Rachel had done.

When Rachel and Hannah got back to the parsonage, the house was empty. Her father's dusty old car was still in the parking lot, so she knew he had simply gone to the church. Rachel went upstairs to pack while Hannah used her cell phone to call home and see if there was any message from Simon. She wished she could call him directly, but he hadn't suggested it, and she felt too unsure of their relationship right now to push him.

"Yes," Martha said when the connection was made, "they arrived safely. And Mr. Simon said to tell you if you called that he'd try to reach you sometime tomorrow."

Hannah had to be content with that. At least he had thought about her. Maybe this was an indication that he was softening.

Next she called David, but he wasn't in his room, so all

she could do was leave a message saying she and his grandmother were coming to Omaha and would be there by six.
"I know you're planning to leave in the morning, but I was
hoping we could have dinner together tonight. I'll leave my
cell phone on. If you get this message before we arrive,
please call me."

The last call she made was to Mark. But he was in court,
so she just told his secretary to tell him she had called and
would be back at the hotel by six.

Then she sat at the kitchen table and waited for her
mother to finish packing. Ten minutes later Rachel came
downstairs carrying a small suitcase.

"I'm ready," she said.

She looked more self-assured than Hannah ever remembered. "Aren't you going to go say goodbye to Father?"

Rachel shook her head. "No, I don't feel like seeing him
right now." At Hannah's look, she smiled crookedly. "Don't
worry, Hannah. I'll call him tonight. I don't want to be
responsible for him having another heart attack."

Five minutes later mother and daughter were on their
way.

Her mother was amazing, Hannah thought in wonder as she
watched Rachel with David.

Tears running down her face, she put her arms around
him and told him how proud and happy she was to meet
him. She touched his face and smoothed his hair and said
over and over how wonderful it was to discover she had
another grandson.

"I know mothers aren't supposed to have favorites, but
Hannah has always been special to me." The look she gave
Hannah was filled with love. "She was my first, you know.
And the first child always occupies a special place in a
mother's heart."

Hannah's eyes filled with tears, and she could see David
was moved by the words, too.

"That means you are my first grandchild. If anything, the
first grandchild is even *more* special than a first child. Dear
boy . . ." She kissed his cheek. "Have I told you how proud

of you I am? Hannah explained about your life. How your adoptive parents died and how you spent most of your childhood in foster homes. You know, a lot of young men would use that as an excuse to lead a wasteful life, but you haven't. You've worked hard and haven't asked anyone for anything. That takes great strength and courage."

Hannah had never loved her mother as much as she did in that moment.

After that the three of them went out to dinner. It was a wonderful evening, one Hannah knew she would remember always. Her mother told David stories about Hannah when she was young and stories about his cousins. Over and over she said how glad it made her to be with him, and how much she was looking forward to getting to know him.

"Hannah tells me you've talked about living in Los Angeles and going to school there. I'm so glad, because I plan to spend a lot of time with Hannah from now on . . . and with you."

By the time they returned to the hotel, Hannah knew she didn't have to worry about David any longer.

He would be coming to Los Angeles.

Thirty-seven

Jenny seemed to be enjoying herself, and Simon was glad. This was the end of their first week in France, and each day they'd been there, he could see her spirits lifting.

Much of her improvement was due to his mother. Madeleine had told him about her conversation with Jenny, and he was grateful that she was able to get through to his daughter when he couldn't. Unfortunately, his mother seemed determined to talk to him, too. He'd been stalling her, but he knew she wouldn't be stalled forever. When Madeleine Ferris wanted something, she never stopped until she got it.

Today Jenny and her cousins had gone to Nice, Simon's uncle Etienne—Madeleine's youngest brother—was out in the south vineyard, his aunt Corinne had gone shopping in town, and Simon had escaped into the library to avoid the heart-to-heart his mother was determined to have.

He browsed the shelves, found a book that interested him, and settled into one of the comfortable armchairs. He'd barely gotten past the title page when the door opened. His mother stood in the doorway. She held a cup of coffee in her hands.

Simon stifled a sigh.

"May I join you?"

As if he had a choice. "Of course."

She sat in a facing armchair and looked at him for a long

moment before speaking. "You've been avoiding me."

He couldn't help smiling. "You noticed."

Now she smiled, too. "I'm your mother, Simon. I love you, and I'm concerned about you."

"I know."

Another long moment passed. Outside the open windows, Simon could hear dogs barking in the distance.

"Have you decided what you're going to do when you get home?"

"What do you mean?"

"About your marriage. About Hannah's son."

"I don't know."

"Dear, I know you think I'm a fossil, and that my ideas are hopelessly old-fashioned, but I'm going to give you my advice, anyway."

He nodded.

"I know you've been angry for a long time. Oh, it's been a well-disguised anger, but nevertheless, it's been there. And I know that anger has been directed at your parents, especially your mother, because of the way she gave you away. I guess I don't blame you for feeling that way, but I feel just the opposite. I've always been grateful to her. If it hadn't been for her, your father and I wouldn't have had you, and until you gave us Jenny, you were the greatest joy of my life." Her smile was tender. "You're going to think this is strange, because what you said, about me not liking Hannah, that was true. But now that I know what she was dealing with all these years, I understand her a lot better and—I know this will be hard for you to understand—I like her a lot more now. She did something courageous when she gave her son up for adoption, something to be admired, not something to be vilified for."

"That's not why I'm angry with her."

"Isn't it? Aren't you projecting what happened to you onto her shoulders? Aren't you blaming her for what your mother did to you?"

"No. I'm angry with her because she lied to me. Because she didn't trust me enough to tell me the truth. Without trust and honesty, what kind of marriage do we have? Certainly not the kind I thought we had."

"I actually understand why she didn't tell you. It wasn't because she's dishonest, I don't think. I believe it was because she was trying to put the pain behind her."

"I don't care what her reasons were. It was wrong of her to keep something so important from me."

"Simon . . ." she admonished gently.

"*You* would never have kept anything like that from Dad." When she didn't answer, he frowned. "Would you?"

She sighed deeply. "I don't know. I do know that as close as your father and I were, we didn't tell each other everything."

Simon stared at her. "What are you saying?"

"I'm saying that there are some things better left in the past. Surely you didn't tell Hannah everything about *your* past, did you?"

He knew she was referring to Kaitlin, whom he had almost married four years before he'd met Hannah. Almost married until he discovered she wasn't the woman he'd imagined her to be. His mouth twisted. And now Hannah wasn't the woman he'd imagined *her* to be, either. "The two situations aren't the same."

"Aren't they?"

Despite what she thought, they weren't. His involvement with Kaitlin had nothing to do with Hannah or their life together. David's existence was different. He impacted their lives, because he was Hannah's child, and he always would be.

"If all that had happened to Hannah was an ill-conceived love affair when she was very young, and she'd chosen not to tell me about it, that would have been fine. It's the fact she had a *child* and didn't tell me about him that I can't get past. How can you just put a *child* out of your mind? What kind of a woman does that?" As soon as the words were out of his mouth, he regretted them.

"Hannah isn't like your mother, Simon," she said softly. "She didn't give away her son because she didn't want him.

She gave him away because she couldn't give him a good life."

"What my mother did has no bearing on this," he said stiffly.

She sighed deeply. "All right, I won't press the point. But just think about what I've said, will you? I'm sure you truly believe Hannah's lie of omission is why you're so upset with her, but I believe the real reason has more to do with your own past than it has to do with Hannah." More gently she added, "Everyone makes mistakes, Simon. I know you wanted to believe Hannah was perfect, but no one is perfect. Like all of us, Hannah is simply a human being with human frailties. It isn't fair of you to expect her to be anything else."

Simon thought about their conversation for hours after she left him. At first he couldn't concede that her argument had a shred of validity, but he finally was forced to admit to himself that there might be some truth in what she'd said.

Maybe it was time to talk to Hannah. He actually reached for the phone, then changed his mind. He didn't want to discuss this on the telephone. They needed to talk face to face. When he got home would be time enough. Maybe by then he'd have come to some conclusion about whether or not they still had a future together.

Hannah stepped back to look at the painting on her drawing table. It wasn't perfect, but it was probably as good as it was going to get. The problem was, she couldn't recall all the minute details she needed to bring the scene to life, and the moment hadn't been captured on film, so she had no other reference than her memory.

But she hadn't painted David and Mark and their first meeting for display. She had painted it for herself, so it really didn't matter whether it was completely accurate. Painting the two of them had been a catharsis of sorts, a way to exorcise some of the anger she still felt toward her father.

One good thing had come of the confrontation with her father: Hannah no longer felt the need to please him or try to win his approval. She now knew that was an impossible task. It was sad, she thought, that she had spent her entire life pretending to be someone she was not. It had taken David's reappearance to teach her that we cannot escape who we are, and until we learn to deal with that knowledge, we can never be whole.

Today Simon and Jenny were coming home. Hannah didn't know what the future held in store for them. Her few, mostly unsatisfying, conversations with Simon during his trip to France had not dealt with their situation. He had simply let her know where they were and what they were doing, and yesterday, what time they were arriving at LAX.

His only reference to their problems came at the end of the call. "Jenny wants to continue staying with my mother."

Hannah had to fight back tears. "I-I was hoping she might be ready to come home."

"I'm sorry, Hannah. She's made some progress in that direction, but I don't think we can hurry her. I think she has to work all this out in her own time."

He hadn't asked about David. He hadn't asked about her trip to Jordan. He hadn't asked about her work.

Most telling, he hadn't said he loved her.

It was the first time in all their years of marriage that they had ended their phone calls with "goodbye" instead of "I love you."

But as disappointing and scary as her relationship with Simon and Jenny was right now, Hannah's relationship with her son was better even than she could have hoped. This was due mostly to her mother and that emotional meeting the two of them had that first night.

Whatever doubts David might have been feeling had been erased by Rachel and her unconditional love and approval. After that night there was no more talk of staying in Florida. Hannah had gone back to St. Augustine with him, helped him sell his truck, and then they'd gone to Tampa to introduce him to Aunt Marcy.

Thinking about that touching reunion brought tears to Hannah's eyes. Aunt Marcy had cried, she'd been so happy.

"Oh," she'd exclaimed to David, "you're so handsome. And you look so much like Jenny."

Hannah and David had stayed overnight. As they got ready to leave, Aunt Marcy made them promise they'd be back soon. Then Hannah and David had flown to L.A. together.

He'd been there for ten days now. They'd found him a really nice, small apartment in Santa Monica, and yesterday, after pulling strings, they'd enrolled him at UCLA, where he would soon begin the fall semester. Hannah had wanted to buy him a new car, but he'd refused, saying he had enough money to buy himself another used truck, that she didn't need to spend any more money on him. The next day he'd made good on his promise. He'd also found himself a part-time job waiting tables at a little restaurant close to his apartment, even though Hannah had said it wasn't necessary.

"I need to feel like I'm paying part of my way," he insisted.

She had never felt more proud of him.

She smiled now, remembering. Yesterday they'd had dinner together, and she'd told him Simon and Jenny were returning today. When they'd parted, he'd kissed her cheek and wished her luck.

"Whatever happens," she said, moved by his concern, "it's not going to affect you and me, David. I just want you to know that. And if things don't turn out as I hope they will, I don't want you to feel guilty. Remember, none of this is your fault."

She sighed, thinking about that passage in the Bible from Exodus 20:5 about the sins of the fathers, only in this case it was the sins of the mother.

"You're too hard on yourself," her friend Jill had said the other day when the two of them met for lunch. "Like Mark said, you were just a kid."

"I was old enough to know right from wrong."

"Yeah, well, knowing and doing are two different things. We all do things we shouldn't, Hannah. What counts is what you do afterward."

Martha had said much the same thing when Hannah haltingly told her about David. She'd hugged Hannah, saying, "You're a good woman, Mrs. Ferris. I'm glad you have your boy back now."

Hannah had had to fight tears at the kind look on the housekeeper's face and her obvious sincerity.

But as comforting as Martha's and Jill's words had been, and as happy as Aunt Marcy and her mother had made Hannah, none of their reactions were a tenth as important as what Simon's and Jenny's would ultimately be.

But that was something that was entirely out of Hannah's hands. From now on, all she could do was pray.

The entire flight home Simon thought about Hannah and David and the future. He especially thought about his mother's advice.

He looked over at her. She was sitting across the first-class aisle next to Jenny. Madeleine's eyes were closed, and she looked tired. Love for her constricted his chest. She'd said he couldn't have found a better wife than Hannah. He wanted to tell her he couldn't have found a better mother. Or father.

Simon's earliest memory was of his father giving him a ride on his shoulders. Simon smiled, remembering how Hugh would pretend to be a plane and swoop around, and Simon would squeal in delight and say, "More, more!"

Sometimes his dad would pretend to be a train and crawl on the ground and let Simon sit on his back. The two of them would call out, "Choo, choo, choo," and Madeleine would smile indulgently as she watched.

He'd had a great childhood. Hugh and Madeleine had been doting, adoring parents. They thought everything he said and did was wonderful.

David hadn't been so lucky.

Simon wondered what David remembered. Did he have any happy memories to sustain him through the bad years?

Once again his thoughts moved to Hannah. Why *hadn't* she trusted him? What was lacking in their relationship that had made her afraid to tell him about David?

By the time their plane landed at LAX, Simon still had no answers. He knew what he wished, but he wasn't sure if it was going to be possible.

Hannah had given Martha the night off. Martha protested, saying she had been planning to fix Mr. Simon his favorite dinner, but Hannah shook her head. "We need to be alone, Martha."

Martha nodded, her eyes immediately turning sympathetic.

After Martha was gone, Hannah decided to go for broke. She uncorked a bottle of Merlot, took out a wedge of Brie to soften, sliced a loaf of French bread, then carried it all upstairs to the bedroom where she'd prepared a small table. She then took a relaxing bath scented with bath oil and dressed in a flowing, violet silk hostess gown that was one of Simon's favorites.

The bed was already turned down, the lights were soft, and fresh flowers perfumed the air.

Maybe what she'd done would appear contrived to him. But it wasn't. It was honest and expressed how she felt. She loved her husband, and she wanted desperately to repair the break in their marriage. Maybe her preparations would show him what was in her heart better than she could ever say.

When she finally heard his car in the driveway, she closed her eyes. *Please, God, help me.*

She was sitting propped up in bed when he walked in. His gaze took in everything, then settled on her. Tears blurred her eyes, even though she'd told herself she wouldn't cry. She swallowed. "Simon," she whispered.

For a moment he didn't move. Then, slowly, he put down his luggage. His eyes never left her face.

What was he thinking? Why didn't he say something?

Simon, I love you so much. Can't you see it in my eyes? Can't you see how sorry I am for the pain I've caused you and how much you and Jenny mean to me?

Later, she marveled at the instinct that made her lift her arms to him. The instant she did, he came to the bed and crushed her to him.

He kissed her as if he were a man dying of thirst, and she was the water that would sustain him. And she kissed him back just as greedily. Soon kisses weren't enough, and they were tearing off each other's clothes.

"Hannah, Hannah!" he cried as he plunged into her.

She arched to meet him, digging her nails into his back and crying out as she climaxed violently. His own release came only seconds later, and was just as cataclysmic. When it was over, he collapsed on top of her.

Much later, holding each other quietly, they finally began to talk.

"I missed you while I was away," he said.

"Oh, Simon, I missed you, too."

He smoothed her hair back from her forehead and kissed her gently. "I do love you, Hannah. You know that."

"And I love you."

"I want us to try to get past this."

"I want that more than anything in the world."

"I have to be honest, though. It's not going to be easy."

"I know. You . . ." She swallowed. "I have to earn your trust again."

"It's not just that. It's Jenny. She's been hurt more than anyone."

"I know."

"Do you?"

"Yes, Simon, I do. But I think she'll get over it once she realizes her place in our family hasn't changed."

"But it *has* changed, Hannah. Yes, you still love her as much as you did before, but she's no longer your only child. She has an older half brother now, and she'll have to share you."

"I know, but—"

"All I'm saying is, don't expect miracles. We still have some rough road ahead of us."

She sighed. "But if we love each other and we show her how much we love her, surely she'll come around. Surely she'll be okay."

"I think she will, eventually, but I just want you to be realistic. If she decides she wants to live with my mother for a while, I want you to give her the time she needs and not push her." He propped himself up on one elbow and kissed her. "Can you do that?"

Hannah's heart twisted. "I'll try."

"The other consideration is David. I like that boy a lot, you know that, but I don't want you to think that we're all going to be one big happy family, because I don't think that's realistic, either."

Until that moment Hannah hadn't realized how much she'd been hoping Simon would say something different.

"Can you live with that, too?" Simon asked softly. "Because if you don't think you can, now's the time to say."

"Yes, I can live with that."

For the first time since he'd walked into the bedroom, he smiled.

They made love again, this time slowly and lovingly. They touched each other with tenderness that slowly grew into passion. And when they finally came together, Hannah's eyes brimmed with tears.

"I love you," she whispered brokenly.

"And I love you," Simon said fiercely. "I'll always love you, no matter what."

Hannah's heart filled with thankfulness. For a long time she'd denied an important part of herself. That denial had nearly cost her her marriage and the respect and trust of her daughter.

Now she had another chance to get things right.

And this time, she was determined to succeed.

Epilogue

~

Three years later

Dear Jenny,

Thanks for your e-mail. I'm glad you're enjoying
going to school in France this year. It's great that you
have this opportunity. I imagine it's a lot of fun room-
ing with your cousin Yvette, too. It's also nice you're
so close to your relatives and can go and stay with
them on the weekends if you want to.

Yeah, we *did* have fun over the summer, didn't we?
I really enjoyed spending that week with you and your
folks in Cancun. I never liked the ocean much when
I lived in Florida, but I have to admit, we had some
fun days in Mexico. Your dad's talking about a trip
to Hawaii next summer. I don't know about you, but
I'd love to go there.

Thanks for the pictures. Boy, you sure are getting
to be one sexy broad. (I'm allowed to say that since
I'm your brother, but if any other guy starts that kind
of talk, you tell him to disappear. I don't trust those
Frenchmen!)<g>

You asked if I still like school. Actually, I love
school. I'm going for a double major, did I tell you?
Your dad and I talked, and since I only needed nine
more hours for a major in mathematics as well as eco-

nomics, I decided to go for it. I've always loved math; there's something orderly about it. Of course, that meant I had to quit my part-time job, but I'd saved up enough money to see me through this last year as long as I'm careful about what I spend. Your dad wanted to help, but he's already doing enough. I'd like to do this on my own.

Yeah, your mother (I know, I still have a hard time saying *our* mother) and I usually meet for lunch on Wednesdays. She's pretty busy now that she's a regular exhibitor at McFarland Galleries, plus she's gotten heavily involved with that adoption-counseling agency I told you about. Your dad is also working with them, and he told me it's made a big difference in his life. I'm glad something good came out of all this, aren't you? Well, other good things came out of it, too, like getting such a sexy broad for a sister <g> and finding my mother, but you know what I meant.

Well, Jenny, if I'm going to get my economics reading assignment done for tomorrow, I'd better hit the books. Have fun at that dance tomorrow night and keep working on your French.

Oh, I almost forgot. Yeah, I *will* think about coming over to visit you on my spring break. If I can get a cheap ticket, I'll be there, bedroll and all.

Your bro,
David